AT
SOMERTON
EMERALDS & ASHES

AT
SOMERTON

EMERALDS & ASHES

LEILA RASHEED

HYPERION
LOS ANGELES   NEW YORK

First Paperback Edition, May 2022

10 9 8 7 6 5 4 3 2 1

FAC-025438-22084
Printed in the United States of America

This book is set in Palatino/Linotype
Designed by Marci Senders

ISBN 978-1-368-08034-7

Library of Congress Control Number for Hardcover Edition: 2014032761

Visit www.hyperionteens.com

SUSTAINABLE
FORESTRY
INITIATIVE

Certified Sourcing

www.sfiprogram.org
SFI-01054

The SFI label applies to the text stock

WITH SPECIAL THANKS TO JULIA CHURCHILL, SARAH DAVIES, EMILY MEEHAN, AND LAURA SCHREIBER, WITHOUT WHOM THE SOMERTON BOOKS WOULD NOT HAVE BEEN WRITTEN.

ACT ONE

CHAPTER
ONE

SOMERTON, SEPTEMBER 1914

Annie—*first* housemaid Annie, she reminded herself proudly—guessed that something was going on as soon she reached the bottom of the servants' stairs. The noise was the first clue: there wasn't any. Usually by the time she came down from lighting the fires, the kitchen was in a scurry and bustle, getting ready to serve breakfast. Plates would be clattering, the footmen rushing here and there, Cook would be cursing the range, Martha would have burned her fingers, and Sarah—but Sarah had left, she remembered. Gone to work in a munitions factory. The thought sobered her, but only for a second. The war would be over by Christmas; everybody said so.

Anxious to know what had brought the kitchen to a standstill, she hurried across the tiled floor, pausing only for a brief glance into the mirror propped on the shelf, which James and Thomas used to check their appearance before going upstairs. She was sure that munitions didn't have half as nice a uniform as the *first* housemaid at Somerton Court did. Certainly by January Sarah would be regretting throwing away her safe job for one that, by all accounts, turned your skin green. With a satisfied touch to her cap, she swept into the kitchen.

"What's going on here?" she exclaimed, seeing that the breakfast was getting cold on the trays, and Cook, Martha, and Thomas were none of them at their usual places. Instead they were clustered by the door in the bright September sunshine, Martha with a dishrag still in her hand. The focus of their attention was a burly young man in a soldier's uniform. Annie was taken aback; khaki was still rare in the village, exotic enough to give her a pleasurable shiver. A second later she recognized the man in the uniform. It was James, the first footman. To Annie's impressed eyes, it was as if the war had waved a magic wand over him, transforming him from dull, everyday James into a glamorous stranger.

"Yes, we're off," he was saying to Cook. "The Palesbury Pals are going to do their bit at last. I can't wait to take a shot at the Germans, pay them back for Mons."

"Well, you keep yourself safe out there." Cook dabbed her eyes with her apron. "I hear French cooking ain't up to much."

"So you're off!" Annie pushed her way past Martha, to James.

"It seems as if everyone's joining up." She looked him up and down. "I must say, the uniform does suit you."

"Thank you." James blushed.

Annie smiled. He'd be back some day, after all, and he might be an officer by then. Decorated, even. You never knew. "Such a pity you're going away."

"Well, I think it's my duty."

"I don't know about that," Cook said darkly. "It's a bloody business, and I'll be glad when it's over."

Thomas spoke up. "We've got to help our allies, haven't we?" As the second footman, he was usually overshadowed by James, but Annie noticed that he seemed to have grown up a good deal in the past months. "It's only right, when poor Belgium's been invaded. I can't stand bullies. Never could. I wish it was me in that uniform, I tell you, James. Feels shameful, not going with you."

"You'll get your chance," said James. "You'll be nineteen soon enough!"

"It's not the age that's stopping me. If Mum and Dad would give their permission, I'd be off like a shot!"

"Well said, Thomas!" rang out an authoritative voice. It was Lord Westlake, who had come in, unseen, through the kitchen door behind them.

Annie jumped to attention. Every single person stood frozen, silent and wide-eyed as the earl joined them. The earl, in the kitchen! Annie could hardly believe it. To the best of her knowledge he had never been in the kitchen before. If anyone had asked her, she would have said he didn't even know where it was. But in he strode, silver-haired and regal. He walked right up to James, who blinked at him like a trapped rabbit.

"I've come to offer you my very heartiest congratulations and wish you all the luck in the world." The earl spoke with energy, and his eyes were bright as a young man's. "Yours is the British spirit we all rely on."

"Th-thank you, my lord," stuttered James.

"No, it is I who should thank you. You are fighting to defend all of us." The earl stretched out his hand. James looked at it blankly. Thomas nudged him. James blinked again and trem-blingly put out his own hand. The earl grasped it and pumped it up and down.

He shook James's hand! Annie exchanged a glance of disbe-lief and amazement with Martha. The earl, shaking the hand of his footman! First the war, and now this. She glanced at the win-dow, half expecting to hear the last trump blow and angels come down to gather everyone up for Judgment Day.

"You're a very brave fellow," the earl said, "and I want you to know that we shall all look forward to your news and will be cheering you on in every way—moral and practical."

He stepped back and looked at Thomas.

"Thomas," he began. Thomas stood to attention. "I know you want to enlist. That shows a brave spirit, and I respect it."

"I wish I could, sir. But my mother won't allow it, what with my older brothers being out there already—"

"I understand. But there are other ways for a man to serve his king and country. For example, by doing a job that frees up another to take his place." He paused, then went on: "As you all know, Cooper left us at the start of the war, and now our next most senior member of male staff, James, is off to do his duty too. But Somerton needs a butler. I want you to be that man, Thomas. You have the dignity. You have the experience. You may be young, but these are unprecedented times. What do you say?"

Annie's eyes opened wide. A butler, at seventeen! It was unheard of.

"Sir!" Thomas managed. "I . . ." He hesitated, and Annie stared at him. Surely he couldn't be thinking of refusing?

Thomas looked around at everyone's eager, encouraging faces.

"I—I'd be honored, sir. Honored."

"Very good." The earl nodded, pleased. "Once more, James, good luck. I would have liked you to use the motorcar to go to the station, but with petrol rationed it seems inadvisable. And what with all the horses being requisitioned . . ."

"I'll walk, sir; it's no distance at all." James shouldered his kit bag and ripped off a crisp salute that thrilled Annie to the core with its military smartness. "Good-bye, sir. Good-bye, all of you. I'll be home before you know it!"

He turned and marched off toward the road. Annie couldn't hold in her excitement any longer, and with Cook and Martha she called "Good luck, James!" after him, until she was hoarse. The earl himself joined in the three cheers that Thomas began, and they watched until James had vanished.

"Well done, that man," said the earl, as if to himself. "Good show. Wish I was going with him."

He turned to the others with a smile.

"And now I shall leave you all to your work. Good day."

He strode away. Silence reigned until they heard the baize door close behind him.

"He wished James luck! And shook his hand!" Martha broke the silence with an awed whisper. "His actual hand!"

"He made me *butler*!" Thomas said, sounding as if he still hadn't gotten to grips with the idea.

"Yes, so cheer up! Think what your mum and dad will say when they hear!" Cook nudged him. "*Mr.* Wright, as we'll all have to call you now."

"Will you?" Thomas looked horrified.

Annie glanced at him. She'd never taken much notice of Thomas. He was a funny sort of lad, always out in the yard, chatting to the chauffeur or tinkering away with some homemade metal contraption or other, getting oil on his hands. He didn't have the pride in his appearance that James took. Still, he was handsome enough—those blue eyes, that strong jaw, and those shoulders. She wanted something more than a footman—well, now he *was* something more than a footman.

"And I've just been made first housemaid!" she said, moving a step closer to him. "The earl must think a lot of us . . . both of us. It's up to us now, isn't it? Together. Winning the war on the home front."

She smiled up at Thomas and fluttered her lashes. To her

disappointment, he didn't notice her. He was looking over her shoulder at the back door. Annie followed his gaze.

She saw a slim, shy-looking girl of her own age, her red hair piled up under a dove-gray hat trimmed with cream silk roses. She held a very battered suitcase in one hand and steadied an equally shabby-looking bicycle with the other.

"Good morning," she greeted them. Annie noted that she was well-spoken—not a local girl. "I am the new parlormaid—Rebecca Freeman. May I know who I report to?"

"As the first housemaid, I expect that will be me." Annie stepped forward graciously.

"Oh," the girl said, sounding startled. "I thought that the housekeeper—"

Cook began to speak at the same moment as Annie. Thomas cleared his throat and they both fell silent, Annie remembering that as butler he now took precedence.

"We are currently between housekeepers," Thomas said. "But Annie will show you the ropes."

"I certainly will," Annie preened; it was nice to be in charge for once. It was her duty, she felt, to make the new arrival aware of her place in the pecking order, and to do this, she had to dismay her with the size of the house, impress her with the dignity of Somerton Court, and utterly overwhelm her with the majesty of its first housemaid. Annie was up to the challenge.

"Now I must warn you, Becky," she began, following her out as the girl leaned her bicycle against the outside wall, "that we expect hard work here, and—"

"Rebecca, if you don't mind," the girl said, glancing up at her demurely.

"I'm sorry?"

"I prefer to be called Rebecca, not Becky."

The girl said this quite pleasantly, stepping past Annie and into the kitchen as she did so, but Annie was taken aback. Surely a new arrival ought to be glad to be called anything at all! She was momentarily lost for words. In the silence, Rebecca spoke up again.

"Excuse me for mentioning it, but I see that the range is out. If the family are in the habit of taking breakfast at nine, I'd think it advisable to start it now."

"Oh, my goodness!" Cook turned in a sudden panic. "The breakfast! All the bacon going cold! Quick, Martha, don't just stand there, get the matches—"

Annie found herself hustled out of the way as Cook and Martha leapt into action. She tried to gather her thoughts.

"I—yes—well—come with me and I shall show you your room."

"Don't you think I should start at once? You'll need some help serving." Rebecca was already putting on a clean apron that she had taken down from the hook behind the door without so much as asking. "If you'll just show me the way up, I can take the next tray."

"Yes, show her, Annie. She may as well get started." Thomas

leaned past Annie to get the tea and coffee. "You'll need to find her a cap; take one from the drawer in Mrs. Cliffe's room."

"I—hmm—very well, then." Annie went ahead of Rebecca, to the housekeeper's room. The key was on a nail by the door; she took it down and turned the lock. The room was barely changed since Mrs. Cliffe had been here; the short stay of Mrs. McRory was like a bad dream. As Annie got the cap from the linen drawer, she tried again to impress Rebecca.

"I don't want to alarm you, but I expect you'll never have worked so hard as you will here. It will be a long way up and downstairs every day—there's the hearth rugs, and the fires, and you'll have to do footman's duties too. We have high standards here."

"Oh, I like high standards," Rebecca said, giving her one of those sideways smiles as she fixed her cap in the mirror. "I have high standards myself."

While Annie was searching for an appropriate reply, Rebecca whisked out of the door. Annie followed, feeling as if she'd lost her edge.

Rebecca gathered up the toast, marmalades, and butter on a silver tray and set off up the servants' stairs after Thomas. As she passed her, Annie had another go.

"You're one of the first women ever to wait at the Earl of Westlake's table," she called after her. "It's quite natural to want to have a little cry," she added hopefully.

"Hush, Annie!" Thomas whispered at her, frowning as he opened the door with one hand. Rebecca followed him out, and the door swung shut in Annie's red face.

Annie stomped into the kitchen and made her feelings known.

"'Prefer to be called Rebecca' indeed! I never heard such airs and graces!"

Martha agreed at once, to Annie's relief.

"I don't know who she thinks she is. After all, she's just a parlormaid." She added darkly, "And if she goes on as she's started, I shouldn't think she'll be one for long."

CHAPTER
Two

"I am really not certain of the earl's judgment in making Thomas butler," said Lady Westlake to Georgiana as they walked down the corridor to the breakfast room. "He is so very young."

"Oh, but I think he is competent!" Georgiana exclaimed. "At least we must give him a chance."

"Yes, but what will people think!" The countess cooled herself with the silk fan she carried as they walked between gilt-framed oil paintings and long windows dressed with floating muslin drapes. Sunlight brightened her profile, as elegant and cold as those of the Grecian statues they passed in the alcoves: the Graces and the Virtues. "I understand we are to have a parlormaid to replace James—such a comedown! A man looks so much better waiting at table than a woman."

"I suppose we have to make every economy to support the war effort," Georgiana sighed. "I wish it were all over, though."

"As do I. The inconvenience is extreme. All the balls have been canceled, and there is nothing doing except these dreary charity events that everyone expects one to preside at. If I have to visit another hospital or draw another raffle in aid of Belgian refugees, I shall simply weep."

Georgiana opened her mouth to say that she had been thinking less of the upset to the social round, more of the horrifying losses that the British army had suffered so far, not to mention the possible danger to those they loved. On second thought, however, she decided there was no point. Her stepmother was unlikely to understand anything that didn't directly relate to herself. Georgiana was uncomfortably aware that the war had not yet touched Somerton; the refused invitations, due to mourning, by more and more of their friends were something the countess did not feel the significance of, or chose not to. The neatly printed lists of dead in the *Gazette*—the names kept getting smaller and smaller, as if they were struggling to fit them all in—these things were just names to her. Georgiana sometimes wished she could be so oblivious. But the truth was that an earthquake had shaken England the day war was declared, and she felt as if she was still reeling, confused, and struggling to find her feet in a landscape that had changed completely.

"I suppose William will join up," the countess said. "It seems to be de rigueur."

"I don't suppose any such thing. William has no sense of

honor or duty; he could never have behaved so unspeakably to poor Priya, if he had." Georgiana still found it hard to speak of her cousin William, the heir to Somerton Court and the title of Earl of Westlake, without becoming breathless with rage. He had forced himself on his son's nursemaid—under the very roof of Somerton—and Georgiana held him directly responsible for her death.

The countess was not listening; she smiled as she entered the dining room.

"Good morning, my dear," she said, pausing to drop a kiss on the earl's graying head. "Michael." She nodded to her son. Georgiana murmured a greeting to her father and glanced at Michael with the same concern that she always felt for him nowadays. He had loved Priya, and though that had been a secret sorrow for her, she knew her unrequited love paled in comparison with the pain that he must have gone through in losing Priya.

They took their seats at the table, and the meal began. Georgiana saw her stepmother raise an eyebrow as Thomas and a young woman with vivid auburn hair swept neatly up under her cap came in and began serving. This girl must be the new parlormaid, Georgiana realized—Rebecca. Georgiana watched nervously, aware that the countess was ready to jump on any error, but soon felt able to relax. Rebecca went about her duties with quiet efficiency, and the initial unfamiliarity of having a female hand pour the tea and slice the muffins quickly vanished, smoothed away by her obvious competence.

Unfortunately, there was still plenty for the countess to

disapprove of, and she did, with a series of small sighs and irritated glances at her husband, who was doing his best to hide behind his newspaper. Georgiana knew that the plates were not as shiny as they had been under Mrs. Cliffe, and there was a very obvious stain on the tablecloth, but she smiled with determination, hoping that Thomas could sense her goodwill and that he would manage his first meal in his new role well, despite the countess's pursed lips.

"The tea is brewed to perfection," she announced, although it seemed much the same as always.

"A pity it is cold," murmured the countess. Georgiana had a strong urge to kick her under the table. She valiantly resisted.

"I do apologize, my lady. It won't happen again," Thomas murmured.

Georgiana spotted his fingers trembling as he poured coffee for Michael. She winced in sympathy. Thomas didn't have the presence of James; she had noticed that he seemed happier chatting with the chauffeur out in the yard or fixing the boiler—no one else seemed to have such a way with the cranky old thing, and though it was hardly a footman's job, let alone a butler's, it certainly saved the expense of calling an engineer. James, she thought, would never have been seen doing such a thing. Thomas would do his best, but she couldn't help thinking he would be happier in a different role.

"Has anything been done about the housekeeper?" the earl said, his mind plainly moving along the same lines.

"Please don't consult me. You know I have enough to do with keeping up the London house," the countess said, opening her post as she spoke.

Georgiana knew the countess had never liked Somerton, had never wanted to live in the country, but she did wish that she took a little more interest and didn't simply complain.

"The experience with Mrs. McRory was so unpleasant," Georgiana began, "that I"—she glanced at the countess, who was, after all, nominally the mistress of the house—"that we hardly like to try an agency again. And the need to economize—"

"Hmm, quite." The earl glanced at Thomas. "Never mind. I have the greatest of faith in our own people."

"Thank you, sir," Thomas murmured.

"Where is the sugar?" the countess demanded.

Thomas looked up.

"I'm very sorry, my lady . . . Cook says there is none to be had in the village."

"No sugar!" The countess's face fell. "I expect it is Lady Amersham. That terrible woman—I saw her motorcar in the village the other day. She has bought up all the dry goods in Shropshire, it appears, and is now coming over to our county. So unpatriotic. This war demands everything from us, it seems."

"The *Empire* demands it, my dear," said the earl, as Thomas and Rebecca retired.

"Yes, of course. The Empire." But the countess's expression was far from happy.

"If sugar is the only sacrifice we have to make to the gods of war," Georgiana could not help saying, "I should be most grateful. Is there any news of Rose, Papa?"

The earl shook his head gravely. Georgiana knew he was as concerned as she was. Rose, his illegitimate daughter, had been brought up without knowing who her father was, working as a maid in the house where her sisters, Ada and Georgiana, were ladies. When the truth had come out, it had threatened to cover the Averleys in scandal. Georgiana was deeply proud of her father for acknowledging and adopting Rose at last. She sensed that Rose was in some ways the dearest of his daughters to his heart, because he felt so much guilt at not having acknowledged her sooner.

"Nothing since the telegram that let us know she was still in Egypt," he said now. "I have spared no effort to contact them, but the War Office is simply too busy to prioritize the messages."

"Oh, I do hope she is safe." Georgiana put down her knife and fork; she had no appetite. "When I think she is really in the center of the fighting . . ."

"At least she is with Alexander," Michael said. "He wouldn't allow any harm to come to her."

"No, I am sure," Georgiana sipped her tea, but put it down almost at once. "I wonder if he too has had to join a regiment. He would detest it."

"Oh, please let us talk about something other than this depressing war," the countess said in annoyance.

"But there *is* nothing else, Mother, and no use pretending that there is." Michael's voice was more serious than Georgiana had ever heard it. "There's nothing to do but to sign up and join in."

"How can you say that? If everyone goes off to join in this madness, how will we ever restore peace?" Georgiana exclaimed.

"For once, Georgiana, I agree," the countess said. "The war *is* madness. I don't think we should encourage it."

"Mother!" Michael's hand shook as he put his cup down. "The war is not a . . . a pushy salesman who refuses to leave. It's a conflagration, a catastrophe. We cannot ignore it." Georgiana could see he was in earnest as he went on: "Since the subject has arisen, I may as well tell the truth. I would not have chosen a war, but now that one is here, I see it as my duty to enlist."

"Well," said the countess acidly, "I am delighted to say that you will not get the chance. You are not of majority."

"I don't see why that should matter. I can shoot a gun, I can ride a horse. I am a British subject as well as any nineteen-year-old. It's dishonorable, Mother, for me to stay at home, when I know what is happening just across the Channel. Even James has gone!"

"Oh, Michael!" Georgiana could not keep quiet a second longer. "This isn't a cricket match. You don't seem to realize you could be killed."

The earl said dryly, "Georgiana, my dear, I would prefer to see my daughter display a *little* more patriotism."

Georgiana could feel her temper rising.

"Real patriotism doesn't involve sending thousands of your countrymen to die," she answered. "What can it possibly matter to us if some Austrian prince is shot in Serbia? How can that possibly be worth the life of a single Englishman, let alone thousands? You saw the newspapers last week—it's terrible, terrible bloodshed. I don't know how you can encourage Michael to risk his life, Papa, when poor little Philip is hardly in his grave." She could hardly keep the tears from her eyes as she thought of it. Philip had not had much of a life, with an older brother like William, and his death from scarlet fever—she blamed William for refusing to bring him home from school even when notified of the outbreak—seemed a particularly cruel blow.

"We all feel that loss very much," said her father quietly. "But a childhood disease is not the same thing as doing one's duty in time of war, is it, Georgiana?"

Georgiana looked at Michael.

"What about killing people? Could you bring yourself to do that, Michael?" Her voice was challenging. "For myself, I think dying would be the easy part. I would rather die than take someone else's life, just to carry out a stupid order."

There was silence as everyone looked at Michael.

"I wouldn't *like* to do it, but I want to do my duty," he said quietly, his eyes meeting hers. "I'd be proud to go. It's what we've practiced for in school, after all—the Officer Training Corps and all that. Besides, the war is here now; it's win or lose. Someone has to go, and I don't have a wife, or a child depending on me. So I of all people am the best fitted to give my life for my country."

Georgiana blinked back tears. It was heartbreaking to hear

Michael's words. She knew Priya's death had hit him hard, but did he really have nothing to live for? Could he think of no one who would miss him? She turned aside so no one would see her emotion. She glanced through the tall window at the lawn sweeping down to sunny fields. It was one of the last fine summer days they would have before autumn set in, she knew, and she gazed at it as if she could drink in all the golden sunshine before it fled from the fields. It was sickening to think of the blood splashed in every word of the newspapers, and to think that the only effect would be not mass protests demanding peace at all costs, but boys like Michael, like James the footman, rushing to the recruit ing offices in some crazy belief that it was their duty to die young.

She came back to herself to hear her father saying: "There is no use asking me to put in a word on your behalf, Michael. You know how I feel: I support any brave lad who wants to fight for his country. But I cannot go against your mother in this regard."

"And I forbid it entirely," said the countess.

Michael bowed his head submissively, but before he did so, Georgiana saw a rebellious glint in his eye. It troubled her. But before she could think too much about it, the countess glanced at the clock, exclaimed, and put her napkin down.

"I must go," she announced, standing up, "or I shall miss the train to London." She nodded to Thomas, who at once left the room to summon the motorcar.

"I hope you will not spend too much money." The earl frowned. "The petrol alone is such an expense. . . ."

"Of course not, my dear, but moderation in all things, even economy. Charlotte may have had her last season, but we should never give up hope. A new dress may change everything."

Georgiana exchanged a glance with Michael. It was hard not to feel sorry for his sister, Charlotte, even though Georgiana had always thought her vain and cold. The countess's determination to get her married off was as steely as any bayonet.

"But, my dear . . ." began the earl.

"It really won't cost a thing. Besides, I shall pay for it myself. I'm sure the government cannot object to that. Unless our army is suffering under a pressing shortage of sequins."

Georgiana sighed as the countess swept away through the door, leaving the earl stony-faced. She knew it was wrong, when so many people were suffering, but she was a little envious of Charlotte. Her own coming-out season was supposed to have been this year. Nothing had been said, but she knew it was postponed, if not canceled. Her father didn't have time to arrange it, and her stepmother would not bother. Charlotte had had three seasons already, three glittering whirls of dance and dress and heart-fluttering romance, before the war. Georgiana had not had even one.

"If only there were a duke with a few thousand a year and he was prepared to marry Charlotte," Michael said, cutting into her thoughts. "Lord Kitchener would just have to parachute him behind the German lines and put my mother at the head of his brigades. We'd be in Berlin by Boxing Day."

Georgiana, who had just taken a sip of tea, choked on an unladylike giggle.

"Michael," said the earl sternly, but there was the hint of a smile in his eyes.

CHAPTER
THREE

LONDON

"'Captain Sir Vivian Osborne and Lady Emily Fintan, by special license from the Bishop of Winchester, et cetera et cetera, at Medbury Church, et cetera et cetera, owing to the emergency of the wedding on account of the regiment being ordered on service in the war, only the colonel, officers and men of the regiment, and the parents of the bride were present.' Well!" The countess put down the *Times*, which she had been reading in the back of the motorcab, and smiled at Charlotte. "That's not what I call a wedding, although without doubt Vivian Osborne is a nice catch for someone of Emily's age. She is a year older than you, isn't that correct, Charlotte?"

"Exactly the same age: nineteen," said Charlotte. The breeze through the motorcar window ruffled her blond curls and freshened her complexion. She knew that people still turned to look after her when she passed. She also knew that nineteen, and three years out, was not the same as sixteen and a debutante.

"Humph." The countess's mouth turned down in dissatisfaction. "You are hardly an old maid—still, the business must be concluded this year."

"No matter with whom?" Charlotte said wryly.

It was true that the news of Emily's wedding had come of something of a shock. They had been friends, but they had also been bitter rivals throughout their seasons. But as Charlotte looked out at the London streets that were transformed by the war, she couldn't find it in herself to feel jealous. At a glance she could see how the world had changed. Lord Kitchener's face, his monumental mustache, plastered the walls, his finger pointing at you . . . you . . . you. Pairs of women patrolled the street, selling Union Jacks to raise money for the war. Every other man seemed to be in uniform.

"Charlotte? Are you listening to me?" The countess tapped her on the knee with her fan.

"I'm sorry, Mother."

"You must keep your mind on the matter at hand. We have a fete, a tea dance, and a dreadful meeting to discuss the charity events for the Red Cross, all this week. Bertie Castleton will be at the tea dance, and Sir Morton Mongredien will be at the meeting. Both of them are charming and I would so like you to get to know them better."

"Don't you think there are now more important things in

life than getting married?" Charlotte hadn't meant to speak so bluntly, but the words sprang from her.

Her mother sat back, and gave her the look that could still freeze Charlotte just as it had when she was a little girl in the nursery.

"There is *nothing* more important in a woman's life than her marriage," she said. "If my example has taught you nothing else, let it teach you that. My first marriage, to your father, brought me fortune. My second has brought me power. A woman is judged on her marriage. She is defined by her husband's position and supported by his money. I thought that I had raised you to understand that without need for explanation."

"You have," said Charlotte quietly. It was true. It was just that the world, from the vantage point of the nursery, had seemed a very different place than it did now. "But . . ."

Her mother raised an eyebrow. "But?"

"But now the war is here, I could do something useful."

"What?" her mother said sharply. "What could you possibly do that is useful?"

"I don't know, but I . . ." Charlotte faltered to a halt. She knew her mother was right. Her useful skills were nonexistent. She could not drive an ambulance. She could not take shorthand or replace a man on the farm. She could not even dress herself without a lady's maid to help.

"You are good for one thing only and that is attracting a husband. And to date you have not succeeded. So let us keep our mind on the business at hand, shall we, dear?"

Charlotte felt as if she had been slapped. Her face reddened. She knew her mother meant only to bring her back to herself, but she had not expected her to be so blunt.

They had arrived at L'atelier. As the chauffeur got out to open the door, her mother placed a hand on her arm and spoke in a low voice as they approached the door.

"Don't be jealous of Emily, dear girl. We will find someone for you, someone who will quite overshadow her catch. War puts everyone in a marrying mood."

Charlotte finally found her tongue. She would never allow her mother to see how much she had hurt her. She had too much pride for that. "I'm not jealous." She disentangled her arm as the doorman opened the door for them and they stepped through. Her cool, sarcastic voice was back, a familiar disguise. "Bickenhill Park is charming, but Vivian Osborne is the most frightful bore."

Charlotte walked through the doors of Céline's L'atelier workshop, the countess at her side. It was like stepping into another world. Mannequins and patrons mingled in an atmosphere of perfumed luxury. Silk, satin, and the scent of perfume seemed to coat the air. She saw many familiar faces among the ladies who were waiting to be fitted, or were trying on gowns, and she also heard foreign voices—French, Spanish, even German accents.

The countess glanced about with satisfaction. "I believe that London is smarter than it has ever been. It must be due to all these elegant arrivals from the Continent. We may no longer be able to go to Paris, but it seems Paris has come to us."

"I'm glad you can see something good in the situation,"

answered Charlotte. Just a year ago it would have filled her with pleasure to be here, choosing a new dress at the most exclusive couturier in London. But things were different now. She followed her mother to a French-style sofa and sat, twirling her parasol idly as she glanced around at the company. Perhaps it was her imagination, but she thought the chattering voices were quieter, more subdued.

Her mother cast a few sharp glances around.

"I would think we'd be seen instantly," she said under her breath. "Really, as an old employer I feel Céline owes us special treatment. If it were not for us she would never have come to the notice of society, after all."

"I expect she has many clients," Charlotte said. "She is so busy nowadays."

"Nevertheless!"

Charlotte could see her mother was preparing to be offended with Céline, and her heart sank; it would be disagreeable to have to smooth over her temper when the couturier finally appeared.

"I wonder how many of these women have sons in France," she said in a low voice, half trying to change the subject and half trying to remind her mother that they were in a situation where many things were more important than being first for Céline's attentions.

"A good deal, which is exactly why we must move quickly, before they are all gone," her mother replied in the same low voice. Charlotte did not reply, but she was struck by how different their thoughts were. However, she was glad that the trick had worked and her mother was distracted, looking avidly around for gossip and badly dressed women to mock.

"Mrs. Verulam is quite wrong if she thinks that turban suits her," murmured her mother. "Oh look, there is the Duchess of Devonshire. I heard the most scandalous story . . ."

Charlotte cleared her throat warningly. Céline was approaching, dressed in a deep purple silk gown so glossy it appeared black. Her face was as fresh and young as when she had been a lady's maid in their house.

"Lady Westlake, and Miss Templeton—I am honored," she said. The countess frowned, but Céline went on at once. "I do apologize for keeping you waiting. Her Majesty has just left."

"Oh, in that case . . ." The countess thawed visibly, and Charlotte smiled. She knew Céline was telling a clever, charming fib—she knew her mother could only bear to be passed over for royalty. She wondered how many other little untruths Céline told, every day, to flatter the egos of her customers—just as she employed subtle techniques and tricks in her dressmaking to flatter their figures.

"We are looking for an autumn wardrobe for Miss Templeton," her mother began. "I do admire these luxurious fur capes." She lifted the arm of one that an obliging mannequin was wearing. "The military styling is so very of the moment, is it not?"

"Yes, I have taken my inspiration from the Russians," Céline replied. "The capes will wear beautifully, and make an impression that is instantly modern."

The two women continued to discuss house gowns and

evening gowns, capes and hats. Charlotte felt her attention slipping—then a bright, familiar voice pierced her like a needle.

"My dear Charlotte!"

Charlotte turned reluctantly to face Lady Emily. At her shoulder was Vivian Osborne—a little plumper and more luxuriant of mustache than she had seen him last. He wore the uniform of the Horse Guards. "What a charming surprise; have you been in town long?" she began.

"We are just here to see dear Vivian off on his tour of duty," Lady Emily said. She added with a simper, "I expect you saw the notice in the *Times*."

"Congratulations," said Charlotte, managing to sound sincere. She added with more warmth, "I am sorry that you have to part so soon after your wedding."

Vivian opened his mouth but Emily spoke over him; from the resigned look on Vivian's face Charlotte imagined it was a regular occurrence. "Oh, not at all, it's simply wonderful to think of him doing his duty. If anyone will be a hero, my Vivian will. And he has given me this dear little locket to remember him by." A length of gold chain flashed between Emily's fingers, and Charlotte saw something dazzlingly jeweled spinning at the end of it. Hardly "little," but almost certainly "dear," she thought. Emily steadied the pendant and showed it to her. Across the front was the insignia of the Horse Guards, picked out in emeralds, and on the reverse was inscribed the familiar quotation *I could not love thee, dear, so much, loved I not honor more.* The whole confection struck Charlotte as impeccably tasteless. She couldn't say so, of course, but thankfully Vivian seized the chance to get a word in edgewise.

"Jolly good show, this war. Looking forward to having a bash at the Boche," he announced.

"Of course you are," Charlotte murmured.

"Charlotte." She heard her mother's clear, sharp tones. She looked around and saw that she was being summoned to try on a gown. She turned back to Emily. "It was so delightful to see you, and once again I offer my congratulations—"

"I expect you know Laurence's news?" Emily interrupted Charlotte hesitated, aware of the malice in her voice, the desire to wound. She and Emily's brother, Lord Fintan, had been very close. What was Laurence's news? she wondered. Was he married? Engaged? In love? She searched for pain in her heart, and was surprised to not find any. She turned back to Emily, amused as she noted Emily's confusion at her lack of curiosity.

"No, I am afraid I've not been honored with his confidence," she said with a brilliant smile. "And now you really must excuse me."

She sailed away without a backward glance, her heart lighter than it had been for a long time. Emily was quite too naïve, she thought contemptuously. Even if she had been wounded, did she imagine that she would betray her feelings in public? She would as soon wear that gaudy pendant.

As she joined her mother, she noticed a slight confusion at the door of the workshop. A tired-looking girl in a ragged dress glanced in, then as quickly shut the door. Céline appeared to have seen it too. She whispered in French to one of her assistants, and the girl at once went after the intruder.

"Who was that?" Charlotte inquired. The look of haunted exhaustion on the girl's face had struck her. She wondered if Céline had abandoned her principles and begun using sweatshop girls like so many of the other couturiers.

Céline seemed hesitant, but she responded to Charlotte's questioning look. "She is a Belgian refugee. She is the only one left of her family; she was separated from her mother and sisters when Antwerp fell, and arrived here alone and penniless."

"Oh, the poor girl!" Charlotte exclaimed.

"There are many like her, sadly. I am providing as many of them as I can with a place to stay, and work if they can manage it. Others will be sent to the countryside—some kind people have offered to take them in."

"How very good of them—and of you." Charlotte looked at Céline with new respect. One didn't imagine common people, even very talented ones such as Céline, having personal lives. But she saw that they did, and that they appeared able to accomplish quite remarkable things in them.

"Not at all." Céline's voice was quiet. "My own parents are here, in as bad a state as you can imagine. My brother was shot by the Germans, and our family home was burned down. They had nowhere to go except to me. Our house in France was directly in the path of the German advance. Many of our neighbors are in the same position."

"I am so sorry," Charlotte said. "Of course, I have seen the pictures of the refugees, but I didn't know—I didn't think—"

"Yes, very sad," the countess interrupted her. "But to return to business, I want to have another look at those capes. The war has changed the fashions completely, and we must be up-to-date."

"Of course, *madame.*" In an instant, Céline's professional demeanor was back. She briskly began to discuss material and trimmings.

Charlotte watched Céline in fascination, admiring her ability to conceal her personal feelings beneath strict professionalism. If Céline could be useful, could help people, could be needed, then why couldn't she? Did she have to be as useless as her mother thought she should be?

Her mother was still talking about dresses. "Yes, I think we will have the silver lining for the military coat, and an edging of mink. As for the day dress, what do you think? Heliotrope, magnolia, lavender, perhaps?"

"Black Chantilly lace," Céline suggested.

"Oh no, no. *Black?* There is nothing so aging."

Céline's next words were spoken quietly, without sensation. Yet for the rest of the day Charlotte could not get them out of her mind. "You must bear in mind, *madame,* that there are, unfortunately, likely to be very many occasions in the near future when mourning will be necessary."

When Charlotte reached her room after dinner—an interminable event, at which her mother had seemed intent on recommending her to a baronet of at least sixty—she went straight to her wardrobe. At a glance she could see dress after dress that she would never wear again. Silk, satin, ruched velvet, sequins and beads glowing with color, crystals scattered on hems like dewdrops, rich embroidery, mother-of-pearl buttons gleaming, the soft kid of handmade shoes, fans like iridescent butterfly wings, gloves in delicate pastels worn only once. Here they hung—useless in this new world of war. As useless as their owner, she thought bitterly.

"MacIvor," she said when her maid came in to help her undress, "how much do you think I could get for these? I mean the ball dresses, and as many of the others as I can spare."

MacIvor studied the dresses with a professional eye.

"It would depend how soon you would like the money, miss. There are people who will dispose of them quickly and quietly, for ladies who have pressing debts, but of course you would receive less—"

"No, I want to get as much as possible." Charlotte thought for a second. "In fact, I have a better idea. I want to write a short note to Céline, the couturier. Will you see that it gets to her tomorrow?"

MacIvor curtsied an acknowledgment as Charlotte sat and wrote:

Dear Madame:

I am sending you several of my dresses, which I would like disposed of, to raise as much money as possible in aid of the Belgian refugees. I believe you are the best person to apply to in

this matter, and will know how to manage it. Of course I would
like my donation treated in the strictest confidence—if anyone
asks, "a lady" is sufficient identification.

She signed it, folded it, and handed it to MacIvor. Then she
began taking dresses out of her wardrobe.

"Miss, you can't mean to get rid of all these!" MacIvor
exclaimed, as the pile mounted.

"I do indeed."

"But what—" MacIvor fell silent, clearly remembering her
place.

"What will my mother say?" Charlotte gave a humorless
laugh. "I don't see what she can say—after all, it's for the war."

She threw herself into discarding the dresses with as much
savagery as if she were hacking through a jungle. Armful after
armful went onto the bed, until her arms were aching with the
weight of them.

"There," she said, trembling slightly. "Please send these to
Céline, with my kind regards."

MacIvor, clearly a little frightened by her mood, curtsied and
withdrew.

CHAPTER
FOUR

Sebastian paced back and forth in the shadows of the lamp-lit alley, his eyes fixed on the bright facade of Claridge's. From here he could hear the music and the laughter. Top hats passed before the light in silhouette; starched shirtfronts gleamed. Just a few months ago he would have been in there himself. Now he was barred, his name kicked about like a muddy football, and all because of that damned photograph.

Hannah Darford had been right; it had been a mistake to publicly embrace Oliver—as he continued to call him, for he could not bring himself to think of him as Daniel Hammerman, and knew that Oliver too preferred to forget the name that reminded him of his father. Sebastian admitted it to himself, as he watched for Oliver to come out. He had been foolish. Just his luck to be caught in a photograph, though at least it had not shown Oliver's face and had thus spared him the same fate. He glanced at his watch. Oliver was late—again. It was ridiculous, he raged inside himself; it was shameful to have to skulk and hide out here. He was not ashamed of who he was. But the whole world thought he should be.

"What the hell is he doing in there?" he muttered to himself. Oliver should be more understanding—after all, weren't they committed to each other? Whatever that meant, in a world that would never acknowledge it.

He waited another weary hour before finally he saw Oliver emerge from the hotel and the doorman summon a cab. Oliver was laughing at a joke that Christopher Carrington was making, and he turned back to shake the man's hand. Christopher's cigar spilled smoke into the air; his undone white tie suggested heat and laughter inside. The two held hands perhaps a moment longer than was necessary.

Oliver let go—or was it Christopher who let go first?—and stepped into the cab. Sebastian hurried, freezing even in his fur coat, to the other end of the alley. The whole thing was a bloody farce. Everything that was degrading about his position came back to him—waiting in the cold, in a stinking byway, for Oliver to finally grace him with his company. After he had talked to everyone else, of course.

The cab drew up, and under the alley's cover Sebastian opened the door and stepped in. Oliver smiled at him. He smelled of wine and cigar smoke. "You're here, finally. I've been waiting for hours," Sebastian greeted him.

"You mean to say you have been skulking about here all evening?" Oliver said disapprovingly. "Why didn't you go somewhere else while I was inside?"

"Where else?" Sebastian snapped, rapping with his cane on the partition to tell the cab to drive on. "You know as well as I that I am barred from every establishment."

"Well, you missed a fine night."

"I can see that. Where were you? You said midnight. It is nearly two!" Sebastian spoke quietly, leaning toward Oliver, though the noise of the wheels on the cobblestones and the glass partition were enough to shield their words.

"Damn it, Sebastian, I can't simply walk out like that. Questions would be asked."

"And hearts broken."

Oliver frowned. "You're becoming very possessive of late."

"And I have no right to be, I suppose."

"That's not what I mean. I have suffered prison for your sake. I have only just been able to enjoy the privileges that are mine by birth, now that my father is dead. I think you might be more understanding."

"I do understand." Sebastian made an effort to keep his temper. "But, Oliver, can you see that it is hard for me to see you go about like this, as if—as if we were not together."

"We are together." Oliver leaned toward him and kissed him. Sebastian wished he did not still smell Christopher's cigar. "But you know as well as I do: we can never be like married people."

"Why not, though?" Sebastian said eagerly.

"Oh, do be reasonable. How? Where?"

"We could find somewhere. We could live in retirement."

"You in retirement!" Oliver laughed, and Sebastian heard a note of bitterness. "What we do is illegal, Sebastian, that's the truth of it. There is nowhere retired enough to escape censure. Especially not now, with everyone looking for spies."

"Well, we cannot go on like this."

"What do you suggest we do instead?"

Sebastian was silent. He knew Oliver was right. And when he thought about it, how many men of his sort had what he dreamed of—a life together with the person they loved? It was impossible. Normal men could get married, did not have to hide what they did from the world. But he was not what the world called normal.

"I am your mistress, not your wife," Oliver said, as if reading his thoughts. "That's all the world will allow us. Do you think I like that feeling? It isn't pleasant to be a mistress: one can always be abandoned; there is never any certainty."

"But you won't agree to step away from all this, to come and live with me quietly somewhere—"

"Sebastian, I repeat: Where?"

The cab rolled to a halt. Sebastian looked out of the window to see they had arrived at his Knightsbridge lodgings. He hesitated. Usually Oliver would come in with him. But he saw at once that there was someone waiting outside. A journalist, he guessed, from the looks of the man.

"Damn it," he muttered.

"One of them?"

He nodded.

"Good night, then."

Sebastian got slowly down. He felt that Oliver should have come in with him anyway. It was madness, he knew it, and yet he wanted Oliver to show that he wasn't ashamed of him. That he believed in them. But of course it was unreasonable to ask him to expose himself. The thought made him angry, angry because he was powerless. He slammed the cab door behind him without replying.

CHAPTER
FIVE

Charlotte opened her eyes to London sunshine. She yawned as the maid went quietly about, opening the curtains and preparing her dressing table. She felt unexpectedly calm, and wondered why. Sitting up, she saw her wardrobe. A faint smile touched her lips. Purging her past had been strangely cathartic.

Her post was by her bed, on the usual silver tray. She glanced at a couple of uninteresting invitations, but the third letter made her start.

The handwriting was instantly familiar. She had read it on a hundred illicit messages, and even now it called up a faint blush to her cheeks. How strange that when she should try to get rid of her past, one stubborn element from it should turn up like this— twice in two days. She opened the letter and read.

Dear Charlotte,

I hope you will excuse this, it must come out of the blue. The fact is I hardly know why I'm writing myself, only that I am off to France tomorrow and it seems I should say farewell, given the occasion, to those people about whom I care. I think that includes you. I don't expect that you care for me any longer, and I understand that, but I'd like you to know that I am going, at least. I am glad to do my bit and hope I shall do credit to the old school and my king and country, of course. Nevertheless, the stories one hears do put the wind up one a bit. That's the truth of it—I am afraid.

I suppose that's why I'm writing to you, really. I don't know anyone else I could admit it to. Mother and Father and Emily just want to hear the usual heroics, and sometimes it gets too sickening to have to keep up the pretense of being quite happy to leave all this behind for the front line. We've kept each other's secrets before. I hope it's not too terribly selfish to ask you to keep one more for me, for old times' sake.

I expect this letter is a terrible mess. Please excuse it. I won't write again, but I wanted to say good-bye and wish you the very best. I want you to know, anyway, that I think of you with a good deal of affection and respect. I hope you feel the same for me.

Laurence, Lord Fintan.

Charlotte read the letter through, and then read it again, and again. So this was Laurence's news. She was shaken. She had expected something so very different.

Her maid was waiting for her to dress. Concealing her feelings, she put the letter back in the envelope and went to her dressing table to begin the day.

As MacIvor brushed her thick, golden hair, she looked at herself in her mirror and tried to organize her thoughts. The letter troubled her deeply. For Laurence to admit fear to her must have taken a good deal. Her heart went out to him; she wondered if he felt as isolated as she did. Perhaps men did have to put on a front, just as women did, every day. Not for the first time, she wished they could have understood each other better—before it was too late.

MacIvor's brush caught a knot in her hair, and she winced. Because it *was* too late. She knew that now; she had known it before she opened the letter; she had known it since she had searched her heart for pain at the thought of Laurence married, in love, and had found . . . nothing. She was glad that he had written to her. Glad that he had trusted her enough, in the end, to speak to her openly and frankly. And it was that gladness that told her, once and for all, that she was not in love with him any longer. The thoughts and feelings she had for him were those that one would have for a dear comrade-in-arms, someone with whom one had fought life's battles—and from whom one could part with no regrets.

I must write to him, she thought, as she rose to get dressed. Perhaps he will know some way in which I could be useful.

CHAPTER
SIX

Ada sat at the back of the tea shop, toying with her napkin. She knew she must look strange to the East End customers—a well-dressed young lady in an unfashionable area of London, and alone. But she had been here enough times, and made sure to tip handsomely enough, for the waitresses to greet her with a smile and the owner to reserve her usual table: two chairs, at the back, away from the windows. They perhaps assumed she was one of the voluntary aid detachment—untrained volunteer nurses, or VADs—from the boarding house down the road. They were often girls from the best families, doing their bit like their brothers.

The doorbell jangled and Ada looked up quickly. A smile flooded her face as she saw Ravi coming toward her. The expression in his eyes as he looked at her made her blush.

"I'm late, I am sorry," he greeted her as he sat down. "I had the devil of a job to get away from the office. There is so much extra war work on."

He reached for her gloved hand and their fingers locked. Ada's tingled as she felt his strong, certain grip. The waitress came to take their order, a smirk on her lips as she looked at them. As soon as her back was turned, Ravi raised Ada's gloved fingers to his lips and kissed them.

"Ravi," Ada whispered. "Some discretion, please!" But she knew her smile was telling a different story. There was a frisson about meeting secretly like this. She knew it was probably wrong of her to feel it, but she had long ago given up trying to resist her feelings. All that mattered was that the principal of Somerville College should not find out that her shopping trip to London was an excuse, her aged aunt an invention. Luckily, she was sure she would see no one she knew here, in this poky tea shop with its grubby net curtains and loud, familiar customers.

"Have you any news of Alexander and Rose?" Ravi asked, a more serious expression on his face.

Ada's smile vanished as she was reminded of daily troubles. "Not a word. I write to the War Office every day, but I hear nothing. Father is doing his best and so is Sebastian, but this awful war seems to have brought everything to a standstill. I trust in her good sense, though, and I know Alexander will allow no harm to come to her."

"Still, you must be worried."

"I am." Ada forced a smile. "But there is so much to distract me. I can never thank you enough for being the person who gave me the courage to go up to Oxford. Of course it was my father who enabled it by agreeing in the end, once it became clear that Rose's marriage would save the estate and mine did not have to, but it was you who first made me think that it was really a possibility. It's all I could have dreamed of—if you were there with me."

"I wish I were, but you know it would be impossible—so many questions would be asked. And we are freer to meet here than we would be in Oxford, where everyone would know us."

"Yes, the city is a wonderful disguise."

"Tell me about your life there. I miss the old place."

"Of course we can't escape the war—students are leaving every day to join up, and you see as much khaki as gowns and mortarboards. But the intellectual life doesn't seem to have dimmed at all; perhaps it is brighter for having something of real, immediate importance to the world to reflect on."

"Ah yes, I remember that feeling of frustration—the ivory tower. Is Connor Kearney still there? His lectures always renewed my enthusiasm for Oxford. He had a unique perspective, as a well-reputed barrister who was also a professor of law."

"Oh yes." Ada's cheeks flushed as she thought of her favorite professor. "What a fascinating man! He argues brilliantly on the side of Irish nationalism. I have never heard these arguments before—of course my father would never allow them spoken at Somerton—and I can't agree with him on every point . . . but he is certainly a powerful speaker, and I don't doubt his dedication to his country. Of course, as a result of his views he has many enemies."

"Yes, he was always provocative." Ravi smiled, remembering. "Is it true that he calls himself a conscientious objector?"

"It is. I think it is very brave of him; it is not easy to make a public stand against war when the atmosphere of the country is so feverish. I worry that he will be targeted, should conscription be introduced. It is already an open secret that the university administration want to get him out of his post."

"Let's talk of something more cheerful," Ravi said, touching her hand. "How do the ladies of Oxford amuse themselves, when not studying?"

Ada laughed. "The women at Somerville are a mixture— some are dreadful, others are delightful. But one can always find interesting conversation. I don't think I have been to bed before two on any night since I arrived there. We sit up drinking cocoa in our pajamas and discussing everything from the vote to the zeppelin. Of course," she added, "this interesting conversation is only with women. If I were seen speaking to a man, even if he were my brother, I would be sent down at once."

"Ridiculous, is it not. As if men and women weren't capable of platonic discussions." There was an amused sparkle in his eye, and he reached out for her hand again. He slid off the soft kid glove and kissed each bare finger in turn, lingeringly. Ada gasped and blushed. A lady's hands were never naked in public. "Just as we are now," he murmured.

"Someone might see," she breathed in reply.

"Tell me to stop, then."

Ada knew she should, but found herself unable to speak, as he continued to tease her fingers. Nothing in her conventional upbringing, she thought, had prepared her for the deep attraction she might feel to the most unsuitable men.

A clatter of china made her start, and she swiftly pulled her hand back, red-faced, as the waitress arrived with their teas.

Sipping tea gave Ada a chance to regain her composure. Ravi seemed caught up in his own thoughts. When he had finished his cup, he spoke. "I want to talk about the future, Ada."

"The future!" Ada gave a small laugh. She looked up, around her. The new menu reflected wartime rationing, and she could see a table full of soldiers by the door. "Does anyone know what that holds, any longer?"

"Perhaps not, but that needn't stop us making plans," he replied. "I am delaying my return to India by staying here. I couldn't be happier, of course, but sooner or later my employer will want me back. I don't want to return without you."

Ada placed her cup on the saucer and looked at him intently. He had never seemed more serious. It was an idea they had discussed many times before, but each time there had seemed so many obstacles. And now—

"I don't want to leave Oxford," she said abruptly. "I have fought so hard to get there."

"I don't mean now," he said. "Of course you should finish your studies."

Ada looked down at the table again. *Studies*, he had said, not *degree.* It touched a raw nerve in her. She could study as much as she liked, come top of her class in everything, but she would never get the certificate that said she was a laureate. Women could attend university, but not graduate. And without a degree, it would be impossible to practice as a barrister, which was what she longed to be. It was a dead end that she tried not to think about. Just to get through Oxford, to use this time as well as she could, to try to be satisfied with studying for her own satisfaction and hope that things would change one day—this was all she could do. Many women spent only one year or two at Oxford. They did not complete the degree program, knowing they would not be awarded the certificate.

Ravi was still speaking. "I want to return to India; my heart is there. And you have often said how you wish you could go back, how you love it as the place where you grew up. I see no reason why we shouldn't go back there together."

Ada could not disagree with him. She did love India. It was where she had spent her childhood; she still felt a longing for the cool hill towns and the rhythm of the monsoon, the languorous heat, the fascinating people. It was embedded in her heart, just as Ravi was. So she did not know why her next words were so evasive. "It is too early to decide. We simply don't know what may happen in the future," she said. "What if they introduce conscription? You may be called up."

"And it may be over by Christmas."

"Do you believe that?"

"I don't know what to believe. I am not a military expert. But

I do know that I want you to think about what I have said. There is no need for a hasty decision. But you know how much I love you . . . how much I want us to be truly together, to love each other properly."

Ada understood him. The thought sent a thrill through her.

"You want that too, don't you?" He touched her hand again, and her skin tingled in response.

"Of course."

"Then think about it, Ada." His voice caressed her. "Please."

CHAPTER
SEVEN

PALESBURY

The streets of Palesbury were full of soldiers. Little boys gathered to stare at the recruiting officer, and British flags hung from every window of the pub. As Rebecca cycled past the old church, she could see a line of men waiting to sign up circling around the churchyard. She could also see the queues that stretched from the baker, the greengrocer, and the general stores. Prices were high; the shipping blockade was doing its work. It gave her an uneasy chill to think that their daily life could be cut off so easily—as if the submarines and prowling battleships were fingers around Britain's throat. What shall we do if we run out of food? she wondered. But there would be time enough to face that trouble when—if—it came.

She got off her bicycle as she reached the little cottage that her mother was renting. Geraniums were bright in pots around the whitewashed walls. Her mother had really made a home here, she thought. It warmed her heart to see it. If only they could stay—but that all depended on her keeping her job.

"Mother," she called, opening the gate. Her little brother, Davy, scampered out to meet her.

"Have you seen, Rebecca, all the big boys are joining up!" he greeted her as he took her bicycle. "They're going to fight the Germans! I wish I could go; I'd shoot a gun, too!"

"Davy, be quiet!" Rebecca hardly ever spoke sharply to him—he was the darling of the family—but she couldn't help herself. The thought that he might have to go, sooner or later . . . She saw the shocked look on his face and regretted her quick words. "I'm sorry, Davy-boy. But don't talk about things you don't understand. War isn't a game. Come on, where's Mother? I've got some things for her!"

Davy led her through, chattering about the games he had been playing that day—all of them seemed to involve explosives in some way, she noted wryly—to the kitchen, where her mother was kneading bread, the baby wrapped in a basket on the floor beside her.

"Oh, Rebecca!" she greeted her, and Rebecca could tell how anxious she had been in the weeks that she had not seen her. She wiped her hands down her apron and came to give her a kiss. "Is everything all right?" Her eyes searched Rebecca's face.

Rebecca gave her her biggest smile. "Oh, yes. I couldn't be better. It's such a shock to see the town in arms, though."

"Oh dear, it's terrible. Those young boys who are enlisting, they can't be more than sixteen, some of them. I am so glad that David isn't old enough to go." She looked back at Rebecca. "So the place is suiting you? You certainly look well."

Rebecca sidestepped the question and placed her parcel on the table. "These are some of poor Master Philip's old clothes. Lady Georgiana thought we might like them for Davy."

"Now that is very kind." Her mother gratefully took up the parcel "But tell me—I've been so worried, what with you not being brought up to this work. Do they treat you well?"

Rebecca looked into her mother's anxious face. Not for the world would she tell her how lonely she felt, how she knew that Annie and Martha giggled at her behind her back, how she found her cleaning brushes dirtied overnight and her fresh aprons spoiled in the morning by someone malicious. Her mother had quite enough to worry about as it was.

"Very well indeed. Lady Georgiana is so kind."

"And the staff?"

Rebecca hesitated. "They're all right. I think it will take some time for them to accept a new face—and a parlormaid at that."

"You answer to the butler? Oh dear, some grumpy old man, I expect."

Rebecca laughed, thinking of Thomas's wide blue eyes and quick smile. Not, however, that the smile was often directed at her. He seemed uncomfortable around her, as did the rest of the staff. Still, she had to reassure her mother. "Couldn't be further from the truth. He's seventeen—"

"Seventeen! No older than you."

"Mr. Cooper went off for war work, you see, and the older footman enlisted. So Mr. Wright was promoted, at least for the duration—or until he enlists too, I suppose."

"Goodness. Well, things have certainly changed since I was a girl in service."

"Yet you're still the best cook I know." Rebecca smiled.

"I know that look; you're trying to get around me. Well, what is it, miss?"

"Do you have any sugar? We're all out, up at the big house, and Cook is in a terrible state."

"Oh, don't tell me! I saw the bishop's wife arriving in her big car; I think she has bought everything in the town. And the prices are shocking. It's a good thing I know how to manage." She bustled around, took several scoops from her jar of sugar, wrapped them up carefully, and handed them over to Rebecca. Rebecca stowed them away. She was determined to make this place work, to show both upstairs and downstairs at Somerton that they couldn't manage without her. She was determined to be the best parlormaid they could hope for.

Rebecca cycled back through the village. The soldiers were parading in the square, smiling and singing marching songs. The whole town seemed to have turned out to watch them, and under the blue sky it seemed impossible that the rifles they carried could ever be used to kill anyone with.

She sighed, not looking forward to going back. Martha would have some snide comment, and Annie would have thought of some new trick to play on her. *But I have to go back,* she scolded herself. *Mother can't afford to keep me, and this is a great chance for me, if I can only show them how much I want the job and how hard I am prepared to work to keep it.*

She was thinking so hard that she was taken completely by surprise when a male voice exclaimed, "Look out!" The next moment the bicycle had run into something, and she was tipped off it. Luckily she managed to catch herself before she sprawled on the path, but the basket fell to the ground.

"Are you all right? Let me help you!" There was a man taking the handlebars, talking in a concerned voice. Rebecca, thinking of the sugar and blushing at the spectacle that she must make, scrabbled around on the ground to collect her things.

"I'm so sorry!" she exclaimed, rescuing the sugar. "I should have been paying more attention—"

She looked up and her voice froze in her throat. The handsome young man holding her bicycle was none other than Master Michael Templeton, the son of the Countess of Westlake.

He looked at her keenly, then exclaimed, "Why, if it isn't Rebecca. You're our new parlormaid, aren't you? I thought I recognized you."

"I'm so—so sorry, sir," Rebecca kept her eyes on the ground. Was she supposed to speak in this situation? Was she supposed to avert her eyes as she did in the house? Surely, surely, bicycling into the young master was a sacking offence.

"Nonsense, it was as much my fault. This is a blind corner. Here, catch hold."

Rebecca looked up to see him holding out his hand to her. Covered in confusion, but afraid to disobey, she took hold of it, and he pulled her to her feet.

"Now then, are you hurt?"

"No, not at all, sir." Rebecca, to her horror, felt tears come to her eyes. She had been feeling so lonely, and he was being so unexpectedly kind. She looked away, blinking desperately, but it was too late.

"I say, are you all right?" Michael asked. He did not release her hand, but drew her closer, off the road, then bent to pick up her bicycle.

"Yes, perfectly. Yes, thank you so much for your help, sir." Rebecca knew she didn't sound convincing. She took her bicycle from him and tried to wheel it away, but he caught hold of the saddle.

"No, wait, don't run off like that." His voice was gentle and concerned. "You should know that at Somerton we never wish to see one of our people unhappy. Is there something I can do?"

Rebecca sniffed, and wiped her eyes and nose with her hanky. She finally felt under control, and could meet Michael's eyes with a brave smile. "I—I was just thinking of my father, sir. He died recently, and I miss him very much."

It was true, although it wasn't why she had been crying.

"I am so sorry." Michael's voice was soft. "I lost my own father when I was a little boy. It's a scar that takes years to heal."

Rebecca felt new tears coming to her eyes. She looked down, and nodded.

"He would be very proud of you, I am sure, if he could see you today," Michael said.

"Thank you, sir," murmured Rebecca. She took her bicycle again. She knew it was unfair to keep him here; he must feel awkward at speaking to a servant like this in the middle of the public highway. "You have been very kind. I must go back now; Mr. Wright will be needing me to help with the silver."

"Of course." He hesitated. "Good-bye, and—good luck, Rebecca."

"Thank you, sir." Rebecca smiled, then walked away with the bicycle. Luckily, the sugar had not spilled at all. She glanced back, just in case he was watching. He was not, he was walking on toward the recruiting office, but she still looked back again, once or twice. Master Michael, she thought, was as gentlemanly as he was handsome—and that was saying a lot.

CHAPTER
EIGHT

SOMERTON

"Excuse me, my lord," said Thomas the next day, appearing at the door of the breakfast room with a troubled expression on his face. "But will Master Templeton be absent for long? It is only that we would like to know how many will be at dinner—"

Georgiana looked up. She caught Charlotte's eye and saw a reflection of her own surprise there. Michael had not mentioned that he was going away.

"Absent?" The earl spoke for all of them. "He is not absent, Wright. Not to my knowledge."

"Er—very good, my lord," said Thomas. Georgiana could see he was not convinced.

"He has perhaps gone for an early ride," Lord Westlake said, noticing Thomas's discomfort.

"He appears to have taken his shaving materials—in fact, everything indicates that he has gone away for at least a weekend, my lord. Roderick only discovered his absence when he went upstairs to dress him."

Lord Westlake looked at the countess. "Did he mention anything, my dear? It's most inconsiderate of him if he has simply gone off on a jaunt."

"No, he said nothing to me. How typical of the boy," the countess sighed. "I shall give him a stern lecture when he comes in."

But the morning passed, and Michael did not arrive. Georgiana spent an anxious day. She told herself that there was no need to worry, that Michael had certainly just gone to visit a friend, and in his usual rebellious way had decided not to tell anyone—but when they went in for dinner, he was still not there.

"I am really concerned now," said the earl, frowning. "My dear, don't you think we had better have Wright speak to the servants discreetly and find out if anyone has seen him?"

"I suppose so. What a nuisance!" the countess replied.

The earl turned to Thomas. "Will you speak to the servants, Wright? Find out if anyone has seen Master Michael?"

The parlormaid, Rebecca, looked up with a startled expression. Georgiana had forgotten until that moment that she was serving the dinner. She was so inconspicuous and quiet—even James could not have done it better. Now, though, she crossed to Thomas and whispered in his ear.

Thomas listened, nodded, and turned back to the table.

"Excuse me, but Rebecca would like to say that she saw Master Michael yesterday in Palesbury."

"You did? Whereabouts?" the countess demanded directly.

"Just by the recruiting office, my lady," Rebecca replied.

Georgiana drew in her breath sharply. The countess put down her glass.

"You saw him by the recruiting office and you said nothing to us?" she demanded in the iciest, and most terrifying tones.

Rebecca trembled.

"I—I didn't think, my lady, that there was any harm in him being there."

"You did not think!" The countess looked around the table with an expression of fury. "Well! Of all the stupidity!"

"Do you have any idea of what he may have been doing in the town?" the earl demanded.

"N-no, sir. I fell from my bicycle and he was kind enough to help me collect my parcels. That's all I know."

"Just because he was seen near the recruiting office doesn't mean . . ." Georgiana was reluctant to say in front of the servants what she knew they were all thinking. But Rebecca seemed to understand.

"I do remember," she faltered, "that he did wish me luck. I thought that was a little surprising, almost as if, as if—"

"As if he were going away for a long time!" the countess finished. "Oh, you idiot girl, how could you not have said anything to us?"

"Thank you, Wright, Rebecca, that will be all," the earl said hastily. The servants left the room and the family was alone. Georgiana looked around at her father and the countess. The look of concern on her father's face and of fury on the countess's did not reassure her.

"The insolence, the disobedience! He has simply flouted my wishes!" The countess got up and paced the room, her silk dress swishing around her ankles like an angry whip.

"You think he has enlisted, then?" Charlotte spoke sharply, betraying her anxiety.

For the first time, Georgiana thought, she and Charlotte Templeton shared an emotion—fear for Michael.

"But he is underage," she said. "Surely they won't take him."

"If they believe him to be nineteen—and he does look old for his age—they will," the earl responded. "Well, I am sorry. I think he should have waited. But he wanted to enlist, and at least it shows he has courage and a manly spirit."

"You surely don't mean there is nothing to be done!" Georgiana exclaimed.

"Nothing to be done? Not at all," the countess responded. "I am going to write immediately to the War Office and demand his discharge. He is not of majority, and I am his sole surviving parent. He is under my command, not Lord Kitchener's! I forbade him to go, and I will not have him disobeying me like this. I will demand a discharge."

"Oh, but, Mother—" Charlotte exclaimed, and at almost the same moment the earl said, very seriously, "My dear, I understand your concern for your son, but think what you are doing.

He isn't a child. He's a young man. He has made this choice, to fight for his country, knowing the risks. How will he feel to be dragged back from doing what he feels is his duty—will he ever forgive you?"

"He is just a child!"

"He is a young man."

"Oh, this is terrible!" Georgiana exclaimed. "We can't allow him to go to war."

"We *can* allow him to go to war," Charlotte said.

"How can you say that?" Georgiana exclaimed. "He may be killed!"

"You don't understand. I am frightened for him, but think how he must feel!" Georgiana was startled by the passion in Charlotte's voice. "You know he was color sergeant in his Officer Training Corps. You know he was top marksman at his school. You know he hates discipline that he does not understand the reason for, but he will dare anything if he only knows the purpose. What greater purpose than this can there be? I cannot imagine a better soldier than Michael, and, well, is it not selfish of us to ask for his discharge just because it would hurt us so much if . . . if he were not to come back?"

Georgiana looked at Charlotte with new respect. She had never heard her speak with such feeling or such intelligence. This season, or perhaps it was the outbreak of war, seemed to have changed her deeply.

"How dare you call your own mother selfish," the countess

said. "May I inform you that my mind is entirely made up. I will write for his discharge at once."

She swept toward the writing desk, opened it, and began to write, fiercely. She looked up to say, "I knew this parlormaid non-sense would come to no good. That wretched girl will have as good as killed Michael if anything happens to him."

"Oh, but how could she have known what he was planning?" Georgiana said.

"I really don't know, but she was the last person to see him, and she did not raise the alarm. That is inexcusable. Oh, to have Cooper back, and everything as it was before the war!"

CHAPTER
NINE

LONDON

The Eagle and Child was thick with smoke; the clink of glasses and the hum of conversation, broken by occasional laughter, filled the air. Sebastian sat nursing his pint, frowning at the scarred table. He disliked being here. It was too obvious; it wasn't the kind of place he liked to bring Oliver to. There were women with mannish haircuts, collars, and ties, some men openly wearing lipstick, flirting with each other. He didn't blame them, but it wasn't where he and Oliver should be. Not that Oliver seemed to mind.

He glanced up as the piano struck up a popular tune, and saw Oliver laughing with the pianist. "Darling," he heard him say. He knocked back his pint and got up, scowling even more. He strode over to Oliver and put a hand on his shoulder.

"I thought you were the police, then," Oliver laughed, but the laugh faded when he saw Sebastian's expression. "What is the matter?"

"You're drawing attention to us."

"'Attention,' the man says. We're in the queerest pub in Fitzrovia and he's afraid we'll stand out." He reached out and plucked a primrose from the vase on the piano, tucked it into Sebastian's buttonhole, and straightened his collar. "Relax, my dear. Enjoy yourself."

The others laughed. Sebastian only scowled more. He pulled Oliver away, noting that he was drunk.

"I was having fun," Oliver protested.

"Come on, these are scarcely our class of people."

"Sebastian, they are exactly our class of people," Oliver said, rolling his eyes.

"That's not what I mean. We may be similar in our proclivities, but—"

"Proclivities! I'm a proclivity now, am I?"

"Don't laugh at me. You know what I mean. We should be in Claridge's or one of the clubs, not in some low dive with these people. . . ."

"You know we don't have that choice." Oliver sounded sullen. "This is what we are; we may as well accept it."

"But I don't! I don't want to be like this. I want us to be . . . to be like Rose and Alexander."

Oliver looked at him and shook his head. "You don't understand, do you? We'll never be allowed to be like that, and . . . well, perhaps I don't want to be. Perhaps I would rather be with people who understand me, who accept me for what I am and don't try to turn me into something I am not and never can be."

Sebastian found it hard to get the words out. "You mean that I don't understand you."

"To be perfectly frank, I'm not sure you do."

"Very well, then," said Sebastian, his voice thick with anger and pain. "If you feel that way, of course there's no more to be said."

He looked at Oliver for a response, but Oliver looked away. Sebastian turned and strode to the door. Halfway there he turned, and raced back to Oliver. He caught him by the arm and pulled him into a rough, passionate kiss. He felt Oliver's lips soft against his own, the delicious smell of him, the pulse that beat in his throat. Then the others started whistling and cheering. Sebastian dropped Oliver's arm as if it were hot, and blundered back to the door. He heard Oliver behind him, saying "Sebastian—" but he didn't wait to hear what it was. He opened the door and plunged out into the night.

He walked for a long time without knowing or seeing where he was going. It's just an argument, he kept telling himself. A little argument. You can turn back now, patch it up. You love him. He loves you. That's enough.

But he knew it wasn't enough.

He stopped, seeing that he had reached Knightsbridge. The streets were dark because of the blackout blinds that were the law now, to guard against zeppelin raids. Standing unseen in the shadows, he saw women in jewels stepping from their carriages and motorcars in front of the theaters and restaurants. The men were in dress uniform and white gloves. In his current mood, one thing struck him with savage force. These couples were men and women. Women and men. Never men and men.

Feeling curiously like a spy, an outsider observing from behind glass, he watched their smiles, their flirtations. What an ordinary scene he was seeing, and yet it was one that was completely impossible for him.

If I go back to Oliver, he thought, what then? What kind of life can I offer him?

He had always pretended that he didn't want what the world offered—reputation, respectability, security, acceptance, the grand old pat on the back—but that was before he met Oliver. Now it was all he wanted. All that he could not, would never be able to, have. A home. A life. A society wedding, damn it. It wasn't just that he wanted these things; it was that he wanted to give them to Oliver. Oliver deserved them.

Some officers had paused on the steps of the Ritz, smoking cigars and conversing in low voices. He heard their soft laughter and took a step forward, as if hypnotized. There were three of them; their uniforms still carried the sheen of new leather and stiff cloth. Volunteers, men who'd rushed to sign up. He'd laughed at these wide-eyed, stiff-upper-lip heroes, but here they were, able to walk into the Ritz, and he was on the outside. Did he need further proof of how far he had fallen? One of the officers caught his eye. He hadn't noticed how close to them he was. He realized, flushing with embarrassment, that he must look like some kind of beggar, lurking in the shadows.

The officer narrowed his eyes at Sebastian, a faint frown showing his puzzlement. With a sudden shock, Sebastian recognized him. It was an old friend of his from Oxford, Vernon Tollemache. Without thinking, he gave a nod of acknowledgement. At the same second he saw recognition in Vernon's eyes. And then they froze.

Sebastian could not find a better way to describe it. Vernon's eyes simply glazed over, cold and hard, as if Sebastian did not exist. He looked away, threw the end of his cigar down. He said something in a low voice to one of the other officers. They all laughed. Then they turned away, Vernon among them, and went up the steps to the Ritz. The door opened, let them in, and shut behind them.

Sebastian stood where he was. He could not bring himself to move. Vernon had cut him—blanked him completely, as if he did not exist. There was no more terrible social judgment. The upper classes had surgically precise ways of dealing with things they found distasteful, monstrous, vile. They simply pretended they did not exist. Sebastian had done it himself, back when he had been one of them. Except he had never been one of them, not really. He had always been living a lie.

He licked his lips and took a soft step back into the shadows.

The first rush of shame and rage had vanished, and he was left with the flat gray landscape of despair.

Of course, this was all he could offer Oliver. Excision, being cut out like rotting flesh from society's healthy body. No. He could not do it.

He turned away. Throughout history there had been one sure path for a man who had nothing left to lose. And tonight, in London, in 1914, Sebastian knew that it would be the easiest thing in the world to find that path.

CHAPTER
TEN

Sergeant Gilbertson, the medical officer at Central London Recruiting Office, was thirsting for a cup of tea. The day had started before dawn, with a long queue of potential recruits snaking down the road and out of the door.

"Take your clothes off," he barked without looking up, as the door opened to let the next young man in. He finished filling out his forms, looked up at the naked man in front of him, and looked again. Most of the young'uns he was seeing here were underdeveloped, underfed, scrawny little things—how could they not be, fed on East End diets. But this man was at least six feet tall, well built, and straight-backed. He already looked like a soldier. He also looked as if he had not slept, or shaved, and as if he had drunk most of a barrel of whiskey. A wilted primrose hung in the buttonhole of the coat he had draped over the back of the chair.

"Age?" he enquired.

"Twenty, sir."

"Name?"

The man hesitated.

"Se—Rupert, sir. Rupert . . . Moore."

The sergeant raised his eyebrow. He could tell a false name a mile off. Probably a middle name. But what business was it of his? The man looked like an excellent recruit for the ranks. Well spoken, too. He wouldn't be the first to join up to escape some scandal or other. Well, if all he did was stop a bullet, that would be quite enough for England.

"Get on the scales" was all he said. He glanced at the weight and made a note of it in the book. "Well, put your clothes on."

He took out the forms as the man dressed again. When the recruit was ready, he cleared his throat. "I'm ready to sign you up. You realize you'll be going overseas?"

"I want to, sir."

"Keen to fight, eh?"

"Not keen to stay." There was a heaviness in the man's voice.

Gilbertson hesitated before continuing with the routine questions. That note in the voice wasn't good. Men who sounded like that didn't last long. They didn't want to.

But there he probably wouldn't last long anyway. Will to survive didn't count for much against a howitzer shell.

Gilbertson filled in the answers—place of birth, British

citizen, and so on—and passed the form back to sign. "There you go. Three years or the duration. Are you ready to take the oath of allegiance?"

The man scanned the form, nodded, and signed. He drew himself up to his full height, raised his hand and repeated after the sergeant the words that would change his life:

"'I, Rupert Moore, do make Oath, that I will be faithful and bear true Allegiance to His Majesty King George the Fifth, His Heirs, and Successors, and that I will, as in duty bound, honestly and faithfully defend His Majesty, His Heirs, and Successors, in Person, Crown and Dignity, against all enemies, and will observe and obey all orders of His Majesty, His Heirs and Successors, and of the Generals and Officers set over me. So help me God.'"

"Very good." The sergeant held out his hand, and the man took it after a moment's hesitation. "Well done, my boy. You're in the army now."

The man nodded. The look on his face was lost, confused. His hand went up, as if unconsciously, to touch the primrose in his buttonhole. Sergeant Gilbertson wondered if he really understood what he had done. If not, he was in for a very rough awakening.

CHAPTER
ELEVEN

OXFORD

"Some post for you, Lady Ada," said the principal as Ada entered the Somerville breakfast room. "News from home, that is always pleasant."

Ada smiled her thanks and took the letter as she sat down. It did indeed have a Palesbury postmark, and she recognized Georgiana's handwriting. She felt oddly reluctant to open it. Georgiana knew nothing of Ravi; Ada had kept it a secret from all but Rose. Georgiana knew, of course, that Ada had scandalously left Laurence, Lord Fintan, at the altar—indeed *everyone* knew, as she had learned from the whispers and glances that followed her everywhere at Oxford—but Georgiana thought that was because Ada had found him *in flagrante* with Charlotte. She did not know that that was only part of the reason. She did not know that the rest of the reason was Ravi.

Ada was uncomfortably conscious of keeping this from her. She played with the letter, knowing that Georgiana suspected nothing, that her own news would be as artless and as simple as ever. It was unpleasant to have to keep secrets like this from those she cared about most. Of course, if she married Ravi and went to India, there would no longer be any secrets in the matter.

If.

She opened the envelope with the paper knife, aware of her housemates' eyes on her. The letter was indeed from Georgiana. The first words arrested her.

We have had a telegram from Rose. She is safe, at least for now, but Alexander has joined a battalion in Cairo—he really had no choice, it seems—and rather than accept a passage home on a military vessel, she has chosen to follow him. We do not know exactly where they have gone, that is classified information, though we must assume it is somewhere in the Eastern Mediterranean. But oh, Ada, when I think of the danger that she will face, now that the Turks have entered the war on the side of the Germans! The whole of the Eastern Mediterranean is a battlefield, and she is in it, somewhere. If only we knew where.

There was more, but Ada did not read on; she was too shaken. She stuffed the letter back into the envelope and looked up to find everyone's eyes on her.

"I—excuse me. My sister. The Duchess of Huntleigh." Her voice trembled. "We have been so anxious for news and it has finally come."

"Oh, I hope the news is good!" said Helen Massey, one of the other Somervillians at the breakfast table, wide-eyed. No one had to ask who the duchess was. Rose's stunning marriage to Alexander, Duke of Huntleigh, had made her a household name. Ada told them quickly what she knew.

"So she has followed him!" the principal exclaimed. "That is, well, of course it is very brave, but it is hardly conventional."

"It does not surprise me," Ada said. "I know my sister, and I know that she would never return to England and safety while Alexander was in danger."

"It is so shocking that this should happen while they were on honeymoon," said another girl, and everyone agreed. Ada was glad that no one seemed to remember, or if they did, to care, about her sister's previous life as a housemaid. Times had changed, she thought. And the world had a short memory. Besides, Rose was so good and kind that no one who knew her could fail to like her. Tears came to her eyes as she remembered how much danger she was still in.

"Please excuse me," she managed, and stood up quickly. She could feel sympathetic eyes on her as she left the room.

She went up to her room for her walking coat, parasol, and hat. She longed for nothing more at this moment than for Ravi to be here, to be able to stroll along the river with him and tell him everything, to cry on his shoulder and be comforted. But he was in London.

She went out of the college. As she did so, she found herself looking at Connor Kearney, who was just coming up the path. He raised his hat when he saw her. His hair was dark, but she noticed that in the dappled sunlight red and gold strands shone in it—a curious but handsome mixture. He was not as old as she had thought him; it was only the gown that gave him an air of serious dignity.

"Lady Ada! Good morning," he said, walking toward her.

Ada murmured a greeting. She was not pleased to have met him. It was intimidating being in the presence of someone so incisively intelligent, so unafraid of voicing his opinions, and even more so in her present frame of mind.

Kearney smiled as he reached her. It lit his face. She caught the scent of his cologne, and cigar. "I wanted to say that I enjoyed your proposal at the debating society the other week," he said. "It was an interesting motion. There was of course no hope that you could win a debate for Indian independence, but you argued for it very cleverly. I think if more people allowed themselves to see beyond their prejudices you would have carried the day."

Ada blushed. Praise from Connor Kearney was rare, and she found herself unusually tongue-tied. After waiting a polite moment, Kearney went on, "I am sorry to say I have come with some bad news, which you will no doubt hear gossip about in the town, so perhaps I should forestall it. It is likely that Somerville may close in the near future."

"Close!" Ada was shocked.

"It will be converted into a hospital for wounded officers," he said. "In this time of national need, we must be ready to make sacrifices."

"And of course it must be the women's college that is to close, not one of the men's." Ada found herself in a towering rage, as if all her pent-up anxiety for Rose had found an outlet. "It was not women who began this war, and I don't think we should have to suffer for it. Men began it—let one of their colleges close."

At once she regretted her outburst. It was unmannerly, and she had made a bad impression on Connor Kearney—a don she so wanted to impress.

Connor, however, did not seem at all perturbed. He simply raised an eyebrow. "But it isn't women who are paying the ultimate price. So should women not be glad to do their bit, as far as they can? To sacrifice their comfort, even if they cannot sacrifice their lives?"

Ada faced him boldly, grateful that he had not taken offense but had turned it into an opportunity for debate. "I am glad to sacrifice for my country, but I ask for equal sacrifice with men. Don't take our education from us as being a nothing, a plaything that we can well do without. Instead, let us go to the front alongside the men, and then you can take Somerville and welcome."

"Bravo! An excellent argument." Kearney grasped her hand and shook it, smiling broadly. Ada was relieved but embarrassed. She let go of his hand quickly, but couldn't avoid blushing. "But I am glad to tell you that none of the students will have to give up their education. You will be moved to one of the men's colleges."

"That is a relief!" Ada's voice shook. She stepped back, afraid that she would betray herself into more embarrassing demonstrations of emotion. "Please excuse me. I want to profit from the sunshine."

"An excellent idea." He raised his hat again as she turned away.

Ada hurried down toward the river. The color was high in her cheeks, and she was not sure quite why—whether because of the news about Rose, or the news about Somerville . . . or simply because Connor Kearney had praised her argument.

CHAPTER
TWELVE

LONDON

Charlotte, sitting next to the countess in the audience of the latest charity concert in aid of the Red Cross, was bored, and guilty for feeling bored. This was war work, she reminded herself: being here was helping men like Laurence. And yet, she thought as the singer's last fluid notes died away and she joined the audience in applause, it seemed as if her mother and her friends had simply taken the opportunity to continue doing exactly what they had been doing—only now they did it for charity. Somehow it seemed too easy.

Her mother nudged her as they got up from their seats and prepared to make their way to the buffet lunch. "Look, there is young Castleton."

"He looks so different in uniform," Charlotte said. It was

strangely shocking to see someone she had once danced with, flirted with, suddenly appear so serious and grown-up. She wondered if he felt afraid, like Laurence—and remembered with a quick shock of guilt that she had not yet replied to his letter. Her mother had kept her in such a social whirl these past few weeks.

"Perhaps we should invite him to stay before he goes overseas," her mother murmured in her ear. Charlotte realized with a start that her mother's thoughts about Bertie were quite different from her own.

"No, Mother, please! He isn't interested in me at all . . . nor am I interested in him." She walked away quickly. Her mother followed.

"What is wrong with him?" she said in a low voice. "You simply can't be so choosy. Not anymore."

"He's dull."

"Well," said her mother, glancing around, "with things the way they are, you may not have to suffer more than a few weeks of his dullness. . . . Goodness, what a look you just gave me. I'm only thinking of your happiness, dear."

Charlotte couldn't find a polite reply. She walked away, not even looking where she was going. It was too horrible to think of marrying someone and calculating on their being killed. She found herself by the buffet, next to a woman in a VAD uniform. Charlotte glanced shyly at her, then realized she knew her. It was Portia Claythorpe, a girl she had never had much time for before the war. She was a bishop's daughter, plump, sweet-tempered, with a rather prim kind of way about her that had irritated

Charlotte. But now, dressed in the flowing white gown of the VAD, even with the ugly apron ruining what there was of her waist and her hair hidden under the cap, she looked admirable. She looked as if she was really part of what was going on, a mysterious creature, with heavy responsibilities—not just a lapdog to be dressed up and ordered around by her mother. Charlotte found herself tongue-tied with admiration. It was some time before she summoned up the courage to speak to her.

"I see you have joined the voluntary aid detachment," she said at last. "You are very brave."

"Oh, I don't know. Someone has to do something for these poor men," Portia replied. "It makes one feel better somehow, being able to be of use."

"You have been abroad, then?"

"No, only here in London. I do hope to go abroad, however. I long to, in fact. I want to do the most that I possibly can to share the suffering of the poor men."

"It must be inspiring work."

Portia smiled tiredly, and again Charlotte had the sense that Portia was in some way on the inside of things, that she was looking out on Charlotte as one looked at a younger sister who knew nothing about love. "It is certainly very hard work. Hard on the body, and on the mind, too." She hesitated. "We received some casualties from Ypres." Her voice lowered. "I know we're not supposed to speak of it, but it was terrible, it was—"

"But it was a victory for us, wasn't it?"

"Yes, but . . ." Portia fell silent as Lady Emily joined them.

Charlotte could guess what she was going to say. *The cost was too great.* She was left with an unpleasant shiver down her spine, and a feeling of both dread and curiosity.

"Portia, you look simply charming," Lady Emily announced. "I would join the voluntary nursing services, but Vivian won't hear of it. He thinks I shouldn't compromise my femininity."

"I never thought that a concern of yours," Charlotte said with a raised eyebrow. Lady Emily had always been the most insufferable suffragette, but it somehow disheartened Charlotte to see her changed.

Lady Emily shrugged prettily. "There are other ways of doing one's bit. I have been selling flags, and handing out feathers. It's a shame to see so many fit young men shirking their duty. In fact," she added, getting out a small clutch of white feathers, "I shall have a word with those two waiters. A woman's touch, you know."

She sallied off. Charlotte and Portia exchanged an expressive glance. Charlotte was longing to ask her more about the life of a VAD, but before she could do so, her mother arrived, Castleton in tow. Charlotte was mortified to see the polite confusion on his face.

"My dear," the countess announced, "I know you wanted to return that copy of Swinburne's poems that Bertie lent you . . ." She went on, overriding Charlotte's protests that she hadn't been lent a book. Charlotte found herself making plans to entertain Bertie at home for a light tea the day before he went abroad, but to her relief, Bertie Castleton interrupted.

"I say, Countess, frightfully sorry to interrupt you, but is Lady Emily quite all right?" he inquired.

Charlotte looked around. She saw Lady Emily by the door; she was holding a telegram that a boy had just brought to her. As Charlotte watched, she turned pale, swayed, and almost fell. The crowd rustled with shock. A man leapt forward to help her to a chair. Charlotte saw Portia go quickly and professionally to her side; she knelt by her, speaking in a low voice.

What had happened? The room was hot and crowded, perhaps that was the trouble, Charlotte thought. A whisper was passing through the crowd. Necks were craned; black feathers on hats trembled. It was Mrs. Verulam who turned to them, her face suddenly showing all its age.

"My dears, such terrible news," she said in an undertone. To Charlotte's surprise, Mrs. Verulam placed a hand on hers. Charlotte, looking into her eyes, was suddenly full of foreboding. "It is Lord Fintan," Mrs. Verulam said quietly. "Laurence. Emily's brother. He was hit by a sniper. A bullet directly through the heart." She added, more gently than Charlotte had ever heard her speak before, "I am sorry, my dear. I know he was one of your set."

Charlotte could not find her breath. Laurence, dead. Laurence, whom she had danced with only months before, had kissed only months before. Laurence, whom she had once thought she would marry. Laurence, whose unanswered letter, his last confession, still lay in her writing case.

"I think we should go home," her mother said, breaking the silence. "Oh dear. Everyone will be greatly upset by this news.

He was so promising." She tucked her arm into Charlotte's, and from that rare gesture of kindness from her mother, Charlotte knew that the news was really true. This was no bad dream or hideous joke.

She followed her mother to her motorcar, in a daze. She had thought there was more time. Time to answer the letter.

"Charlotte? Are you all right?" Her mother leaned toward her as the car drove off. Charlotte was jolted against the soft leather interior. She still could not speak. She clung to the ivory handle of her parasol as if to a life belt.

"I just can't imagine it," she managed to say. "A bullet through the heart."

"Don't try."

But Charlotte could not stop trying. Laurence, debonair and handsome in a ballroom or a debating hall. She had never seen him in his uniform, and she could not call an image to mind now. Somehow she had to take that lively, scornful, ambitious young man whose tie was always perfectly knotted and imagine him in a muddy field, with a bullet through his heart. Her hand went to her own heart, unconsciously. A memory, sudden, unbidden, of a shoot at Somerton a couple of years ago, came to her mind. Explosion after explosion cracking the sky, and the birds tumbling down, all soft-feathered like fainting women in ball gowns, the dogs running up with them. Even then, death had seemed clean.

She stared out of the window. All she could see was black. Black on hats, on armbands, on dresses, on parasols. So much black.

"Charlotte," her mother said again.

"I am quite all right, mother," Charlotte made herself say.

"I know you cared for him." It was the closest to concern that Charlotte had ever heard from her.

"It isn't that."

"I blame myself. I should never have encouraged it. You were too young."

"No, mother. I did care for him once, but that's all over. It's simply that . . ."

"He was one of us. One of our set."

Charlotte wanted to say that that was not it either, that she was stunned because she realized now that there were no sets, only millions of men suffering and dying, that this pain was only part of a web that connected everyone in Europe, perhaps in the world. But what her mother said next drove it out of her mind. "After the shocking way that Ada treated him—"

"Oh, Ada!" Charlotte's hand went to her mouth. Ada had been engaged to Laurence, had nearly married him. She had been as close to him, in her own way, as Charlotte had. This news would be a blow to her too, Charlotte knew that. She could not allow her to find out in the most brutal way, through the newspaper report that would surely follow the death of a peer.

They were pulling up outside the Mayfair house. Charlotte got out as quickly as she could. As soon as the butler opened the door, she ran up to her room. "MacIvor," she said breathlessly to her startled maid. "I must send a telegram at once."

CHAPTER
THIRTEEN

OXFORD

The lecture hall filled with discreet noise as chairs scraped back and the women collected their books. Ada was one of the last to stand up; her cheeks were flushed and her heart was beating fast.

"Professor Kearney." She accosted him at the door.

"Lady Ada?"

"I want to tell you how much I passionately disagree with everything you have just said in your lecture," she said. She knew she was speaking too fast, but she could not hold her tongue. Kearney looked at her in surprise and she was aware of her fast breathing. "And how much I admire you for saying all of it," she finished.

Connor Kearney laughed. His eyes crinkled, and he seemed

a long way from the fiery speaker he had been a moment ago. "I take it you are against an independent Ireland."

"I think it would be an absolute injustice to the Ulstermen."

"And what about the injustice of cutting the head from the shoulders of a great nation?"

"Ireland's fate is bound to England's—"

"In spite of what the Irish people want."

"And now, in the midst of this crisis, is exactly the wrong time to pursue Irish nationalism."

"The wrong time for England, perhaps. For Ireland, it may be perfect timing."

"Oh, you are insufferable!" she exclaimed. Then she flushed, realizing how inappropriate her tone had been. To her relief, Kearney was laughing again; he did not seem to have taken offense.

"Do walk as far as the bridge with me, Lady Ada," he said, moving toward the door. "I am sure your reputation can stand it, and it is always delightful to talk to someone who has strong feelings and is not afraid to express them."

Ada was about to reply, but as they reached the door of the lecture hall, a telegram boy came running up to them, his feet pounding on the parquet floor.

"Excuse me, miss—are you Lady Ada?" he inquired breathlessly.

"I am," Ada said in surprise.

He handed her a telegram. Ada took it automatically. Her

hands gripped it and she suddenly felt a wave of dread roll through her mind. Telegrams meant so much these days. But there was no one she loved at the front, was there? Unless Michael had been sent . . . or Rose—oh, please let it not be bad news about Rose! She tore the envelope open, her fingers trembling so hard that the thin paper inside almost ripped in half.

LAURENCE KILLED IN ACTION NOVEMBER 1 STOP
WANTED YOU TO HEAR BEFORE THE PRESS STOP
AFFECTIONATE SYMPATHY STOP CHARLOTTE

Ada did not realize that she had gasped aloud until she heard Kearney's concerned voice. "Lady Ada? I am afraid you have had some bad news."

His voice brought her to herself again. Memories of Laurence—his strong arms around her as they danced, his cool confidence, the way he'd stepped in to save her from those horrid duns demanding William's debts, the passion of his kisses— flooded into her mind. Numbed, not knowing what she was doing, she turned the telegram over as if something might be written to explain it all away, to say it was a joke. But there was nothing. *Killed.* The word was stark and simple.

"There must be some mistake," she murmured to herself.

"Won't you sit down? You look faint."

Ada accepted his help to lower her to a nearby chair. His grip on her arm was strong yet gentle. The telegram boy had gone, backing off in wide-eyed sympathy. They were alone.

"I'm sorry," she managed. "It was just the shock. We were—I always thought . . ."

"So many of these telegrams, and more every day. I'm very sorry," he said gently.

Ada looked down at the telegram again. Charlotte's kindness in telegraphing struck her. She knew that it must have hit Charlotte as hard as it did her—perhaps harder. They had been rivals for Laurence, in a way. But what had happened had left them both knowing their own hearts better than ever before.

She became aware that Kearney was speaking to her again. "Shall I call a cab? I expect you will want to go home to Somerton as soon as possible. If there is anything I can do to help—"

"Home!" Ada sat forward. "No, no. Oh . . ." She blushed as she realized what he had assumed. "No, it isn't anyone close to me."

"Oh! I am glad. I thought from your reaction, that it might be—"

"I am not engaged," she said, quickly. She thought guiltily of Ravi, but that was a different matter. "It is someone I used to be close to . . . in a way. An old friend."

"That hits very hard too," he said. "I know that."

Ada looked up to his sympathetic face. She saw that she was understood. "It does hit hard," she replied, quietly. "I can't seem to imagine it. It seems there must be some kind of mistake. He is so young—was so young."

She found herself suddenly in tears. Kearney's arm was

around her shoulder and he was murmuring kind, comforting words. Ada sobbed until she was exhausted.

"Oh, I have been so silly," she managed at last, wiping her eyes with her handkerchief. "I am sorry."

"Not at all, there is nothing to apologize for. Let me see you back to Somerville."

"You're very kind," she replied.

They stepped out into the street, Ada conscious of his reassuring presence. She felt that she owed him an explanation, and yet it was all such a shock to her, so confusing, so horrible, so chaotic, that she did not feel she could even explain it to herself. The vigor of their pleasant argument had slipped away like the sun behind a cloud. All that was left was the dreary certainty that someone she had once cared for was dead.

"He gave his life for his country," she said, speaking almost to herself. "I don't think he would ever have regretted that."

"He must have been an honorable man."

"I believe he was. Oh, I can't bear that he should have died in vain. It makes me feel I should have the courage to make the same commitment. And yet . . . how am I to do that?"

"Surely by helping to establish women's place in every part of England, in public life and in private, so that when this war is over, we may all rise renewed." Kearney looked at her for her response.

"You have put it so well," she murmured. She felt that he had expressed her feelings. She did not want to die for her country, but to live for it.

"I understand your patriotism," he said softly.

Ada glanced at him, realizing it was a veiled reference to his own feelings for Ireland. "Do you know," she said abruptly, "there is something about you that reminds me of him."

"Of your old friend?" He looked at her with a smile in his eyes. "I'm flattered."

"That is, you are quite different from him," she said, stumbling. "There is just something . . ."

She trailed off. She could not, of course, tell him what it was. That she felt safe with him, just as she had always felt safe with Laurence.

They walked in silence until they reached Somerville. Ada's mind could not settle; she kept seeing the words of the telegram in front of her: *Killed*. How could they apply to Laurence? Why, she'd seen him just a year ago. How could he be gone?

"I don't think you should be alone this evening," Kearney was saying to her. "You must find someone—friends who will understand. Are you listening? Ada?"

She looked up, startled at the use of her first name. He looked at her seriously.

"I am concerned about you," he said.

Ada managed a smile.

"Thank you. I shall do as you say, but now I must go, or I am afraid I may break down again—so silly."

"Of course." He stepped back at once, and Ada went quickly up the stairs to her room. Alone at last, she placed the creased telegram onto the table. Silence surrounded her. She wished now that she had not let Kearney go. She wanted to talk about Laurence to someone. In the end she snatched the writing paper and began to write to Ravi. She poured out her heart—the sorrow she felt at Laurence's death, how impossible it was to believe that he was dead.

I can't believe he has gone forever—so young, so full of life. When I think that all over England families are suffering far worse than I am, when I think that women are losing men they love as much as I love you, I can't bear to think of my country suffering so. Laurence and I had many differences, but I always admired his patriotism. I feel so powerless, so angry that I cannot do something to defend my country also. How strange that it should be Laurence's death that should make me realize that is how I feel.

Before she could have second thoughts, she sealed the letter and went downstairs to put it in the post.

She could not relax that afternoon, even when her housemates came back from their lectures. She knew from the whispers and the glances she caught in her direction that the news had spread. All of them knew that she and Laurence had been engaged—that she had thrown him over on the very day of the wedding. It was not news that could be kept secret, and nor was his death. She found herself getting angry, resentful of their curiosity.

Evening fell, but instead of growing tired she felt more and more restless. She threw on her coat and went out into the rain.

Through the wet, gleaming cobbled streets she walked, without paying attention to where she was going. Everywhere she looked were recruiting posters and khaki uniforms. England was on a strange, new, terrible path, and she was pulled in its wake. All she could think was that she, like Laurence, loved this country— the rain, the stone, every bit of it. And she could not think of leaving it.

CHAPTER
FOURTEEN

SOMERTON

Georgiana came into the hall, and stopped as she saw the door of her father's study was still closed. In the drawing room the new parlormaid, Rebecca, was dusting. She quickly turned to leave as Georgiana came in.

"No, wait, please—I wanted to ask you. Has the earl been in his study for long? I wish to speak to him and would like to know how long he is likely to be."

Rebecca curtsied. "The earl is with Mr. Bradford," she said. "They have been inside for an hour already."

"Mr. Bradford!" Georgiana said thoughtfully. He was the earl's lawyer. She wondered if this meant he was taking steps to change his will and disinherit William. She hoped so.

"Very well, thank you, Rebecca." She turned aside, ready to wait until he was free. She wanted to ask her father if there was any news of Michael. Even saving Somerton from William had slipped to the back of her mind; her fear for Michael and Rose, both in grave danger, had taken over every thought. The shocking death of Lord Fintan, which the countess had written to them about, had brought home to her how much real danger both faced. I cannot rest until they are both home safely, she thought.

On an impulse she went into the music room. She had once loved to play, just as Rose had loved to compose, but now, with managing the house, she had so little time for it. She sat at the piano stool and began playing a composition of Rose's, "Eastern Dance," from memory. Tears came to her eyes as she played. It brought back memories of an earlier time, before the war, when Somerton had been a happier place.

She became aware that someone was standing in the doorway, and brought the music to an end. Turning, she saw Thomas hovering.

"Yes, Thomas, what is it?" Discreetly she wiped the tears from her eyes.

"Excuse me for disturbing you, my lady. The countess telephoned and desired me to inform you that she is returning from London today, but that Miss Charlotte will remain to attend some charity events with Mrs. Verulam."

"Oh, goodness!" Georgiana was overwhelmed at the thought

of yet more work for the already stretched staff. "So her room will need preparing, and we will have to have a full waiting service at dinner, otherwise she will be displeased. Do you think you can manage it? Shall I send to the village for extra staff?"

"Untrained staff are more trouble than they're worth, my lady, if I may say so," Thomas said. "We'll manage."

"I do so appreciate it."

She followed him with her eyes as he walked away. He looked tired and overworked, and most of all, she was not sure that he enjoyed the job. He did it, but without passion. Georgiana was troubled; she wanted everyone at Somerton to be happy.

But before she could think how to achieve that, she heard the door of the study open, and the earl and Mr. Bradford came out, deep in conversation. Georgiana got to her feet at once and made for the corridor, ready to intercept them. The two men paused at the foot of the stairs. Thomas hovered, ready to show the lawyer out.

". . . yes, it all seems in order. Yes, indeed." The earl shook his lawyer's hand. He was smiling, which made Georgiana's hopes rise.

Mr. Bradford bowed, and the earl rang the bell. As soon as Mr. Bradford had left, Georgiana half ran over to her father. The earl clearly saw the question in her eyes and smiled, although he looked sad.

"Well, my dear, it is done," he said.

"You have changed your will?"

"I have." The earl's voice was heavy. "I wish it did not have to be done, but there was no choice. I cannot let William take possession of Somerton Court on his accession to the title, not now that I know him for the cad that he is."

"His accession to the title? You mean he will still be Earl of Westlake?" Georgiana asked. The thought left a sour taste in her mouth.

"I am afraid so."

"But how can that be just!" Georgiana said. She could not bear to think that the title of the Earl of Westlake—her father's title should pass to a man who was a gambler, a drunkard, a rapist, and in her view no better than a murderer.

"I am afraid that justice and the law do not always coincide," the earl said with a humorless smile. "The title is not mine to bequeath: it was bestowed upon my ancestors by a previous monarch of England, and it passes, according to the law of the land, to the most direct heir in the pure male line. Since I have no male children, I count as a dead end. The next in line, strange as it may seem, is William. The title could not be taken from him even if he were convicted of murder—and in my view he should be, for what he did to that poor nursemaid. Titles do not care if they lodge in an honorable man or a cad."

Georgiana said angrily, "Well, I think it's simply unspeakable. It feels like a stain on our family, that such a man as William should be the earl."

"I know it, but there is nothing to be done. At least I have taken the estate away from him. Thank heaven it was not entailed. The house and land of Somerton, together with the majority of my fortune, will pass to my firstborn grandson."

"That, at least, is a relief," said Georgiana. She sighed. "I do wish that all this was not happening at once. Have you had any news of Michael?"

Her father snapped his fingers. "In all the business discussions, I actually forgot. Yes, I think I have traced him. He is in a training camp in Kent. I shall go down as soon as possible." He shook his head. "He is a brave boy, but his mother is firm. He must come home."

CHAPTER
FIFTEEN

"Mr. Wright, you must let me help you with the silver," Rebecca said, appearing at the door of the butler's pantry. She was breathless after having run down the flights of stairs from the countess's rooms, but she was satisfied that she had left the place in perfect order and ready to welcome the mistress of the house.

"Thank you," replied Thomas, who was already sweating with the hurry and hard work of getting everything ready for the countess's arrival. "But I think you have plenty to do already, preparing her room."

"It's done. I did it as soon as I heard she had telephoned."

"Is the sweet jar filled up? And the flowers?"

"Yes, with lavender comfits and yellow roses, just as she likes.

You really must let me help you; you don't have time to do all this and your usual duties as well."

"I think I'm capable of deciding what I have time to do, Rebecca."

Rebecca came into the room and boldly shut the door. Thomas turned to her in surprise. Rebecca was aware of how close they were together, and her stomach was suddenly full of butterflies. But she pushed bravely on, knowing that if she didn't speak now, she would be putting up with this behavior for the rest of her time at Somerton. "I must say my piece, Mr. Wright. I feel that you are trying to prevent me from doing duties that are rightly mine, as parlormaid, and I won't have it."

Thomas raised an eyebrow. "That's a very high-handed way to speak to your superior."

"I have to speak out if I see the house being run in a way that's not efficient and that will lead to problems."

"Oh." Thomas's sarcasm was deep. "And you think that I am doing such a thing?"

"I do. As parlormaid, I am engaged to fulfill the duties of a first footman. Not simply dusting and preparing rooms, but pantry work, keeping the library in order, silver polishing, brushing the gentlemen's clothes—all the things a footman would do. And you are not allowing me to do those, and you are keeping them for yourself, and as a result, you are overworked and nothing is getting done well."

"Very well. To be honest with you, I don't agree with the post of parlormaid. I think there are some jobs that women are simply not fitted for."

"Oh? And what gives you this insight, may I ask?"

"Rebecca, I am in charge here, and I expect you to obey orders. Otherwise you can find another place."

"So that's how it is, is it?" Rebecca felt her face flush as red as her hair. "Well, Mr. Wright, I'm pleased to tell you that you are a fool."

She jerked open the door and stalked out, her blood thumping in her head. It took her only a few paces down the cool passage to regret her temper. She couldn't do with losing her job, and she was bound to lose it now.

The bell jangled above her head. Rebecca looked up: the countess. She hastily tried to calm herself, tidying her hair and smoothing her hot cheeks. Then she took a deep breath and went upstairs to answer the bell. Work didn't stop just because she was upset.

She found Lady Georgiana in the countess's bedroom. The countess's furs were spread on the bed.

"Oh, Rebecca." Rebecca saw at once that Lady Georgiana looked tired and tearful. "Moth has got into the countess's furs! Oh, what are we to do? This would never have happened when Mrs. Cliffe was here."

Rebecca looked closely at the furs. "They must have been put away without the mothballs, my lady." She knew how serious it was—the furs were worth hundreds, and if they were ruined, the countess's temper would be unspeakable and everyone's life made a misery. Her mother had told her a good deal about the care of furs, learned when she was in service herself.

"Yes, that will be Annie. I can hardly blame her—she is not trained for this work. But oh, what are we going to do." Lady Georgiana sat down on the bed, tears in her eyes. "Once they're in, it's impossible to get them out."

Rebecca took a deep breath. "I think, my lady, that there is something I could try. My mother used to be a lady's maid, and she told me about it. If you place the furs in a box of ice, the eggs will freeze and die."

"Ice! Won't that harm the coats?"

"No, my lady. They will dry before the countess even notices. I can simply take them down to the ice house."

"Are you sure?" Lady Georgiana looked doubtful.

"Quite sure, my lady."

"Oh, well, in that case, please do it at once."

Rebecca quickly and carefully removed the furs from the wardrobe. Lady Georgiana watched.

"I can't thank you enough," she said. She managed a smile; her eyes met Rebecca's. "I'm sorry I was so silly. It's just the strain . . . everything seems to be going wrong at once."

"I know, my lady. Is there . . . is there any news of Master Michael?"

"There is." Lady Georgiana's face lightened. "I think we will be able to bring him home—that is, if his battalion is not posted abroad first, and if the army do not take it into their heads to be stubborn and not let him go. But I—I wish it had never happened. He will feel it very much, being brought home like this. It will hurt his pride."

"I couldn't be sorrier that I didn't try and stop him enlisting. But I simply didn't know, my lady, please believe me."

"Of course not, how could you have? Please don't take the countess's words to heart. She was simply upset, afraid for her son . . ."

"Naturally, my lady." She looked down, and bobbed a curtsy. That was hopeful, but she knew how kind Lady Georgiana was. The countess might not be so quick to forgive. "I'd best go and start on these furs, my lady. Will there be anything else?"

"No. No, thank you. That is . . ." Lady Georgiana hesitated. "How are things downstairs, Rebecca?"

Rebecca thought before answering diplomatically. "Everyone is doing their best, my lady, but of course it's very hard on Cook having to manage the upstairs staff as well." She wondered if she should mention Mr. Wright's reluctance to trust her with footman work, then decided it would not be fair. They had to sort out their own differences.

"Yes. I do think that we need a housekeeper, whatever my father says. These moths only prove it. I just don't know where to look for one."

"Perhaps you might write to the previous housekeeper?" Rebecca suggested. "I understand that Mrs. Cliffe gave excellent service. She might know someone, perhaps, or at least be able to give some advice . . ."

"What an excellent idea, Rebecca!" Lady Georgiana's eyes brightened.

Rebecca curtsied. "Will that be all, my lady?"

"Yes. Yes, and thank you Rebecca."

Rebecca went downstairs with the furs, feeling more cheerful. Lady Georgiana was a treasure, she thought, and she would do all she could to help her. As she came to the foot of the servants' stairs, she heard Annie and Martha gossiping as they scrubbed pans. She walked down to the kitchen knowing what she would see: Cook doing all the work as usual while Annie leaned against the table and Martha swilled dirty water round the same pan again and again.

". . . got a cousin in the War Office, well, he's the errand boy there. He says that this war is all the bankers' doing." That was Annie. "They'll make money selling to both sides."

"Well, what can you expect from a pack of Jews?" Cook replied. She turned to the door and saw Rebecca standing there. "Oh, Rebecca. Take this tea up to the library, will you, and hurry up before it goes cold."

Rebecca didn't reply. The weight of the furs in her arms suddenly seemed to overwhelm them, their musty smell to suffocate her.

"Did you hear me, hoity-toity? Don't stand there gaping; you'll catch flies. Whatever are you doing with those furs anyway?"

Thomas was coming up behind them, and Annie said, giggling, "Oh, Mr. Wright, Rebecca thinks she's too good to carry the earl's tea upstairs. I expect I'll have to do it."

Rebecca turned and almost ran, away from the kitchen, out to the refreshing freedom of the garden. Her heart pounded, and the furs dragged at her arms. Just as she thought things were going well, she was reminded that everything could come crashing down at any moment.

CHAPTER
SIXTEEN

Georgiana stood with the countess at the drawing room window, watching as the motorcar approached down the long drive. The trees were bare and the frost looked almost like snow covering the lawns. The message from her father had come that morning: he was on his way back, with Michael. Relief fought with fear about how Michael would be feeling. Georgiana knew him so well, and knew that pride was key to his character.

She looked down and realized she had torn the rose in her corsage almost to pieces in her nerves. If only Ada or Rose were here. At this moment she would have even been glad of Charlotte's company—but she was still in London. The countess complained about her failure to write, but Georgiana sensed that she was really quite pleased about it—the countess was sure that it meant Charlotte was spending all her time with the suitable Bertie Castleton.

As soon as the car drew close enough for her to be sure that her father was not alone in it, she turned and almost ran to the door. Thomas was just opening it, and Rebecca was standing by, ready to receive the driving coats, hats, and goggles. The chauffeur opened the door, and the earl got out, followed the next moment by the person Georgiana had been longing to see—Michael.

"Oh, I am so glad you're home safely!" she exclaimed.

Michael's scowl silenced her. "I expect you had a hand in this," he said in a low, furious voice. "Don't think I'm grateful!"

He exchanged a single, resentful glance with the countess and then stalked off up the stairs. The countess seemed about to call him back, but the earl stopped her with a hand on her arm. "Better to let him be, my dear," he said quietly.

The countess clearly made an effort to control herself. The earl beckoned Georgiana toward them. "I must speak to you in the study," he said.

Georgiana followed him in, nervously. The study was reserved for stern talkings-to, or for official meetings. She was never comfortable here.

Her father waited until the door closed behind them, and then stood before the fireplace, his hands behind his back. He looked, Georgiana noticed, as if he was holding in some great excitement. There was something indefinably younger about his expression, a suppressed spark that, oddly, made her heart sink.

"I have to tell you that I shall be going away, just for a month or so," her father began.

"A month?" Georgiana said in surprise. "But then will you be away for Christmas?" Her heart sank. Even though she knew Christmas would not be the same in wartime, it still seemed a shame not to be all together as much as possible.

"No, I hope to be back before then."

"Are you going to London?" The countess did not seem surprised; she was used to her husband leading quite a separate life when he wished to.

"Yes, to London, and then"—the earl looked self-conscious—"to France."

"France!" Georgiana exclaimed.

Her father glanced at her quickly, and now she saw that he was embarrassed. Embarrassed, but defiant. In fact, she thought with growing anger, he reminded her of Michael.

"Yes, while I was in London I bumped into my old friend Horatio—he is an admiral now—and he happened to mention that Field Marshal Sir Douglas Haig was in need of some advice regarding the Indian troops who are currently fighting in the area, and as you know, I have some expertise in that field—"

The countess frowned. "I can't pretend I am pleased, but surely you won't face any real danger. You won't be at the front, will you?" Georgiana could see real concern beneath her cold words. The earl seemed to hear it too, and he reached out and took her hand affectionately.

"My dear, I will be quite safe. They will keep an old man like me out of harm's way, believe me."

"That is almost worse," said Georgiana.

Her father looked at her, and she saw hurt in his eyes. But she could not keep silent. The whole horrible stupidity of it, the ridiculous, murderous bloodshed—and it seemed that now her father was as foolish as Michael. She took a step backward, her voice trembling. "Your power and influence might have been used to try and stop this war. But instead you are just like Michael, a little boy wanting to see a fight. I am sorry, Papa. But I cannot say I think you are right to go. I don't. I don't want anything to do with it."

She turned and went out of the room. She managed to keep her tears held back until she reached her own room, and was mercifully alone.

CHAPTER
SEVENTEEN

Rebecca laid out Michael Templeton's evening clothes on the bed, taking special care to crease nothing. She smoothed down the silk of his dinner jacket and made sure the white tie was placed exactly where Thomas would know where to find it. She wondered how Master Templeton was feeling. She hoped that he was not too angry at being ordered home. If only she could comfort Michael as he had comforted her that day in Palesbury. But of course, she thought, if he knew the truth about her he would probably want her sacked too.

The door burst open and she turned with a gasp of shock to see Michael Templeton stride in. One look at his face told her that he was on the brink of tears of fury. He caught her eye, and she saw him struggle to disguise his feelings, but he couldn't. "Excuse me—I didn't realize—" He backed away again, but Rebecca, full of sympathy, went toward him.

"No, please, sir. I'll leave."

She was about to go past him when she caught a glimpse of his face in the mirror. There were tears in his eyes. Her heart seemed to twist, and without thinking she turned to him and said. "Sir, are you—please let me comfort you."

"I'm a fool," he said thickly.

"No, no—"

"I am. Damn it!" He swallowed, forcing back tears. "Brought back like a child! I wouldn't have believed Mother would do it. I wouldn't have believed it of Georgiana. I'll never live this down. The servants must be laughing at me, I expect."

"None of us think less of you. On the contrary, we admire your bravery."

"You're very kind."

"I'm only speaking the truth, sir."

"I'll apply for a commission as soon as I'm nineteen. My birthday is near enough."

"Did you see France, sir?" Rebecca couldn't help asking.

"No such luck." He smiled, and it transformed his face. "Got as far as a training camp in Kent. Played at soldiers for a while. I felt as sick as a dog when my mates went off to the front. I thought I was going too, but I was called into the sergeant's office to see the earl standing there." His voice darkened again. "My mates will be facing bullets and bombs now, and I—I'm dressing for dinner. I feel ashamed."

"Sir, there is nothing to be ashamed of," Rebecca said, gently. She reached out to lay a hand on his arm. He smiled at her.

Behind her, someone cleared their throat. Rebecca realized in an instant how compromising their position could look. She turned, her throat tightening as she thought that it might be the countess.

It was not the countess. It was Thomas. Rebecca had never seen him look like his. His eyes snapped fire, and though he was standing as discreetly as a professional servant should, there was a look about his shoulders that made her think that every muscle was tense. He was furious. "Excuse me for disturbing you, sir," he said with the quietness of a tiger.

"Not at all," Michael said at once. "Rebecca was kind enough to help me remove this lint from my sleeve." He flicked an invisible piece away from him.

Rebecca edged away from Michael, grateful beyond words for his defense.

"Very good, sir," said Thomas. Rebecca could hear he was not convinced. "Rebecca, you are wanted downstairs to help lay the dinner cloth."

He went into the room to help Michael Templeton dress. Rebecca hesitated outside the door for a second, then scurried to the servants' stairs, feeling as close to despair as she ever had. She had just reached the door when Master Templeton's opened and Thomas came out again. Glancing left and right to see if they were alone, he came straight up to her. Rebecca, frightened at his expression, took a step back.

"What was that?" he said in a low, furious voice.

"I—" Rebecca stared at him startled at the passion in his voice.

"Was he taking liberties? If he touched you—"

"No!" Rebecca was horrified at the thought. "No, we were simply—I was telling him I was sorry for his disappointment, having to come home. I—I know it was very familiar of me, and I'm sorry . . ." She trailed off. She had thought that Thomas's anger would be directed at her, but it seemed he was more concerned for her safety. "Please, don't worry," she said softly. "I was quite safe. Master Templeton is a perfect gentleman."

Thomas met her eyes, and she knew he saw she was telling the truth. He nodded. "That's good," he muttered, looking a little embarrassed. "Well . . ." He backed away, and returned to Master Templeton's room. Rebecca stood where she was until the door shut behind him. Then she went through the servants' door and onto the stairs, feeling even more miserable. She had not been in the house more than three months and already she had made the countess detest her, and now the butler thought of her as a flirt.

CHAPTER
EIGHTEEN

SUSSEX

Left, right, left, right—the pounding rhythm of the march was in Sebastian's head, drowning out his thoughts. The rolling Sussex countryside was all around him, but he didn't look up; he kept his gaze fixed on the back of the head of the man in front of him. His legs were dead and aching, and it was an effort to lift them, but he forced himself, bringing each boot down on the road with fierce determination. The pain blotted out any thought, any feeling. The pain was good. The pain was what he had enlisted for. It drowned out the other pain, the pain that welled back up like blood from a wound that wouldn't heal, every time he had time to think and feel.

"Company . . . halt!"

Sebastian fell out with the other men, and, with them dropped down onto the grass verge to rest his legs and catch his breath. His feet were swollen, and he knew that if he took his boots off he would never get them back on again. The sweat was running down his face and his head was thumping, even though the air was cold. He took out his water bottle and swigged from it.

He became aware that the lad next to him was prodding him in the side, gesturing, without the breath to even speak, for his water bottle. Sebastian had a savage impulse to ignore him, but then he caught sight of the boy's white face. *It isn't the poor lad's fault anyway,* he thought. He handed him the water bottle.

The boy gulped the water down gratefully. "Thanks, chum," he managed, eventually. "I'm dead beat."

Sebastian didn't reply. The boy sat up with an effort. "Another ten miles, heaven help us. Still, I suppose we'll be glad of the practice when we get to France."

Oh great, a talker, thought Sebastian. He grunted and looked away. All he wanted was to be left alone, to march, to shoot, to follow orders and obey and drive his wretched heart so deep underground that he forgot he had ever had one.

But the boy didn't seem to notice. He sat up on his elbows, looking across the downs toward the sea. "Blimey, that's the Channel. Never thought I'd see it up close. Never thought I'd cross it, come to that. Still, I suppose that's why I joined up—to see the world. How about you?" The lad looked questioningly at Sebastian.

Sebastian shrugged. There was no way he could avoid answering, though, without drawing even more attention. "Just want to do my bit," he muttered.

"Me too. I wish I'd known how hard it'd be, though! Never done anything like this. Makes me realize what a good place I had. Still, too late now." He lay back again. "My father was gamekeeper on the Millrace estate in Warwickshire. The local regiment was up to strength, so I came down to London to try my luck. Not sure I don't regret it now." He laughed, shakily. "I remember the woods and the fields there," the boy went on. "It was a good life: we always had enough to eat, and I'd have gone into my father's job if I'd have stayed."

He went on, describing an estate that was so like Somerton that Sebastian found himself feeling homesick. Somerton's rolling hills, lush copses, the river that curved around the hill so the stone house was framed like a jewel, all came to his mind's eye as the boy talked. The boy finished with a sigh, "Still, this war might be over soon enough."

Sebastian did not reply. He could hear, or perhaps feel, something trembling through the ground. A dull and distant booming. It troubled him.

"You're a prodigy, though, aren't you? Crack shot, you don't seem to think anything of the route marches. You been in another regiment before this?"

Sebastian was suddenly on his guard. He had to reply, to put the boy off the scent. Enlisting as a private soldier, he was aware that he had the advantage of having been in the Officer Training Corps at Eton that the others didn't. Most of them had never handled a gun before, were not used to long marches on little food, whereas he had been to several summer camps, practicing semaphore, drill, musketry, tactics, and map reading. If the boy put two and two together . . . "I expect I'm just used to it."

"Is that right? What were you before you signed up?"

Sebastian did not know what to answer. He'd told some lie on the official form—what, he could not remember. It struck him that he would have to do a lot more lying in the time to come. Luckily, he did not have to lie now.

"Right, men, back on your feet!" came the shout down the line. Sebastian braced himself and struggled to his feet. After a moment's hesitation, he reached out to help the lad up. It was strange to clasp his hand in a friendly way, he thought. Back in his old life, he would never have touched someone from a lower class like this so casually. They would never have had this simple, friendly conversation. Except Oliver—but then that was different.

"Thanks, chum. I'm Joe," the lad told him. "Joe Brown."

"Rupert Moore," Sebastian told him. That was the one lie he had down pat. Rupert was his middle name, and Moore was an old family name on his mother's side.

He looked out to see the sparkling blue of the English Channel. He frowned, trying to work out what the distant, dull booming was. It sounded too powerful and far off to be waves.

"Listen—hear that?" he found himself saying.

Joe listened for a second in silence. "Odd, isn't it? Like something big, rocks or something, dropping far off? What do you reckon it is?"

"Oh . . . perhaps just artillery exercises," Sebastian said, looking away. He had realized in just the last few seconds what the relentless, pounding noise was, and in a flash he decided it was better not to speak of it.

They fell in and started off again. The crunch of boots marching along the road, the puffs and groans of the men, drowned out the distant noise. But Sebastian felt he could still hear it, as close as the blood in his head. He knew that he had heard the sound of the guns, the barrage of firing all the way from the trenches in northern France, where they were heading. The thought was stark: If it sounded this much like hell from here, all the way across the sea, what would it be like close up?

CHAPTER
NINETEEN

LONDON

Charlotte trudged up the hill toward the hospital. A chilly rain spat down into her face; wind whipped her hair. She couldn't be colder, she thought, or wetter. And despite the constant cold that she'd had ever since she started living in the hostel and working at the hospital, she couldn't be happier.

It was ridiculous, she thought, amused at herself. Really, Charlotte, said a voice in her head rather like her mother's, what is the matter with you? You weren't happy in a ball gown designed by Céline; you weren't happy kissing the handsomest man of your acquaintance; you weren't happy when your bed was made by someone else and you had a warm, scented bath whenever you liked it; you weren't happy when you didn't even know what a black beetle was, let alone had to squash several before you could have your morning wash. No. Clearly what you wanted was chilblains and blisters, scrubbing bedpans, preparing dressing trays, and treating the most repulsive wounds. What are we to do with you? She laughed out loud, and a man who was walking past her glanced at her nervously. It was such a novelty, she thought, to walk through the poorest area of London and have no one look twice at her. Perhaps this was what men felt—this confidence, this freedom.

She remembered her interview; it already seemed like a long time ago, though it had only been a month. Portia had told her what she would have to say, but she had not been prepared to stand for the entire ten-minute period. The matron who interviewed her had looked like a folded paper crane in her pristine white uniform, and her voice had had as many sharp creases in it. At first Charlotte had found herself blushing angrily, resentful of being treated like a servant, but as the minutes passed, with her answers given meekly and received coldly, her feelings changed. She began to feel a certain amusement at herself. Am I really so concerned with my own self-importance? she wondered. There was something comforting in the world being so topsy-turvy.

Still, it had been mostly pride that had made her sign up to work in the East London hospital alongside Portia. She didn't want Portia—Portia, of all people!—to look down on her, to laugh and say that Charlotte was a coward. So she had pushed down her nervous doubts and signed the paper the matron held out to her. Her one comfort had been to get her uniform made at L'atelier.

Portia had not approved.

"You're not going to a ball, you know," she had said as Céline held up samples of red silk to make the cross on Charlotte's apron.

"I know that. But I don't see that being dutiful and good and so forth has to mean being frumpy."

"Well, it doesn't seem very appropriate, that's all." Portia frowned.

"What do you think, Céline?" Charlotte appealed.

"I agree with you, Mademoiselle Templeton," Céline had said, flitting up and down with her needle and thread to make the extra gathers. "The soldiers are in need of cheering up. Every man I have ever met likes to look at a pretty girl well dressed. Indeed, if it were up to me I would prescribe French hats for the nurses as most essential medicine."

Portia rolled her eyes, but Charlotte saw her smile.

"There, you see?" she teased her—teasing Portia! She had never imagined such a thing possible. "It is my patriotic duty to get the best-cut uniform I can, and learn to do my own hair as well as any lady's maid."

"Oh, very well, but I wonder if you will feel that way after a week working at the First General Hospital." She glanced around L'atelier and added, "But having said that . . . I *would* like a new pair of gloves."

Now, a month later, Charlotte smiled to herself as she entered the bare, cold little cloakroom and shook the rain from her coat. Portia was a nice old thing after all.

She took off her coat and hung it up. Servants must live like this all the time, she marveled. It was so cold, so barren, so lacking in any luxury—and yet she had a job to do. It was enough to make her want to sing despite the calluses.

On the wall was the notice that asked for volunteers for active service overseas. She glanced at it sideways; it was both magnetic and frightening. There were two or three names already written up. Going overseas would be the last straw, she scolded herself. Mother was angry enough about the nursing as it was.

She went onto the ward. Before she had begun working here, she'd imagined peace and stillness, silent sisters, men lying still and pale in their beds. Nothing could have been further from the truth, which was constant noise and activity—but the early mornings, when the men were often still asleep, were as close as it came to what she had imagined.

"Good morning, Nurse," said Sister briskly. Charlotte wondered if she would ever get used to the thrill of being addressed as Nurse, though she knew she was only an untrained helper. It was wonderful to have the cloak of a job title, something that made her feel she was capable and strong—that she could be listened to, the way people would listen to a man. It was exciting to feel that she didn't have to flirt to be wanted, that she could simply be that cool, capable, sexless creature called a nurse—and get a kind of respect she had never had before.

She went off with the others, working as fast as possible to get the regular jobs out of the way, trying to ignore the shivers that told her she was on the brink of flu. The ward rang with the groans and shouts of men who were coming around from operations, the endless whine of the gramophone, popular songs such as "When Irish Eyes Are Smiling."

It was only an hour from the end of her shift, and she was in the chilly sluice, helping one of the men wash and shave, when Sister looked around the door and said, "Come and see me when you are done there, Nurse."

"Yes, Sister," Charlotte said, wondering what she wanted.

She found Sister at her desk, filling out the ward records. The woman looked up at her, and Charlotte was struck by her cool professionalism. "Nurse," Sister said, "go to that man in the bed at the end. I want you to ready him for an amputation."

Charlotte's heart thumped. She had never before had to do this, and she wondered how she could find the right words to say to a man who was about to be made a cripple. But there was nothing to do but obey. She went down the ward, wishing she were anywhere but there, and opened the curtains. She saw a boy with bright blue eyes and curly brown hair, his leg out in front of him, bandaged. She saw the greenish stain on the bandage that she had come to learn meant gangrene. He couldn't be any older than Michael, she thought. The thought twisted at her heart.

"Are they going to cut it off?" he said, straight out.

Charlotte couldn't find words; then she made an effort and said, "Yes. I'm sorry."

"Don't be sorry. It's better than what happened to my mates." He lay there watching her as she placed the instruments on the table, aware that he was looking at the saw blade, at the pincers and the tweezers and the speculum, and at the chloroform that would mercifully mean he would not know anything of the operation. Outside the curtains, the ward rang with noise, busy footsteps and commands, shouts of pain, but here she and this boy seemed closed inside a cocoon.

"What happened to your mates?" she asked. She didn't realize what she was saying; she wanted simply to divert his attention from the knives.

He did not reply. She turned to look at him, and saw that his eyes weren't fixed on her but on something, somewhere, very far distant.

He came back to himself, and smiled. It was not a real smile, just the skeleton of one, she thought.

"It's hell out there," he said calmly. "You don't know until you've seen it for yourself."

Charlotte stood, not knowing what to reply. For a moment she was there with him—the low moans were shrieks of fresh, raw pain; the distant thumping and banging were not the orderlies moving trolleys but the guns booming ever closer. She remembered how she had felt when she had first heard the news of Laurence's death.

She started as the curtain was whisked aside and the medical officer, sweating and in a rush, came in, followed by Sister. "Nurse Templeton can assist at the amputation," Sister said, "unless of course you don't think you're up to it, Nurse?"

Her frank doubt pulled Charlotte back to herself. "I'm quite happy to assist, Sister," she said spikily. She moved to take hold of the bandaged leg, as Sister bent over the boy in the bed, cotton wool and chloroform in her hands. The doctor was quite coolly selecting his tools for the job, and as Sister counted down from ten to zero, Charlotte saw the boy's hands flop down, and the smell of gangrene seemed even sweeter and more sickening.

All I have to do is not let go, she told herself, as the doctor moved the boy's gown aside and made his first incision.

Afterward, she remembered only the last moments of the operation, when the limb she was holding was shaking back and forth and the doctor was sawing like a man removing a tree limb. She'd never realized, she thought, that it was so *difficult* to cut a man's leg off. The ridiculous thought floated across her mind. *It should be better managed.* She almost giggled, light-headed with horror and fear and revulsion, at the various ideas that occurred to her about how to perform a more efficient operation. A wave of faintness passed through her at the sound of the saw cutting through bone, but she fiercely fought against it. She was not going to let herself down. She was not going to let Sister see her weakness. She remembered the way she'd smiled over a breaking heart at Mrs. Verulam's ball last season, and tried to access that same, stone-cold part of herself. Pretend to be strong, and you will find yourself stronger. She hardened her heart and her gaze.

Then there was a sudden shudder, and she was holding not a boy's leg, but just a leg.

"Thank you, Nurse," said Sister.

It was over. Charlotte helped Sister place the limb on the trolley. She made sure not to look at it, not to think. The boy lay white-faced, unconscious. On the trolley, the foot stuck up, as if it were the leg of a wooden puppet. Ridiculous, she thought. She felt completely distanced from herself, as if she were watching the scene from high above. This war is simply ridiculous.

She started as Sister placed a hand on her shoulder. "Well done," said Sister quietly. "You may go, Nurse."

Well done. Charlotte hung on to the words as she went off down the ward. Sister's praise was rare. A new feeling surprised her. It was pride in a job well done.

She made it as far as the cloakroom before the exhaustion hit her. Aching in every bone, she leaned against the wall, trying to summon the energy to walk back to the hostel. In a moment, she promised herself. There was no hot bath waiting for her. Just freezing water, sleep if she was lucky, then wake to break the ice in the water bowl and start all over again. She noticed the bloodstains on her skirt for the first time. She would have to try and get those out, and was it cold water or hot that made it stain?

And yet she was somehow, almost inexplicably, *happy.* A boy perhaps younger than Michael would be crippled for life. But he would most likely *have* a life, and she was part of the reason for that. Despite everything her mother had said, she was being useful. And she could do more. She was sure of it.

Her eye fell on the notice asking for volunteers to go overseas. With a great effort, she pushed herself away from the wall, walked on blistered feet over to the paper, took the pencil that lay on the windowsill, and wrote her name down.

CHAPTER
TWENTY

OXFORD

Ada pressed her fingers to her temples, trying to concentrate on the essay she was writing and ignore the sound of laughter and conversation that she could hear from her fellow students' rooms. It was a bright, sunny afternoon, and she wished she could be with them, but she was determined to make a good job of the essay before her. It was for Connor Kearney. She knew he expected great things of her, and she was determined not to let him down. But other thoughts, other worries, kept creeping into her mind. She had been to see her father off at Waterloo Station, on his journey to France. Georgiana had not been there. She had wished him the best of luck, trying not to show her anxiety. Still, he must have sensed it, for he had placed a hand on her shoulder and said gently, "Don't worry, my dear. I shan't be in any danger, I shall be well behind the front lines."

"Of course. I'm just sorry Georgiana couldn't come."

"I don't think she approves."

"No, I don't suppose she would."

"But you do, don't you?"

"I understand your desire to do something for your country. I wish I could too."

"Dear girl. You will find someone who loves you, and all this restlessness will be gone once you are married."

The words had twisted like a knife in her heart. He did not understand her at all. And there was nothing to say about it, because he was stepping onto the train, waving. She waved too, and the train whistled and let off steam. Then she was standing alone in a sea of people, waving to the great machine that carried him away from her.

She put her pen down just as a knock on the door disturbed her. She got up to find the chambermaid there. "Post, my lady," she said, dipping a curtsy before hurrying back downstairs to her work.

Ada recognized the handwriting at once. Ravi. She hesitated before opening it, though she was hardly sure why. They had always been able to speak freely to each other, had never had to fear what the other might say. But he had taken so long to reply. She sensed something was wrong.

She tore it open, telling herself she was being foolish. She began to read it quickly. Very soon a blush of anger and pain came to her face, and she could hardly bring herself to read on. Certain phrases leapt from the paper and lodged in her heart: *Should I be jealous of this Fintan? He has clearly been closer to you than I suspected. . . . cannot offer you the impeccable English gentleman, and I begin to fear that is really what you want. . . . Your desire to sacrifice all for your country is hard to swallow when your country is oppressing mine. . . . do not understand why you should feel so much for Lord Fintan, if you really were not in love with him.*

"No, no, no!" Ada exclaimed aloud. She threw down the letter. It was such a horrible misunderstanding. She could read between the lines of Ravi's letter and see that he was smarting with jealousy. She turned to her writing desk and pulled out the Bradshaw rail timetable. The next train was in fifteen minutes. She had time to put on her hat and throw on an overcoat, and a few minutes later she was walking briskly to the station. There was only one thought in her mind: She could not allow Ravi to feel like this for a single moment longer than necessary.

As the train steamed down the track toward London, Ada stood by the window, unable to relax. She peered out at the landscape flitting by. It was not fast enough. She longed for winged horses to pick up the carriage and whisk it into the air, carry her to London, and set her down at Ravi's office. She had the address written down on a piece of paper in her reticule; she clutched its ribbons tightly. It would be beyond everything to simply show up at India House; she couldn't believe she was being so shameless.

As soon as the train pulled in, she ran down the steps and across the platform. The clock was tolling out twelve o'clock. If she hurried, she might meet him coming or going from lunch.

The bustling crowds blocked her way. On all sides she could hear military music, the rattle of trams; through the forest of hats she glimpsed recruiting posters—eager men in uniform, even posters calling women to war work. Soldiers with kit bags, veterans back from the front with a dazed look in their eyes. VADs like flocks of doves, their red crosses like bloody wounds. As many of the hurrying workers in the street were women as men, she noticed, of all classes. War had given everyone a purpose.

She found herself outside Ravi's office. Not sure what to do, knowing she could not go in and boldly ask for him, for fear of getting both himself and herself into trouble, she crossed the road and walked up and down a few times, trying to stay out of the way of the crowd and watch the entrance of the building at the same time. The doorman now and then opened the door to make way for gentlemen to leave. None of them were Ravi.

She heard the church bell toll one o'clock. She watched anxiously as younger men left the building, in pairs and singly, going to their lunch. What if he left with a friend? She hadn't thought of that, and she unconsciously wrung her hands. She wouldn't be able to approach him—and then the door opened and he came out, jogging down the stone steps, his top hat gleaming, in every way the athletic, intense man that she loved.

She began to follow him along the road, waiting for a moment when she could cross. How could she accost him in the street? She would look like a common prostitute. She hesitated, and as she did so, he turned down a quieter street. She seized her chance, rushing across the road. She followed him into the street, and saw he had stopped to light a cheroot. He looked up, and saw her. "Ada?" he exclaimed. She could see in his face that he felt guilty.

She did not reply. She simply ran to him and threw herself into his arms. He dropped the cheroot and pulled her tightly to him. Their lips met with a passion that Ada found both exhilarating and terrifying. His arms were so strong, so determined never to let her go. He stopped kissing her to whisper, "I'm sorry I'm so sorry, Ada. I was afraid for our future. I was afraid—"

"Don't let's think of the future," she replied. "Let's think of now."

This time it was he who pulled her into the embrace, with renewed passion, as London drummed past the end of the street, a desperate, hopeless rhythm.

CHAPTER
TWENTY-ONE

SOMERTON

Georgiana walked toward the stables—so empty now that the army had taken all their horses. It was hard not to feel a pang as she crossed the normally bustling courtyard. So much had changed, she doubted things could ever go back to how they once were.

She looked into the stables. Michael was where she had hoped she would find him, sitting on an upturned barrel, deep in thought. In his hand, she saw, was a copy of an old schoolbook: Caesar's *Gallic Wars*. He looked up, startled, as her shadow cut across the sunlight.

"I thought I might find you here," she said, trying a smile. "Doesn't it seem empty, now that they have taken the horses? Poor Beauty, I wonder where she is now."

Michael looked away.

"Please, Michael. Let's not quarrel. I understand how you must feel, I do. But we were so frightened for you. You don't understand—perhaps you don't understand—how much we care about you." She swallowed. That had been a hard speech to say; it was so difficult not to give her heart away, not to say the wrong thing.

"Everyone is making sacrifices," Michael answered finally. "I only want to make mine. It's not as if anyone would miss me— not now."

"But we would. We would miss you so much. It would— life would never, ever be the same if anything were to happen to you."

Michael looked at her in sudden surprise. Georgiana pressed on. "You are going to sign up as soon as you are nineteen. We can't help that. But you know . . . you may never come back. So let's not spend what may be our last days together quarreling."

He met her eyes finally, and she saw respect in them. "You're right," he said quietly. He got up and came toward her. Georgiana was aware of how close they were together, how much more like a man than a boy he was now. "You're right, as always, Georgie. I don't know what I'd do without your good sense and your kindness."

He put out his hand. She clasped it, and they shook hands. The gesture was so formal, yet so intimate. She hadn't realized how much stronger his grip was than hers.

"You are a very good friend to me," he said.

"Of course I am—how could I be otherwise?" She swallowed. Pain and pleasure mingled. It was the sweetest thing to see the warmth when he looked at her, but would she ever be more than a friend?

They began to walk slowly back to the house together.

"But I don't want you to think," she went on, "that just because I want peace, I would stand by and do nothing. We are in a crisis, and I want to help. I just wish I could see some way to do it without leaving Somerton. I've come to love it so much here." She paused. She could see that Thomas was just opening the door and showing a man out. She did not recognize him. "Is that one of Mr. Bradford's colleagues?" she said to Michael. "I hope there isn't some new problem with William. What with Papa abroad, it would be difficult to deal with."

They sped up their pace without needing to exchange a word.

They went up the broad marble stairs. Thomas was ready to bow and open the door for them. Georgiana went straight into the drawing room, eagerly looking to see who was there. She stopped, shocked. The countess was sitting on the sofa, sobbing into her handkerchief.

"What is the matter? Mother?" Michael went to her side.

"It's over—there's no hope—"

"Who? What has happened?"

"Sebastian. Oh, my baby!" The countess's voice was hardly audible.

"Sebastian!" Georgiana exclaimed. "What has happened to him?"

"He has joined up. He has gone into the army, under a false name."

Georgiana and Michael exchanged a shocked glance over her head.

"But how do you know?" Georgiana asked as gently as she could. She had never seen her stepmother so distraught. She knew that Sebastian was her favorite child. There always seemed to be some secret between them.

"It is my fault," the countess said instead of replying. "I do not understand it. How could he do it?" She began to sob again.

Michael drew Georgiana aside. "I think my mother should see a doctor," he murmured. "She seems hysterical."

"Yes, of course," she replied in the same quiet tone. She crossed to ring the bell. Turning back, she went on, "But Lady Westlake, how do you know this? I cannot imagine Sebastian would do such a thing. Is it true?"

"Yes. I hired a private detective to follow him. The man has just reported back to me."

"You hired a detective to follow him?" Michael sounded furious. Georgiana made soothing gestures at him. Now was not the time to get angry about her intrusion into Sebastian's private life.

Michael took a deep breath. "I understand your concern, Mother, but Sebastian is not dead yet. Let's not give up before we have begun the battle, shall we?" He raised his eyebrows at Georgiana—*Was that diplomatic enough?*—and she beamed at him approvingly. "I shall telephone the earl and see if he can discover anything more about what has happened to him."

He turned and walked out. Georgiana could have cheered at his self-control, but she restrained herself. Instead she told Rebecca, who had appeared in response to the bell, "Please bring a glass of water for the countess." She glanced back at her step-mother; it seemed she was somewhat recovered, so Georgiana did not ask for the doctor to be called. The less gossip the better.

She turned back into the room. The countess was perched on the edge of the sofa, dabbing her eyes. "I do not know why all my children are so willfully disobedient," she said. Georgiana was relieved to see that she seemed back to her old self, though there was a sadness in her voice where once there would have been only asperity.

"Charlotte is not," she said, hoping to encourage her to think of the bright side.

"Oh, indeed! I have just received a letter from her. She has signed up as a VAD."

"Charlotte, nursing?" Georgiana was both shocked and pleased.

"Yes, in some of the worst hospitals in London. I don't know how she can do it. I could have got her a lovely little job on the board of some charity or other. I dread to think what she will have to see in the course of nursing. Certainly when I was young no right-thinking young man would ever have married a girl who had so compromised her womanhood."

"Well . . . perhaps today's young men think differently," said Georgiana thoughtfully. Charlotte's action filled her with admiration. Her stepsister had more in her than she had ever supposed.

CHAPTER
TWENTY-TWO

SOMERTON

"Annie," said Thomas, frowning as he came into the kitchen, "have you seen anyone but me opening the silver cabinet? Or with the key?"

Annie looked around from the mirror, where she was adjusting the flowers on her hat. It was her afternoon off, and she was looking forward to getting to the village and seeing what was going on, exchanging gossip with the postmistress. By the look on Thomas's face, there would be gossip indeed. "No," she said. "Has something gone missing, then?"

"We're short of two teaspoons. Of course they might simply have slipped down the back, but . . ."

"Or someone might have made off with them!" Annie exclaimed. This was delightfully shocking. The silver spoons were worth a good deal, and it would be a sacking offense at the very least. The police might even be called in.

"I don't like to think that."

"None of us are thieves, Mr. Wright," Cook said. "We're all long-standing staff, as you know; every one of us has been here long enough for our honesty to be beyond question."

"When did you find them missing?" Martha asked.

"Just a few days ago."

"And no one new has been into the silver room?" Annie asked. "No one?"

Thomas hesitated. Annie read his expression.

"Except Rebecca!" she said, and drew in her breath. "Oh, do you think."

"I don't think anything. Polishing the silver is her job," Thomas snapped. "Just because she is the newest arrival, it means nothing. I wasn't sure about her at first, but her work has been excellent so far, I have to admit."

"Well, it would be," said Martha.

"Of course! To throw you off the scent!" Annie exclaimed.

"Now, now," Cook said. "She's a good girl, as far as I've seen."

"I want to think of these spoons as lost, not stolen," Thomas said firmly. "I shall speak to everyone at dinner tonight and ask them to look for them. If they come back again, no more will be said about the matter."

"You think what you like, Thomas," Annie said, heading for the door. "We won't say I told you so!"

"It's Mr. Wright, not Thomas." Thomas's last words followed her down the path. Annie smiled to herself. He'd get over it.

She walked down the road to the village, enjoying the winter sunshine. The sky was full of birdsong and the hedges were still thick and green.

But once she reached the village, it was easy to see that things had changed, that the war was on. The recruiting office was still open, though everyone who could enlist already had. Posters everywhere urging her to do her bit, save food, build bombs. It was all so exciting!

The post office looked as it always had, with red-berried holly hedges bringing a splash of color to the scene. The village was crowded with bicycles and people on foot; a square of soldiers paraded by the fountain.

The postmistress was busy talking to her daughter, who was doing the rounds now that the postman had gone to the front. "I say it's misdirected, and ought to go back where it came from."

"I don't think it's misdirected; just the name's written all wrong."

She put the letter down where Annie could see the address. Annie scanned it and read:

Miss R Freudemann
C/o the housekeeper
At Somerton Court
Palesbury

At once she realized what had happened. Rebecca had given a false name. She wasn't Freeman, but Freudemann. A German!

Annie thought fast. She wanted her suspicions confirmed. Without speaking to the postmistress, she turned and went out again.

She walked down to the cottages. She could see some children playing in the road. She remembered that Rebecca had taken some castoffs of Master Philip's down with her. And that little boy, who had the same red hair as her, was wearing clothes that looked very familiar . . .

"I have a message from Rebecca Freudemann," she said. "For her brother. Do any of you know him?"

She saw the boy's head turn toward her, and he opened his mouth to reply, then was quiet as he clearly remembered he was not supposed to answer to the name.

"Sorry, miss," said the oldest child. "We don't know anyone called that."

"Never mind," she said with a smile. "I must have made a mistake."

She wandered off to the village square, now and then glancing back to where the children were still playing. A few moments later, she felt a tug at her dress. She looked down. It was the boy with red hair.

"Miss," he whispered. "I know her brother. I could take the message for him."

Annie's suspicions were confirmed, and she thought the

penny she took out of her purse was well spent. "There you go; your sister sent you that," she said.

"Cor, thanks, missus!" He was so excited, she noticed with a smile, that he hadn't thought to correct her when she said *your* sister. He raced off with it. Annie, full of her news, set off back up to Somerton Court. So Rebecca was German! She couldn't wait to tell Martha. She felt a little stab of guilt when she thought of the little boy's trusting face, but she stifled it. This was for her country, after all.

CHAPTER
TWENTY-THREE

FRANCE

France was noise, thought Sebastian, crouched under the wet bivouac sheets on the back of the lorry. The rain, hammering down in the pitch-black night; the rattle, distant and almost lost in the heavy rain, of a machine gun; the growl and squelch of the lorry's tires as they inched forward toward a trench, unseen, possibly nonexistent; the whine of some missile overhead; the dull underground tremble and boom of the artillery.

Someone rapped on the side of the truck, and Sebastian pulled aside the sheeting and looked out to see their corporal, Morrison, squinting up through the rain. He had a lot of respect for Morrison; he was an old-timer from the Boer War, and he knew the ropes.

"Moore, Brown, all the rest of you—down. We're here."

Sebastian jumped down, followed by the others in his platoon, some with more grumbling than others. Joe looked around, and Sebastian saw his own doubt mirrored in the boy's pale face. "Cor blimey, Corporal, are you sure? This don't look like a trench to me."

"Welcome to the front, boys." The corporal gave a bark of humorless laughter. He looked at Sebastian. "You, lad, you're a sensible chap—come with me. Two of us are less likely to get lost."

He turned and plodded off through the squelching mud into the dark. Sebastian shouldered his pack—he'd come to hate the thing—and followed him down the walls of sandbags. The walls were collapsing in the rain, and he could see trickles of mud pouring through. Joe was right; it didn't look much like the textbooks. Mind you, it wasn't raining in the textbooks, and it appeared that all it did in France—or Belgium, wherever the hell they were—was rain.

The corporal paused, and only when he pushed a rickety door open did Sebastian see that they were standing in front of the dugout. It was built from sandbags too, and the rain hammered on the tin roof. Inside, there was a broken table, a flimsy chair, and a scrawny, red-haired lieutenant with a twitch.

The corporal snapped off a salute. "Corporal Morrison, sir, reporting for duty with B Platoon."

"Good show, good man." The lieutenant rubbed his pink eyes. "Just got here myself, replaced Second Lieutenant Carlyle. We've, ah"—he picked up a printed message from the table, and Sebastian saw his hands trembling violently—"ah, just had orders from HQ, move out against the enemy and take the machine-gun emplacement west-southwest, so get your men ready."

A sortie? thought Sebastian. It was madness. The night was lightless; they wouldn't be able to move in the mud. And they had only just arrived from Étaples—it was their first time in the trenches.

"What, now?" said Morrison, then added, "Sir? What—now, sir?"

"Yes, now. Those are the orders. God knows how we're going to manage it. Must do it, though."

Sebastian swallowed his horror. It was obvious that the lieutenant was badly shell-shocked, and as sorry as he felt for him, he couldn't be let near the men. He backed out with Morrison, who let out an expressive whistle as soon as the door was shut.

"Right," he said, and Sebastian knew he understood completely what a cock-up the whole business was. "Get the men together while I have a look at the map."

"We're going out there, then?"

"No help for it."

Without replying, Sebastian marshaled the exhausted, shivering men into some kind of order.

"This can't be true, chum?" Joe whispered to him. "They can't send us straight out."

"Afraid they have," muttered Sebastian.

"Bloody hell. It's murder," said Jim Kelly, another of the platoon.

"Chin up," said Sebastian, though he didn't feel the enthusiasm he tried to put in his voice. "We're trained for this; we're fresh and ready. Those poor German bastards have been stuck in the trenches for days; they'll be exhausted and demoralized. We can do this, and if we pull it off we'll be a lot happier here without that damned machine gun spitting down the trench every time we stick our heads out of the dugout."

"Well, that's true," said Jim, looking more enthusiastic. He scurried away to get his kit bags. "Come on lads! For Blighty!"

Sebastian felt Morrison's eyes on him; he suddenly felt embarrassed. Perhaps he had spoken out of turn.

"You'd better look out, lad," said Morrison, unsmiling. "Carry on like that, you're going to get promoted." He shouldered his rifle and plodded off down the trench. Sebastian followed him with mixed feelings. He hadn't meant to encourage the men. He had done it without thinking, out of habit.

A few hours later, they were in the thick dark of no-man's-land. The ground had been churned into some kind of muddy sea by shell holes, punctuated by the tattered remains of barbed wire and the burned-out skeletons of gun carriages.

"Bloody hell, I think we're lost," Joe muttered to him out of the darkness. "I haven't seen the others for a while."

"At least it's stopped raining," Sebastian replied in the same tone.

"It's a marvel how you keep your spirits up in this hell."

"Oh well, it could be worse. Could be Eton."

Joe's silence hit him at once, and he realized what he had said. He swallowed, feeling sick. But he heard a huge grin in Joe's voice. "Don't worry, sir. I'll keep your secret."

Sebastian didn't have time to thank him. There was a chattering noise and the blackness exploded with fire. Sebastian dived and pulled Joe with him. They ended up in a shell hole, Sebastian shivering, Joe shuddering and on the brink of tears, while the gun swept around them. They heard cries, screams.

"Is that us? Is that us screaming? Or is that them?" Joe was shaking.

Sebastian was sweating with fear too, but he made himself move and look over the lip of the crater. He could see the machine gun, not fifty yards away, tearing the night to shreds. It didn't seem guarded.

"If we can sneak behind it, we've got a chance," he said, sliding back into the mud.

"Got to be bloody joking!"

Sebastian grabbed him and pulled him close. "Listen, if we don't shut that gun down, we're dead men. As soon as dawn comes we'll be sitting ducks. I don't think he knows we're here. Now is the best chance we've got."

Joe nodded silently. Sebastian let him go, relieved—the real terror had been thinking of being stuck here in the shell hole, in the dark, unable to help himself, powerless, with Joe gibbering with fear next to him. If the boy could be made to act, to do something, he'd live. If he froze in fear, he'd die.

"I'll take out the machine gunner. You deal with anything else." He pushed a grenade into Joe's hand. "Got it?"

Joe nodded dumbly. Sebastian didn't look into his eyes, afraid that if he saw fear there he would panic himself. There was no time for fear.

They scrambled out of the shell hole on their bellies and

wormed through the mud toward the emplacement. They made it twenty yards before there was a blast of light and Sebastian shut his eyes and tried to play dead. But the signal flare had gone up beyond them, and when he squinted he saw a sight he would never forget—men collapsing to their knees, like ninepins, like hay when the reaper slashes the stalks. All lit in a way he hadn't seen since the darkness and vivid fire of the Caravaggio paintings that hung on the staircase at Somerton. How strange that he should be thinking of Somerton now, he thought, numbed, but the image was gone as fast as a bullet, and survival was back. *Now,* he thought, while the German was busy scything through the rest of the platoon. He scrambled across the destroyed earth to the wall of sandbags, slid around it and into the trench. There were Germans in the trench, but they were firing the other way, toward the main platoon, and he was able to step up behind the machine gunner. His pistol was in his hand, and this was the moment he had tried not to think about. Could he do this? Could he shoot a man in cold blood? Or should he simply wait to be shot first? This was his chance to allow the war to take him. To give his life and go down in a bloody moment of insanity.

He was looking over the gunner's shoulder, and in that second he saw Corporal Morrison, in the last of the flare's light, fall to the ground riddled with bullets. The last thing he saw was the blank astonishment on the man's face, the grizzled gray stubble on his chin. Those eyes. The look in them would haunt him forever.

He pulled the trigger.

CHAPTER
TWENTY-FOUR

Charlotte stepped off the train, shivering. Portia followed her. Number 34 General Hospital was supposed to be around here somewhere. But she couldn't see anything that looked like a hospital. Just dirt roads, stray cats, gray skies, and soldiers here and there. The wooden huts seemed like a kind of cancer that had overrun the skin of the country. And underneath everything was the shudder of the guns. The only refreshing thing was the smell of the sea that came over, across the railway and the dunes.

"I suppose this must be Étaples," said Portia, looking around her.

They had traveled together, across the Channel and through Boulogne, down the railway to Étaples. Étaples was the key base for the forces allied against Germany, a huge complex of huts all thrown up in just a few months. Every soldier who went to the front went through here. The crossing had been rough, and Charlotte could see her own exhaustion mirrored in Portia's eyes. When they had first set sail from Dover there had been blue skies, seagulls dipping and swerving overhead, and soldiers singing and whistling to keep their spirits up. As she looked down at the white wake of water, she had felt nervous but excited also—she was finally going abroad, finally going to be in the thick of it. Forty-eight hours later, that optimism seemed a long way away. She ached in every muscle and wanted nothing more than a hot bath in scented water, and then bed, to sleep forever. But that was not what was in front of her.

"I can't see anything that looks like a hospital," she said. "Only those huts over there."

"Do you think anyone will come and meet us?"

"I should think not." Charlotte tried to sound more cheerful than she felt. "Let's walk; it will keep us warm at least."

Portia picked up her case with a small sigh. Charlotte did the same, but as she stepped down from the platform, she saw a horse and cart approaching. On the flapping tarpaulin sides was painted the distinctive red cross.

She put out a hand to alert Portia and they waited until the cart reached them.

The woman who stepped down from the cart looked about fifty. A sister's badge was pinned to her cape. "You must be Nurse Templeton and Nurse Claythorpe. We are glad to see you," she said.

Charlotte murmured a polite reply. She expected to be asked to step into the cart, but instead the sister walked a little way away and gestured to them to follow her. Charlotte and Portia did so, and Charlotte was surprised to see the sister speak a few words of French to the stationmaster. A moment later they were in his office, and with a very Gallic bow he left them.

Charlotte looked around, noting the spartan surroundings. Everything here seemed washed of color, she thought, just as a man's face was colorless when he was afraid.

"I shall get to the point, since there is little time. I want to ask you if you will do something rather unconventional for us," Sister said.

Charlotte raised her eyebrows. She was fairly sure that Sister did not have in mind any of the unconventional things she had already accomplished.

"Of course, Sister, we will do anything we can to help." Portia spoke for both of them. "That is why we are here."

"The thing is . . ." The sister hesitated. "You are not needed here, that is, not as much as you are needed elsewhere."

"You wish us to transfer?" Charlotte said in surprise. This was a normal occurrence, and she wondered why the sister was making such a meal of it.

"Yes, but not to one of the other general hospitals. We are short of staff at Hidoux Farm Casualty Clearing Station. It is not usual to send VADs so close to the front line of fighting, and it is not ideal. But would you be willing to go? Now?"

Charlotte did not know what to say.

She knew that CCSs could at times come under direct fire. She knew that the conditions there were likely to be more chaotic, worse than here in the relative safety of Étaples. She felt as if things were moving too fast for her. But this was war.

"Speaking for myself, Sister," said Portia after a moment, "I am ready to go."

Charlotte found both of them looking at her. She could not refuse. She could not look like a coward, not now. "I will go too," she said.

"Thank you, Nurse Templeton. I appreciate it greatly." Sister's tired face blossomed with a smile. She was not so old, Charlotte realized. Simply exhausted.

But she could feel panic rising inside her. She'd thought she could cope. But that was back in England, when she could go home whenever she liked. This was different. There was a channel full of German submarines to cross if she wanted to escape; more than that, there was her pride. She couldn't bear to fail now; it would be too humiliating. Her mother would be proved right: She was no more fitted for nursing than a butterfly for baking bread. She should know her place and her limits. But just a few months' nursing in London had shown her a new life, a new future in which she could be needed and useful. And she would not give that up without a fight. Like all the men who arrived here, she had gone too far to turn back.

CHAPTER
TWENTY-FIVE

Sebastian opened his eyes. The ground trembled with distant artillery fire, but the silence—the comparative silence—was almost deafening.

He sat up with difficulty. He ached everywhere and was covered with bruises from the day before. As he got up to wash, it all came back to him: Morrison's eyes, the shock in them as he died. Crawling about in the blood and the dirt, the body of the machine gunner on top of him. Finally, he'd gotten out and found Joe, wounded in the leg. There were German fighters coming in from above, strafing the trench. It was clear they couldn't hold it. He'd gotten Joe back through no-man's-land to the shelter of a shell hole, then to their own trench. There had been wounded men, screaming men, shattered men. And then—

He stopped, aghast at his own insanity, as the memory of yesterday swept over him.

"I'm going back for Morrison," he'd told the lieutenant. Shells exploded, pulverizing the ground beyond the safety of the trench.

"Are you bloody mad?"

"I'm not leaving him out there." He'd looked around at their shocked faces. "You know as well as I that if we don't get his body back now, he won't be there tomorrow. He'll have sunk into one of those hellish mud holes, or the rats will have had him, or the shells. I'm going back."

"I'll come with you." That was Joe.

"No." He'd told Joe that firmly, with the authority he remembered from his other life—a life of giving orders to servants. "You're to stay here. I won't risk anyone else's life. But Morrison deserves better than a mud grave."

He'd gone out there. Wriggling on his stomach, forcing down the part of him that screamed he should turn back, that he was risking his life for a dead man, that he was tempting fate, that he wanted to *live*, goddamn it. The beams of light swept across the churned earth: he saw limbs, bodies, ragged scraps of metal and flesh and wood and leather all tossed together as if God had shaken the world in a cocktail tumbler.

Morrison lay in a half-flooded shell hole. He was stiff with rigor mortis. Sebastian waited for the searchlights to pass, then ran. Like a rabbit, he thought, remembering hunting at Somerton. He'd never go on a shoot again, not if they begged him.

How he got the body back was a mystery to him. One

movement at a time, dodging search beams. It took hours. Finally he was back in the trench. He sat, too exhausted to move.

"Going back for a bloody dead man." That was Jim Kelly. He sounded almost angry.

"Shut up, Jim. You'd want someone to do it for you." That was Joe.

That was all he remembered. Now here he was in his dugout, and some bastard was shouting his name outside. No lie-ins in the army.

He came out, blinked in the sunshine. "What is it?"

He didn't recognize the smart, slick-haired young officer who stood there like a vision from another world.

"Rupert Moore? You're to go back to HQ, see the colonel."

Sebastian nodded, blankly. It was probably something he'd done wrong. There had to be something. The whole thing was a farce, and farces had to end eventually.

He dressed and joined the staff officer in his motorcar. He was too tired to talk or even think as they bumped along the rain-washed, pitted road. His uniform was stiff with mud and blood. His head thumped and he wished he had a drink of water. Across the ruined earth, pools of still water lay, and from them the wrecks of gun carriages protruded, along with the torn stumps of trees and here and there a bloated corpse, as if such a thing were quite normal. Sebastian sat in silence, glad that the wind noise prevented speech. Slowly, his mind put itself back together. He began to feel uneasy. If this summons was because they had found out who he was . . . *what* he was . . . He swallowed down a sudden desire to vomit.

On the horizon, the shape of a château revealed itself.

He had seen houses like this on holidays in the French countryside—long, long before this had happened. He had dined in them, drunk champagne from their cellars, listened to stories told in accented English, and fallen in love with the elegant, easy luxury they surrounded themselves with. As they neared it, he saw the windows were blown out. Then he saw that much of the roof was gone too. It was as shattered as everything else here.

"Any idea what this is about, sir?" he asked, trying to keep his voice calm.

The driver shrugged. "Ask them when you get in." He motioned him out and Sebastian obeyed. He had a heavy sense of fate; there was no running away from this one.

The reasons he might be here cycled through his mind. If it came out that he'd used a false name, if it came out about who he was, what he'd done . . . His feet crunched on broken glass as he crossed the elegant hall of the château. There were shattered mirrors and empty frames, and a shell seemed to have gone through one wall and out of the other.

He entered the colonel's office and stood to attention. This might be the last time I do this, if I'm found out, he thought, and found the thought somehow demoralizing.

The colonel looked up with a wintery smile. "Ah, Private Moore, isn't it."

"Yes, sir," said Sebastian warily.

"Jolly good. Jolly good. I hear you had quite an adventure last night."

"I suppose you could call it that, sir." Sebastian kept his tone light, wondering where this was leading.

"I have a report from Private Brown, but would you like to tell me in your own words what happened?"

Sebastian recounted the night's events, aware that a staff lieutenant was typing along with his words. He itched to see what was being taken down. What had Joe said?

"Excellent. Excellent. Well, that was a brave action, and you'll be glad to know the machine-gun emplacement was retained and the sortie was a great success. And Morrison's family will be more grateful than words can say. To have his body to bury will mean the world to them."

Sebastian nodded heavily. The memory of Morrison collapsing to the ground flashed into his mind again, and he closed his eyes, feeling an almost physical pain.

"I am therefore promoting you to acting corporal, with every expectation that the role be confirmed and made permanent following the war."

Sebastian jerked his head up, astonished. "I—I'm very grateful, sir" was all he could find to say.

"No need. My pleasure." The colonel smiled his chilly smile again. "Dismissed. And have a good rest before rejoining your platoon."

He saluted. Sebastian responded. It was the strangest thing, he thought. This colonel—this perfect English officer and gentleman—would drop his hand in disgust if he knew who he was saluting. But here he wasn't Sebastian Templeton, the debauched and disgraced. He was Rupert Moore, the good soldier.

"Thank you, sir," he said, and turned away at the colonel's nod.

Sebastian walked away, past the broken windows, open to the bare countryside, still trying to process what had happened. They weren't onto him. They weren't after him. They'd promoted him, of all things. He was surprised to find himself feeling a surge of pride—actually smiling.

He hadn't signed up to be good at this. He'd signed up to get killed. But here he was, alive, and others were alive because of him. He laughed and shook his head wonderingly. He'd scrabbled in the mud of no-man's-land and come up clutching a precious jewel—life.

He stopped on the terrace of the château and looked out, trying to imagine this landscape back to how it once had been: peaceful, the tall trees lining the avenue, the fresh smell of grass. But it was impossible to bring it to mind.

Don't get too complacent, he thought. It was well enough to have helped others and found a reason to stay alive—for now. But this was just the beginning. There was still plenty of time for him to get killed—or to get found out.

CHAPTER
TWENTY-SIX

LONDON

Ada and Ravi walked together, so close that, she thought, they might have held hands. No one would notice. No one would care. Everyone had other things to think about. They were all hurrying, heads down, in their uniforms or to their overloaded jobs, struggling to get butter and sugar for their families, or glancing nervously skyward for zeppelins.

"And so Somerville is to be requisitioned without a doubt?" Ravi asked. They had been talking in low, familiar tones. Ada realized she had come to think of these streets as theirs, this crowd as theirs. They could be alone here, lost, invisible in the East End, down by the docks.

"Despite all our objections, yes. We're to move to Oriel

College, and no doubt the male students will make our lives as unbearable as they can. They resent us."

"Do you ever think that it might not be worth it? All this . . . and you won't even be allowed to have a degree or to practice, at the end of it."

"If I don't take what education I can, I won't be able to show how well we women deserve degrees and to work as men's equals."

"It might even be easier in India, you know. Mrs. Sorabji has set a fine example for female lawyers, and I am sure I could introduce you."

Ada was silent.

"I want to ask you something." His voice was strained, and she saw his hands were clenched in his coat pockets.

"Anything."

"You love, me don't you?"

"Need you ask?" She stopped, startled at the question, and turned to him.

"You do?" He searched her face with his eyes.

"Yes. I do." She tried not to feel a little, a very little, as if she had been forced into saying it.

"Then"—he glanced down toward the glittering Thames, and up toward St. Paul's "will you marry me, Ada? Now? As soon as possible?"

Ada was silent. She didn't know why she wasn't able to speak, why it felt as if someone were clutching her throat. It was sheer joy, she knew it was—joy that they should finally be together.

"Of course I will," she said finally, her voice trembling.

The flash of fierce happiness on Ravi's face resolved all her doubts. She was laughing, exhilarated, as he swept her into his arms and kissed her. She did not care that the world was staring, she would not even have cared—as she pressed herself against him, answering his kisses with equal passion—if the countess were to walk past at this very minute.

"Your father will not approve," Ravi said, when he finally released her.

Ada laughed without humor. "That is an understatement. But I will have to face it. He must learn that I am not his little girl anymore."

"I do feel for you. As much as I love you, I detest the idea that I should separate you from those you love."

"Perhaps he will come round in the end," she said with confidence she didn't feel. "But if not . . . well"—she swallowed—"we will be a long way away from everyone and everything I knew before. So it should be easy to forget about it . . . when I know how happy we will be together." In her heart she was not sure that was true.

"And I will do everything to make you happy. You will have more opportunities, and though the society isn't what you have been used to, it has its own advantages." He spoke eagerly. She felt with a pang how much he wanted her to be happy . . . and another when she thought of how every member of her family would be deeply unhappy with her action.

Ravi was still talking, arm in arm with her as they walked

along through the crowded street. "My salary is enough for a pleasant house in one of the better quarters. Of course it won't be what you are used to, but I think you will enjoy it. There are some very educated women—and men, of course—there, and I see no reason that with your reputation and class you would not be accepted as a legal professional."

"It sounds more advanced than England."

"Ah—it is so much *more* than England in every way," he said, his face alight with passion and pleasure. "The mountains are higher, the plains are greater, the rain is more powerful, the cities are older than those in England. I can't tell you how small this country seems to me in comparison. And the sunsets! I cannot wait to show you India."

"You forget I lived there until I was seventeen," Ada said with a smile, trying not to mind his criticism of her home. She knew he did not mean it, that he was simply swept up in his feelings.

"Ah, but that was different," said Ravi. "Now you will see it through Indian eyes."

It was a casual comment, and he went on speaking, telling her with passion of the great dusty plains, the noble Himalayas, the cool beautiful tea plantations, the sensation of seeing an elephant step silently from the dusky jungle, the chatter of parakeets like jewels in flight, the intricately carved temples and statues—and yet that one comment stayed with her through the afternoon and even on the train as she traveled back to Oxford, an unfading echo. *That was different.*

She watched the soft countryside—so small, this island—pass

through the train window. Horses galloped across a field and rooks wheeled above the copses. She blamed herself for remembering that one comment. And yet there it stayed, and she knew in her heart that it stayed because it was true. Would she ever be able to see India through Indian eyes, as he believed? Did she even want to?

She was deep in thought as she stepped down at Oxford. She hardly noticed the walk back to Somerville; it was automatic. Her thoughts were with her family. The more she thought of it, the more troubled she felt at the idea of leaving them. It would create a rift. Georgiana would feel abandoned, especially with the inheritance question so uncertain. She did not like to go away with Rose's fate still uncertain. Her father in particular would be inconsolable, furious. But was it fair of him to stand in the way of her happiness?

A flash of anger and resentment at all the ways in which her life was limited—not allowed to vote, as if she were a child or a lunatic; allowed to study but not to be awarded a degree even if she were a better scholar than any of the men; not allowed to do the work she longed to do; treated as if she were unable to look after herself, meaningless without a man to complete her—went through her. And her father had been part of all of this. No matter what she did, no matter what she achieved, she would still be nothing to him but his daughter: a chattel to be disposed of, an ornament rather than a person. Let him be furious, she thought. I don't care. I owe him nothing.

She came to the end of the road and could see the bulk of Somerville in front of her. A few steps later she recognized the girl who stood in front of it, her veil over her eyes—her clothes all black. It was more the way she stood, the way she moved, that was familiar, for there was nothing in the clothes of mourning that reminded her of her sister.

"Georgiana?" she said, and she broke into a run.

Georgiana turned toward her, and as she reached her Ada saw that she was crying.

"Georgie, what's wrong?"

"Ada, you must come home. Come home now." Georgiana threw herself into Ada's hugs, sobs choking her. "It's Papa. He's dead."

ACT TWO

CHAPTER
TWENTY-SEVEN

SOMERTON, DECEMBER 1914

The weather could scarcely have been more appropriate for a funeral. There was a dull, cold, gun-metal gray sky, and frost that made the ground like rock. Georgiana stood with Michael at the door of the church. Her hat was draped in embroidered lace, veiling her face, and her hands were buried deep in a sable muff against the cold. They were waiting for the funeral procession to arrive. The congregation was seated in the church. Only Georgiana and Michael were left, standing on the threshold, between the wide-open oak doors. A cold breeze blew in and swirled dead leaves around their feet, stirring the branches of holly and ivy that wreathed the church. Christmas had come and gone and she had barely noticed the day passing, caught up in the horror of the news about her father. Only the fact that the church was decorated reminded her of it.

"This awful frost," Georgiana said to Michael, her voice low. "The grave diggers will find their job very difficult, I am afraid."

"Try not to think about it," he replied softly. "It is not something you should concern yourself with now."

Georgiana did not reply. She knew he was right, but she could not stop worrying—as if she had been guilty of some inconsideration toward the workmen. She knew it made no sense, that she could hardly be considered responsible for the late-December weather. And yet she couldn't stop her mind darting after every anxious thought. Were the servants prepared, would the refreshments be adequate for all these people who had traveled so far? Were the flowers as they should be? What if there had been some mix-up, what if the cortege did not arrive—and most of all, where was Ada?

She still found it painful to think that Ada had not come directly back with her. It had almost been a scene, there in front of Somerville College.

"I must collect my books," Ada had said, once her first tears had died down.

"You don't need to," Georgiana had replied, shocked at the idea. "How can you even think of studying at a time like this?"

"You don't understand. I must keep on studying. If I fall behind, all this will have been in vain."

Georgiana stepped away from her sister. "I don't pretend to understand you. But I see clearly that you care more for your books and studies than you do for your family. Very well, have it your own way: come in your own time. But I am going back to Somerton now."

Georgiana forced herself to breathe deeply. Deep down, she knew that feeling anxiety and anger was easier than allowing herself to feel grief. She knew that if she once allowed her mind to linger on the fact that her father was dead—dead so brutally, so suddenly, with no chance for her to tell him that she loved him—she would break down completely. And she could not do that. She had to be calm, dignified—an Averley. It was what her father would have expected of her.

"I wonder what the weather was like when it happened," she said quickly, to Michael. Her voice sounded shrill in her own ears, but she didn't dare stop talking, in case she began to cry. "Perhaps it was a fine day; perhaps that was why they decided to tour the trenches. And perhaps that was why the sniper could see him so plainly—perhaps the sun flashed from the gold braid on his cap. Just think, if it had been overcast, perhaps Papa would still be alive." She fell silent, unable to trust herself to keep speaking calmly.

"Georgie," said Michael. He didn't say anything else, but just the way he said her name was like a comforting arm around her shoulders. Georgiana knew that he understood the way she was feeling, perfectly. She had to swallow a sob.

"I am sorry, but I can't help wondering. The official communications are so . . ."

"They're damned brusque."

Georgiana nodded, carefully, so as not to spill tears.

"I do hope the doctor is looking after the countess," she said, once she had composed herself again. "I worry so much when there is laudanum to be given. It is such a strong sedative, and—"

"Oh, Georgie," said Michael, and this time he did take her hand. She looked at him in surprise. "I hate to see you worry like this. It's the last thing that should be on your mind. I'll take care of my mother, and whatever else I can."

"You are so kind," Georgiana said softly. When, she wondered, had Michael become so grown-up, his hand so much larger and stronger than hers? She pushed the thought away, and glanced down toward the road. Where was Ada? She knew the funeral was today.

The sound of approaching hooves, a hollow music like forlorn applause, broke into her thoughts. The funeral procession was coming up the lane at last. Nodding black plumes could be glimpsed over the hedgerows. He voice faltered and all thoughts of Ada, all thoughts of everything except the ceremony ahead of her, faded away.

Michael squeezed her hand wordlessly. Then he released it and walked down to the lych-gate to take his place as coffin bearer. The assembled mourners bowed their heads as he passed. Even the crows in the bare trees seemed to cease their cawing in respect. Georgiana could see down the path to where the bearers were taking their places around the simple box in which her father lay—mahogany, with his coat of arms discreetly gilded on the lid. It would be laid to rest, Georgiana knew, in the mausoleum with all his forebears. It was so hard to understand, she thought, that it could really be her dear papa in there. Surely he was still in France and this was some kind of a bad dream. Surely there would be a chance to see him again, to wipe away the memory of the disagreement under which they had parted. She tried to bring the memory of his face to mind, but all she could see, all she could focus on, was the coffin under its velvet pall. If only Ada were here.

She turned away and walked back into the church, right up to her pew at the front. She held her head high; none of these people should say that her father's daughter had let him down at his funeral. She seated herself and waited for the coffin to arrive. She pressed her lips together so as not to cry as she saw the seat next to her, empty. Ada, who should be at her side now, had not even written or telegraphed to let her know when she could be expected. There had to be some explanation, but what?

She looked up as Mrs. Verulam, resplendent as a mourning peacock in black satin and a hat trimmed with ostrich feathers and jet beads, rustled toward her. "My dear," Mrs. Verulam murmured, "I think there is a little *contretemps*; your presence might be helpful."

Georgiana got up, too startled to reply, and followed her back to the church doors. As she reached them, she saw that she was right. The coffin was still at the bottom of the path. It was hard to see what was going on, among the identical sleek black suits and the shadows, but she made out the priest's white surplice and heard his raised, pleading voice. He seemed to be trying to calm two of the bearers.

"But what on earth is happening?" she said. "Can they possibly be arguing?"

"It does appear so," Mrs. Verulam murmured.

Sudden fury flared up in Georgiana. This was unacceptable. Nothing should be allowed to mar this most sacred hour.

Without another word, she set off down the path toward the coffin. As she approached, she saw and heard what was going on.

William was there. He had not been invited, but he was there, in full mourning. His red hair bristled, and Georgiana noticed his nose was as swollen as a strawberry—a sure sign of drink. He was squaring up to Michael, who was not backing down.

". . . and I say that the earl would not have wanted you to bear his coffin," Michael said, clearly keeping calm with a great effort.

"How dare you? You're not even an Averley. I am the earl's heir." William, bigger and broader than Michael, tried to push him from his place. Georgiana saw that Lady Edith was there, too, dressed in flowing weeds, and holding Augustus (with some difficulty, since he was wriggling and complaining) prominently in her arms. Georgiana had never seen her without a nursemaid before; this was clearly done for show.

Georgiana stopped abruptly on the path, the rambling gravestones to each side, like witnesses. Each one of the dead here had been linked to the great house at Somerton, as a tenant or a servant or one of the family. The church had been roofed and given its stained glass by one of her ancestors. Georgiana felt a heavy responsibility.

"William," she said, surprised by the authority in her own voice. William turned, startled, to face her. "We will allow you and your family in the church." Georgiana's hands were shaking with the effort of speaking calmly and coolly. She clenched them into fists, hidden by her muff, and raised her voice so that Mrs. Verulam, still watching from the church, would be able to hear every word. It was important to make things clear, to forestall gossip. "As Averleys you and your family may pay your respects to my dear father. But he did not name you as one who would have the honor of bearing his coffin. Therefore, please be good enough to stand back and allow my father's funeral to take place in peace."

William looked inclined to object, but a whisper from Lady Edith checked him. He stepped not back but forward, and strode up toward the church, scowling. Mrs. Verulam's face was a frozen mask of disapproval as she stepped aside to let him pass. Lady Edith followed him at a much slower pace, now and then dabbing her eyes, through her heavy lace veil, with a jet-black handkerchief. She paused when she reached Georgiana.

"I do condole with you on the passing of your father," she said in a stage whisper. "No matter what injustices he has done to my own dear son"—Augustus squirmed—"I cannot help but feel for you. Such a tragedy! But there, we must not question divine will."

She swept on toward the church. Georgiana held her breath and counted to ten. At a nod from the undertaker, the sad, steady drum began again, and the bearers shouldered the coffin and began the slow march up to the church. Georgiana turned and went before them to her pew.

Just as the priest reached the pulpit, and as the gloomy organ music booming through the cold stone arches was about to come to an end, Georgiana heard hasty footsteps coming up the aisle. She looked around to see Ada, elegant in black silk and a dramatic sweep of lace, hurrying toward her. Despite everything, Georgiana couldn't repress a huge smile of relief. But, as quickly, her relief turned to anger. How could Ada be late for her own father's funeral? How could she put her studies ahead of her family, especially at a time like this?

Ada took the seat reserved for her next to Georgiana. She looked straight forward, her chest rising and falling as she recovered her breath. The organ heaved its last sigh.

Georgiana glanced at Ada once more. Through the veil, she could see that tears were running silently down her sister's face. Georgiana looked ahead again, her own heart wrung. But to touch her hand in comfort and sympathy—even to reach out for comfort and sympathy herself—seemed impossible. The gulf between them had never felt wider.

CHAPTER
TWENTY-EIGHT

Rebecca came up the stairs from the kitchen as fast as she could, trying not to let the tray of sandwiches she carried slip. They only had half an hour before the family would be back from church, and everything had to be ready and perfect to receive the guests. She checked the flowers with a glance as she came through the hall and made a small exclamation of annoyance. The yellow roses were still in the Lalique vase, even though she had sent Annie and Martha up to replace all of them with lilies half an hour ago, and the water was filthy. She went into the white drawing room, where the table was set for the refreshments. Annie and Martha were standing in the middle of the room, arms full of flowers, whispering excitedly to each other.

Rebecca didn't usually protest when she saw them slacking—after all, it was hardly her place to do so—but today all the memories of her own father's funeral were uppermost in her mind. Poor Lady Georgiana had looked exhausted as she left for the funeral, and Rebecca was determined that her life should not be made more difficult, today of all days. "Come along, you two, get a move on!" she challenged them, putting the tray down on the table. "The family will be back any minute!"

Martha gave her a malicious look. "Very well, Miss Freeman—or should I say Miss *Freudemann*?"

"What?" Rebecca felt a shock go through her at the sound of her old name. "What did you say?"

But Martha had already swept past her. Annie scurried after Martha, having the grace to look embarrassed. Rebecca stood where she was, her heart thumping painfully in her chest. She had to confront them. She had to stand up to them, deny it. But she could not bring herself to lie. She was tired, she realized, so tired of pretending she had nothing to hide. But her job depended on it—

A scream from Martha and a smash knocked those thoughts out of her mind.

"Oh no!" she exclaimed, visions of shattered crystal and scattered flowers filling her mind. She raced into the room, and stood, dumbstruck. Everything she had feared was there—the vase had smashed on the edge of the marble coffee table and the water was dripping from it onto the Persian carpet—but there was one element she had never imagined. Martha and Annie stood as if frozen, and in front of them, backed up against the fireplace like a hunted deer, was a girl—a stranger.

Rebecca was speechless for a moment. She took in the girl's appearance almost unconsciously. She wasn't quality; that much was clear from her hat and, after a moment's observation, from a thousand other little details, not merely in her dress but in her appearance. Her wide, terrified blue eyes, her cheap gloves, and the way she stood, like someone more used to being in a still-room than in a drawing room, all proclaimed that she was no official visitor.

"A ghost!" Martha trembled. "An apparition!"

"Nonsense," said Rebecca sharply. She realized that she recognized the intruder: she was one of the innkeeper's daughters, at the Averley Arms. She had seen her often enough, running errands around the village, though she did not know her name. "What are you doing here?" she said, making an effort to keep her voice calm and soothing. "And how—how did you get in?"

"I'm here to see the family." The girl's reply was strong and clear. "I found a window open, and I'm here to see them, face to face."

"She's come to kill us all in our beds—" Martha began.

"Martha, please!" Rebecca took a deep breath. Again she spoke gently, putting her hand out to the girl. "Come downstairs, for heaven's sake. You can't see the family, not now. The earl is dead, didn't you know? The funeral is today. If you're found here, there'll be the most awful trouble."

"The earl is dead, she says!" The girl gave a harsh laugh. "Do you think I care? I wish he'd died before this war ever started!"

"Hush, for heaven's sake!" Rebecca was horrified, and the thought crossed her mind that the girl might be insane. She crossed to the girl, took her arm gently, and tried to steer her toward the door. "Come away—have you no sympathy for poor Lady Georgiana? And the countess?"

"Haven't they any for me? At least they've a body." The girl shook her off, her voice trembling. "I've nothing to bury—not even any right to grieve. No one knows, oh, no one knows how much we loved each other."

The words came out as if wrung from her, and Rebecca's heart twisted in sympathy. The girl *was* mad, she realized—mad with grief. Clearly, she had lost someone close to her. Perhaps not a husband; perhaps they hadn't even been engaged. There were tragedies like this every day, she knew. She put an arm around the girl's shoulders. "My dear," she said softly. "I am so sorry for your loss. Wouldn't it be better to come downstairs with me and compose yourself? Then you can speak your piece to the family clearly, without breaking down."

The girl hesitated, and Rebecca was sure that her childish trickery would never work. But she had underestimated how tired the girl was, she realized. She remembered that exhaustion herself, from when her father had died—days of not sleeping, of raging, until she was so sore at heart that she longed for anyone to put an arm round her and tell her it was all right, that she could stop grieving without letting him down. The girl shuddered and relaxed against her arm. Rebecca found herself almost carrying her to the servants' stairs. As she passed Annie, she turned and whispered fiercely, "Get the mess cleared up; get this room to rights. And don't breathe a word of this to anyone, you two!"

She hoped, as she steered the girl from the room, that she could rely on Annie and Martha to hold their tongues. It seemed unlikely, but she had other things to do. The girl had to be gotten downstairs before the family arrived, at all costs.

Just as they reached the door of the drawing room, Thomas came in. He started in astonishment as he saw them. "Rebecca?" He looked both angry and anxious. "Who on earth is this woman? Get her out of here! The first motorcars are coming up the drive!"

"Don't you order me about!" The girl roused herself at his words. "If my James was here as he used to be, he would never have stood for it."

James! Rebecca remembered the footman she had never met, who had left the day she arrived. By the stricken look on Thomas's face, she knew that he did too.

To her relief, he changed his tone at once. "I'm sorry, miss. I didn't know who you were. But if you come downstairs with me and Miss Freeman, we'll see you have everything you need . . ."

Rebecca kept walking the girl toward the baize door, and Thomas came to flank the girl on her other side. Distantly, she heard the noise of people entering through the front door: clear, upper-class voices. She hastened her pace, her heartbeat quickening. They were at the baize door, Thomas still talking calmly, politely. The door was open, and they were through. But the sound of it closing behind them made the girl start. She turned and began trying to fight her way upstairs again. Rebecca had all she could do to stop her from pushing her way back through. Luckily, Thomas was just behind her. Together they managed to get her down into the servants' quarters, but not without Rebecca's face being covered in scratches and her cap knocked sideways. Thomas managed to get the girl's arms behind her back, and steered her toward the housekeeper's room.

"Can you get my key from the hook and unlock it?" he gasped. Then, to the girl: "Gently, miss, I don't want to hurt you!" Rebecca hastily slipped the key from the nail on the wall and unlocked the housekeeper's door. Thomas pushed the girl in, and Rebecca slammed the door shut behind the three of them.

"I can't leave Annie and Martha up there—they'll never manage." Thomas was out of breath, the girl still struggling.

"I'll stay with her—you lock us in," Rebecca answered.

"Right—here goes." Thomas pushed the girl toward the housekeeper's chair, with a brief "Sorry, miss," and caught the key as Rebecca tossed it to him. He darted out of the door before the girl could turn around, and slammed it behind him. Rebecca heard the door lock. The girl spun to face her, and Rebecca took a step backward, thinking for the first time of the danger she might be in. But the girl simply put her hands to her face, began sobbing heavily, and collapsed into a chair. It seemed she was defeated.

Rebecca stood, catching her breath. She watched, full of pity, as the girl sobbed. This was such a tragedy; no wonder the poor girl was in such a state. She had never met James, but she had helped the others put up parcels for him and had seen his cheerful, short letters pinned up in the kitchen. This girl had clearly loved him very much.

"What's your name, dear?" she said, once the sobs had begun to die down.

"Jenny. It was going to be Jenny Carter. He promised me that."

"I'm sure he did," Rebecca said gently. She knew how hard it was—a love affair still young, not told to the parents yet. Where did that leave poor Jenny, with no right to weep at the funeral? "I am so sorry for your loss," she said. "But how can it be the family's fault?"

Jenny looked up, fierce and resentful. "They encouraged him! He was so cock-a-hoop at the earl shaking his hand! I told him to be careful, but he said he'd do anything for a master like that." Her voice shook with passion. "It isn't f-fair. The earl gets a grand funeral; my James gets n-nothing. He's missing in action. He'd never have gone if it wasn't for the earl egging him on. He cared for me so much." The girl began sobbing, softly and hopelessly. "And he's gone, he's gone."

Wordlessly, Rebecca went to the girl and knelt before her, taking her hands in her own, pressing them kindly. She sensed that the girl simply needed to talk to someone, anyone. She listened as the girl cried and told her everything—how they had courted, how he had promised to marry her as soon as he got leave, how she hadn't wanted him to go but he'd been so set on the idea of being a hero, living up to the ideal . . . and now there was nothing, not even a body to bury. Rebecca listened and felt like weeping herself.

"Do you have something to remember him by?" she asked finally, thinking of James's few possessions that he had left behind, and wondering if she could give Jenny something to keep.

Jenny looked into Rebecca's eyes. She gave a brief, bleak smile. "Oh yes," she said. "That's the trouble."

It took Rebecca a moment to understand what she meant. Then—with a shock of sympathy—she understood. No wonder the poor girl was so desperate. What was she to say? *I'm sorry* sounded callous—what was there to regret in a baby born out of love? But what was there to celebrate in a baby born into shame and poverty, with a father dead before he knew of its existence?

"Perhaps it may not be so bad," she said in the end. "Have you spoken to his parents?"

"No, nor to my own. I know what they'll say."

"They may not. It may not be as you fear." Rebecca looked up into her face, wanting so much to give comfort. "His parents will be grieving; think what it could mean to them to have a grandchild. And your parents . . . well." She thought of her father, his stern, kind love. "My father would have been angry, but my mother would have talked him round, and they would both have understood in the end."

Jenny did not answer. Rebecca was silent, unable to think of another thing to say that might help. She had tried to be comforting, but the fact was, Palesbury was a small town. Not all parents were as loving as hers. Jenny would be thought of as ruined, and that would make it hard for her to find work, impossible for her to find a husband to care for another man's child . . . The future seemed bleak.

After what seemed like a long time, there was a knock at the door, and Rebecca heard a key turning in the lock. She got up and met Thomas at the door. Jenny did not move.

"Is everything all right?" Thomas greeted her in a whisper.

Rebecca nodded. His eyes searched her face, full of warm concern.

"I should never have left you here with her in this violent state," he said in the same low voice. "She could have attacked you or anything. I didn't think. I'm a fool."

"There was nothing else to do, and I was quite safe."

"Still, it was wrong of me. I'll never do it again."

"She is so much better now; I don't think she would ever have harmed anyone," Rebecca said quickly, anxious to defend Jenny.

Thomas looked over at Jenny. She had stood up while they were talking, and she was now standing at the window, her back to them, looking out through the diamond paned windows.

"I'm very sorry, miss, for your loss," Thomas said gently. "James gone—I can hardly believe it. I must go up again, but I had to come and pay my condolences." He went on, his voice trembling. "We all respected James so much. He was like an older brother to me."

Jenny nodded distantly, still looking out of the window. Rebecca crossed the room so she could see what she was looking at. Framed in the diamond pane was a corner of the drive, and they could see the earl's motorcar. Lady Georgiana was just getting out of the car, leaning on Master Templeton's arm. Rebecca was too far away to see his face, but there was something about the tender, attentive way he bent over her that made Rebecca feel as if her heart were a violin, and that a string—a minor string, but still one that had been lovingly tuned—had just snapped.

Jenny turned away from the window. In her face was nothing but weariness and resignation. "You needn't worry. I won't make a scene. I know you are right and it would be foolish," she said. "I'll go home, and perhaps . . . perhaps it won't be as bad as I fear."

She went toward the door. Thomas stepped aside to let her pass. Rebecca followed, still worried about her. But Jenny seemed genuinely composed. She stopped at the kitchen to say, "You have been very kind, I thank you both."

Rebecca followed and saw her out of the back door. As she stood on the step, she whispered to Jenny, "I know Lady Georgiana will help you out if she knows the truth. She's kindness itself."

Jenny looked up at her. "She knows what it is to love. I see that," she answered quietly. "I suppose they are human after all."

Rebecca watched her walking away. Her heart felt twisted inside her, with pity for Jenny and pain at the knowledge that Master Templeton loved Lady Georgiana—even if her mistress did not know it.

She sighed. Turning back into the corridor, she was startled to see Thomas still standing there, waiting for her.

"I think she means it, sir," she said. "She won't make any trouble."

"I believe you." He hesitated. The sunlight came through the kitchen window and glinted on his dark gold hair. "I want to thank you, Rebecca. If it were not for your quick, clearheaded actions, this could have been a very unpleasant scene."

Rebecca blushed with surprise at the praise. "I was only doing my job, sir."

"You did it well. I'm grateful—and I'm sorry about what I said about parlormaids. You've proved me wrong."

He smiled at her. It astonished Rebecca. She had never seen him smile before, not like this. It lit up his eyes; they were the exact same color as a summer sky. It was a color she could not forget as she went about her duties for the rest of the day, and at night when she lay down to sleep, she found the last thing she was thinking of was his smile.

CHAPTER
TWENTY-NINE

OXFORD

Ada sat, silent, with eyes that longed to weep, on the train as it made its way down the country toward Oxford. Her gaze was fixed on the window, and on her own reflection, fragile and ghostly, in the glass. Her back was as straight as she had learned to carry it since the nursery, and she swayed back and forth with the motion of the train, her wide-brimmed hat like the head of a flower on a tall, slender stalk. She longed to lean her aching head against the cool glass of the window. But well-bred women did not do that, and besides, she was not alone. In front of her sat two men, one in civvies and one in uniform. She guessed they were colleagues, one perhaps on leave. They had a newspaper; she caught snatches of their conversation.

". . . say it was a terrible thing, people killed in Great Yarmouth."

"We're not safe even here. . . ."

On the front page of the newspaper was an image of something Ada had seen only once or twice before the war: a zeppelin. The dark, smudged shape was like a stain on the paper; there was something ominous about it. It was strange that something so vast could move so silently, invisible among the clouds of night. Her eyes kept returning to the image. It was like a pit whose depths she could not see.

The train swayed and the *clack-clack* of the wheels on the track beat at her mind. She had always enjoyed the rhythm of the train, but now, through her pounding headache, it felt like torture. She had had a headache for days; she always did when she had been crying.

I must compose myself, she told herself. I am going back to start Hilary term. I must concentrate. I must remember to smile.

But she knew that Oxford would never be the same again, not after what had happened.

After Georgiana had left Ada at Oxford before their father's funeral, Ada had spent the whole night packing, getting her books in order. Then, so early in the morning that it was still dark, she had set off down the street, exhausted, carrying her case, to catch the first train to Somerton. The trees overhead were invisible, but whispered softly as she passed the Thames. The moon was bright and shone down on the cobblestones and on the water. And then she saw him—first by the light of his cheroot, just as she had that day so long ago when they had first met. She knew him by his shadow, by the way he moved. He was walking across the bridge toward her.

She quickened her step, and climbed onto the bridge where he was standing. He tossed his cheroot aside as soon as he saw her. "Ada, darling. I heard the news yesterday—a rumor in India House. I am so sorry." He wrapped his arms around her and stroked her hair.

"Thank you . . . yes, a terrible shock." Ada hardly knew what she was saying. She knew she could be seen at any moment by a don out for a moonlit stroll, but somehow she no longer cared. "We never imagined . . . we thought he would face no danger. It does not feel real."

"It's the most awful thing." Ravi's voice expressed everything that his words could not. He took her case from her. "Come, let's go to my rooms. This place is not private."

Ada followed him, too tired to think about the danger of being seen. He was talking as they went, telling her how as soon as he'd realized that the rumors of a visiting advisor being killed in action by a sniper's bullet must refer to the Earl of Westlake, he had come straight to Oxford.

"I couldn't bear the thought of you facing this alone," he said, pausing before a tall town house. "It's not much," he added, apologetically. "I took the first thing I could find."

They went up the narrow, steep stairs, and he let her into his room. Ada looked around. This was the closest she had ever been to him, the most intimate glimpse of his life: his razor on the washstand, his shirt hanging in the wardrobe, and it somehow made her want to cry. She wanted so much to know him with such intimacy like this, every day. But now . . . how could she go to India, with Somerton reeling from the blow of her father's death?

"Don't light the gas," she said quietly. "Just open the curtains so we can see the dawn."

He obeyed. The pale dawn light flooded in.

"Ada," he said, with such deep warmth, and moved toward her. She put out a hand to forestall him, resting it on his broad chest.

"Ravi, I—"

"Please, I know your heart must be full. Don't feel that you have to speak unless you wish to." He moved her hand gently, and stepped closer. She was close enough to lean her head on his chest; she could smell his sandalwood scent.

"I simply cannot understand it," she said. "He was adamant that he would face no danger."

"The word in army circles is that he was touring the battle-field, looking for improvements that could be made to the trenches. He wanted to do something for the men, to make their lives easier."

"My poor father." Her voice broke. "How like him to think of others. Oh, I must go back to Somerton." She turned away, but he followed her.

"You look exhausted," he said. "Rest for a moment, please."

She longed to simply sink into his arms. But it would not be fair. She had to say it, and she did, in a rush. "You must know this means we must postpone any plans—"

"Of course you will not marry until you have properly mourned your father."

"Not only that." She paused. "Ravi, I have been thinking, ever since I saw Georgiana and heard this news. My father is gone; the countess is from all I hear prostrated with shock and grief. I cannot leave Somerton without knowing whether it is in safe hands for the future. I cannot leave my sister without support."

"But you must let go of the past," he said quietly, firmly. "Your family has always prevented you from being who you truly are. Your title has been nothing more than a millstone around your neck."

"That is not quite true."

"You said—"

"I know it has felt so sometimes." She clenched her hands. "Ravi, please try to understand. Whatever my family is to me, whatever Somerton is to me—it is part of my self."

"And what about me? Am I not also part of you?" His arms went around her, his lips touched her neck. "I have tried to be; I long to be. I will be your family; I will be your Somerton."

"I wish you could be," she murmured, her eyes aching with tears. "But I fear nothing can replace them."

"What are you saying? Ada, think carefully—"

"I have been thinking. I have been thinking for months. Let

me ask you something." She turned to face him, and stepped back, her hands resting lightly on his. "Will you give up any thought of returning to India, will you stay here with me?"

There was a long silence. She could see the emotion on his face.

"You know I cannot."

"Then you know how I feel."

"You mean you will not go to India with me." His voice trembled.

"I mean that no matter how much I long to go to India with you"—she hesitated, not wanting to say the words that she knew she had to say—"I know that I would not be happy there. I could not live with the guilt of abandoning my family and my country in their hour of need."

"But you will abandon me," he said bitterly. "That is what you are saying, isn't it? You are saying that you . . . that you . . ." He paused; she could tell he was on the brink of tears and was struggling to hold them back. "That you will not marry me." The words came out fierce and angry. "That everything you said was a lie. That you do not care for me. That you do not love me—"

"Stop!" she cried out. Her hands were up as if to defend herself from a blow. A moment later he was covering her hands with passionate kisses.

"Ada—I am sorry—I didn't mean it—I am a brute. Forget I said it, forget it. We can start again. We can forget all these insane words. Please, forgive me."

She leaned against him and let her tears soak into his shirt. Finally gaining control of herself, she looked up at him. "We cannot start again. You know it. You know that if I were to come to India, or if you were to do the impossible and stay here, we would always be having scenes like this. In the end it would destroy us. You know that, Ravi; please, have the courage to admit it."

He held her tight. After a long time, his answer came. It was what she had asked him to say, what she had known he would have the integrity to admit, and yet it broke her heart.

"Yes. It is true."

They clung to each other, without words. The sunlight brightened on the wall, but Ada had never felt less as if dawn were breaking. Dawn should come with hope and strength, she thought. Not tears and silence.

A small noise told her he was crying. Her heart felt as if it were being wrenched in two. She felt such great love for him, such passion and such heartbreak. She kissed him, whispering how sorry she was, how much she loved him. He returned her kisses; she tasted his tears. She knew they should stop, but she could not bear to. It seemed too cruel that they should be brought together, then driven apart, without ever knowing each other as deeply as they longed to. The kisses became desperate; she found her fingers unbuttoning his shirt, his hands plunged deep in her hair, her dress slipping from her naked shoulders . . .

"Tell me to stop," he murmured, as he had done once before, but now there was no tease in the words, just an intensity that made her tremble with desire.

"I don't want you to stop," she replied, and as he lifted her and carried her to the bed, she knew with all her heart that it was the truth.

As she gazed from the train window it was as if she could still feel his kisses on her skin, burning her. She would never forget what they had done, she thought. It was a precious jewel, locked deep in the black velvet of her memory. She knew that over the years to come, she would be able to touch it, caress it, gaze into its shining depths. No one could snatch this memory from her.

Through the window, she could see they were coming into Oxford. She tried to see the rooming house where they had been, where it had happened. She had heard the rattle of the trains passing; it must have been close to the railway line. She remembered saying to him, *I have always longed for this. I will never regret it.* And later, *If only I had known. If only I had known that it would be so perfect.*

And even later, *Good-bye. Good-bye forever, my darling, good-bye.*

The train slowed at the platform. The men stood, and one of them politely handed her case down. Ada wanly smiled her thanks and followed them out of the carriage.

She took in her beloved refuge. Oxford. She had arrived here with such joy, every time, but now she could see nothing but the gray misery of a land under siege, a dark future, shapeless and terrifying as the shadow of the zeppelin. She would have to go back to university, work, work, work, as if Ravi had not left, as if he were not even now taking ship from Southampton.

In time the pain will fade, he had told her.

I will never forget you, she had replied.

No, but the pain will fade. And he had kissed her. They had been standing at the station. Anyone could have seen. Ada did not care. What was there left to lose now?

She picked up her case and, head high, walked out of the station. The crowd parted before her, some giving her curious glances, others indifferent.

If only they knew, she thought with a bitter, reckless glory. If only they knew how free I feel.

CHAPTER
THIRTY

FRANCE

The CCS was in a half-ruined, rain-sodden little farm from which all the animals, people, and evidence of life had long since disappeared. It was strange how quickly it had come to seem like . . . well, not exactly home, Charlotte thought as she hurried across the yard, but familiar.

She entered her hut, a shack built up in the ruins of the barn, and collected her leather motoring coat and muff. She was glad that she'd invested in them, buying them at Boulogne from a VAD who was leaving to go back to England to care for her elderly parents. She thought with a moment's regret of her beautiful furs, left behind in England, and then pushed the memory away. That was then; this was now. Fur would be sodden and heavy, worse than useless on the regular ambulance runs to the front line to collect the wounded.

She came out of the hut and ran over to the waiting ambulance. She scrambled up next to the driver, a grizzled, chain-smoking bus driver from the East End called Sid. The first time she had been in the ambulance, even though its rusty, mud-encrusted exterior had given her some idea of what it might be like traveling inside, she had been dismayed to find that there was no seat, except for a rusty oilcan. She was used to it now, after many trips down to collect the wounded from the dressing stations where they were taken immediately after battle, but still felt very exposed; it was little more than a wagon with an engine bolted on and canvas sides to the back part where the wounded traveled.

Sid shoved the ambulance into gear and it shot off violently, nearly throwing Charlotte off her seat.

Charlotte had known before she arrived that they could not use headlights so close to the front for fear of being spotted by planes or snipers, but she hadn't realized exactly what that would mean, driving over muddy, slippery, potholed roads in the pitch dark, between the churned fields at either side. Back and forth they lurched, the ambulance sticking frequently, now and then dark shapes looming out of the night—the wrecks of other cars, a single, blackened, leafless tree that had somehow escaped a shell. On the horizon, the sunset left its last glow, and the thundering of the shells was their compass. Charlotte clung to whatever she could, fixing her eyes on that distant scene, frightened but also desperate to get there and help.

"Who are we picking up this time?" she asked Sid.

"B-Four Trench, they've been in the thick of it."

"Poor boys. It must be time for leave for some of them at least."

"We should be so lucky. Nineteen fifteen's looking like the year we dig in and stay dug in."

Charlotte didn't reply. It was depressingly likely to be true. After swaying back and forth across France and Belgium for most of 1914, the front line had solidified, as if stuck in the mud. Neither army was gaining ground. It was starting to look as if it would be a long war.

So I must do my best to help, and keep the men's spirits up, she told herself determinedly. But she had never been so exhausted. It was painful to feel that what she was doing was not the nursing she had found so rewarding in London, but a desperate, rushed patching up of broken and torn bodies until they were well enough to be loaded onto another train and dispatched back to the general hospital at Étaples. It was only now that she realized that in London she had been caring for men who were stabilized, who were already as likely to survive as they ever would be. There had been few deaths there. Here, when the men came right out of the battlefield, hemorrhaging and in shock, there were too many deaths to count. Too many to remember their names. Tears stung her eyes, partly from sheer tiredness, as she thought of it.

On and on they went—and then she realized the red glow was not the sunset. It was the dressing station that they were heading for. The dressing station itself was on fire.

"Oh Lord!" she exclaimed, knowing it must have been a direct hit. Adrenaline sizzled through her; she sat up, all her self-pity vanished. Sid seemed to realize at the same moment; he swore and put his foot on the accelerator.

It was more tense minutes before the ambulance got close enough to stop. The heat from the flames hit Charlotte as she jumped out, and the glow gave an eerie brightness. Distantly she could hear the crump of exploding shells and the whine of shrapnel. She almost fell over a soldier who was sitting with his back against a ridge of earth, silent and shivering with shock. Charlotte could only guess at the extent of his injuries; she wrapped a blanket around him and helped him drink water.

"Over here!" a man shouted out to her, and she stood up to see stretchers being lifted out of the trenches. The man who had shouted came running up to her. She could not see his face through the crust of dirt and blood, but red-gold hair glinted in the flames.

"We've got men who need help here," he told her.

She noticed that his accent was American, but had no time to think about it further. More men were coming from the trench, some stumbling on crutches, others leaning on each other. Some had to be carried; there had been no time for stretchers, and they were simply laid into the back of the ambulance, screaming in pain. Charlotte and the American helped position them more securely.

"Watch out!" Charlotte snapped as he almost let a badly

burned soldier slip. She didn't dare to think how many of the wounded would survive the trip back to the hospital. The most important thing was to get them out of the way of the firing before another shell wiped them all out.

"That's the lot." Sid came running past her, toward the driver's seat. "Get in, now!" Charlotte jumped into the back of the ambulance and reached out a hand to the man who had been helping her. For the first time, as he struggled to get onto the step, she realized he was hurt.

"Oh—your arm!" It was clearly broken, tied up in a sling. Now she understood why he had been so awkward.

He climbed up next to her with a grunt of pain and effort. A shell exploded to their left, and Charlotte ducked, jumping at the noise. The ambulance moved off with a jerk and she was thrown against the American man. She heard him gasp with pain. There was a patch of space on the boards, and he sat down, and pulled her down too—onto his lap. Charlotte jumped up as if she had been burned.

"Sit still, ma'am!"

She had no choice: the ambulance reeled across the road and threw her off balance, back into his arms. She clung to him, furious at the position she was in, aware that she had to keep her dignity as a nurse at all times. Then a shell burst directly overhead. She couldn't stop herself shrieking in fear. His arm tightened around her; she found herself clutching at him. But the glare of the explosion had shown her the chaos inside the ambulance. She had to do something. She felt for her first-aid bag and crawled on hands and knees to each of the men, giving them what help she could in the shaking darkness. By the time they had left the explosions behind and the road had grown smoother, she had worked her way back round to the American.

"Who put this sling on?" she demanded, turning her fear into anger. "It's a filthy mess."

"Me, ma'am. Sorry—not a medic by training."

"You're not a medical officer?" She looked at him again. In her flashlight's beam she made out an insignia on his torn uniform: wings. "You're a pilot!"

"Shot down behind the German lines—bailed out, broke my arm coming down in a tree. Got to the dressing station, but looks like the enemy followed me." He smiled through the pain.

So he'd been shot down behind enemy lines, made his way back to the British side with a broken arm, and *then* helped her get the others into the ambulance. Charlotte was impressed despite herself.

"Well, I hope you haven't done any permanent damage" was all she said. You couldn't get close to the men, especially not one as cocky as this. If she showed him how impressed she was, he would lose all respect for her. She wondered what an American was doing in the war—his country was still neutral—and then a bump in the road sent her gasping into his arms again. She fought him off furiously.

"If you dare to take advantage—"

"Don't worry, ma'am, I'm a man of honor. I'll marry you first chance I get."

Charlotte was breathless with indignation. Luckily the ambulance pulled up at that moment, and she didn't have to think of a cutting response. She jumped down and began assisting the orderlies with unloading the wounded men. Then it was back to the routine of chaos, helping the medical officer perform emergency operations, administering sedatives and water and comfort, cleaning and bandaging wounds, and always with the screams of pain and always, always, someone calling for their mother. There was no time to think, no time to stop, no time to do anything but try as hard as she could to save as many lives as she could.

It wasn't until much later that the medical officer in charge, Dr. Field, told her to go to her hut and rest.

"There's still so much to do," she replied. Distantly, someone was moaning in delirium.

"There's always so much to do," he told her. His face was gray and lined with exhaustion. "Go and sleep now, or you will be no use tomorrow."

Charlotte nodded, knowing the older man was right. She turned away and went up the ward toward her hut.

"Hey, there."

A familiar voice spoke up from one of the beds. She turned and saw his blue eyes smiling at her. Cleaned up, he was handsome. A sprinkle of boyish freckles covered a once-broken nose.

"That was a fine job you did there, ma'am. Name's Flint, Flint MacAllister." He held out a bandaged hand. "Yours?"

Charlotte drew herself up, despite her aching feet. She was glad to find she still had the energy to put him in his place. "You may call me Nurse Templeton. If you must call me anything at all, that is—and I'd rather you didn't."

She spun on her heel, shaking with exhaustion, and stalked off to her hut. She collapsed on the camp bed and fell asleep without even removing her uniform.

CHAPTER
THIRTY-ONE

SOMERTON

Rebecca made her way down the servants' stairs, her basket of mending in one hand. It was a relief to be sure that this afternoon, at least, she wouldn't have to keep putting it down to run around answering bells. Of course, she reminded herself, it was for a sad reason—all the family were at the reading of Lord Westlake's will.

It still seemed impossible to realize that he was gone. She had only seen him a couple of times, while waiting at table, and he had never spoken to her. Still, she had heard the kind way he spoke to his family, and he had never seemed a harsh master. Lady Georgiana must be heartbroken, she thought with pity. It had been so hard when her own father died, she remembered; how she had longed for someone to talk about it with. But there had been no one. Mother had needed her support; Rebecca couldn't let her feelings show. She had needed to be cheerful and keep things going for her and Davy. And now . . . it felt as if she had pushed the grief so far down that she could not imagine speaking of it to anyone. But it was still there, like an underground river.

She walked into the kitchen. Instantly she was struck by the atmosphere. Annie and Martha were talking to Thomas—or had been, until she came in. The instant they saw her, they stopped. Annie was pink in the face. Martha had her arms folded tightly. Cook looked furious. The other servants were silent and serious.

Rebecca stopped on the threshold, shifting the heavy basket into her cradling arms.

"Is something the matter?" she asked, thinking at once of the war. Had there been some bad news—had the Palesbury Pals taken another beating? Or one of those terrible zeppelin raids that seemed to come so randomly?

Thomas looked up at her. He seemed troubled. "Unfortunately," he began, "we are unable to find—"

"Oh, do tell it straight, Thomas," Annie interrupted. She stepped forward and pointed at Rebecca. "We know you stole them spoons."

Rebecca, shocked, took a step back. "I didn't! I've not stolen anything!" She looked at Thomas in appeal. "How can you let her say that? It's a lie!"

"Well, you tell us who it could have been, then," Cook said, tutting at her. "No, I won't hold my tongue, Thomas. You're too kind to her. You know no one else had the key to the silver cabinet."

"It's not true!" Rebecca's shock was replaced with anger. Color flooded into her face, and she felt on the brink of tears, which only made her more angry. "It's a barefaced lie; you should be ashamed of yourself."

"That's enough." Thomas barely raised his voice, but the note of authority quietened everyone. "I won't have Rebecca accused like this, with no evidence. She's been a very good worker here, better than you two put together, Annie and Martha."

Martha opened her mouth, but Thomas raised a hand.

"I've had enough of all these rumors and gossiping. If the spoons have been stolen, that's a serious crime. I'm not just talking about being dismissed without a reference; I'm talking about the police, and prison." He waited for his words to sink in. There was dead silence. "So it's no small thing to make these accusations. I am going to get at the truth once and for all."

Rebecca tightened her grip on the basket.

"I am going to search the servants' rooms—all of them." He glanced around. "Does anyone have any objections?"

There was an uncomfortable silence. Roderick looked as if he might want to object, but no one spoke.

"Very well. I shall do it now. Cook"—he turned to her—"I want you to make sure no one leaves this room until I return. And I want no talking, either. No more bullying of Rebecca, and no more accusations. We'll know the truth soon enough."

"Yes, sir," said Cook. Rebecca noted that it was the first time she had called him sir. She gave Rebecca a cold glance, and Rebecca knew that she in particular would be watched.

She slid into a seat, still clutching the basket. She knew she wasn't guilty, and yet she was still afraid. Annie and Martha were out to get her. She wouldn't put it past them to have planted the spoons in her room.

CHAPTER
THIRTY-TWO

PALESBURY

Ada walked down the High Street from the railway station to Mr. Bradford's offices, which were in the shadow of Palesbury Minster's tall bell tower. The road curved gently, and through the gaps between the stone cottages and the slate-tiled roofs she glimpsed countryside that was sunny, though the cobbles underfoot were still slippery with the morning's rain. A few passersby glanced at her, and she knew she looked out of place in her London-purchased clothes: the scoop neck and her daringly short skirt, skimming her calf. Some recognized her and tipped their hats or smiled a welcome. Others raised an eyebrow. In London it had become normal for well-bred young ladies to walk around alone wherever they liked. War work demanded it. But here in Palesbury it still seemed to be something out of the ordinary. Ada found herself resenting the glances. She walked faster, her hands buried for warmth in her muff.

It was a bitter feeling to think that she had given Ravi up to stay here in England, where everyone would turn their backs on her if they knew the truth. Oh, how I hate this country sometimes, she thought. With its small-minded hypocrisy, its smug self-satisfaction. Even the weather hasn't the moral courage to commit to rain or shine. The thought made her smile for a moment, but her smile died as she remembered the passion of the monsoon and the uncompromising heat of the Indian sun. She had given that up forever.

She arrived at Mr. Bradford's offices just as the clock was striking one, and saw her father's motorcar drawn up outside it. It caught her throat to think that he would not be stepping from it. Instead she saw black-swathed figures getting out. One was the countess, though hardly recognizable. She seemed to have lost weight, and leaned on Michael's arm. There was something fragile about her that Ada had not seen before; clearly the loss of her husband had hit her badly. Ada felt sympathy; she had never gotten on with her stepmother, but she did not deny that she had loved the earl in her own way, and that the disappearance of Sebastian must be plaguing her mind.

Georgiana followed them. Ada was startled, but pleased, to see how grown-up she looked. As Georgiana approached, she noticed the new strength and gravity in her face. Georgiana had had none of the usual coming-out, and yet she seemed to have grown into herself, grown into a young lady, without the benefit of the London round. Ada was glad to see it—but she couldn't help feeling guilty that she had not been there to help Georgiana over the past months.

She redoubled her pace and met them at the door.

"Ada, I am so glad you are here," said Georgiana. "For once."

Ada's own greeting died on her lips. She swallowed down the hurt as Georgiana walked past her into Mr. Bradford's chambers. His secretary showed them in, bowing deeply. Ada hung back before going into the office, and held Georgiana back too.

"Georgie, I want to apologize for my lack of consideration at the funeral—and before," she said quietly. "I know I must have seemed very uncaring, but please believe me when I say that it has only been that . . . I haven't known myself. I haven't known what was important."

Georgiana looked quickly into her face, and Ada saw warmth there. Dear Georgiana, she could never stay cross for long. But to her surprise and pain, Georgiana looked away again. "It hasn't been easy for me either," she replied quietly. "I don't wish to think badly of you, Ada, but I cannot help it—I do. You put your own aspirations before your family. That hurts me."

She removed Ada's hand from her arm and walked into the office. Ada stood where she was, feeling hollow. She had never seen Georgiana so upset before. Perhaps, she thought with a stab of guilt, I have taken her for granted.

She followed her into the office. There was nothing to be said or done for the moment. She only wished that Georgiana could know what she had given up to be here.

They seated themselves, Ada murmuring greetings to the countess, Michael, and Mr. Bradford. The black satin and lace, the heavy veils of the countess, the dark oak paneling, the smell of old books, and the heavy windows blocking rather than admitting the light—it all made Ada feel as if she were suffocating. She swallowed the feeling down.

"It is for a very solemn and tragic reason that we are gathered here today," Mr. Bradford began, with much coughing and clearing of his throat. Ada allowed her attention to wander as he went through the forms of politeness. Her father had been such a loving, permanent presence in her life. The thought of going on without him was hard to bear; it made all other pains seem small.

Outside the door she heard raised voices. At first she thought it was mere street noise, but the voices continued. She heard Mr. Bradford's secretary exclaiming—"irregular!"—and then a voice she recognized well, one that made her draw her breath in sharply and sit up straighter. It was William.

Mr. Bradford paused in his reading. Michael caught Ada's eye. There was a tautness about his jaw that told her how he was striving to keep his temper.

"I demand to be admitted," William was saying. He had a voice like a bull bellowing. "I am the new Earl of Westlake, and I demand to hear the will. On behalf of my disinherited son, my poor wronged Augustus—"

"Let him in," said Michael.

"Are you certain—?" Georgiana began.

"Yes. I won't have him going around saying that we are doing things in an underhand manner. Damn him, he's a blackguard, but we had better let him in."

"I must agree with Mr. Templeton," Mr. Bradford said, adjusting his spectacles nervously. "It is not my personal opinion . . . but certainly, I think, to avoid a scene . . ."

"Lady Westlake?" Ada appealed to her, but the countess, invisible behind her veil, merely shook her head wearily.

"Very well." Ada looked to Mr. Bradford. "Please instruct your secretary to allow the Earl of Westlake entry." She could not hide how much she disliked using the title for William.

Mr. Bradford pressed the bell, and a second later the secretary appeared at the door, looking flustered. William was behind him, and barged his way in, cane flailing, as soon as he saw a crack.

"Sir, I apologize! I was unable to —" The secretary was clearly caught between his duty to his employer and his deference to an earl.

"That's all right, Simpkin. The Earl of Westlake is welcome here." Mr. Bradford bowed stiffly. William strode in with a triumphant glance around him. Ada looked coldly in front of her and did not meet his eye.

"Very good. I knew a little authority would work," William said, as Mr. Bradford placed a chair for him. He sat on it, cane in one hand, looming as if he was taking over the entire room. Ada detested him, and she could see in Georgiana's pressed-together lips that she felt the same. "Go ahead, Bradford. Let us see what my uncle has to say."

Mr. Bradford read on, nervously. There was a good deal of legal preamble before he came to the main point:

"... I leave the estate of Somerton Court and its income to my firstborn grandson. My three daughters, Ada, Georgiana, and Rose, are to share my wealth, goods, and chattels equally. My grandnephew, Augustus, shall receive ten percent of the income from the estate for his lifetime. All of this shall be subject to the provision that Fiona, Countess of Westlake, shall be allowed to continue to live in Somerton Court as if it were her own house, until she no longer wishes to. I also request that, for the duration of the current war, the house at Somerton be made use in whatever way my family shall think fit, for the benefit of the nation."

There was an uncomfortable silence after Mr. Bradford finished speaking. Everyone was wondering what William would say.

"Very well." William's voice was quiet and steady. He was sober, Ada realized, and this was quite a frightening thought. It meant he was serious. "Very well. So the old man thinks he can cheat me, does he? Well, we will see about that."

"Don't refer to my father with such disrespect," Georgiana spoke out, her eyes flashing.

William looked at her and laughed. "He's dead, and I'll speak of him however I choose, you little brat."

Georgiana drew back as if she had been slapped. Ada was aware of a quick, violent movement and saw Michael rising from his chair and stepping toward William, his fist clenched and drawn back. William half rose, but Michael's punch connected before he could. The countess screamed, as William went flying backward over his chair and cracked his head on the bookshelves. Georgiana jumped to her feet, as did Ada, shocked—and yet wishing she could cheer. Michael stood over William, his collar awry, breathing hard.

"Get up," he said, his voice crackling with the effort to control it, "and get out."

William struggled to his feet, clutching his nose. Blood trickled down from under his hand, and the look he gave Michael was full of hatred. "I'll summons you for this," he told him thickly. "And every one of you, as witnesses."

"Get out!" Michael shouted.

William made for the door. He shoved past the secretary, who had come with the offer of water, and out of the door. Ada saw, before the front door swung closed, that a small crowd had collected and was watching—as William came out, holding his nose, there was an ironic cheer.

"I'm sorry," said Michael. He looked shamefaced. "That was foolish of me."

"I wish you'd hit him even harder!" Georgiana burst out. "That hateful man—I am ashamed to think I am related to him. I can hardly bear that he should be Earl of Westlake."

"It's unspeakable," Ada agreed. "He shames our family, and he brings shame on the title."

"Lady Averley! The countess—" Mr. Bradford's voice was panic-stricken.

Ada turned, and noticed her stepmother slumped in her seat.

She ran to her side and saw at once that she was on the brink of fainting. "Some water, please, at once!" she said over her shoulder.

The water was brought, and Ada gently revived the countess so that she could stand, and Michael escorted her to the motorcar. Ada and Georgiana lingered a moment longer with Mr. Bradford. "Do you think he will really challenge the will?" Ada said to the lawyer.

"It is hard to say. He may do." Mr. Bradford looked very worried.

"I shan't let him have Somerton," Georgiana said hotly. "I could never look Thomas in the face if I had to tell him William would be his master."

"Never fear, Georgie. It shan't happen. I will make sure of it," Ada said.

Georgiana looked at her directly for the first time. "But what can you do, Ada, to stop it happening? And . . . do you care enough to try?"

She turned and walked quickly from the room. Ada followed her a moment later, her eyes brimming over with tears. She had never thought her sister would doubt her so much.

CHAPTER
THIRTY-THREE

SOMERTON

Rebecca sat on the same chair she had been sitting on since Thomas had gone upstairs to check the rooms. At the far end of the table, Annie and Martha sat in sullen silence. Cook fidgeted by the sink. The other servants had backed up against the wall, waiting. The atmosphere in the kitchen was heavy and sharp with nerves. Everyone was wondering what everyone else had to hide . . . and no one, Rebecca thought, was under more scrutiny than she was.

She sat straight-backed, meeting none of the curious glances that she could feel crawling over her skin. Instead she looked at the raindrops glittering on the kitchen window. Never had she longed so much to be back in Manchester. Smoky, dirty Manchester! She had hated it, lived for trips to the countryside.

But at least no one had looked at her as they did here. There, in the city, immigrants were not unheard of. The pork butcher was German. The seamstress was Dutch. There was a port, and Africans and Indians often came into the city from the ships, though they kept themselves to themselves. But Somerton was different.

She started as she heard footsteps coming down the stairs. A moment later, Thomas appeared, framed in the doorway. Everyone looked at him, including Rebecca.

He cleared his throat. Rebecca could see that he wasn't happy.

"I have made a thorough search," he said, "and I have found nothing. No spoons."

There was a moment's silence, and then everyone began to speak at once. Thomas raised his hand for quiet.

"That doesn't mean that we don't have a problem," he said. "The silver is missing. That's very serious, and I ask you once again—if anyone knows anything, come clean now, and I shall do my best to be understanding. But for now, we have no proof that anyone in this house is guilty of theft. So I don't want to hear any more accusations."

"But, sir—" Martha began.

"*Enough*, Martha!" Thomas hardly raised his voice, but the whole kitchen fell silent. "Have I made myself clear?"

"But sir, she's a spy!" Annie burst out. She pointed at Rebecca.

"A *German* spy," Martha joined in. "Annie saw it on a letter."

Rebecca laughed. She couldn't help herself. The accusation was so ludicrous, and yet—somehow—she had been expecting it. Something like this had been bound to happen. She felt the pit of her stomach, like a dark hole. It had been going too well. It had to end.

"Brazen hussy, laughing in our faces!" Cook exclaimed.

Thomas was looking back and forth between Martha and Annie and Rebecca, the look of astonishment and disbelief on his face showing he was lost for words. Now he found words. "I beg your pardon, Annie? What kind of nonsense is that?"

"It's not nonsense. The postmistress knows. Everyone in Palesbury knows."

"Have you got any evidence?"

Annie was silent.

"Well?" Thomas's voice was slowly changing from astonished to angry. "None! You have none, have you?"

"I saw it on a letter—"

"You saw *what*? Was it addressed to Miss Freeman, spy, care of Somerton Court?" Thomas said sarcastically.

"I don't know about a spy, sir. I don't like to accuse people without reason. But one thing's for sure. She's a German," Martha said solemnly.

There was a hiss of shocked breath from everyone.

"Why, nonsense," Roderick said. "Anyone can see she's as English as you or I."

Martha gave him a withering glance. "The Germans don't look different, you fool. They look the same as English folk."

"I've had enough of this," Thomas snapped. "I don't want to hear any more wild accusations against Rebecca. It's nothing more than jealousy—yes, because she's a hard worker and a good worker too. It's bullying, and I will not have it in my staff. The next person I hear spreading lies about Rebecca Freeman can consider themselves sacked without a reference."

There was dead silence. Rebecca felt herself blushing with both embarrassment and relief. She blinked back tears.

"I hope I make myself clear. Now, back to work. The family are due back at any moment."

The staff looked at one another, then went silently back to work. Martha looked as if she wanted to protest, but Annie pulled her away.

Rebecca got up. Her mending hadn't gotten done after all, she noted dully; she would have to do it tonight. She was almost at the door when Thomas said, "Rebecca, a word, if you please."

This was it. She was bound to be sacked. She knew Thomas was a good man, she thought, as she followed him to his pantry, but when he heard the truth there was no way he would allow her to remain.

Thomas shut the door behind them. Rebecca looked up at him, her eyes aching with the desire to cry. She had already decided what she would do if this moment came. She wouldn't lie. She was proud of her father, no matter what anyone else said.

"I am sorry you have been treated this way," Thomas said gently. He looked at her, and she had to look down; his eyes were just too blue, and it hurt to think that they would never be so kind again. "Martha and Annie have taken a dislike to you."

She remained silent.

"I want to ask you, is there any truth in any of what Martha is saying?" Thomas went on at last.

Rebecca did not answer for a long moment. Then she looked up at him. She would do this bravely, cleanly, quickly. "Yes, there is," she said quietly.

Thomas's dark eyelashes flickered, the only sign that he was startled. Rebecca swallowed and went on. "My real name is not Freeman. It is Freudemann. My mother decided to change it on the outbreak of war, when we had to move to the country. We were afraid people would take against us if they saw we had a German name. My father is—my father was . . ."

She had to stop and swallow.

"He emigrated here from Germany as a young man," she said quickly, not looking up at Thomas, wanting to get it all over with as soon as possible. "He thought he would find a more tolerant society here. He was Jewish, you see."

She listened to the silence, then went on. It was somehow a relief to be saying all this. She knew that when she looked up and saw his face—pitying, or disgusted, or disappointed—it would all feel so bitter, but at least she could go on now.

"He had an architect's business in Manchester, designing mansions for the manufacturing classes. Then he became ill. He died last year. We found out only after he died that his partner had defrauded the business. Everything had to be sold. When war broke out, my mother decided that we should change our name and move somewhere where no one knew us."

She looked up, finally.

Thomas's expression surprised her. He was looking at her gently. "I am sorry," he said gently. "You must miss your father very much."

Rebecca swallowed hard. She did not trust herself to reply, but she knew her expression said it all.

"I want you," said Thomas after a moment's thought, "to take the afternoon off."

Rebecca was so startled that she said, without a thought of crying, "But sir, how will you manage?"

"We'll manage, don't worry." Thomas smiled at her. "You're a great help, Rebecca, but I'll manage without you, for one afternoon only. I wouldn't like to try it for longer, and that's the truth. Now, you forget all about work for this afternoon. Go for a walk, or rest, or see your mother, or whatever you like. I'll try and get some work out of Annie for once. And don't worry."

He nodded to her, and stepped out of the pantry. Rebecca, left alone, tried to take in what had just happened. *Wouldn't like to try it for longer!* That meant—that had to mean—that he wasn't going to sack her. Even though he knew the truth. She thought of the mischievous grin that lit his face like a ray of sunlight. And she realized that the most wonderful thing about not leaving was that she wouldn't have to leave *him*.

CHAPTER
THIRTY-FOUR

FRANCE

"What a beautiful day," Portia said, as she rolled bandages and placed them on the metal trays, one by one. "It feels as if winter might finally be over."

"I hope so, for the troops' sake," Charlotte replied. She glanced down the ward. It was a rare moment of peace. Half the beds were empty, for now, and they had the chance to catch up on work, to make every bed as well as it should be made, even to rest their feet for an instant. The windows were open to let in the fresh air and sunlight. Most of the men were sitting up in bed, reading or simply resting. Others—the mobile ones—had gathered around the bed of Private Trent, a painfully young, stick-thin lad who had been badly gassed and even now could not sit upright without pillows to prop him, his face bandaged almost completely, with just holes for eyes and mouth. It was touching, thought Charlotte, that the soldiers came to him, knowing he couldn't move to join in the conversation.

She looked back at the dressing trays and saw what was missing. "I'll fetch some more iodine." Charlotte got to her feet and set off down the ward to where it was stored.

As she passed the group, she saw a flash of reddish gold hair and heard a voice that had become very familiar in the short time that he had been there. ". . . and I fold! All yours, pals. Never did have luck with five-card. Reminds me of a game I played back in Texas. 'Cept it was a hell of a lot hotter and the drink was a sight stronger." He winked at Charlotte as she passed, raising his teacup as if to toast her. Charlotte looked away quickly, annoyed at having been caught noticing him. She could still hear him as she went up the ward. There seemed to be no end to his stories. She was annoyed to see that Portia was smiling as she listened. She reached her and set the bottle of iodine down with a thump.

"I do think it's too much that that awful American should still be here. I wish the medical officer would make up his mind what to do with his arm and send him on."

"Oh, I like him," Portia replied. "He has such exciting stories, and you must admit that it's something out of the ordinary. I'll be sorry when he goes."

"I won't. I think he's entirely too full of himself." Charlotte sat down and started rolling bandages, trying not to hear Flint's drawling voice going on about gunfights and horse breaking and saloon bars. "What is he doing here anyway? The Americans are not involved in the war."

"No, but there are plenty of volunteers. To hear the way he tells it, he was flying in an aerobatic show in London on the outbreak of war, and one of the generals saw him loop the loop and wrote off to Buckingham Palace requesting that this man should be got by hook or by crook as a pilot, since it would be absolutely impossible to win the war without him—"

"How insufferable!" Charlotte interrupted. To her annoyance, Portia was laughing. "Oh, it's a pack of lies, of course."

"Well, you must admit," Portia said, "that he certainly keeps the men entertained. Since he's been here, ward morale has gone up greatly. I've never heard so much laughter. And we all know that morale is the single most important factor in recovery."

Charlotte pressed her lips together. Portia was right; she couldn't deny it. It was Flint who jollied the men along, Flint who made sure Trent was the center of the poker game. She had to admit it, poor Trent might well have succumbed if it hadn't been for Flint's blustery kindness. She had seen it happen before—men giving up simply because they had nothing to live for.

"Well," she said, feeling she had to gain some victory, however small, "I won't have gambling on the ward, at least. It's immoral," she added primly, pushing thoughts of certain flutters at Ascot out of her mind. When your friends' parents owned the horses it was almost impolite not to bet a shilling or two, after all. She got to her feet, annoyed by Portia's smile, and went down the ward toward the group. As she did so she could see how the men were laughing, and how cheerful they all looked. It seemed a pity to break the game up, but she pushed on. Flint looked up, saw her, and was gracefully on his feet in a second.

"Nurse Templeton, do join us, please." He offered her a chair.

Charlotte blushed furiously. As if she would join in a common card game!

"Excuse me, Captain MacAllister," she said to Flint, loudly and with all the authority she was used to using with servants, "I don't expect to see gambling going on in the ward. Please stop immediately and find yourself some . . . wholesome entertainment instead." She wished she had been able to think of a less ridiculous word than *wholesome*.

The men rolled their eyes and there were some groans, but Flint glared at them until they stopped. He was never anything but exquisitely polite to her, Charlotte thought grudgingly. It was very irritating.

"I do beg your pardon, ma'am. I want to assure you we were not playing for stakes. I never do, not since I lost my fortune at Flagstaff."

"Mr. MacAllister's telling the truth, ma'am—I mean, miss," said one of the other soldiers. "There's no money involved; we were just playing for fun."

"Let us go on, do, miss," joined in another officer, who had one eye completely bandaged.

Charlotte felt like a fool, and more than that, she felt like a spoilsport. She was about to give in, but Flint interrupted the men. "Now, let's not forget how much we owe to the nurses. If it wasn't for ladies like Nurse Templeton, we'd all be dead. So if she says no cards, no cards it is." He reached for the cards and scooped them up. With only one hand free, he was clumsy, and his own cards spilled onto the floor. Charlotte found herself kneeling automatically to collect them. She handed them to him, not knowing what else to do, and his smiling, warm blue eyes caught hers as their fingers brushed. She was aware of heat in her cheeks and a fluttering in the pit of her stomach.

"You had three aces," she said, her voice smaller than she'd meant it to be.

"I never count my losses," he replied.

He helped her to her feet. Charlotte was aware that she had come close to losing her poise. She dusted herself off and, without another look at him, turned and walked away, hardly knowing where she was going. She felt his eyes on her all the way down the ward to the sluice. She grabbed a bedpan at random and began washing it angrily.

She was halfway through, water splashing her uniform, her hair straggling down from under her cap, when she realized he had followed her and was standing at the door of the sluice. She stood up quickly and angrily, aware that she had probably never looked less attractive in her life—tired, bedraggled, holding a bedpan, for heaven's sake!

"I wondered if you'd had any time to think about my proposal of marriage, Nurse," he said with a half smile.

Charlotte stood dumbstruck, for a second. Then she burst

out. "Mr. MacAllister, you may think you are extremely smart and amusing, but let me tell you, your constant harassment is ill-judged and offensive. I am not an American"—she did her best to give the word the necessary contempt—"and I am used to certain standards of behavior in gentlemen, modesty, courtesy, and . . . and I certainly will not stand for any cheek!" She finished, wishing she could have found something better to say. One should never lose one's temper; one should only be cool and calm and collected.

"Apologies, ma'am," he said, at last. His smile had vanished, and he looked sad, and tired, and older than before. "I never meant to offend you—I meant the opposite, really. I know my manners ain't exactly drawing room. I guess I'm not used to being around a lady like yourself—well-bred, I mean. I sure am sorry, I only meant to make you smile."

He looked so downcast that Charlotte found herself wanting to hug him. It was awful to see his smile vanish, and now she could see the tiredness and pain that was underneath it. She felt she had been, in Michael's words, a cad. "Oh, Captain MacAllister, I am the one who should apologize," she said. It was an effort, but she felt better for saying it. "I—I am a little tired, and not in the best temper. I am sorry, and I would like you to go on with your poker game."

He made a slight gesture of denial, but she interrupted before he could speak.

"I mean it. Please. I can see how much pleasure it gives the men, and heaven knows they need it."

She even smiled. It took a good deal to wrench it out of the embarrassment and misery she felt, but she did.

Flint's smile returned at once, brighter and bigger than before. It was like a lighthouse beam flashing out of the night, full of reassurance and safety. As long as I see that smile, she was surprised to find herself thinking, I know things can't be *all* bad.

"Are your tales true?" she said, abruptly.

"Most of them . . ."

She almost laughed.

". . . are mostly true."

This time she did laugh. He laughed along with her.

"Nurse?" Dr. Field's voice came from the ward. Charlotte hastily wiped the smile off her face.

"Coming, sir," she replied, and went past Flint to the door. She could feel him watching her as she went up the aisle toward the sister, and couldn't hide a blush—nor, although she told herself it was silly, could she help feeling quite pleased that she had ordered the uniform from L'atelier after all.

CHAPTER
THIRTY-FIVE

SOMERTON

Breakfast at Somerton would never be the same again, Georgiana thought, as she watched Thomas, in his black bands of mourning for the earl, go quietly about the business of pouring tea. No one spoke. Michael, she could see, had as little appetite as she did, and the countess was in her room once again. Even when mourning was finally over, she could not imagine feeling happy again.

"Has your mother everything that she needs?" she said to Michael as soon as Thomas had left.

"I think so. The doctor says that there is little to be done; it is her spirits and not her body that are failing." He sighed. "She keeps talking about Sebastian."

"That is something, at least."

"But she speaks of him as if he were already dead."

"Oh." Georgiana was shocked and saddened.

"I think she feels strongly that she has failed in some way. The earl's death has been such a shock, and with Charlotte and Sebastian both in France . . ." He trailed off. "She blames herself. She thinks that if she had managed them better, they would have stayed."

"I don't think so. They did what they saw to be their duty," Georgiana said quietly. She looked up as Thomas reentered the room.

"A letter, my lady. I'm afraid it seems to have been delayed, however. It is in a bad condition."

Georgiana took the crumpled envelope from the silver tray that he offered her. The address was blurred with water damage, and she opened it gingerly, trying not to damage it further. Inside, the writing was half obliterated. She frowned at it, trying to work out what it said. Words came into focus . . .

"It's from Rose!" she exclaimed.

Michael put down his cup. "Thank heavens, at last."

Georgiana tried her best to decipher the rest of the writing. "This was sent months ago, though. She writes about some battle, but of course all the details have been censored. But I am sure Alexander is safe; it would be impossible for her to write in such an easy tone if he weren't. . . . Something about more journeying, and something about a ship? I can read hardly any of it." Frustrated, she put the letter down. "But at least she is safe—or she was when she sent this." The thought of how much time might have elapsed between the sending and the receipt of the letter made her spirits sink.

"Rose has so much courage," Michael said. "If anyone comes through it all right, she will. Don't fret, Georgie."

Georgiana nodded. She placed the letter on the table. Reading Rose's cheerful words, even though she knew that she must have been frightened when she wrote them, had made her mind up. She would not allow her father's death to crush her. She would try her best to carry out his will.

"Michael . . . will you walk with me for a moment?" She stood up. "I have an idea. I would like to sound you out about it."

"With pleasure." He got up and took her arm. Together they left the breakfast room and walked down the marble hall toward the ballroom. Georgiana looked about her, noticing the dust sheets. It was painful to see, as if Somerton itself were in mourning for the earl.

"You see," she told Michael, "so many of the grand rooms are closed off already; we simply don't have the staff to keep them in order. It would be simpler just to shut a wing, but," she sighed, "that seems like defeat."

"I agree," Michael said.

"And yet it feels absolutely unjustifiable to have Thomas working so hard to try and keep the house up to the position it had before the war."

"It's a lot of trouble for him, and for the rest of the staff."

Michael looked around, and Georgiana knew he too was noticing the dust sheets shrouding antiquities and artworks.

"And at a time of national economy." She paused, and threw open the great double doors to the Adam ballroom. "And there's this wonderful room," she said with a sigh. The statues placed here and there, examples of classical beauty, the fluted columns, the high ceiling crowed with gilded stars, the Caravaggio that hung at one end of the long room. "It seems a crime to simply shut it up like a mausoleum. My father wouldn't have wanted that. He wanted it used for the benefit of the nation."

"But how?" Michael asked. "It is a home. Not a practical home, I'll admit, but it is not fitted for anything else that I can think of."

Georgiana swallowed. She knew what she was about to propose was ambitious. "Well, we know that so many buildings have been requisitioned for public use," she began.

Michael nodded. "But you can't want the War Office hacking the place to bits, I'm sure."

"No, I don't. Anything but that. But we must somehow fulfill my father's last wishes. I . . ." She hesitated. "I thought, what about a hospital?"

She rushed on into Michael's silence.

"Just think how many beds we could fit in this room! If we laid down carpets, the floor would be hardly damaged at all. And how wonderful for a convalescing soldier to wake and see all this beauty around him, and the fresh air just outside the doors, so easy to open them and sit on the terrace, or stroll down into the gardens. Don't you think? Oh, please tell me you agree," she ended plaintively, since she could tell nothing from Michael's thoughtful expression.

"But Georgie, what do you know about running a hospital?"

"Nothing at all, but I'm sure we would have advice. And you would help, wouldn't you?"

"Of course I would. I think it's a wonderful idea—"

"Oh good!"

"But I can see so many potential problems." He looked at her, his eyes warm and amused. "You never see problems, do you?"

"I know I'm not very sensible, but please don't mock me," she said.

"I wasn't! I meant it as a compliment—a very sincere one."

Georgiana blushed and looked down.

"You see only possibilities, and only good in people."

Georgiana savored the compliment. But before she could decide whether the note of warmth in his voice was more than friendship, there was a slight cough at the door. Georgiana turned. The parlormaid was there, discreetly in the shadows.

"Yes, Rebecca, what is it?"

"There is a telephone call, my lady"

"Oh, who is it?"

"Mr. Bradford. He wanted to speak to the countess, but since she is sleeping and the nurse says she is not to be disturbed, I thought . . ."

"Thank you, Rebecca," Michael said. "I'll take it." He nodded to Georgiana.

Georgiana caught his sleeve. "Do think over what I've said. You can persuade your mother, I know."

"I'll do my very best."

He walked out after Rebecca. Georgiana, left alone, looked around the ballroom, the shrouded chandeliers that had once blazed with light, the dull floor that had once been waxed to a sheen, the silent, mournful piano. It was so empty. She hadn't danced here since her father's wedding to the countess—it seemed so long ago. Every day, she woke and saw her mourning clothes laid out for her. The funeral was over; now there was nothing to aim for, just a long sad future. She knew that her father would never have wanted her to be depressed like this. He wanted things to be done; he wanted to improve things for people. If she could only make the dream of the hospital come true, it would be what he had wanted.

"Some bad news, I'm afraid."

She turned with a start. Michael was back, frowning as he walked into the room.

"What is it?"

"A letter has come to Mr. Bradford's offices. It is from William—well, from his solicitor. A well-known London firm, the one that secured the settlement in the Cumberland divorce case."

"And?" Georgiana asked, suddenly feeling afraid.

"He is challenging the will."

"But on what basis? How dare he?"

"Simply put—I don't pretend to understand all of it—he argues that he needs an income to keep up the dignity of the title. He can call on precedent. He argues that it would be unfitting and contrary to the spirit of your father's will to leave him without an income."

"So it's money he wants?"

"It appears so, yes."

"Oh, the monster!" Georgiana turned away, unable to hide her contempt and fear. "But do you think he will succeed?"

Michael shook his head. "I can't say. All I know is that Mr. Bradford said that we must take it seriously. I am sorry, Georgie. I wish I had better news."

Georgiana looked around the beautiful ballroom. It felt suddenly as if her dreams had been dirtied. "It can't happen," she said. She made up her mind. Whatever her differences with Ada, that all had to be put aside now that so much was at stake. "We must write to Ada. She may have some idea of what to do."

CHAPTER
THIRTY-SIX

FRANCE

Of all the day, Charlotte thought, this time—the hour just before dawn, when the darkness seemed for the first time to promise to become lighter—was her favorite. Even the worst of the men had fallen into some kind of exhausted sleep, and although she was tired, she savored the moments of calm and quiet, knowing her shift would be over in just a couple of hours. She even had leave coming up—a whole two days, at St. Malo.

She walked noiselessly up the ward, checking the men one by one, with a glance.

Her eyes had grown accustomed to the dark, and the first gray stirring of light was enough for her to know what they required. She could tell just by listening which men were breathing with difficulty, which were awake and perhaps thirsty.

To left and right men lay, sleeping, breathing through nose or mouth, some groaning or whimpering in their sleep. If my mother could see me now! she thought, and smiled. She had never been allowed to enter a man's bedroom before; now here she was surrounded by twenty of them. Of course, her mother thought nursing a very indelicate profession. If only she knew the truth: romance was very far from Charlotte's mind. . . . She quickly dismissed any rebellious feelings that tried to suggest that that might not be the entire truth.

She paused by Private Trent's bed. She always liked to check him first; the poor boy was so piteously wounded. His whole face was still swathed with bandages. She knew he must be going through terrible pain, but he never showed it. He reminded her of Michael: his build was the same, the fresh pinkness of his unburned skin, too—though what lay beneath the bandages that swathed his face she did not dare to, could not bear to, think. He'd hung on to life for so long, and he could hang on longer, but what about when he got back? she wondered, looking down at him. Left like that, at eighteen, perhaps younger. It was cruel.

She bent down to check his breathing. The dark hole in the mask was silent. She listened for the feeble rasp of breath. It didn't come. Charlotte's own breathing snagged, as if on barbed wire. She stood looking down on him, willing herself not to give in to tears. She took his wrist, but even before she felt for the pulse, the coldness of it told her what she already knew. There were not even any eyes to close.

A movement in the bed next to her made her start. Flint

turned toward her, his hair tousled, blinking in the new light. He raised himself on his good elbow and looked at her, then at Private Trent. A second later he had swung himself upright and was standing by her side, his arm around her. Neither of them spoke. Charlotte let her cheek rest on his shoulder. She could feel tears running down her face, soaking into his pajamas. She'd blame herself for her unprofessionalism later, she told herself. For now, it was simply comforting not to be alone—to be with him.

"I'll write to his next of kin," said Flint softly. "Save you a job, Nurse."

"That's good of you," Charlotte managed. She would have to put together Trent's few possessions: his bloodstained uniform, his revolver, his kit bag. There would be paperwork. "Poor Trent. I wonder if he had family."

"He had a girl," he replied. "He asked me to write to her too. I think he knew he didn't have long."

Later that day, they buried him. The chaplain read a hurried service. Charlotte stood there in her best uniform, her eyes down, as the earth rattled onto the coffin. Distantly the guns kept booming. Opposite her, Flint stood. He seemed ill at ease, and she knew it was that he disliked to stand still. Every time she saw him he was in action, laughing, joking, alive and vivid. He was so different from every man she had ever met—especially from cool, suave Laurence—and yet he was fascinating. He made her laugh, and she had never known how important that was until now, when laughter was in such short supply, and sometimes the only thing that kept them going.

The war has changed me, she thought. Only now was she beginning to realize how much.

After the funeral, they walked back together, behind the chaplain. In the thornbushes, blackbirds sang. "I like to hear the birds," he said. "They're like stubborn civilians who won't leave their homes. I admire their courage."

"Are there blackbirds where you come from—in your hometown?"

"I don't come from a town. I come from the middle of nowhere—a ranch in Texas. There are eagles."

"Of course," Charlotte murmured. Eagles were exactly what she would have associated him with. He didn't strike her as a man who could be easily tamed. But then who would want to tame a man, when wilderness was so much more interesting? "However did you end up here, in this war, really?"

"Well, ma'am, we fell on hard times—to tell the truth, it was my father that lost the fortune in Flagstaff. The fortune, and the ranch. Left me nothing but a few worthless shares in an emerald mine."

"Shares in an emerald mine sound hardly worthless!" Charlotte exclaimed.

He grinned at her. "Only worth something if there are emeralds in the mine . . . and I fear there weren't in this one."

"I see."

"All the horses were sold. So I had to find something else. I found flying."

Charlotte smiled, hearing the love in his voice. "I can tell you don't regret the horses."

"Ma'am, a horse is a horse, but up there . . ." He gestured to the sky: it was blue and birds wheeled in it. "Well, there's nothing like it, being so close to heaven. I love it—and I'm good at it too."

Charlotte smiled again. He was certainly more blunt than the men she'd met before, but she was beginning to see that he wasn't boastful—just honest. There was something refreshing, she thought, about a man you could trust to tell you the truth when it really mattered.

"I joined an aerobatic show that bit was true enough We came across to England as part of Wild Bill's circus, then set out on our own. We were performing in London, giving duchesses thrills by looping the loop over Buckingham Palace, when war broke out."

"And a general specially requested you be brought in to stop it."

He laughed.

"I just told the men that for a joke—they were so thrilled to meet one of these mythical beasts called Americans, I thought I'd give them a story to fit. No, the truth is I thought, well, I can't miss an opportunity like that, and besides, I'm the best damn pilot they'll ever see; they need me. So here I am. And I just can't wait to be back in the sky."

"I can understand that," Charlotte said with a small sigh. "It must be wonderful to feel so free."

He turned to her with a bright smile. "I'll take you up as soon as I can, if you'll let me."

"Will you really?" Charlotte was suddenly breathless with excitement.

"Ma'am, it'll be an honor."

"But isn't it quite dangerous?" Charlotte lowered her lashes and glanced at him, wondering how he would react to such obvious flirtation. Laurence would have smoothly promised to protect her against anything—and then forgotten all about the promise.

"Only if you don't know what you're doing—and I know what I'm doing. Besides, ma'am, I suspect you're being coy with me. You strike me as the kind of girl who ain't scared of a thing."

Charlotte laughed outright at the way he'd so quickly seen through her. They were coming up to the ward. Charlotte sped up her pace. "Then as soon as I'm back from leave," she tossed over her shoulder, "I'll hold you to that promise."

CHAPTER
THIRTY-SEVEN

LONDON

"I am flattered that you chose to confide in me, Lady Ada," said Connor Kearney, as they walked across sunny Norwood Square. "Rest assured that I will do everything I can to help."

"I know I can trust you," Ada replied.

It had not taken her long to decide to take him into her confidence, once she had heard from Mr. Bradford what the situation was. She had not expected him to be so ready to offer personal help, and the fact that he knew Hannah Darford had come as a surprise—it appeared that he often engaged her to work for him, since Oxford would not award degrees to women and therefore she could not represent clients in court herself. But he had at once recommended Hannah as a specialist in inheritance law.

"I enjoy any legal challenge, but it is not my primary field," he had told her. "Miss Darford will be the best person for us to apply to, especially as you have prior acquaintance."

That was why they were here—to visit her at her office, at Number Twelve Norwood Square, newly acquired since Ada had visited Hannah before going up to Oxford. She remembered that Hannah had spoken of wanting to get a residence of her own, to replace the rooms she was renting.

It seemed a pleasant place, Ada thought, glancing around her. Certainly, it was not Mayfair. The countess would have called it decidedly middle-class. But it was light and airy, and the plane trees and cherry trees that lined the small central park waved their leaves in the breeze and gave shade to nursemaids and babies. A few motorcars were parked by the side of the road, showing that it was certainly a respectable address. The kind of place where she and Ravi could have been happy together, had he stayed. She winced at the sudden pain. She was almost glad that William was making trouble; it helped to have something to concentrate on, to take her mind from it. That, and she had begun to study, almost ferociously, for her examinations. Filling her head with Latin and Greek drove Ravi out of it at least until the night, when she lay down to sleep. That was when she could not hold back the tears.

"You seem interested in the area," Kearney said with a glance toward her.

"I am, frankly, curious," said Ada, calling up a responsive smile. She paused to collect her emotions, then went on, as gaily as she could, with half the truth. "I admire Hannah Darford so much; what she has achieved is extraordinary. It seems that even her house must be special somehow." She looked up at the town house. It certainly did not look special—a wisteria and a couple of faded geraniums in a pot were the only things that stood out.

"Only in that it is her own, outright—not her husband's." Kearney rang the bell.

"Is she married, then?" Ada looked at him in surprise. "I had not heard."

"No, excuse me—I should have said *a* husband's. She is not married."

"It doesn't surprise me," said Ada with a sigh.

"No?"

"No. Love doesn't seem to fit with liberation—not happily, anyway."

She was glad that the door opened and Connor could not follow his inquiring look with a question. She had expected a maid, but at once realized that the lady in the old-fashioned long skirt and tie—very 1910—and pince-nez was no such thing. The severe expression on her face softened at once into a smile as she saw Connor. "Oh, Mr. Kearney! Do come in. Miss Darford is expecting you."

"Thank you." Connor stepped after her, over the threshold. "Lady Ada, may I introduce Miss Evesham. Miss Evesham is Miss Darford's secretary."

Ada exchanged greetings and they followed Miss Evesham into the house. It was clearly set up as an office, but the feminine décor struck Ada at once. In contrast with Mr. Bradford's offices, the house was painted in soft, light shades, modern paintings hung on the walls, and elegant flower arrangements were laid out on almost every surface. Bright light poured through large windows, and artfully placed mirrors and crystal reflected it. And yet there were several serious-looking filing cabinets and a substantial desk in the Directoire style. It was feminine without being frivolous.

"How delightfully modern!" Ada exclaimed.

"Isn't it? I admire her taste." Kearney looked around with obvious pleasure.

"A place like this—so clearly a *woman's* office—makes me feel that we have won the battle already." Ada smiled. "Sadly, that's a dream."

"But not a dream for too long, I hope." Hannah Darford, quick and businesslike and smiling as always, came through the door toward them. She shook hands with both Connor and Ada, firmly. "Lady Ada, I condole with you on your loss. It is a terrible thing."

"Thank you," said Ada quietly. Most people had already given their condolences, in person or on black-edged cards. But now and then she met someone who had not, and it seemed to rip open the wound again. She knew that Connor was looking at her, concerned.

They sat down, and Hannah Darford glanced at them questioningly. "I understand that this is a matter of inheritance, pertaining to the late earl's will?"

"Yes," Ada said. "It's a worrying matter. My cousin William—he is now the Earl of Westlake, but a horrible wretch—is challenging my father's will. He asserts that he should be entitled to income from the property. I have his letter here."

She handed it over, nervous about what Hannah would say. As she read it, Ada couldn't help watching her face, anxious to see what her judgment would be. Hannah took her time, but finally she said, "Humph!" and placed the letter back on the table.

"Well, Miss Darford?" Kearney said.

"He has no chance of success," Hannah replied.

"Exactly what I thought," Kearney said.

Ada, full of relief, looked from one to the other. Kearney was not smiling; he looked thoughtful. Hannah was frowning.

"And . . . there is more, isn't there?" Ada said. "I can tell it is not that simple."

"I expect he had no thought of success," Hannah replied. "The precedents he cites are weak. The man is a gambler, is he not? Yes, I can see from your expression that he is." She looked at Kearney and they both smiled.

"It's a gambler's move," Kearney said. "He gambles that you may be frightened by the letter, frightened enough to simply give him money, in order to persuade him not to pursue the house and land—your home. I expect that if you fail to be frightened, he will turn to his next move, which is to embarrass your family as deeply as possible, in revenge. Your sister Georgiana is not yet married either, is she? It could be very unpleasant for you all if he has nothing to lose, and goes about sullying the Averley name. A man who has no reputation of his own to lose will have no reason not to lie and spread rumors to destroy the reputations of others."

"He means to blackmail us," Ada said. She was shocked, and she had thought nothing could shock her. She felt herself trembling with rage on Georgiana's behalf.

"He does," Hannah said. "There is nothing more dangerous than a man who has nothing to lose."

"So, we give him something to lose," Kearney said.

"But what?" Ada looked into their faces and guessed the answer. "Money. You mean that we offer him money, in return for a pledge—"

"A *legally binding* pledge," said Kearney, nodding along.

"—not to speak of the matter again?"

"Yes. Our response is to ask him to cease all threats and blackmail, to give up any claim on the income, and in return, we offer him . . . oh, say, three thousand pounds?" Kearney raised an eyebrow at Hannah, who nodded and shrugged.

"Three thousand pounds!" Ada was almost breathless. "But where are we to find such a sum?"

Kearney and Hannah looked at each other, then at her.

"My dear, did you not understand the terms of your father's will?" Kearney said, sounding for a moment very Irish indeed. "I am surprised at you!" He smiled. "You are a rich woman. Your father has left you and your sisters the sum of his account at Coutts. I expect you will be able to cover it and still have plenty left over."

"I must confess, I had not thought of it. I have received letters from the bank asking me to send them my instructions, but it seemed so unimportant compared to everything else . . ." Ada trailed off. She was not used to thinking of herself as rich, but she guessed that since Alexander had cleared the family's debts on his marriage to Rose, her father had been careful to arrange his rescued investments with more foresight than previously.

"It is more important than you think," said Hannah. She glanced around at her office. "The only reason I have been able to establish myself here in the legal profession is because of my late father's will. He intended the sum as a large dowry, but I have used it to support myself in business. I cannot expect to earn as much as a man would, so I am lucky to have independent wealth."

Ada sat in silence for a moment. She had, in fact, not quite grasped the implications of her father's will. There had been too many other things to think about. Now, she thought of all the things she would like to spend money on. An office like this. A trust to help other women into university and the professions. A charity to relieve poverty-stricken women. With money, one could do anything. Even, it appeared, get rid of William's threats.

"I will do it, of course. Please, draft the letter to William's solicitor."

Hannah did not move immediately. Connor looked at her. "Are you sure, Ada?" His voice was soft. "I was too hasty and unfeeling in the way I spoke; I was thinking as a lawyer faced with a problem, and not considering that it is, after all, your money."

"Quite sure," Ada said. "Thank you, but . . . Somerton is very important to me. My family is very important to me." She swallowed, remembering Ravi again, and closed her eyes briefly to stop the tears coming.

Hannah rang the bell.

"Miss Evesham, please take dictation," she said when the secretary entered.

Once the letter was done and signed, Kearney stepped through the door into the outer office. Ada hung back, and turned to Hannah. "Thank you so much, Miss Darford. You have been so helpful."

"Not at all." Hannah hesitated, then went on, sounding almost embarrassed. "I wonder if I might speak to you . . . on an entirely different matter?"

Ada nodded, wondering what it could be.

"Have you heard anything from Mr. Sebastian Templeton?"

Ada shook her head.

"Nothing, and we are all so worried. But why do you ask?"

"The truth is, my brother Daniel is very anxious to know what has happened to him."

"Daniel . . . ?"

"Oh, excuse me. You would have known him as Oliver. You may not have heard, but my brother is a . . . very close friend of your stepbrother, Sebastian Templeton."

Ada hesitated. She had heard dim rumors of something between Sebastian and Oliver—but she had never heard the full truth. "If I could tell you anything," she said, "I would. But I am afraid we know as little as you do. If I do hear something, I will be sure to contact you."

Hannah nodded heavily. "Thank you."

They walked out into the outer office. Miss Evesham gave them her wintery smile and they stepped down into the street.

They continued in silence for some time. Ada could hear the sound of a distant military band. She was deep in thought when Connor spoke. "It was very courageous of you to give up so much of your money," he said, glancing at her sideways. "I hope you didn't feel that you were pressured into doing so. I would not have thought less of you, nor would Miss Darford, if you had chosen to keep it."

"Perhaps I should have." Ada sighed. "It is so hard to know what is right. I could have benefitted other people with it."

"And better enabled yourself to practice as Hannah does."

"Yes." Ada swallowed. "But no, I know I have done the right thing. I do owe my father this, and more, I owe it to Georgiana. I owe it to Somerton."

"I believe you are right."

They walked on in silence for a moment. Then Connor, who had seemed deep in thought, spoke. "You have heard of the new reform bill?"

"The Bill for the Representation of the People? Of course I have. It would give all men, even the working class, the right to vote. And also women over thirty—if they own property, of course."

"Well, once the war is over, I assure you that nothing will

be able to keep it from passing into law—and taking you, Lady Ada, one step closer to your goal of legal and societal equality with men."

"You think so?" Ada felt a flutter of hope.

"I do."

"But there is so much opposition to it in both houses of Parliament."

"There is, but the fact remains that the vast majority of the men fighting and dying abroad for their country at this moment are currently not allowed to vote. Imagine their feelings! The need of the whole country to work together during this emergency means that there will be no rebellion against this injustice until the war is over, but once it finally *is* over, it will be impossible to deny them their obvious right. It will certainly pass, and it will carry women with it. There would be revolution if it did not."

A passing nursemaid, hearing the word *revolution*, looked startled and speeded up. Ada smiled. "You give me hope," she said.

"It's justified hope. I believe that equality will come to pass in our lifetime. That may or may not happen, but I do believe, Ada, that I will be there to shake your hand on the day you cast your first vote."

"Anything is possible," she said, the color high in her cheeks. And despite losing Ravi, despite everything, she felt a flutter in her heart at the thought of the future.

CHAPTER
THIRTY-EIGHT

FRANCE

"How wonderful it is to be away from the front!" Charlotte exclaimed, throwing back her head to smell the fresh air as they walked along the path that led to the dunes. They had just arrived at St. Malo, and she almost could not believe that no last-minute emergency had arrived to ruin the holiday. She felt revived already.

"Yes, and to have time off for once!" said Portia. "Can you believe it? It seems so long ago when we had nothing to do all day but dress and answer letters, and maybe lunch or play tennis—"

"It is like another life." Charlotte shook her head, disbelieving. "And we never appreciated it, and always yawned! If I had a day like that again, I should fill it with the most wonderful things. I'd ride, and have a wonderful bath, then I would walk down Oxford Street all alone, and go to the pictures—"

"Shocking!" Portia teased her.

"I would, all alone!" Charlotte's laughter faded. "Although I don't suppose they are doing much of anything fun in England now."

"No, I suppose not." Portia's sigh was as tired as the lines round her eyes. "Oh, do you remember the balls, though, and how we'd dance till daylight? I wonder if we will ever dance like that again."

They walked on in silence. Charlotte felt the heaviness of war pressing down on her, as it always did if she wasn't actively trying to keep her spirits up. She almost wished she were back on the ward; at least Flint kept her laughing. There was a single last dune before them, between them and the sea, and tired as she was, she broke into a run. "Race you to the top!" she shouted.

Laughing and protesting, Portia struggled after her. When she finally reached the ridge, her legs aching, Charlotte was glad she had run. The broad sand swept down to crashing waves, seagulls danced above the water like needles stitching an invisible tapestry, and the wind slapped her in the face until the tears came. She was grateful; she needed an excuse to have tears in her eyes.

She slid down the dune, and Portia came breathless after her. "Charlotte, you are quite shocking!" she told her as they reached the bottom. "What will they say at the tea shop when we arrive looking so bedraggled?"

Charlotte shrugged and laughed, brushing sand from her skirt. "They'll think I have been rolling in the sand dunes with a handsome officer."

"You are naughty!" Portia brushed sand off herself too. "I think it's frightful, the things that go on. Some of the VADs have no shame."

"I can't blame them for having fun while they can. Everyone is so afraid."

"Even you? You always seem so capable," Portia said, as they walked on toward the little tea shop that had opened in one of the wooden huts.

"Of course," said Charlotte. She didn't say, though, that what she was most afraid of was not the war, the bombs, the wounds. What frightened her was the thought of what might happen after the war. She had no idea. She could not imagine it.

They went into the tearoom. A couple of off-duty medical officers were sitting talking at a table. Portia and Charlotte sat down; Portia picked up the menu and began studying it.

Charlotte sat, and looked out of the window at the sea and the wind-whipped dunes. Inside she felt hollow. She wished she were back on the ward. There were dressings to be changed, work to be done, sad memories to be pushed away.

"Pity about MacAllister," she heard, almost at the same moment. "He's an excellent chap."

It was the medical officers. They were chatting as they drank their tea. Neither of them noticed Charlotte's sudden, still attention.

"Indeed. One of the best."

"Yes, and a good pilot by all accounts."

"Makes it all the worse."

"You think there's no hope, then?"

"Not a chance. The break's a nasty one, and he didn't have it set soon enough. I blame the delay at the front. Dr. Field at Hidoux has been trying his best, but there's no way he'll be going back to flying."

"No way of steering a plane with an arm like that."

"I'm afraid not. The nerves are gone in three fingers, entirely."

Charlotte sat, silent, cold as if ice had poured over her. She thought of the conversations she had had with Flint, the tales he'd told her about growing up motherless, with a drunken father on a ranch. How he'd loved horses, found his solace in them, until he found his one true passion: flying. How he dreamed of starting his own aerobatic show, how he longed for the day when he'd be up in the air again—"above all this," he'd said, gesturing with his free hand, a gesture that seemed like a bird taking flight.

And they were saying he would never fly again.

Portia looked up from the menu. "Is everything all right?" she sounded concerned. "You look pale."

Charlotte managed to nod. How could she tell him? She didn't know. But she knew she would not let anyone else break the news to him.

CHAPTER
THIRTY-NINE

OXFORD

Ada came down the creaking, wooden stairs from her room in Oriel College. The principal's door was ajar, and she hesitated, hearing the sound of voices from within. Hannah, and Connor Kearney. She was nervous. She knew that William's solicitor had replied, but she did not know what the details were.

She went in to find the parlormaid laying tea and the principal talking warmly to Hannah while Connor, unusually restless, examined the books. He turned at once as soon as he heard the door swing open.

"I am so sorry to keep you waiting," Ada greeted Hannah and Connor, and took the seat the principal offered her.

"Hannah and I were just discussing old times," the principal said with a smile.

There was an awkward pause. No one was willing to begin discussing the Averleys' private business before the principal, and yet she was expected to be present to chaperone Ada. If only she knew, thought Ada with some contempt, that there is no need for that anymore—it is quite too late for my chastity!

Luckily, the principal was a reasonable woman. She stood up and said, "I understand you have private business to discuss. I shall retire to the conservatory. I am sure that Miss Darford is unexceptionable company."

They watched her go; then Ada, unable to contain her curiosity, turned to Hannah. "You have had a reply? What did he say?"

"I am sorry; the news is not good." Hannah passed the letter to Ada. Ada read it, her heart sinking as she did so. The words were clear and cold, obviously written by the lawyer and not dictated by William. *The sum is too small. It is insulting. The earl has the intention of traveling with his family to America and wishes to invest in the oil fields there.*

"I don't understand," she said, feeling cold inside. "Why is he saying that he wants to go abroad?"

"Because the cad wants more money," Connor said.

"Well, how much does he want?" Ada exclaimed.

Connor and Hannah exchanged troubled looks.

Hannah said. "I am afraid he will not settle for less than ten thousand. And that will leave you very little for yourself."

"But that doesn't matter. Surely we must get rid of these threats at all costs."

"Lady Ada, with respect, I don't think you've been much

used to thinking about money," Connor said. "Your share of the inheritance is hardly over ten thousand pounds in its entirety—leaving aside the small sum that your father left to provide for you while you were in education. That will support you very well for the rest of your life, and enable you to do whatever you like—to practice law, to help others—but if you give it away, you will be forced to either earn your living in whatever way possible, or to marry for money. It isn't an easy decision."

Ada was silent for a moment. "Forgive me, but I think it is," she said finally. "I cannot accept this threat hanging over Somerton. It is my home, it is . . ." She stopped, not trusting herself to even hint at all she had already given up for Somerton, for her family. "The money seems a very little thing in comparison with other things. Did you not say that the bill will pass? Well, I trust that once we have the vote, no one will be able to keep us out of professional life. I believe that you are right. The bill will pass, and I will be awarded my degree one day, and then I will be able to honorably earn my own money."

"Your faith in the future is admirable," Connor said, his eyes shining.

"Be that as it may, it is a big decision," Hannah said.

"The decision is made. Give him the ten thousand." Ada stood up. "Please, just let me write to my banker now, and you can take the letter for me."

She went upstairs and wrote the letter. Folding it and placing it in the envelope, she did not pause to ask herself if she was doing the right thing. She knew she was.

When she came back down, the principal was in the room again and was talking to Hannah. Connor opened the door for her. She wondered if he had done it so they would have a moment to speak quietly.

"You are quite sure?" he said, as she handed him the letter. They were hidden by the door and the shadow, and she was keenly aware of how close together they were, how intimate this moment was.

"Yes, I am."

There was an almost eager, boyish look on his face as he looked at her. "You are noble, Lady Ada, in the truest way."

Ada was surprised to find herself blushing.

CHAPTER
FORTY

FRANCE

Sebastian lit a cigarette and, as the first dawn light touched
the skyline, drew the smoke into his cold, aching body. He had
never been a smoker, had never enjoyed the taste or the smell.
But things were different here. When all around you was mud
and rain, rats and human remains trodden deep into the earth, a
cigarette was something that was warm, at least, a small star to
focus on. It filled his belly and gave him something to concentrate
on. More than anything, it stopped his hands shaking. He knew
there were many others who smoked for the same reason.

A shadowy shape passed him in the trench, with a muttered
"Good luck, Corp."

"Good luck, pal," he replied. The light was slowly draining
into the sky, and he could see the silhouettes of the barbed wire,

the guns, the German dead end they had been facing for days. It was hard to imagine that in just over an hour—no, less than an hour now, it would be over, for good or ill.

This was it. He thought of Oliver. Those days seemed so far away, the sun-bathed days before the war. If they could see each other again, could he explain? Was he the same person he had been then? He wished he could have said something, could have written. But every time he had sat down and tried to place his feelings on paper, in the muddy dugout, there hadn't been the time, or the words hadn't flowed, or someone had been shot, or a message had come from staff, asking him to count the iron rations remaining—some such make-work nonsense. He'd never written, and now, as the scene before him brightened inexorably, he knew he never would.

He could see the face of his watch, the luminous numbers glowing faintly. Time to call the lieutenant.

He left his post and went back to the dugout. All along the trench, he passed men leaning on the fire step, silent and watching, rifles at the ready.

"Good luck," he murmured as he passed each one. The words seemed so frail, so useless. He was surprised they didn't laugh at him. But instead they echoed them back to him as if they truly meant something. Just last night, Joe had said to him, "We can only trust in God now, sir." He hadn't known what to reply, but in the end all there was to do was agree.

He knocked on the door of the dugout and pushed it open.

The lieutenant sat at the table, his hands out in front of him.

He was looking at the door, silent and still. His face was shadowed, a silhouette.

He should have been invalided out, thought Sebastian. His nerves were clearly destroyed. Too late now.

"It's time, sir," he said.

The officer took his time replying. Sebastian watched him nervously. He began to sense that all was not well. He was sitting very still.

"Sir?" he said. He didn't want to think of what would happen if the man refused to go. He would have to force him out at gunpoint.

He took a step closer. Then he saw the razor.

Sebastian stood still for a second, taking in the dark pools of liquid on the table, on the floor, the drip-drip of something that was not the rain through the leaky roof. There was notepaper in front of the officer; there was a pen. If he had written anything on the paper, it had long been blotted out by the blood.

"Corp?" A nervous voice at the door. It was Joe. Sebastian turned around and went for the door, to stop him coming in. The shock of what he had seen made him tremble. The man had killed himself rather than face what was waiting for them over the top.

"What's up, Corp? Where's the lieutenant?" Joe was nervous.

"The lieutenant won't be coming with us," Sebastian replied. He didn't give Joe time to ask another question, but made his way to the trenches. And the bastard's left me with this, he thought. He realized that the lieutenant's death meant that he would be the one to lead the men over the top. That meant he was first in the line of fire. He did not examine the fact too closely, for fear that he would panic. But he knew what it meant. In just a few minutes he would almost certainly be as dead as the lieutenant.

He glanced at his watch.

"Synchronize watches." He gave the order in a low voice, and it passed down the line. "At oh-seven-oh-five hours, we're going over. You know the drill: we're going to advance in perfect order, directly toward the German line."

There were a few hollow chuckles. Sebastian knew he had to say something.

"The guns will shred the wire for us," he said, louder this time, more firmly. Remember giving orders. Remember in the old days, when you had nothing to worry about but the knot in your tie. "We know our job. We do it well. We're professionals, and everyone back in England is depending on us. Wives, mothers, sweethearts." And then he began speaking from his heart, from everything that he had thought of over the long nights and days of danger. The thing that had kept him out there. "You think you're marching across no-man's-land to Germany. But that's not what's on the other side of no-man's-land. What's on the other side of no-man's-land is England. Peace. Home. And a better England than the one you left, the best so far. Because if we don't get up and march across that land, this war will never be over. The only way to get home is to advance."

The guns began firing at that moment. The sound was incredible, a barrage of fire and thunder over their heads. Sebastian sank into the noise, allowed it to possess him. He placed his foot on the fire step. When the guns fell silent, that was when he would leap forward, leap up as if he were mounting the saddle of his favorite hunter, and he would go forward, as if Oliver were waiting for him on the other side, and that lazy, long-ago, sun-drenched day when they'd first kissed.

I want to live, he thought. It was a shocking, sudden thought. He wanted one more day with Oliver. He wanted to take his hand and kiss him and tell him he was sorry for the way they had parted. He'd been wrong to give up on their love. But it was too late.

The guns fell silent. The smoke floated above the battlefield, as if the roaring silence were visible.

"Forward!" Sebastian shouted. He sprang ahead, up and over the trench. Anything after this was a bonus, he knew. Life he didn't expect to have.

Bullets skipped past him like hailstones. He glanced back once, to check the men were following. They were. A wave of them, fire spurting from their rifles. He pressed his own trigger, felt rather than heard the bullets sputtering from the barrel. He'd taken three steps now at least, three steps of life he'd never counted on, three lucky steps, three steps he should be grateful for, staggering between the remains of bodies and gun parts and the churned hard shell holes. Four. Five. Why weren't the Germans returning fire? Then the smoke changed color, from white to yellow. From the acrid cordite smell came another smell, sweet and choking. Gas.

Sebastian realized what it was just as he felt it catch the back of his throat. He dropped to the ground at once, crawling under the clouds. Silent in terror and desperation, he struggled to tear his sleeve, to rip off cloth for a mask. He pressed it to his nose and mouth and the cloud rolled above him, into the ranks of soldiers. His eyes burning, he saw through tears figures collapsing, choking, vomiting, clawing at their throats and eyes. *Joe!* He wanted to scream out to him, but he couldn't even breathe. The wind eased the deadly cloud onward.

Sebastian crawled across the ground, heading directly into the gas. He knew that that it was suicide: the cloud was thickening, and sinking down around him, so the little air he'd gained from going close to the ground would soon be used up. But the gas was coming from the German lines, and his only chance of stopping it, of stopping the screaming hell all around him, was to reach its source and destroy it there.

He rolled into a filthy shell hole, the hollow giving a little more breathing space. Above, he could hear screaming now, gasping, hideous sounds. He pulled up his rifle and fired into the cloud of gas, as if it were a solid enemy. The Germans would be behind it, advancing, he knew. He could not tell if any of the bullets had struck home.

Then the wind changed. The gas clouds fluttered, parted. For a second there was a clear line of sight. Sebastian saw men advancing toward him, carrying machines with nozzles. That was where the gas was coming from. Panic snagged in his throat like barbed wire. He wanted to turn and run. But if just one of his bullets hit home, killed the man carrying the gas, he could save all his platoon. He had to go on.

He leapt to his feet and ran forward, firing. The gas filled his eyes; his eyes were burning, screaming. He saw the shocked eyes of a German soldier, who raised the nozzle toward him. The rifle burned his hands, kicking with every bullet. Sebastian kept his finger on the trigger. He could no longer see; he could no longer breathe. Bullets skipped around him. It took all he had not to turn and run. Instead, he forced himself onward, even though the Germans were concentrating their fire on him now.

Oliver, he thought. I want to see you again.

He took step after step, until he could see nothing more and was firing into blackness and pain. Then something hit him hard in the leg, and again in his side, and he collapsed to his knees. Even then he kept firing, his finger holding down the trigger, until he finally lost consciousness.

CHAPTER
FORTY-ONE

SOMERTON

Rebecca finished laying the dining room breakfast. The plates were gleaming, the silver and crystal sparkled. She drew back the curtains so that the sunlight bathed the room. It was such a beautiful view, she thought. It refreshed her every day to see it. She knew that her mother was happy here, and Davy was getting big and strong in the country fresh air. If it wasn't for the shadow of the war, and the troubling fact that there was a thief in the house, she would have been perfectly happy, she thought. Even Lady Georgiana was happy, now that the news had come that Sir William—it was still hard to think of him as the Earl of Westlake—had actually booked his passage to America on the *Europa.*

She turned away. There was still work to be done. She went

downstairs to the butler's pantry, where the morning papers, still wet, were waiting to be ironed. She scanned them for the news. Another big push on the western front was rumored. It was hard to imagine what it could be like, there. The newspapers dealt in figures, trumpet blasts of propaganda. It was impossible to imagine shell fire, impossible to imagine the dead men behind each number. She thought of Jenny and James. That was what was behind the figures—a brave footman, never coming home again. She hastily finished the ironing and placed the newspaper to go up with the breakfast, it would never do to cry on it.

As she came out, she realized the kitchen was quieter than usual. Thomas—Mr. Wright, she had to remember to call him— was in the kitchen, talking to Cook, as she came in.

"Hello," she said. "Is breakfast ready to go up?"

There was no answer. Annie dabbed a tear from her eye. It was Thomas who spoke.

"It will be. Annie, please will you finish Martha's work. I know it's not your job, but just for once I would appreciate it."

"What's happened?" Rebecca asked. "Where's Martha?"

"Martha won't be coming back," said Cook. "She's done a silly thing—a very silly thing."

Rebecca, eyes wide, went on with assembling the trays for the family. As curious as she was, she could see that Cook was upset, and she didn't like to pry.

"She may as well know," said Roderick. "And it's only fair, after she was accused like that."

Annie shrugged an angry shoulder.

"The spoons have been found," said Thomas, quietly. "The man who buys the kitchen scraps from Cook was arrested in a town north of here, trying to sell them to a pawnbroker—luckily the man smelled a rat when he saw a crest had been filed off. He admitted that he was given the spoons by Martha. She smuggled them out, hidden among the food scraps. They were splitting the proceeds."

"I can't believe it of her," Cook sniffed.

"Oh!" Rebecca was shocked. "So Martha is . . ."

"Not coming back," said Thomas. He added. "I want to apologize to you, Rebecca, on behalf of all of us. It was wrong that you were accused without evidence. I'm sorry it happened; it shouldn't have happened, and I will make sure it never will again."

"I'm sorry too." Cook, unexpectedly, came up to Rebecca and pressed her hand. "I do feel such a fool for believing her."

A murmur of apology came from all the other servants. Even Annie, grudgingly, mumbled, "I didn't mean any harm."

Rebecca felt tears fill her eyes, but they were tears of relief and happiness. It looked—it actually looked—as if she might be able to stay.

"You're all so kind," she said, dashing the tears out of her eyes. "And now," she added, getting a professional control of herself, "shall I take the breakfast up?"

She went off down the corridor, but she was aware of Thomas looking after her, and she was embarrassed by the big happy smile on her face.

When she reached the breakfast room, Lady Georgiana was

already there, reading a letter. Rebecca hesitated. Lady Georgiana looked up.

"Excuse me, my lady—I wasn't expecting anyone here so early."

"Please don't apologize." Lady Georgiana smiled at her, though she looked troubled. Rebecca went about her work, laying the breakfast out on the sideboard. "I expect you have heard about Martha," Lady Georgiana said, behind her.

"I have, my lady. I'm very sorry about it." Rebecca finished her work and turned around.

"Yes, it is terrible, the poor foolish girl. And it leaves us even more understaffed, as I'm sure you realize. Even more in need of a housekeeper—someone to take the reins."

"Was there ever a reply from Mrs. Cliffe, may I ask, my lady?"

"I have it in my hand." Georgiana held up the letter. "She writes very kindly, but in haste—she is about to go to France herself, to tour the battlefields as research for a war novel."

"She must be very brave," Rebecca said, unsure whether to be horrified or in awe.

"She is indeed. Like her daughter." Lady Georgiana gave a small sigh, and Rebecca knew she must be thinking of Lady Rose, so far away and in such unknown circumstances. "Anyway, she tells me to trust my judgment and make the appointment I truly feel is best. What do you think of that?"

"Well," said Rebecca, pausing to consider, "I think it's good advice, my lady, but it doesn't get us much further. Of course, hasty decisions are likely to work out badly, but we need someone as soon as possible. There are all kinds of little jobs that need doing, that we are falling behind in because there is no one with a housekeeper's authority to see them and order them done. So I do think you should listen to her advice, my lady, and make the appointment. We will all support your choice."

"Thank you, Rebecca. Very sensible, but then you always are." Lady Georgiana smiled, and Rebecca turned away with a curtsy. As she walked from the breakfast room, she could feel Lady Georgiana's thoughtful gaze resting on her.

CHAPTER
FORTY-TWO

OXFORD

"Lady Ada." Someone was knocking at Ada's door and calling her name. She forced herself out of sleep. A glance around the room reminded her that she had fallen asleep while revising; scribbled notes and open books lay everywhere.

"Who is it?" she asked sleepily. She got up and pushed her hair out of her eyes, threw her dressing gown on, and went to the door. "I'm not dressed. What is the matter?"

"Please open the door." It was her housemate Helen Massey. Ada, surprised by the urgency in her voice, opened the door a crack. She saw Helen's wide brown eyes, full of shock. "You must see this. I am so sorry."

Ada took the newspaper that was thrust at her through the crack of the door. The print was still wet. It took her only a second to scan the front page and take in the facts: the picture of the *Europa*, and the stark black headlines. *German torpedoes sink British liner. No survivors. Earl of Westlake, Lady Bridlington, prominent MPs among the dead.*

"Lady Ada? Are you all right?" That was Helen Massey again.

"Yes—yes, thank you," she said faintly. She felt sick. The horror of what had happened refused to seem real.

"Is there anything I can do?"

"No—please leave me. Thank you."

Ada sat down heavily upon the bed, still holding the newspaper. Despite their differences, she had never wanted this to happen. And poor little Augustus . . . she put a hand to her mouth in horror. How could this be? William, Edith, and Augustus, all gone.

"I must go to Somerton," she said aloud. She leapt to her feet and began to dress, hurried and frantic. She could not let Georgiana down again. More horrible thoughts whirled around her head. Had she killed them by sending them to America? Was their blood on her head? She checked the Bradshaw: the next train was in half an hour. She would have to run.

She was halfway to the station, breathless and agitated, when she heard a motorcar slow next to her and Connor's voice said, "Lady Ada?"

She turned toward him.

"Please, get in, I can see something has happened." He opened the door for her, and she stumbled into the comforting warmth of the car.

"I need to go home," she told him.

"To the station, Reeves," he told the chauffeur. The man nodded and they sped away. Ada, breathless and close to tears, willed the car to go faster.

"What has happened?" he asked, concern in every line of his face.

She simply held out the newspaper. He took it, while she stared out of the window, able to think of nothing but the dark, cold water flooding in.

"My God," he said softly.

"I've killed them," she blurted out. "It is my fault."

"No. No, you must not think like that." He put down the newspaper and took her hands. The intimacy of this did not strike her until much later; at the time it seemed completely normal. "He would have sailed for America with or without your money. His debts were too pressing for him to stay in Britain."

She could only answer with sobs.

"We are at war," said Connor, his voice graver and more tender than she had ever heard it before. "There is danger everywhere. You did not send the German submarines into Irish waters. No one will blame you, and you should not blame yourself."

She knew he was right, and yet it weighed on her.

"I must go home," she said again, almost to herself. "This has put everything in confusion."

"If you don't mind me asking," he said abruptly, "have you any idea who the title now passes to? Who will be the new Earl of Westlake?"

"I don't know. I am sorry, I can't think—"

"No, no, of course not. I am sorry to have brought it up."

"But of course you are right to." Ada made an effort and pulled herself together. "Whoever it is will have a connection with our family, even though they will not inherit the estate. I had not even thought . . ."

"Will you do something for me?" he asked. "Will you put this matter in my hands? I know that Mr. Bradford is a good lawyer, but I want to do something for you, Lady Ada. I would like to help you. As a friend."

"I would be honored, but are you sure you have the time?" She felt so relieved that this would be one thing neither she or Georgiana had to worry about.

"All the time in the world. Some of my clients have dropped me since the unrest began in Ireland—it seems I am tainted by my connection with the Gaelic associations," he said rather bitterly, then smiled. "But I am glad, because it gives me the opportunity to help you. I shall discover the new earl, and let you know all about him as soon as I can. Besides," he added, "I want you to concentrate on the examinations. I want you to do as well as I know you can, and it will be hard to do that with this uncertainty hanging over you."

CHAPTER
FORTY-THREE

SOMERTON

"It is such a horrible thing," said Georgiana. She could still not take it in, even though it had been a week since the news. She watched as Rebecca carefully arranged the tea things.

"Well, let us hope some good comes of it. Let us hope that the news Mr. Kearney is bringing us is good news, that the heir to the title is as far from William as can be imagined," said Ada.

"I am grateful to you for coming up," Georgiana said to her. "You must have so much more on your mind."

"There is never anything more important than Somerton on my mind."

Georgiana looked down. She would never say she doubted her sister's word, but she could not forget her previous behavior.

"Will there be anything else, my lady?" Rebecca asked the countess.

Michael Templeton answered for her. The countess spoke little these days; she gazed from the window with listless eyes. "Thank you, Rebecca, no."

Ada followed Rebecca with her gaze.

"That girl seems very competent."

"She is," said Georgiana, glad to be on a pleasant subject.

"This Mr. Kearney of yours is late," said Michael, who had wandered close to the window. "Ah no, wait—here is the car."

Georgiana readied herself, her heart beating fast. She had heard so many praises of Connor Kearney's intelligence from her sister that she felt almost frightened to meet him. It was strange that Ada should like him so much, she had said to Michael, since their views on Ireland were completely opposed.

"They disagree on everything but the important things," he had said with a smile.

But the wiry, energetic, handsome man who walked in through the door, his eyes twinkling with good humor, was not as old as she had imagined him, nor was he anything like an imperious don.

"Mr. Kearney, what a relief—I mean, what a pleasure," she said when they were introduced. She did not fail to notice Ada's heightened color when she introduced him, or the way he looked at her sister.

"I am honored to make your acquaintance," he said to Georgiana. Looking around at the assembled people, he said,

"Shall we get straight to business? I expect you have guessed that I come with news."

"You have found the new earl?" Georgiana said. He held a leather folder; she could see parchment inside it.

"Exactly right." He opened the folder, and passed it first to the countess, who examined the document, then passed it to Ada. When it reached Georgiana, she recognized the parchment in a second. It was the Averley family tree. A name was highlighted: Francis Wyndham.

Mr. Kearney was speaking. "You will remember that the title passes back to the descendants of the previous earl—your grandfather, Lady Ada. William was the only male heir of that line, and on his death and the end of his line in Augustus, it passes back once more, to descendants of your great-grandfather."

Georgiana shivered suddenly; she had never really thought of this title, like a living, immortal thing, swimming up and down bloodlines until it found its host. Perhaps it is more alive than we are, she thought. Longer-lived, certainly.

Kearney was still talking, his finger tracing the soft parchment, as he described the way the title had met dead ends and then new branches. ". . . and so Mr. Francis Wyndham is the new Earl of Westlake."

"But who is he?" said the countess. She was sitting forward, suddenly attentive. Mr. Kearney turned to her. "What kind of man is he?"

"Certainly a gentleman, your ladyship, and seemingly one of means. He has a large estate, Sandbourne, near Southampton.

He has a staff officer post that keeps him in London."

"Married?"

"No, he is a young man."

"And his character?" asked Ada. "I hope he is not another William."

"I have heard nothing against him—although you must understand a week is not a long time in which to find out all a man's secrets."

"We must have him here," said the countess with sudden strength. "We must welcome him to Somerton and accept him as us. As the earl, he will no doubt want to be acquainted with the family and people of his estate."

"But it is not his estate," said Ada sharply. "It is to go to the firstborn grandson, we know that."

"Yes, of course. But nonetheless." She raised herself from her chair. "I shall write to Charlotte." She swept from the room.

Georgiana exchanged a glance of amused, embarrassed horror with Ada; for an instant it was as if there were no gulf between them. Mr. Kearney looked puzzled. Michael came to the rescue—Georgiana had begun to expect it of him—and quickly engaged him in talk about hunting.

"I want to thank you so much for your help, Mr. Kearney," Ada said. She had come down to say good-bye to him. Now she found herself inexplicably tongue-tied.

"It has been a pleasure to help a friend." He smiled, and she saw that he looked tired. "And a welcome distraction."

"I hope that things are not too difficult for you at the moment."

"They are not pleasant, certainly. I had a very difficult meeting with the dean and I expect to have more. They would like to have me pushed out of my post, but I won't let that happen. They are acting on suspicion and prejudice. I never allow those to win."

His chin jutted as he spoke. Ada sensed a powerful determination in him.

"But let us change the subject to something more pleasant. Yours is a beautiful estate," Connor said, turning to look out at the view. "What a charming view; one really feels at peace here."

"Of course, you have never visited Somerton before!" Ada exclaimed. "It seems hardly possible."

"Quite possible, I'm afraid. Your father would not have approved of me, I fear."

"Oh, I am sure—"

"I don't doubt he'd have made me welcome, but we would never have seen eye to eye on anything." He laughed.

Ada smiled. She knew that he would have been able to stand up to her father—more than that, to meet him on his own level. Connor, she had come to realize, did not think of himself as anyone's inferior, social or otherwise. Nor did he feel the need to justify himself, or to earn anyone's respect. It was an attractive trait.

"Well, good-bye." She held out her hand. He touched the tip of her fingers, then hesitated. He said, with an obvious attempt at being casual, "By the way, as I said previously, Captain Wyndham is not married."

"You did mention it." Ada was not sure what comment she was supposed to make to this.

"If I were to give you advice—not legal advice, but solid, worldly-wise advice—I might suggest it would be a good idea to marry him."

Ada's eyes opened wide and she looked at him. He went on, bluntly. "I know the title means a lot to you, and you would be a logical match." He hesitated. "And of course, having given up your fortune to Sir William, you must make provision for yourself. I would be, er, concerned if you were to find yourself without protection. . . ."

Ada looked away, pressing back a smile. My goodness, he is in love with me, she thought. She was shocked to realize it—and equally shocked to realize that she did not mind a bit. In fact, she found herself rather thrilled by the idea. The man she had looked up to for his intellect, his courage, his skill in debate, was blundering in his speech, all because he desired her, and it confused him. It was both surprising and exhilarating to find that she had such power.

"I don't intend to marry anyone," she said quietly, stepping toward him so that there was no chance of Thomas overhearing at all. "Marriage is not for me, not now, at least. It closes more doors than it opens, loads women with golden chains. But"—she smiled, aware for the first time of how he looked at her, and lowered her voice so that it was clearly for his ears only—"there are plenty of possibilities in life apart from marriage."

He stared at her in amazement and then smiled.

"You never cease to amaze me, Lady Ada," he said quietly.

CHAPTER
FORTY-FOUR

FRANCE

The light was the first thing he became aware of. The light, and the pain.

It was a dull, sore ache, deep in his eyes. His eyes were closed. . . . no, they were not closed, because when he tried to open them, the light—pale, creamy, and pink-tinged as sunlight through a magnolia petal—did not change to images.

He was so deeply tired that it did not seem to matter, at first, that he could not see. He could hear birdsong, a blackbird, perhaps, trilling up and down with almost unbearable sweetness. There was a gentle breeze, warm sun. Distantly, he heard a regular squeak, like a gate that needed oiling. Shadows moving against the light were like boughs of a tree. As all this became clear, he found himself anxious to see where he was.

He lifted his hands to his eyes and felt bandages. His throat was dry, so dry that when he tried to speak he could not. After trying for what felt like a long time, he managed a croak.

The light changed. A shadow leaned over him. A soft female voice said, "Are you awake? I will bring you some water."

A moment later, he felt strong, gentle hands helping him sit up. Water touched his lips and ran down into his throat. It was like an explosion, more painful than delicious. He could only manage a few sips.

"Don't rush; take it slowly," the woman said. She had the kind of voice he had not heard for a long time: well-bred, delicate, charming. She reminded him of days before the war.

Perhaps this is heaven, he thought. What else could heaven be, really, but the past? At least it was not hell. That was the trenches.

But surely it could not be heaven, or he would not feel such eagerness to know where he was. Heaven was an end of everything—no more striving. Just contentment. It had never appealed.

He reached out, using all his strength, until he found her arm. The soft flesh, the downy hair—all this told him he was alive.

"Where am I?" he managed.

"This is the CCS at Remy Farm—the casualty clearing station."

"Remy Farm!" He hadn't hoped for luck like this. "The others—Joe—"

"I'm afraid your battalion was pretty badly hit."

He read the unspoken, understated message. He remembered his last sight of Joe—stretched, choking, on the ground. His eyes involuntarily closed as if to physically shut out the memory. The light fluttered, darkened, lightened.

"Please take the bandages off now," he said, remembering them. "I want to see where I am."

The nurse did not reply. Sebastian was still holding her wrist. He felt her pulse, fluttering like a trapped butterfly. He could hear her breathing, soft and gentle. He felt something—some unspoken message, in the catch of her breath, in her trembling pulse. The silence seemed to last forever, but really he was pushing away the knowledge, trying to fend off the future that swam toward him like an ocean flooding in, a knowledge he had had, deep inside him, buried until the wave of knowing washed it clean and clear from the sand. He had known, he thought, from the moment he awoke.

"I am sorry," she said, and from her voice he could hear how young she was, how frightened, how sorry. "Mr. Moore, I am sorry to tell you like this, but I am afraid . . . taking the bandages off would not be of any use to you. You are blind."

Act Three

CHAPTER
FORTY-FIVE

SOMERTON, APRIL 1915

Georgiana walked up the grassy slope of Selcut Rise, a hill in the
grounds of the estate. The countryside was spread out, in warm
morning sleepiness: patchwork fields, the dark line of the river
and the railway curving alongside each other, the three spires of
Palesbury, and the distant haziness of the smoke of Birmingham.
That smoke was the only thing, thought Georgiana, that reminded
her they were at war.

Ada was just behind her. Georgiana was aware of the distance between them and felt it painfully. Once they would have
walked arm in arm, and there would have been no secrets. Now
there seemed to be so much unsaid. She had been touched that
Ada had visited Somerton on hearing of the sinking of the *Europa*,
and it was good to see her again once more, even though she

could only stay a day. But there was a long way to go before she could feel really at ease with her sister.

Ahead of them Michael walked, pushing the countess in her bath chair. Georgiana was not sure how ill she still really was, but she certainly seemed to enjoy the attention. Her eyes didn't linger long even on Michael, though—the one figure upon whom everyone's attention was focused was a man she had not seen until yesterday, but whose arrival she had been awaiting with a mixture of hope and fear: the tall, slim, dark-haired man in officer's khaki. Francis Wyndham.

She could hear Michael talking to him, telling him the history of the hill. "We think it may have been a Celtic barrow. Some local historians were once interested in excavating it, but my stepfather—the late earl—would not allow it. He didn't hold with disturbing the dead."

"A very considerate man," said Captain Wyndham, nodding his head.

Georgiana smiled. Yes, Captain Francis Wyndham was turning out quite well. She hadn't known what to expect, really—but so far he had been very pleasant. He had charmed the countess by telling her that his father had been an old dancing partner of hers and had often spoken of her beauty, he had pleased Michael by turning out to be a good cricketer, and his behavior to the servants had been as polite as she could have wished. *That* was the real mark of a gentleman, she thought. Only Ada was still treating him with a certain frigid reserve. Georgiana was sure she had chosen to walk behind so that she could observe him.

The thought annoyed her. He had done nothing to deserve her distrust. She sped up to walk with the others.

"Do you know, for the first day this year I can really believe that summer is here," she said as she reached them. "I do wish we could have spared Roderick to bring the chairs and then we could have picnicked."

Michael gave her a laughing glance. "Good old Georgie, you are so optimistic. I don't believe you've even seen that gray cloud in the west. Thomas may be needed sooner rather than later." He glanced behind them, where the butler followed at a discreet distance with the umbrellas.

"Oh dear! You are right." Georgiana sighed, then added in an apologetic tone to Francis, "Besides, it really was not possible. You understand, I am sure. The staff shortages . . . economies . . . A year ago things would have been very different."

"A year ago, things were different for everyone," he said with a slight bow.

She stopped to catch her breath, and for a moment everyone was still in the windy silence, the song of the lark the only thing to disturb the peace up here. Georgiana looked around, and she could see—perhaps better than anyone—how the grounds had been neglected. Nearly all the groundsmen had signed up, and though the remaining staff had kept the fields and the kitchen garden going, the topiary was sadly neglected, the maze was more of a forest, and the summerhouse on the lake, she knew, was inaccessible for the weeds—even if all the boats had not been hauled up waiting for repairs that never seemed to happen.

"What a magnificent view," Francis said. He looked out over the hills. "I can see why you love your home so much, Lady Georgiana."

Georgiana smiled. "I hope you will consider it your home too," she said impetuously.

Ada, who had strolled behind Francis while Georgiana was speaking, raised an eyebrow at Georgiana over his shoulder. Georgiana felt herself blushing; she knew that Ada was advising her not to wear her heart on her sleeve. But Ada had quite the wrong idea if she thought she was attracted to Francis—handsome though he was. She merely wanted to make him welcome, and put behind her all the bad memories William had created.

"You are very kind to praise it," the countess said to Francis. "But I suppose Sandbourne, your estate, is much larger than this?"

Ada coughed, and Georgiana did blush this time—her stepmother's questions were so pointed. She had been trying to find out the size of Francis's fortune all the way up the hill.

"Oh, no—hardly." Francis's self-deprecating laugh left it unclear whether he was simply being modest. He looked embarrassed. "Now that we are away from the servants, and all together, there is something I must say to you. I . . . I am so grateful for the kind hospitality you have shown me, and I really hardly know how to tell you this . . ."

Georgiana turned to him in surprise, wondering what he was about to say. He was almost blushing, as he went on, blundering through his words: "Really, you must understand that I have no intention of acting on this information, no intention whatsoever of taking any advantage, not until the natural course of events is run through, and I have no doubt that will be a very, very long way in the future . . ."

"I don't follow," said the countess, her voice clear and sharp as cold water.

"It is quite embarrassing," Francis went on, and now he was really red in the face. "The only thing that allows me any comfort is the certainty that both Lady Ada and Lady Georgiana are certain to find marital bliss in a very short time—one can hardly doubt it with such charm and beauty—"

"My dear chap," said Michael, looking at him in astonishment, "do get to the point. Whatever it is can't be so bad, can it?"

Francis cleared his throat and looked around at the attentive faces. "The fact of the matter is this. My lawyer, upon hearing from Mr. Bradford, took it upon himself to investigate the matter further. He was startled—I may say shocked—to discover a single copy of a very old document, witnessed in the reign of Queen Elizabeth, which without reserve places an entail on the estate of the earls of Westlake."

There was silence. Georgiana stared at him, not fully understanding. "But no, there is no entail; that is how my father was able to separate the title from the lands and house—"

"I am afraid this document has gone unnoticed, hidden in the archives of a cadet branch of the family—my own, in fact—for centuries. You will remember that the Civil War was a chaotic period in history, and in this time it seems that the document was lost, or misplaced, and the truth was simply not understood."

"Do you mean to tell me," said Ada, so calmly and politely that Georgiana knew that she was angry, "that you have accepted our hospitality only to assert that the very house you are staying in, and the land surrounding it, are your own property?"

Francis went even redder. Georgiana wanted to feel sorry for him, but she was too shocked. The news was extraordinary—but not impossible. Certainly not impossible. A sick feeling began to form at the pit of her stomach.

"I am certain there must be some mistake," Ada said.

"I am afraid there is none." Francis's voice was icy cold, and Georgiana knew he had taken offense at Ada's tone. "I am sorry to have surprised you like this; perhaps I should have written formally, but I felt that as we were family—"

"Oh, of course!" Georgiana exclaimed quickly. "We are simply so very surprised, you see, so . . . we . . ." She knew she had to say something, despite the shock, something polite. But for once, words simply failed her. Michael was equally dumbstruck, and the countess, though her bright eyes were watching everything, was silent.

Francis spoke instead. "Believe me," he said, "I have no intention of pursuing any course whatsoever, as I say, until the appropriate time comes to pass, which as I say, I am sure will be many, many, many years from now." He glanced at the countess in the bath chair. Georgiana was surprised to see that, far from being upset at her death being discussed so openly, the countess looked more alert and satisfied than she had for months. She sat up straighter in her chair and addressed Francis directly.

"But do you mean to say that you get everything? Excuse my bluntness. I want to be quite sure I understand this."

Francis spread his hands apologetically.

"That is exactly what he means," said Ada, "that is, if he can produce this document."

That was exactly the thought that had been in Georgiana's mind, but she would not have dared to express it to Francis's face. He was, after all, the Earl of Westlake, and it was as good as questioning his word as a gentleman. Even so, she was hugely relieved that her sister had voiced the unspeakable. There was something to be said for her education after all, she thought.

"I am not surprised at your reaction, Lady Ada," Francis said, forcing a smile. "I will, of course, have my lawyer come to see Mr. Bradford with the document as soon as possible."

"No, don't do that," said Ada coolly. "Mr. Bradford is a very good man, but as I'm sure you are aware, he is a mere country solicitor. I would prefer you to have the document sent to *my* lawyer—Mr. Connor Kearney. You may have heard of him."

The expression on Francis's face showed Georgiana that he had. Her relief and gratitude to Ada grew. Surely this was all a horrible mistake, but it was important to get things clear and settled. Somerton could not be given away to a stranger without some legal scrutiny.

"Of course," he said, fumbling a bow. "I had not realized you were acquainted—of course I have heard his reputation—"

"Yes, he is an excellent lawyer, and I am sure he will be able to find out exactly what the situation is," Ada replied with a smile that was dazzlingly insincere.

There was an awkward silence. Georgiana racked her brains for some way to get them all away from each other without appearing rude. Michael saved the day. "Oh dear, is that rain?" He put his hand out and looked at the sky with such an innocently concerned expression that despite everything, Georgiana had to bite back a laugh.

"I feel it too," she joined in, playing along. She turned to Thomas, who came up at once with the umbrellas. Thomas spread one over Michael and the countess's bath chair, and handed another to Francis. He took it and at once stepped forward gallantly to spread it over Ada and Georgiana.

"Thank you, Mr. Wyndham, but I am quite capable of carrying my own umbrella," Ada said with a faint smile.

"Yes, but please do indulge me." He fell into step next to Georgiana, speaking over her head to Ada—both were taller than her. Georgiana raised her skirts to keep them from getting damp, noting enviously that Ada's more modernly cut dress did not trail so badly in the grass. "I understand that you have just taken examinations. You must be relieved that they are over."

"I shall be relieved when I see that I have passed them, and passed them well," Ada said coldly.

"Ah, indeed . . . indeed." Georgiana could see that Captain Wyndham was seeking for some other way to engineer a polite conversation, since Ada was clearly not prepared to discuss her studies. Glancing around him, he went on:

"Perhaps you could tell me the name of that little copse—it does look charming, set between the two slopes there."

"I forget. I expect it will be in the inventory when Mr. Bradford goes through the list of *your* property."

"Ahem—quite." Captain Wyndham was silent for a moment, then tried again. "I notice the stone here has a very charming golden shade; Palesbury Minster quite glows in the sunlight. Do you know its composition?"

"I am afraid not."

"Ah, because I thought perhaps it was partly mica—"

"I really could not tell you, but I expect you will be able to find a guidebook to the area in the bookseller in Palesbury when you return home tomorrow."

"Oh, Captain Wyndham must stay a week, as we had planned!" Georgiana exclaimed, wincing at the hurt expression on Captain Wyndham's face. After all, an honest mistake by the lawyer—she could not imagine any other explanation—was hardly his fault.

"That is very kind of you to say, Lady Georgiana." He looked at her with gratitude in his soft brown eyes.

"It is up to you, of course, Georgie," Ada said carelessly.

They went on without speaking for some time. Georgiana wished she could think of something to say, but the whole situation was too horribly awkward. Ada would twist anything that

Captain Wyndham said, and she really could not think of two words to put together—the extraordinary news had robbed her of all ideas. They went on in silence until they were nearly at the house, when Captain Wyndham spoke. He addressed himself over Georgiana's head, to Ada. "Lady Ada, I feel we have begun on such an awkward footing, and I would like to make amends."

"For what, Captain Wyndham? If what you say is true, you are simply the unwitting beneficiary of Fate—as we are its victims."

"Fate," said Francis desperately. "There is so much of that in wartime."

"So much everywhere. It is in the nature of Fate." Ada was being curt, and Georgiana wished she could think of something witty to say that would break the tension of the conversation.

"Ah—ha-ha. Yes, of course. I meant to say . . . don't you feel that Fate really does rule all our destinies? Whether we win, or whether we lose."

"Perhaps," said Ada. She picked her pace up, as they reached the flatter ground, so that he had to trot to keep up with her. "But there is no reason to give up in the face of difficulty, Captain Wyndham. I personally find adversity quite invigorating."

She looked back at him, her eyes clearly indicating her anger. They had reached the lawn, and Georgiana, half-dead with embarrassment for poor Captain Wyndham, who had only been trying to make the best of an awkward situation, scampered after her with a murmured excuse. She glanced back once as she followed her sister into the drawing room. She saw Captain Wyndham standing alone on the lawn, looking quite hangdog, under the broad umbrella's wing. But her attention was caught by the countess. She had stood up from the bath chair . . . one of the few times she had been on her own feet since she had received the news of the earl's death.

"Mother, are you sure you are able—" Michael said, stepping forward to support her.

"Quite able, dear. I would like to walk." She stepped forward with surprising energy and passed Georgiana on the threshold. Georgiana, astonished to see her walking after so long, thought she looked as if she had renewed purpose and energy. And she thought she could guess what had caused it.

CHAPTER
FORTY-SIX

It was a trying lunch for Ada. She sat, doing her best to hide her anger, opposite Captain Wyndham, as Rebecca and Thomas served the usual wartime fare: everything less than it had been before, and not as good. The spoons, too, were the second-best set, she noted. The whole house had a tired, anxious air to it—a sense that it was trying, and failing, to keep up with a past that had become a burden. She did not envy Georgiana, here day after day. But that did not mean she was prepared to let this impossible cad, this Francis Wyndham, steal their home from under their noses. Whoever should have the first child—and at this rate, it seemed likely to be anyone but her—she wanted her father's will to be respected, not set aside.

Finally lunch was over, and she got to her feet, hoping that she would have some time to speak to Georgiana and Michael alone before her train departed. Luckily, the countess—who had made a marvelous recovery, she noted—attached herself to Captain Wyndham's arm.

"I want to show you our rose garden," she announced. "I expect you have someone special—someone you might want to take a few blooms to—"

"I do not," said Captain Wyndham clearly enough to be heard by the entire table. Ada clenched her fists; the man was simply impossible. Was he expecting a bride to come with the property? She went after Michael and Georgiana into the yellow drawing room and shut the door behind her.

"Well!" was all she said, but it was expressed with feeling.

"Do you mind if I smoke?" Michael asked, almost at the same moment.

"Please do; I wish I did myself," Georgiana sat down on the sofa, her hands clasped in her lap. "What a terrible upset! I can hardly bring myself to believe it."

"Whereas I shall not be making the effort," said Ada firmly.

Georgiana looked up. "You think his lawyer made a mistake?"

Ada exchanged a glance with Michael. Georgiana was kind-hearted to a fault.

"Yes, a mistake, or a downright lie," Ada said. "You think the best of everyone, and I hope you are right, but I am more cynical, I'm afraid."

"Please don't apologize for it," Georgiana said with feeling. "I was so pleased when you said what I dared not. I—I am sorry, Ada. I thought you didn't care about Somerton. But we would not have known what to do without you. Do you think Mr. Kearney will really be able to find out the truth?"

"I haven't the least doubt of it." Ada spoke gently; she was touched by her sister's words.

"I simply can't understand it," Georgiana went on, still clearly trying to imagine a world in which Captain Wyndham was not a complete scoundrel. "How on earth can this document have slipped through the net? And can they enforce it now, after it has been in abeyance for so many centuries?"

"Well, the estate has always passed directly down the line, so the entail has never in fact been asserted in all this time," Ada said. Then, catching herself, she added, "If indeed he has clearly understood this document and is not simply wishing himself into an inheritance."

"I am as suspicious as you are," said Michael, and then raised a warning hand. The countess's voice could be heard: she was approaching down the corridor, and Francis, though silent, had to be presumed to be with her.

"I must call Rebecca to help me with my luggage," Ada said abruptly. In fact, she did not trust herself to be in the same room with Francis Wyndham a moment longer.

"Oh, do stay, Ada, it will look so . . ." Georgiana pleaded.

"Dear Georgie, I've long given up caring how I look." Ada smiled. She placed a kiss on her sister's cheek, shook Michael's hand, and went out. Her apology to the countess was perfunctory, but she noticed that the countess seemed perfectly well and not at all distressed by her departure.

After she had packed, she came downstairs, Rebecca following with her cases. She was surprised to see Francis in the front hall. The door was open, and Roderick had the motorcar ready, but she paused as Francis stepped out of the shadows to meet her. He was very smooth, she thought, looking him up and down. Very sure of himself.

"Lady Ada," he said, smiling. "I thought it was my duty to speak with you before you depart. I so dislike the idea of us being on unpleasant terms, especially when I have such an esteem for you . . ."

Alarm bells rang in Ada's mind. She waited.

"I did not expect such an encounter, I must admit. I had been told that you were beautiful, but I did not expect the strength of character, the clarity of your intelligence, your passionate affection for your family and home . . ."

He must be quite desperate to marry, thought Ada. He is actually attempting to flirt with me in the entrance hall. She was sure, then, that there was something unsound about the alleged entail. Why, otherwise, would he be so keen to ingratiate himself with her, if not to have another claim to the property should the first one fail? But the difficulty would be in proving it.

". . . has made such a strong impression on me. I really couldn't bear it if I let you go away thinking ill of me." He reached for her hand, and she let him take it. "I am so glad," he murmured. "Your little fist should never be clenched in anger against me. I hope I will never do anything to deserve it . . . may I call you Ada?"

Ada had heard enough.

She said clearly, but in a low voice, "I can see exactly what you are doing, and I may as well tell you now that it is in vain. I am not interested in marriage."

He dropped her hand as if it were hot.

"I know you will say you mentioned no such thing. Please don't take me for a fool. I don't take you for one. I take you for a clever man. But perhaps not a wise one."

She waited for him to speak; when he did not, she continued, making each word very clearly enunciated.

"Lady Georgiana is no fool, either, but as I am sure you have noticed, she is tenderhearted. However, there is no danger of anyone taking advantage of her. I am extremely protective of my younger sister."

"I—"

"Please, there is no need to say anything. I merely wish you to understand that—and to understand that I will investigate your claim of an entail thoroughly. I shall be back at Somerton soon enough, and I hope that you will find your stay here . . . relaxing."

She walked past him, knowing that he would find it no such thing. She knew he was watching her as she stepped into the motorcar and settled her veil against the glare and the dust. He was a dangerous man; she believed it, but had no proof. She hoped that her warning would induce him to leave Georgiana alone, and Michael, she was sure, would be as good as a guard dog. The engine roared into life, and she was carried away down the drive, toward the railway station, her veil fluttering in the wind. She could not wait to tell Connor what had happened.

CHAPTER
FORTY-SEVEN

Georgiana sat looking at the accounts, in the ledger that had been started by Mrs. Cliffe. Her elegant handwriting filled most of the book, and gave way only for a few pages to Mrs. McRory's spiky scribble; then Georgiana's own nervous hand took it up. Georgiana's head quite hurt with trying to make the numbers add up. It was almost impossible to see how they would be able to maintain Somerton in the way they had before the war. And that would mean putting people out of work, in such a difficult time for everyone. Her own inheritance was not in her control until she was eighteen, or, she thought, she would have spent it on this.

A steady housekeeper with a commitment to Somerton, and a sensible approach to budgeting, was exactly what she needed, she thought. But where was one to be found? She had not forgotten

Mrs. Cliffe's advice, but the trouble was she was not sure what her instincts said to her. If it were not for Rebecca, she thought, things would be even more difficult.

She put down her pen, on impulse, and decided to go downstairs and find Rebecca. If anyone would see how to make the accounts make sense, it was her.

She glanced from the window before she went down. The countess was strolling amicably with Captain Wyndham on the lawns. Georgiana was glad of it; it saved her making an effort to be at ease with him.

She went downstairs and into the kitchen. It was the afternoon, and she expected to find the servants resting, perhaps doing some mending. As she walked along the corridor, she heard voices from the kitchen. She did not recognize the man who was speaking, and then remembered: Of course. Francis's valet.

". . . The truth is, Lady Ada's not the match he thought she would be." The man sounded malicious.

"Go on with you! What about her money?" That was Annie.

Georgiana colored suddenly, and sped up her pace. The man had to be stopped from gossiping about her family. But his next words stopped her in her tracks.

"What money? She's given it all away, hasn't she?"

"What do you mean?"

"Just what I say. Friend of mine's a footman in London, and a few months back he hears that Sir William—the Earl of Westlake as was, that went down in the *Europa*—is hiring. Well, no one expects him to pay, but it turns out that he *does* pay, and seems to be pretty flush as well. So my friend asks around, and what do you think? Lady Ada's only paid him over her inheritance to get him to leave off his claims on Somerton. So she's got no dowry. And since Sir William died intestate, the whole lot goes to the Crown." There was an audible slurp of tea. "And my friend's glad now he didn't go for the earl's cash! He'd have found a watery grave on the *Europa* along with his master."

Georgiana had heard enough. She stood where she was, her breath coming fast. So Ada had given up her inheritance for her family, for Somerton. She had never imagined; she had thought that William had simply been frightened off by Connor Kearney. She found tears in her eyes, but they were not of sorrow, but of pride.

She turned and went back upstairs without making her presence known. She had not left Somerton since her father's funeral, but she knew now that she had to go to Oxford.

CHAPTER
FORTY-EIGHT

OXFORD

Ada walked up the hall toward the notice board where the examination results were posted. Her heart thumped uncomfortably, and she felt sick with anxiety. She had purposefully waited until the first scrum of students had departed—some throwing their caps high in celebration, others slouching away with hunched shoulders that told quite a different story—so that she would not be bothered by the male students, who too often seemed to resent the women in their midst.

Finally she was here, and she could no longer put off the moment of truth. She looked up at the list. There were the names of two of the best of the male scholars, and below them . . .

"Are you proud?" She turned to see Connor smiling at her.

She had not noticed him in the shadows. "Because I am proud of you—very."

"I'm third in the year!" she said, hardly believing it. "Third!"

"And if your year had not been so disrupted, I am sure you would have been first," he said.

She smiled up at him with tears in her eyes. He touched her cheek and brushed the tear away. She blushed under his touch; it was so intimate. There was something so pleasurable in this uncomplicated, tender relationship. He was not Ravi. But he was exactly what she needed right now.

"You are a marvel," he said softly.

They walked together through the empty hall, toward the exit and the sunshine.

"How will you celebrate?" he asked her.

"With my sister. She has written that she wants to visit me—I expect her today and will meet her from the train."

"That pleases me very much."

"And you? How will you be spending today?"

His smile died. "Writing a good deal of letters in support of a friend of mine, who is falsely accused of buying guns from the Germans to aid Roger Casement's revolt."

"I am sorry," she said, shocked.

"Yes, things are bad. I have been barred from giving more lectures."

"But why?"

"There need be no reason, only fear and suspicion. I was never a member of the establishment, and everything about me is suspect, from my religion to my politics. I want an independent, united Ireland and I am not ashamed of that. But some of those who want the same are joining forces with the Germans and accepting arms from them. That makes all of us who are outspoken about our views potential traitors. Although how one can be a traitor to a flag one doesn't recognize as one's own, I do not know."

"Be careful," said Ada quietly. As they spoke they had left the college and stepped out into the quadrangle. She could see two students looking over toward them, drawn by Connor's loud voice. She turned back to him. "Connor, I worry for you."

"Don't," he said with a smile. "I have been playing this game for long enough, and I will outwit them in the end, never fear."

He bowed slightly and walked away. Ada watched him go, her heart tightening with anxiety. But she had to go and meet Georgiana. The clock was booming out the hour: it was twelve already, and her train was due in at ten past.

She found Georgiana just stepping off the train. Ada sped up to meet her, smiling as she noticed how her little sister had grown over the past year. Her hair had darkened to auburn and her figure had filled out. More than this, she had an air of dignity, of competence about her. Georgiana seemed nervous, but she smiled when she saw Ada. Ada felt a rush of pleasure and relief; there was something open in her expression that hinted that she was forgiven.

"Dear Ada, how lovely to see you."

"Georgiana, I'm so glad to welcome you to Oxford," Ada replied, slipping an arm into her sister's.

They walked together along the riverbank, Georgiana glancing around at the punts, the straw boaters of the students, and the old stone bridges.

"It is so strange for me to be here," Georgiana said thoughtfully. "I never understood your passion for studying, and the very thought of Oxford frightened me. But I can see it is a beautiful, peaceful place."

"I love it here," Ada said simply. "Some of my most wonderful memories are of this place."

"And some of them are of Somerton," said Georgiana, stopping and looking at her.

"How can you doubt it?"

"I will admit, I did doubt it." Georgiana toyed with her parasol, clearly embarrassed. "I thought, that when you did not come back with me to Somerton . . . well, I felt abandoned. It seemed to me that anything mattered to you more than us, more than Father, more than Somerton."

"Oh, Georgiana!" Ada exclaimed. She was deeply hurt, and yet she could see why her sister had thought it.

"But then I found out the truth," said Georgiana. There were tears in her eyes. "You gave your fortune to William, didn't you?"

"How did you know?"

"Never mind, I see it is true. Oh, Ada! You could have done so much with that money. Don't think I don't know. I have been struggling with the accounts at Somerton, and I know that money is a necessary evil."

"It was not an easy decision." Ada swallowed, remembering

what she had given up: independence and ease. "But I will earn my own money. I believe that after the war we will have more liberty, and soon female professionals will be accepted."

"I hope you are right. You have fought so hard for it, and you deserve it." Georgiana placed her hand on her sister's. "Please forgive me, Ada. I see now that you do care for your family as much as you care for your studies. I misjudged you. I am sorry."

Ada found her vision blurred by tears. She could not bear that secrets should separate her from her sister, whom she loved so much.

"I was not late for Father's funeral because of studying," she blurted out.

And then she was telling Georgiana everything. About Ravi, when their affair had started, how it had gone on—and how it had ended. Georgiana listened, eyes wide with shock and then soft with pity.

"Please don't think of me as a fallen woman," Ada finished. "I do not think that of myself. I am glad I had the chance to know what it is to love someone, and to be loved. So many do not have that joy."

"Oh, Ada" was all Georgiana said, but she embraced her sister, and Ada knew that she did not judge her.

Georgiana released her finally, her cheeks wet with tears. "You have done so much for your family," she said.

"Not as much as you have," Ada replied.

"I? I've done nothing. I wish I could, but everything seems so frighteningly difficult to me. I know who I would like to see housekeeper, but I don't dare appoint her in case it goes wrong. And I want so much for Somerton to be a hospital for the war, as Father wished, but I feel so incapable of organizing it—"

"But, Georgie, you are the most capable person I know!" Ada exclaimed. She took her sister's hands and looked into her eyes. "You have been the guiding hand at Somerton for months. No one could know better than you what the best thing to do is. Have confidence in yourself, just as I have confidence in you."

Georgiana smiled up at her, blinking back her tears.

"Thank you, Ada. I will try."

CHAPTER
FORTY-NINE

SOMERTON

The sun came in through the diamond-paned window and made the mahogany linen press glow with a deep, rich light. Rebecca held up a fine linen sheet, monogrammed and embroidered with the Averley crest. A patch had begun to wear away, and the sun glinted through it.

"You see," she said to Mollie, the new tweeny who had been taken on to replace Martha, "the sheets start to wear away at the bottom, where the feet go. But we needn't waste the sheet; we simply cut it down the middle here"—she traced a line, enjoying the soft feel of the cloth—"and sew it back to back."

"Goodness, won't the ladies and gentlemen mind?" Mollie was a perky, freckled thing, good-humored, but Rebecca was already beginning to realize she was a real gossip. "I thought they'd want all new things. What's the point of being a lady if you can't have new sheets whenever you fancy?"

"There's a war on, you know," Rebecca said reprovingly. "Lady Georgiana's more sensible than to waste good cloth. Now set that aside and go on checking the pillowcases—if you can see daylight through the cloth, they need mending."

"The countess, though, I bet she'd like to do things properly," Mollie went on, holding up the pillowcases one by one. Rebecca winced at her rough handling, but at least she was willing. You couldn't be too picky, these days, with most girls preferring factory jobs. "She looks like a good sport."

"Mollie!" Rebecca was scandalized at her tone, but amused as well. She stifled her desire to giggle; it was more important to make a good job of this mending.

"Sorry," Mollie said, but it wasn't long before she burst out again. "I can't stop thinking about the *Europa*. It must have been awful, going down like that and drowning. Them big ships are just not safe."

"Well, don't think of it," Rebecca said. She remembered the look on Lady Georgiana's face when she'd heard the news. It was not something she wanted to see again.

"I can't help it, though! I've always had a fear of drowning, ever since—"

"Rebecca?" Rebecca looked up to see Annie at the door. "Lady Georgiana wants to see you in the drawing room, at once."

"Me?" Rebecca put down her mending, trying to think what could have gone wrong.

"Yes, you." Annie hesitated. "Do you want me to get on with this mending meanwhile?"

"Well—thank you." Rebecca was touched. Things were still awkward between her and Annie, and she wished they were not. But she was glad that Annie seemed to be trying to make amends for her behavior. She was not so bad, she thought, just easily led. It was all down to not having a housekeeper to keep the female staff in line. Cook couldn't do it all, she thought as she went up to the drawing room, stopping to tidy her cap and straighten her cuffs. What was needed was someone with authority, someone who knew how things should be done upstairs as well as in the kitchen.

She went to the drawing room. Thomas opened the door for her. She tried to guess from his expression what she was summoned for, but he was impassive. She walked in to see Lady Georgiana and the countess sitting next to each other on two of the elegant regency chairs that were set between the grand French windows.

"You wanted to see me, my lady?" She dipped a curtsy, aware of the dust in the air. It was impossible to keep the place clean, and she was nervous in case the countess was going to blame her for it. But she looked in the best of humor—quite self-satisfied, in fact. If she were a cat, she would be purring.

"Oh, Rebecca—I am sorry to disturb your afternoon," Lady Georgiana began, her sweet voice somewhat nervous. "I wanted to discuss some things that are quite important. . . . As you know, we have not been able to find a suitable housekeeper. . . ." Rebecca saw that she kept glancing at the countess from the corner of her eye, as if looking for reassurance. She became aware that Thomas was tense, and she sensed his excitement. Some big news had been broken to him, she realized. Something was up.

". . . in short, it has not been easy to find someone who has the necessary authority and experience to be housekeeper here at Somerton Court. We wondered if you would be prepared to take the post—temporarily, at least?"

Rebecca was so shocked she could not speak. Lady Georgiana hurried on. "I know you have not been with us long, but I have the utmost confidence in you. You work hard, Thomas has given us the best report of you, but most of all I feel you *understand* Somerton. Does that make sense? Would you be willing?"

"I would be honored, my lady," Rebecca managed to say.

This meant everything to her. Her job was secure now, and even if they found a permanent housekeeper after the war, she would have had experience at the highest level in one of the grandest houses in the country, and that would stand her in good stead. And as housekeeper she had a real chance to prove herself, to show that she knew how things should be done and to do them. Now she understood why Thomas was so excited. She wondered if he had recommended her. They would certainly not have offered her the post if he had not agreed. She wished she could throw her arms around him and hug him and thank him—

"Oh, I am so glad," Lady Georgiana said, with such clear relief that Rebecca almost laughed. "We really were quite desperate." The countess's foot was tapping impatiently, and Rebecca was sure that she would have something to say to Lady Georgiana about appropriate tone with the servants, as soon as they left the room. "Now, to turn to the next subject. It does seem awful to land you with this at once, but I want . . . I want to attempt something quite different, and I will need all your help to get it right. I want . . . to turn Somerton into a hospital."

"A hospital, my lady!" Rebecca looked up, startled.

"Yes!" Georgiana's color was high; she sat up straight and talked quickly, clearly full of enthusiasm. "My father wanted it, and I feel we must do our bit. What better way to do it than this—to share the beauty of this house, and give it to those who have fought so hard for us. This is a perfect place for recuperation, and we have rooms of a large enough size to take at least a hundred and fifty beds, I am sure of it." She glanced at the countess, and Rebecca nervously followed her gaze, certain that the countess would be against the idea. But on the contrary, she beamed.

"I'll do all I can to help, my lady," Rebecca said.

"Wonderful! I knew you would. It will mean so much organization, but we will manage it together, I am sure. And one more thing—I have another great favor to ask you. I would like to welcome Captain Wyndham—"

"The Earl of Westlake," said the countess reprovingly.

"Yes, of course, how silly of me." Georgiana blushed. "We would like to welcome him properly, as an earl should be welcomed, to the village as well as to the house. Especially if"—she hesitated—"if he is to have an even closer connection with this house, I think it so important for him to get to know Somerton."

Rebecca dipped a curtsy; she was not sure what Lady Georgiana meant, but she was pleased at the idea of a big event.

"I want to organize a charity fete, to help raise money toward the conversion of the house—buying beds and so forth—on the grounds. We haven't done such a thing for a long time, and everyone has been so sad . . . so many losses." Her voice almost trailed off, but she rallied. "I think it would be the perfect thing to welcome Captain W—the Earl of Westlake."

Rebecca nodded, a lump in her throat. A thought had been nagging at her as Lady Georgiana was speaking, but she was not sure if she dared voice it. Then she made her mind up. She had waited too long already. This was the perfect opportunity, and she was not going to waste it for want of courage.

"I wondered, my lady, if I could ask you a favor? I don't want you to think me cheeky, or that I'm putting myself forward—but when you spoke of wanting to do something for the soldiers, I thought I must ask."

"Of course, Rebecca, please ask." Georgiana's eyes opened wide in surprise.

"It's just that . . ." Rebecca's mouth was dry, and she swallowed, suddenly wondering if the question would give the wrong impression of her. "You know that James is missing in action, of course."

"Yes, poor James. We can only hope for the best," Georgiana replied.

"Well, he's left a girl. Jenny—Jenny Adderley. The poor thing's distraught, of course. But there's worse—and I know it's wrong, my lady, I don't want you to think I don't—but it's how it is and can't be changed. Jenny . . ." She couldn't find the words; she regretted starting the sentence. The countess would have her head for even mentioning such a thing in the hearing of Lady Georgiana, who was not even formally out yet. "She's . . . she's . . ."

Thomas broke in, stammering and embarrassed, but doggedly keeping the conversation afloat. "She's done something that she'd like to regret, but the fact is, miss, that in a couple of months Jenny is going to have—"

"'That is quite enough!" The countess almost rose to her feet, her cheeks flushing red. "Really! How dare you introduce this subject into my hearing!"

"Please, Lady Westlake!" Georgiana said firmly. Rebecca looked at her in surprise; she sounded quite firm, and there were spots of color in her cheeks, but she was not embarrassed. "I want to hear it. Jenny is going to have a baby, is that what you wanted to say?"

Rebecca nodded dumbly. "If your ladyship were to show her some kind of favor," she murmured, "just to show people that she shouldn't be cast out . . . And we've taken up a collection, below stairs. We wouldn't ask in the normal way of things, but with James gone . . . he told her he'd marry her as soon as he had leave."

"I cannot allow this to proceed—"

"I will be very glad to visit her," Georgiana said, still with those red spots in her cheeks. "I remember what happened to our nursemaid Priya, and I will not allow such a tragedy to occur again."

The countess sat up straight, her eyes blazing. "Have you thought, Georgiana, how it will appear for you to countenance a fallen woman? Your reputation, as an unmarried girl?"

Rebecca saw Georgiana flush at the words *fallen woman*. Something about them had wounded her, she thought, but she could not guess what it was. Lady Georgiana's next words were firm and clear.

"This is wartime, Lady Westlake. Everything is different now. James has given his life for his country, and are we not to look after his dependents? That's not Somerton's way."

"Thank you, my lady." Rebecca put all her heart into the words.

"That's quite all right, Rebecca. You may go. Please do think of what we can do to make this fete really special."

As soon as they were back behind the safety of the baize door, Rebecca and Thomas exchanged a look. Rebecca let out a deep breath she'd been holding. "Thank you, Mr. Wright, oh, thank you!"

"For what?"

"They'd never have given me the post if it wasn't for you, I know it."

"Nonsense, they just asked me my opinion and I gave it honestly." Thomas was smiling broadly at her. "No, I want to thank *you*—for standing up for Jenny. That was something!"

"What else could I do? The poor girl. I wish she had said

something to Lady Georgiana herself—I don't like to speak behind her back—but I'm sure it's the best thing for her in the long run. I know Lady Georgiana is kind."

"Yes, but did you see the looks the countess gave her? I expect she'll be getting a dressing-down about now."

"She won't let it stop her doing what she believes is right." Rebecca fell silent, remembering that they were gossiping. But it was too hard to keep her tongue. "Mr. Wright, sir, this fete will be a lot of work. Are you sure we can manage it?"

"I'm not worried about the fete. I'm worried about the hospital!"

"Oh, goodness." Rebecca had almost forgotten. "Do you really think Captain Wyndham will be pleased by the surprise?" She covered her smile with a hand at the look Thomas gave her.

"I think he's got his own plans for this house and land."

"Do you think—" Rebecca stopped talking as Mollie came up the stairs toward them. She was embarrassed, aware of how she'd dropped her guard entirely with Thomas. She wished it didn't feel so delightful not to be entirely professional for once. And she couldn't forget the warmth in his eyes when he'd praised her for standing up for Jenny. She thought it would keep on lighting her heart, like a little candle, for a long time yet.

CHAPTER
FIFTY

FRANCE

"Time for your break, Nurse Templeton," said Dr. Field, as he came onto the ward.

"In a moment." Charlotte continued making the bed. The sheets were getting more and more stained and worn, she could see. She wondered when they could expect a new delivery—perhaps not for weeks. She heaved the heavy mattress over to air. A man had died in this bed just yesterday.

"Now, please." The man stopped by the bed and waited for her to leave.

"But the dressing trays . . ." She put a hand to her forehead, as a wave of sudden exhaustion overcame her. "Yes, sir."

As she left the ruined farmhouse where the wards were and

walked toward the old barn where the mess room had been set up, she heard the medical officer's footsteps behind her, and turned to face him. She had always liked him; he reminded her of the earl in some ways—a reassuring presence. The earl himself had reminded her of her own father.

Now, however, he looked concerned. "Nurse Templeton," he began in a low voice, "you must be sure to take your breaks when you are able. I have noticed you are reluctant."

"I just want to be useful."

"But you cannot be useful if you are exhausted."

Charlotte was silent. She knew he was right.

"I want you to take your home leave as soon as possible," he told her. "I can see how tired you are. VADs were never meant to work in such danger and under such pressure, and though you have done well, you need to recuperate. Do you understand me?"

"Yes, sir." She could hear the distant drone of an aircraft ahead. One of ours or one of theirs? she wondered. Somewhere, someone would be getting hell as that aircraft dropped its bombs. The thought was exhausting.

"Good." He nodded to her; she noticed how deep the lines on his face were and how his gray hairs had multiplied. "Now go and take your break."

Charlotte went to the mess room, full of mixed feelings. She knew the more experienced man was right, but she also did not want to follow his advice. She was unable to imagine her life without work now, she realized. She did not want to go back to a life of tennis parties and balls and boring young men. She was afraid that if she took home leave, her mother would see to it that she never escaped again.

"Post for you, Nurse Templeton," said the orderly, coming into the mess room with a handful of letters. Charlotte took them, seeing the Palesbury postmark. Coming on top of her last thoughts, it did not fill her with joy.

"You never seem very eager to get your letters, Charlotte," said Portia teasingly. "Not like us."

"She's bluffing," said another of the VADs. "I'm sure Charlotte has a special young man somewhere, don't you, dear?"

"Perhaps closer than you think," said Portia.

"I don't know what you mean," Charlotte said. The last thing she wanted was for her and Flint to become a subject of common gossip. It was so impossible, after all—he was not to be relied on; there was nothing serious about him at all.

She opened the letter. It was from her mother, on Somerton-headed paper, and her heart sank at once. The confident handwriting swaggered across the page, as if to remind her that its loops and curls still enchained her, lassoed her like one of Flint's horses.

My dear Charlotte,

I am deeply disappointed that you have not yet come home. I really do not think that leave can be a problem, not for someone as well connected as you are—if only they know that you are being summoned home for the filial duty of looking after me, they will let you go instantly. But I must insist, now, that you return to Somerton.

My dear girl, I know how you must feel. And I blame myself. Your seasons were a complete disaster, it is true. It is so hard to understand why, though I don't believe you should have shown yourself interested in Fintan so early. Men enjoy a chase. But still, you should not feel obliged to bury yourself out there in France. I really don't dare to imagine how indelicate the work must be. No Templeton woman has ever worked, and I don't think we should let standards fall simply because there is a war on. No, I am not so ready to give up, believe me. I know that I will never see my darling Sebastian again, and it makes me more determined than ever to do my duty to you, my only daughter. Fortunately, Fate has put it in my power to do exactly that.

The new earl, Francis Wyndham, visited the other day. Until now he has been a little out of our set, though perfectly respectable of course—but it appears not only has he the title, but a claim to the house and land as well. So the obvious course is for you to marry him. He is a very presentable young man, a perfect gentleman, quite unexceptionable. He has a staff post which keeps him in England, and I would like you to come back to Somerton at once and get to know him better.

You need simply confirm the date of your arrival and I will have Thomas meet you at the station.

Warmly,

Your mother, Countess of Westlake

The countess's magnificent signature covered most of the page.

Charlotte was barely conscious of reading to the end of it. With shaking hands, she tore the letter across and across again. Portia looked up, startled. "Is everything all right at home?" she said, her face full of concern.

"Perfectly." Charlotte stood, crossed to the fireplace, and pushed the letter into the fire with the tongs. Her hands were still trembling. How dare her mother order her about like this? How dare she assume she would be willing to jump to attention, to marry whoever was put in front of her? She was so dismissive of everything Charlotte had achieved, it was as if none of it meant anything to her. Charlotte felt tears in her eyes, hard as stones. She realized only now that she had been hoping her mother would see her differently after her nursing—would respect her. But no.

She was in no mood, crossing back to her hut, to speak to Flint. But there he was—and the way he threw down his cigarette and crossed to walk beside her, she guessed he had been waiting for her.

"Please, I'm not in the mood for jokes, or card games, or whatever else it is," she said, trying to move past him.

"Me neither." His voice was serious, and she looked up in surprise. The evening twilight shadowed his face, but she could tell that something had occurred.

"I wanted to tell you that my news has finally come through. I'm to be sent back to England, to a rehabilitation center. There are surgeons there who are hoping to straighten out my arm some more." He gestured with his broken arm, which was still bandaged.

Charlotte's heart sank. She realized how much she would miss him, how much he brightened her life here. But her mother's words rankled: *You should not have shown yourself so interested in Fintan so early.* She was certainly not going to make the same mistake twice.

"I see," she said with a bland smile. "Well, I'm very glad."

"Are you?" He sounded hurt and Charlotte was fiercely pleased, even knowing that she shouldn't be.

"Of course. It means you are better, doesn't it?"

"I guess so. Though I don't understand why they don't simply send me back to my unit. I just want to get up in the sky again."

Charlotte did not know what to say. She couldn't lie to him. He deserved the truth. She had been putting it off because she could not bear to tell him that he would never fly again. Time and again she'd begun the conversation, but she had never been able to bring herself to come out with the truth. And now she felt that if she spoke to him again, her real feelings—how much she would miss him—would come pouring out. She tried to walk past him. He stopped her with a movement of his body.

"Damn it, Charlotte, don't you have anything else to say?"

"What else is there to say? I wish you the very best of luck, of course."

"Oh, of course. Well, I guess that's it, then." He stepped back. Charlotte had expected—had wanted—more resistance.

She hesitated, feeling like a fool and knowing it was her own fault. "Good-bye, Nurse." He turned and walked away. Charlotte watched him go, caught between fear of losing him and fear of what would happen if she called him back. The light was sinking; the candles in the mess room windows glowed from the dark. Sister would come out of the ward at any moment and all privacy would be over.

"I'll miss you," she said, her voice sounding like a stranger's in her own ears.

He didn't skip a step, didn't hesitate, simply wheeled as if he were on a parade ground and came back to her at the same sure, swift pace with which he had walked away from her. Charlotte stood watching him, not understanding what he was going to do—until he was close enough for her to hear his breathing, sense his smile, smell his warm body. He swept her into his arms— she had no chance to do anything but utter a small gasp—and kissed her. Charlotte, lifted off her feet, breathless with shock, felt him take possession of her completely, his strong arms, the bristle on his chin, the rasp of his uniform shirt, and his brass buttons pressing into her skin. She allowed him to kiss her passionately, until she was able to get her breath back—and then she responded, more passionately than she had ever kissed anyone before. Her hands slipped under his shirt, careful against his bandaged arm, finding scars old and new, the tempting, mysterious lines of his muscles—like a hidden treasure that she was exploring for the first time. She barely had time to realize how long she had been longing to do this, how exquisitely pleasurable it was to press herself against his body, barely time to begin to feel delightfully frightened by the force of his kisses, to wonder how they would ever bring themselves to stop, when the mess room door opened and Sister's familiar voice called: "Nurse Templeton? Are you out there?"

Panting for breath, they let go of each other. Charlotte almost giggled, as she heard Flint's breath rasping against her cheek, heard him murmur, "Damned woman—!"

"Yes, Sister," she replied, her voice only trembling slightly.

"Who are you with?"

"Officer MacAllister came out for a breath of fresh air and turned a little faint." She went forward into the light.

"I see, well, I hope he is quite recovered now. I expect you back in the ward at once, Officer."

"Yes, ma'am." Flint, doing his best to look faint, started back toward the light. Charlotte caught his arm and held him back.

"I have to tell you," she whispered. It was not the moment she would have chosen, but Sister was still there, silhouetted in the door. "I overheard the MOs talking. I wanted to say before, but . . . you won't be able to fly again. Your arm is too damaged. I'm sorry."

He was silent.

"Nurse! Must I come out there and find you?"

She couldn't see his face in the darkness, so she pressed on. "I wanted to tell you before."

"I understand." She heard the catch in his voice. "Thank you. I'm glad you were honest with me."

"It's just too unfair." Charlotte's voice shook at the understatement.

"I'm alive, aren't I?"

Charlotte hesitated. She wanted to give comfort but knew there was nothing else she could say. Then he spoke again. There was only a small tremble in his voice. "Damn it, Charlotte, I wouldn't have my old arm back for anything. If I hadn't lost it, I wouldn't have found you."

Tears rose to Charlotte's eyes. No one had ever said anything so loving to her before.

His lips touched hers, gently as two flowers brushing.

"I'll write," he said softly. Then he walked back to the ward. Charlotte hesitated before following him. She was sure of a tongue-lashing from Sister, teasing from the VADs. But she didn't care a bit. She was as full of happiness as the sky was full of stars.

CHAPTER
FIFTY-ONE

LONDON

Summer seemed to have finally come; the sun was warm and the Thames sparkled. On the other side of the river, the Houses of Parliament were mirrored in the shimmering Thames, the intricate Gothic spires and turrets making the building look like something between the pipes of a great organ and an iceberg—it was both beautiful and dangerous, like a spiky shell cast upon the edge of the river. That was where Ada longed to be, one day. One day, she thought, she would stand for a seat in Parliament. One day—once they had the vote.

She glanced at her pocket watch. The jeweled face told her the same time that Big Ben did. Connor was late. That wasn't surprising; they'd had to travel separately from Oxford so as not to excite suspicion. Their affair was delightful: she enjoyed every moment of it, and there was not the intense pain that she had suffered with Ravi. They understood each other perfectly.

She strolled on, her lace parasol shadowing her face. When she reached Cleopatra's Needle she would turn and walk back again, and he would be there, she was sure.

She was nervous and excited about the afternoon ahead. He had told her he would take her to see some friends of his who lived in Bloomsbury—intellectuals and artists. Ada wondered if she would pass muster with them. She was aware of being very naïve still. She had done so little, achieved nothing. But she was sure she could . . . if the brutality of the war did not rip everything to shreds. The posters caught her eye, one after another: *Enlist Now. Men of England, will you stand this? For King and Country.* So stark, so certain.

Cleopatra's Needle was in sight. Connor was not there. Ada paused, at a loss. He had never been so late before.

Could he have grown tired of her? The question sat in front of her; she could not avoid it. Was everything he had said about equality a hypocritical lie? She couldn't believe it, but the color came to her cheeks nevertheless.

I will wait another ten minutes, she told herself.

And then what? she found herself replying.

I will think about that when the question arises, she replied firmly.

She turned and walked away again. Her footsteps were not so confident now, however, and she couldn't repress her anxious thoughts. She had believed she could have it all, could meet a man on a level of equality in all ways. She had thought Connor was the exact man who would be able to live up to her hopes—mature, intelligent, principled, and with a sense of humor. But what if she was wrong? Or what if the difference in their views had really come to seem like an insurmountable obstacle to him? She knew how strong the anti-Irish feeling was at the moment. Everyone was nervous that the Irish nationalists would take advantage of the war to rebel against the English. That would divide the army's forces and could potentially lose the war. There could be no higher stakes. The situation was a powder keg, and everyone knew Connor was a firebrand, a passionate speaker for Irish nationalism. While she understood the depth of his feelings, she felt that an independent Ireland would be disastrous for the Protestant minority living there. It was England's duty to protect them.

Ten minutes was up. She turned and walked back to Cleopatra's Needle. Connor was not there. The newsboy was watching her curiously. She turned without meeting his gaze and walked quickly away, heading back to Waterloo Station.

By the time she arrived back at Oriel, she was no calmer and no more sure of what to believe. The door to the principal's room was ajar, and she came out, with a disapproving expression on her face that Ada had come to recognize. "Lady Ada, I must tell you that it is quite unacceptable for you to go away for a whole day without informing me first," she began. "The rules of the college clearly state—"

Ada had listened to a similar lecture many times before. This time, she could not keep her temper. "I am sorry," she replied, feeling anything but. "But I find these regulations simply ridiculous.

Why, when the entire country is caught up in something so serious, must we harp on something so petty?"

"It is by no means petty. The rules are here to safeguard your reputation."

"I call that petty. I don't intend to live by my reputation, but by my intelligence and ability."

She turned before she could hear the principal's reply, and went upstairs almost at a run. Entering her room, she tore off her gloves and hat. A moment later she saw the letter on the bureau. She crossed and picked it up. Not Connor's writing. The disappointment struck her hard. Almost without thinking, she tore open the envelope. The note inside, on plain paper, was hastily scribbled, but the words caught her attention instantly. It was dated the previous day.

Dear Lady Ada,

I am sorry to tell you that our friend Connor has been arrested. He telephoned me this morning and asked me especially to contact you. As you know, his forthright expression of his political views places him under suspicion at this time of war, and it appears allegations have been made that he is closely linked with gun runners in the south of Ireland. I am confident that this is lies. However, the matter should not be taken lightly. I hope you will be able to come to London as soon as you receive this. I will have need of your help in preparing a defense.

Kind regards

Hannah Darford

Ada did not hesitate. She turned and ran out of the door, pausing only for her hat. Her coat and her gloves she left behind her, and the last thing she heard was the shocked exclamation of the principal echoing down the path as she ran as fast as she could, back to the station.

CHAPTER
FIFTY-TWO

SOMERTON

The sun had come out, and Rebecca's prayers were answered.
Sunbeams slanted between the gray clouds, pushing them aside
as if refusing—for today, at least—to think of the war, of mud
and khaki and everything sad and dutiful. The wind caught the
streamers of red, white, and blue bunting and fluttered them so
that they seemed to glitter. A huge banner proclaimed the garden party in aid of the Red Cross, the military band was tuning
up under the tent, festooned with tendrils of rambling roses.
They were all in khaki, but the sun blazed off the brass instruments and gleamed in the polished wood of the cello and bass.
The lawn had been perfectly mowed—this part, at least. Rebecca
knew that they hadn't had the manpower to do the other side
of the house. But what did it matter? As far as she could see,

everything looked just as it must have before the war—just as it should.

"The bunting looks wonderful," Georgiana said, pausing by the table where Rebecca was setting out the homemade jams that they were selling to raise funds for the Red Cross. "How did you manage to afford the cloth?"

Rebecca blushed. "To tell the truth, my lady, it's the house-maids' old petticoats. I put them by just in case."

"How clever of you!" Georgiana clapped her hands, as the countess glided up to them in deepest black, the brim of her hat shading her complexion. She looked well recovered, Rebecca noted, though there were lines on her face and tiredness in her eyes that no cold cream or hat could hide. "Did you hear that, Lady Westlake? Rebecca manages so well."

"I must admit that the preparations have gone better than I could have hoped," the countess said, to Rebecca's amazement. She even allowed her a wintery smile. Rebecca curtsied her thanks. She knew that this little, from the countess, was praise indeed, and from the glance Georgiana gave her once the countess had turned away, she knew that she too appreciated it. Certainly the countess was in a good mood, she thought. But before she could glean any hint of the reason, Michael came up, Thomas following him, carrying the cream and strawberry cake.

"Rebecca," Michael began warmly, "it was such a considerate thought of yours to have the cake. Really, at the grand old age of nineteen I thought I'd never get another."

Rebecca curtsied again.

"It's nothing, Master Templeton. Thomas tells me we have always had a birthday tea for members of the family, and it seems a shame to miss the tradition just because of the war."

"I do agree," Georgiana said. "The war shouldn't stop us having fun."

"But I wondered if you'd mind if I donate it to the cause?" Michael asked her. "It would be a wonderful guess-the-weight prize. I expect there are plenty of families who would be even gladder of it than I would be."

"Not at all, sir, what a lovely idea!" Rebecca beamed. She had found her centerpiece for the table. Once Georgiana, Michael, and the countess had walked on, she helped clear a space for it and Thomas set it down carefully, cream glistening as it slipped over strawberries and sponge, on the crystal cake stand. Rebecca, her head to one side, wreathed white Somerton roses around its silver base.

"There," she murmured. "Now, shouldn't the jam jars be in a pyramid? Oh, I don't know, perhaps it should all be on the other table after all—"

"I think you should leave well alone," said Thomas, a smile in his eyes as he looked at her. "It looks perfect, Rebecca—er, Mrs. Freeman."

"But don't you think the sandwiches would be better by the apple juice? I do hope Annie remembered to strain it."

"I said, I think it's perfect. Now, look—the villagers are arriving."

"Oh dear!" Rebecca jumped to attention. The first visitors

were coming in through the arch of bunting, shy at entering the grounds of the great house, children clinging to their mothers' skirts, fathers stiff in their best clothes. So few fathers, she noted. So much black—gloves, hat ribbons, the borders of the children's aprons. The war cast its shadow still, she thought. VADs walked among the crowd, rattling their collection tins. She saw her mother and Davy, and smiled a welcome, but didn't go over to greet them—she felt too much on duty for that.

She brushed down her dress. She was still self-conscious in the smart black gown that she was allowed to wear as housekeeper. A small pearl brooch, one of the few things she had been able to keep from her life before, was at her throat.

"I sometimes wish I was still in a maid's uniform," she found herself confiding in Thomas. "I always worry I might be taken for a lady, and that would be so embarrassing."

"What do you mean, 'taken for'?" he replied teasingly.

Rebecca looked at him reproachfully. "Please don't laugh. I am not a lady; I'm a servant."

"Nonsense, you're a perfect lady. If you weren't, do you think that the countess would have allowed your appointment for a moment?"

"Oh, but . . ." Rebecca faltered, remembering how strongly the countess had seemed to be against her.

"Her ladyship's bark is worse than her bite," Thomas whispered, just before the villagers thronged in, on a wave of happy laughter and conversation. "She wanted to see you prove yourself—and you have. By the way, I overheard her saying at dinner that she was very impressed with the way you managed to save her furs from moth. Now it's time for you to enjoy yourself."

He tucked a spray of rosebuds into the waistband of her skirt. Rebecca, blushing, couldn't find words to protest. As the gardens filled with people, she walked among them, consciously checking that everything was going as planned, but in reality delighted and in awe at the event that she and Thomas had created together. Everything seemed to be running well; nothing had gone wrong. Mollie hadn't put her thumb in the butter or spilled the tea down the bishop's wife; everyone was mingling in the correct groups, happily without embarrassment. There was just enough juice—they'd used all last year's apples and thinned it as much as possible with spring water—the biscuits made with the new margarine were not really dreadful, and most of all the sun was shining and the band was playing. Children lost their shyness and began playing hide-and-seek among the rhododendrons. Above it all, like a gracious hostess, the great house, Somerton Court, stood. Rebecca looked up at it, the elegant pillars, the wide windows. It was beautiful, she thought. She remembered her father without unhappiness for the first time, remembered how he had pored over drawings of grand houses, pointed out the golden mean—proportions—to her, explained how beauty was all a matter of substance, and balance. The right stone, the right ratio to the windows. He would have loved Somerton Court, she thought.

She looked down, and saw a man and woman who could only be Jenny's parents; they stood aside, and from the grim expressions on their faces, she guessed that they feared being ostracized for their daughter's actions. She saw the father looking around, scowling in case he caught gossip or curious glances. But then she saw Lady Georgiana making her way toward them. The expression on Jenny's father's face changed, comically, as he realized that Lady Georgiana was going to actually speak to them. Jenny's mother curtsied clumsily, looking half scared, half defiant.

Rebecca longed to be able to hear what was said, but what she saw was enough to reassure her. Lady Georgiana spoke quietly, she smiled, and she took Jenny's mother's hand and pressed it. Jenny's father's expression softened into surprise. Jenny's mother seemed inclined to start crying, but Jenny's father silenced her with a gentle touch on the shoulder. Rebecca could tell, from Lady Georgiana's expression, that she was offering support and help.

Good old Lady Georgiana, she thought. I knew she would do what she could.

She turned as she heard the band fall silent and the vicar call for silence. The countess had climbed onto the bandstand and stood there, shaded from the sun, looking out like a captain over an unruly sea. Everyone fell silent and turned to face her.

"I am delighted to welcome you all to this garden party in aid of the Red Cross," the countess began, her voice carrying without difficulty across the lawn. "We must not forget the men whose benefit this is all ultimately for . . ."

Rebecca's attention wandered; she watched the crowd, wondering how they would react to the news they were about to hear.

". . . We have taken a good deal of thought before we made

our decision to hold this party," the countess went on. "But we feel that this is what my dear husband, the earl, would have wanted. We have decided to turn Somerton Court into a hospital. From next month, we will be receiving cases for rehabilitation."

There was silence, and then solemn applause.

CHAPTER
FIFTY-THREE

Georgiana watched as the fete went on. The villagers were enjoying themselves, and the friends of her father whom she had invited were spending money, especially on the raffle where the first prize was signed first editions of Mrs. Cliffe's latest novel. All was going well, and yet she could not be happy. It was strange, she thought, how everything managed to continue without her father. She could not have imagined a day like this a few months ago. She still could not really understand what had happened. At times the mourning that she woke up to every day seemed like a dream; at other times she hated it, and felt guilty for hating it.

"You look sad," Michael said, at her shoulder. She looked up, startled.

"I am just thinking about my father," she said, managing a smile. "Oh, I am sorry—I shouldn't be so downcast on your birthday."

"I wish you never had to be downcast at all," he said seriously.

"How can we help it?" Georgiana said sadly. She did not say the other thought that was on her mind: that sooner or later Michael would be off to the front. She could not hold him here, now that he was nineteen.

Michael had begun walking, and she followed him, almost unconsciously, into the maze of white rosebushes. They had not been properly cared for since the gardener left, and the long sprays of roses had grown out of control.

"Have you seen that the *Times* reported the arrest of Connor Kearney?" she said. "It seems that Hannah and Ada have pre-pared a good defense for Mr. Miller to present."

"Yes, it's all trumped up slander against the poor man," Michael agreed. "I am proud of Ada. In this feverish atmosphere it would be easy for a wrong judgment to be brought."

"The *Times* calls Mr. Kearney a conscientious objector. I should like to be one of those—but being a woman, one is not even allowed to serve, let alone refuse to serve."

"You begin to sound like Ada."

"I don't think I will ever be as forceful as she is. I don't have the intelligence, and I daresay I care too much about dancing and dresses and so on to be a real suffragette. But I do find it hard to have no say whatsoever in what is happening—when so many people I love are being taken from me." She stopped as she found herself face to face with a very overgrown patch. "Oh, I don't think we can get through here. If only we still had a gardener, he would have kept the path clear."

"Well, let's find a new path. Don't you remember when you used to scramble through hedges? It wasn't so long ago." Michael ducked under the roses and turned back with a tempting grin.

"My dress . . ." Georgiana hung back, but she couldn't repress a smile.

"Come—I'll help you." Michael reached out to her, and, giggling despite her sadness, she ducked under the roses.

"That was quite exciting," she said, glancing back at the offending foliage. "I don't know why, perhaps just because I wish every obstacle in life were so easy to overcome."

"Things will not always be so gray, dear Georgie," said Michael gently.

"But when will they change? I suppose this war can't go on forever, but what if it does? I can't imagine the future, and that makes me sad and afraid."

"Would you rather I did not apply for my commission?" he said abruptly.

Georgiana hesitated. The sudden question had thrown her; she did not know what to reply. Of course she would rather he not, but she had seen enough of the pressures upon him to know that would not be an easy choice. He would be choosing to be scorned by everyone; he would be embarrassed to meet women in mourning and men in uniform. Most terrible of all, he would feel that he was not doing his duty.

"I . . ." Her voice faltered. Could she really be so selfish as to ask him to remain at home? "I would rather not lose someone else dear to me, so soon after losing Father."

"I might survive, you know," he said teasingly.

"Don't," she said, her voice choking in her throat. She caught his lapel, and he held on to her. They stood close, in silence, in a green thorny embrace, heavy with the scent of roses. Georgiana knew that he understood there was too much to say. Too many fears. Too much knowledge. A few months ago, they had not known what war meant. Now they did. Now they knew how likely death was, how they did not dare cling to the painful chance of life, in case the heartbreak that was almost certain to come crushed them utterly. All this, and the feelings she had for him, that she could not properly find words for . . .

"I'll wait," murmured Michael after what seemed like a long time. "I shan't apply at once."

Georgiana rested her head against his chest. She could find no words to express her gratitude. At least one fear was gone, and her heart felt lighter already.

Walking back toward the sound of music, she searched for a subject that would not bring the war back to them. "Do you think Ada might marry him?" she said. "I wonder; they certainly seem to be close."

"Mr. Kearney? I don't believe he is the marrying kind," said Michael.

"And I don't believe Ada is, either. Yet she deserves to be happy."

As they came out of the maze, the band was playing and Georgiana was struck by the strange light, the long dark shadows and the intense golden sunshine, as if a storm were about to break. Against the gray clouds, birds shone white as they glided on the wind. Couples were dancing to the band's music.

Captain Wyndham came to meet them. "Will you dance, Lady Georgiana?" he said.

"Oh, I . . ." Georgiana blushed. He was certainly very handsome. She hesitated, then smiled. "Why not?"

He swept her off across the grass. Georgiana allowed herself to be carried away, to imagine herself for a moment in a ballroom. Captain Wyndham was the most wonderful dancer. Michael, she had to admit, had never been as sure-footed. There was still something boyish and awkward about him, whereas there was no doubt that Captain Wyndham was a man, and a most elegant and sophisticated one at that.

"You must love your home very much," he said as they danced.

"I do," Georgiana said, looking about them at the beautiful gardens. "I wish I never had to leave it."

A moment later she regretted what she had said; it was tactless to bring up the inheritance. She had not been thinking about it; it had simply been the truth.

Captain Wyndham leaned close to her ear. A faint, masculine scent, full of the mystery and glamor of the ballrooms of her dreams, lingered on his collar. "If I have my way," he murmured, his warm breath caressing her neck, "you will never have to."

Georgiana looked at him, startled. There was a wealth of implication in the words. She found herself blushing as she looked into his dark, velvety eyes. Was it her imagination, or was there tenderness there?

A sudden commotion at the edge of the crowd drew her attention. Children scattered, squealing. Georgiana saw Thomas heading over to the source of the confusion—then the crowd stirred as if it were the surface of a lake changed by something moving beneath it.

"An entertainer!" cried someone.

"Did we engage an entertainer?" Georgiana said to Captain Wyndham, perplexed. But then she saw what was causing the excitement. Two women, one dressed in flowing Arabic robes, a baby in her arms, the other in a stained traveling dress, stood under the arched entrance to the fete. Georgiana stopped, transfixed for a second—it could *not* be—and then she heard the Englishwoman's voice, exhausted but so familiar that it sent a thrill of recognition down her spine.

"Excuse me—I am looking for the Earl of Westlake. Please, is there anyone from the family here?"

She turned toward Georgiana as she spoke, and Georgiana's mouth opened in wordless shock and delight. The dark brown hair, the lily-like head, so graceful, and the Averley chin—

"Rose!" she shrieked, with a complete lack of all dignity. She left Captain Wyndham's arms and ran toward her sister, her hat lost as she went. She flung herself into her arms, into a confusion of strange, incense-like scents, familiar warmth, and heard Rose's happy laughter, bordering on tears.

"Oh, dear Georgie! I can't wait to tell you—we've had such an incredible journey!"

CHAPTER
FIFTY-FOUR

FRANCE

Charlotte's shift was nearly over. Outside, the sun was setting. She moved wearily around the ward, tidying up and making sure that the men all had water, and were comfortable for the night. Outside, the last train to carry the wounded back to the general hospital rattled toward them.

She had almost made up her mind to transfer back to England. She was exhausted in mind and in body. With Flint gone, she did not even have the energy that his presence always gave her. As much as she wanted to help, the war was wearing her down. Even her mother would be a relief.

Back in the mess room, she looked at once at her shelf, where letters were placed when they came in. Nothing. She tried not to feel hurt. There were many reasons he might not have written immediately. But, she thought as she went to make herself the inevitable, endless Bovril, he might also have discovered that his feelings had changed. War was not the real world, and perhaps everything looked different from England.

"Oh, Charlotte." Portia came in, and Charlotte's eyes went at once to the envelopes she held. "Two for you just came with the last train. From home."

Charlotte's heart leapt as she took the letters; it fell as she saw the postmark and heard Portia's words. Both were from Palesbury, and she recognized her mother's handwriting on the first.

"Bad news?" said Portia sympathetically.

Charlotte glanced up at her with an ironic smile. "From my mother, so almost certainly."

Portia smiled understandingly, and Charlotte opened the letter. It wasn't pleasant to face another telling-off; she was sure that her mother would want to know what had happened to her, why she had not replied to her last letter. She was right.

Dear Charlotte,

Did you receive my last letter? I can only assume it has gone astray. I must insist that you return at once. The situation is quite critical. Rose has arrived after the most extraordinary journey, looking quite shocking, and bringing an unspeakable Arab woman with her, who is nursemaid to her baby son, Edward. Yes, Rose has a son. You will instantly recognize the significance of this. She will be expecting him to have the house and land, as my husband specified in the will. But as the estate is entailed, he will certainly be set aside in favor of Earl of Westlake's more valid claim. I write this simply so that you are forewarned, I don't expect real opposition from her—she is too concerned with writing to Alexander, who is serving somewhere on the eastern front, to pursue her son's interests herself. No, the real danger comes from Georgiana. Captain Wyndham has been paying particular attentions to her. I am sure that you will know how to detach him from her, but it is essential that you give up this sulk and come back to Somerton. Do not delay. Come immediately, and wire your arrival time from London. While in London, you should also collect some new dresses, which I have ordered for you, at L'atelier. Everything may depend on the next few days. If it will persuade you, I will even allow you to continue with your nursing while you are here, since the house is to be converted into a hospital—in fact, it might be a good idea, as these things do impress the men. At any rate you must get out of France before you are absolutely unsexed. Think how terrible it will be to be a spinster. Dear Charlotte, do be reasonable and come home at once.

> *Your mother, Countess of Westlake*

Charlotte put the letter down, a little dazed by the mixed feelings it had aroused in her. She was surprised at how relieved she felt at Rose's safe return. She had never liked Rose, but she could see now that she had treated the poor girl unfairly, driven by her own unhappiness. She had assumed competition where there was none, and with distance she suspected that it had unconsciously galled her to see Rose finding something to excel at—her musical compositions—when she herself felt she had no real purpose in life. But now . . .

Even surrounded by death and sorrow, she was happier than she had ever been before. Nursing had shown her where her talents lay. And she thought of Rose quite differently—not as a rival, but as one more unfortunate person caught up in this awful war, the war that had given her own life meaning, but that she wished more than anything had never happened.

No, it was not possible to hate Rose. She had no energy for it, no desire to hate her. Besides, being away from her mother gave her perspective. She fervently hoped that Georgiana would be happy with this Captain Wyndham, if she really liked him and it was not just her mother seeing what she expected to see. As for Somerton, she did not want it. It had never been her home. But how like her mother to try and snatch it from Georgiana, who had always loved it!

She angrily crumpled the letter up, her resentment at her mother's tone flooding back into her. As if she would run home at her bidding, simply to throw herself at a man she had never met! The whole thing was an insult.

She tore open the other letter. The handwriting was badly formed and she frowned, trying to make out what the writer meant to say. Then she realized, and her cheeks flushed with pleasure and delight.

Dear Charlotte

Well, I have landed up in the finest place on God's earth! It's like the garden of Eden here, with a grand old house in the middle of it all, and that's where I'm staying, with some of the kindest, nicest people on earth looking after me. Can you believe the old earl left it in his will that the house should be used for the benefit of soldiers during the war? He must have had an enormous heart. Well, I have never been too good a writer, and making do with my left hand only worsens it, so I will close, only saying that this is my address and I hope you will remember to write to me. Fine as it is here, I would like to see you again, that would be like a ray of sunshine in my life.

Captain Flint MacAllister

Charlotte flipped the envelope over, only to confirm what she had guessed already. Flint was at Somerton! She could not decide which astonished her more—the fact that the house had become a hospital, or the fact that Flint had been sent there, of all places. Nothing could have been luckier, she could go straight home and straight to him . . . but was that the right thing to do?

She hesitated, folding and refolding the letter as she thought. She knew, none better, how desperate the need was for medical staff here. But she also remembered what the medical officer had said. She could not continue forever on the front line. And if she could keep going with her nursing, as her mother had promised, she would still be helping.

Her heart made the decision for her. She slipped the letter into her pocket, snatched up a pen and her mother's letter, and scribbled a hasty reply on the bottom.

Dear Mother,
Please expect me soonest.
Charlotte

She put the letter into a fresh envelope, stamped it, and, stopping only to drop it into the post tray, raced back to her hut to pack.

CHAPTER
FIFTY-FIVE

SOMERTON

Rebecca hurried along the main corridor of Somerton Court. She passed rooms that had been drawing rooms, which were now filled with neat white beds. Her mind was still whirling with all the changes that had happened, all the new things that she had had to adjust to. The first men had arrived a week ago, just twenty officers and the VADs with them. It was difficult to juggle the often conflicting orders from the countess and from the sister who was in charge of the hospital. But she could see at once how glad the men were to be here, in the heart of the countryside, with the fresh air and the peace and quiet that she knew they had been missing. There was no doubt in her mind that Lady Georgiana had done the right thing.

Today a new batch of men was arriving. She reached the hall, the ring of her footsteps changing as she stepped from parquet to marble. Outside, the motor ambulance was drawn up, and the VADs were helping the men from the ambulance up the stairs, into the house. Lady Georgiana was standing on the steps, ready to greet them.

"Welcome!" Lady Georgiana said. Rebecca could tell she was nervous, but her smile came from the heart. "We thank you for all you have done for us, and we hope you will make a full recovery at Somerton."

The men murmured their thanks, one by one, as they passed through. They seemed quite overawed. Rebecca went ahead of them, leading them to the appropriate wards. It was still strange to see prim, practical hospital beds set up in the yellow drawing room and the white drawing room and the ballroom.

"In here, sir," she said, helping a VAD settle a man on crutches into a bed under a Velázquez depicting a battle scene. She wondered how the soldiers felt about that, but it was too late to do anything about it—she could dust-sheet it later if there were complaints.

Behind her, she could hear Lady Georgiana and Captain Wyndham—she could not get used to calling him the earl, though she would have to remember when she wrote place cards for dinner—talking as they followed after the VADs to see that the soldiers were comfortable. They paused just outside the door, and spoke in low voices. Rebecca, helping arrange blankets, guessed they did not realize she was there and could hear them. She pursed her lips. The earl was up here at Somerton far too frequently for her liking. She was sure that he was trying to make an impression on Lady Georgiana. It was a hunch, that was all, but she had taken a dislike to the man. There was something so oily in the way he spoke to Lady Georgiana.

"It has been an easy enough transition into a hospital, don't you think?" she heard Captain Wyndham say.

"It could have been much worse. Rebecca and Thomas are so well organized."

"I am so glad that this part, at least, of your father's will could be fulfilled without controversy."

"As am I," Lady Georgiana replied. Rebecca could tell from the tone of her voice how much she appreciated the thought. There was a pause; then the earl went on in a lowered voice:

"I am afraid your sister will never forgive me."

"Rose? Oh no. I don't think she holds a grudge on little Edward's behalf. We are"—Georgiana hesitated—"sorry, of course. As devoted aunts, we want everything good for our nephew."

"I am glad to hear it, but in fact I did not have Rose in mind. I am concerned that Lady Ada is going to some extremes to try and prove my lawyers have made a mistake. It is understandable, of course."

"Oh . . ." Rebecca could hear the embarrassment in Georgiana's voice, and her desire not to say anything that would offend or hurt. Tucking in the blankets, she wished she could say, *You're too soft on him, my lady.*

"But let us speak of more pleasant things," Captain Wyndham went on, steering smoothly away from the subject. "I was delighted to hear that the Duke of Huntleigh may soon be able to get compassionate leave to visit his wife and son."

"Oh, yes!" Georgiana's warmth and enthusiasm rang in her voice. "It has been so awful for her, to receive these letters all blacked out by the censor. It seems truly cruel that the men are not allowed to write where they are. I know it is necessary, that the information could be intercepted by the enemy, but still— Rose trembles at the news of every engagement in the east."

"My heart goes out to her. I—" He broke off as Rebecca, who had finished her work, walked out of the room. Rebecca saw an unpleasant expression in his eyes as he looked at her; he was standing very close to Lady Georgiana, and she was sure that she had disrupted some plans he had for flirtation. She met his gaze boldly, and wished she dared stick her tongue out. There was no way she was going to let him wheedle his way into her Lady Georgiana's affections.

"Would you like me to see about the extra medicine stores now, my lady?" she addressed Georgiana. "The doctors were talking about needing more space. . . . I'm sure we can make room in the kitchen for things that are not dangerous in any way."

"Yes, that's a good idea, Rebecca." Lady Georgiana's blush was fading. She looked up, and Rebecca followed her gaze, as some soldiers walked into the room, gazing around openmouthed at the paintings and the high ceilings and gilded cornices.

"Cor blimey, Bert," one of them said, in a strong Cockney accent, "look where we've landed up. Bloomin' Buckingham Palace!"

"Oh, are you lost? May I help you find your ward?" Lady Georgiana went toward them, her back turned to Captain Wyndham.

"Here, you. There must be some mistake," Captain Wyndham said to Rebecca. "We are an officers' hospital. These men must be sent away at once."

Rebecca bridled. "No, sir," she said as calmly as she could, "Somerton Court Sixty-Sixth General Hospital will be accepting both officers and men. It is not unprecedented."

"But good God, woman! You can't expect gentlemen to live side by side with . . . with . . ." He gestured at another load of ordinary soldiers who were coming up the hall. "Tommies."

"They have been doing so in the trenches, sir." Rebecca was angry enough to let it show in her voice.

Captain Wyndham took no notice. "Why was I not consulted about this?" he demanded.

"Because, Your Lordship, you are not the master of Somerton Court," said a voice.

Rebecca, startled, looked up and saw that Thomas was approaching. He had spoken quietly and with a pleasant smile, but Rebecca could feel the tension in the air. She swallowed as he reached them, hoping that there would not be a scene. Captain Wyndham blinked, looked away, tried a contemptuous laugh, and then, seeming to realize he was faced with hostility from two sides, turned and quickly walked off.

Rebecca caught Thomas's eye and they both breathed out in relief. A scene had been averted—for now.

"That was brave of you," she said to him under her breath.

"Not at all. He's not master here, and he may never be," Thomas replied in the same tone.

Rebecca smiled her agreement. She turned away, but Thomas spoke her name, calling her back.

"Rebecca—may I speak to you? Privately?" Thomas took her hand and drew her aside, into an empty room, without waiting for an answer. Rebecca's pulse speeded up. "I want to ask you a question, and I thought I should grab my chance," he said in a low voice.

He is not going to propose, Rebecca told her fluttering heart, sternly. Really, don't be silly!

"Of course, Mr. Wright."

"Thank you. I can trust you with anything, I feel, and I can't tell you what a relief that is." He pressed her hand. They were very close together. She could feel his warmth, knew that his heart was beating fast too. She did not trust herself to reply.

"I want to ask you a great favor. I need to go away, just for one day. I daren't ask for leave; they'd want to know why. Can you cover for me?"

"O-of course." Rebecca hoped her faltering voice didn't betray her disappointment. "But may I ask why?"

"Certainly. It's nothing underhand, but I wouldn't like it to get out, until I was sure." Thomas sounded embarrassed. "I am going to Manchester to be interviewed for a job."

"A job!" Rebecca was shocked. "You mean—you mean you're going to leave?"

Thomas let go of her hand, and looked down. "The thing is, Rebecca, I want to make something of myself. Something more than a butler. I know many would say that I'm lucky to be doing what I am, that I should stay where I am, but I'm still another man's servant. I want to have my own business, my own money. I want to be my own master. I know the war's making everything difficult, but there'll be a world after the war, and I want to be ready for it. So I want to go and train as an engineer. I've saved up the money, and there'll be plenty of work while the war's on. When it's over, well, I'd be ready to set up my own business. My old man was a coach builder. It's not that far from coaches to motorcars; you just take out the horses. This job I'm going for is just as an apprentice, but it's guaranteed work, and it'll take me forward in life. I don't want to spend my life here. I can't sign up—my parents won't hear of it and I won't cross them even when I come of age—but I don't want to spend the war opening doors and ironing collars, either."

Rebecca nodded silently. She understood how he felt. But she wondered if it would be easier to bear if she didn't. "Of course I will cover for you," she said quietly. "I shall say you've gone into Palesbury, to the dentist, will that do?"

He grinned. "I'll fake a sore tooth the day before. Thank you, Rebecca. I knew I could count on you."

He squeezed her hand one more time, and walked out of the shadows, back to the stairs. Rebecca followed him. Just as she reached the bottom of the stairs, and he was at the baize door, it whisked open. Annie was on the other side of it. Rebecca's quick fear that she might have been eavesdropping vanished as soon as she saw her flustered expression and heard her words. "Oh, Mr. Wright. There's an officer here, come all the way from London. He wants to see a Corporal Moore? Rupert Moore? Something about a medal?"

CHAPTER
FIFTY-SIX

The bath chair's wheels trundled along parquet, then were muffled by carpet, then clattered onto marble. Sebastian had learned to distinguish the sounds, had learned to listen more carefully in the past few weeks than he ever had before. That, he thought, was a silver lining. But he couldn't find it in him to appreciate it.

He fought against an urge to shout at the VAD who pushed his chair. To tell her, *I'm not bloody crippled, you know. Just blind.* Yet even though his other injuries were long healed, he had to sit here, a burden, a problem to be moved from one place to another, an object of pity. Powerless. That smarmy staff officer, that Wyndham, who'd spoken over his head to the nurse, his voice dripping with pity the way a wound dripped blood. If he'd had any spirit left, he would have punched the man. Run his bath chair over his foot. The thought brought a half smile to his mouth, a lip jerking upward like a fish on a hook. Not really a smile, but better than nothing, he thought.

Soft footsteps behind him. The swish of a skirt.

"Corporal Moore," the VAD began. Her voice was soft and startled as a butterfly taking flight. They were all so bloody gentle, he thought, and full of pity. "Wouldn't you like to join the other officers in the garden? It is a lovely day."

"No thank you."

"If you like, I could take you on a tour of the house and gardens. We are in—"

"I don't care where we are."

"But—"

"I said I don't care where we are!" He thumped his fist against the arm of his chair, taking a perverse pleasure in hearing her intake of breath and her step back. If they thought he was their pet, they could think again. This lapdog bites. "What the hell is the good of a tour if I can't see a damn thing? If you want to do me a favor, leave me alone. And get everyone else to do the same."

"Sir." Her voice was hurt, and she backed away. The door closed behind her. Sebastian was left alone.

That was a brutish thing to do, he thought. The sun came full on his face; he was facing the window, he guessed. The sound of birdsong and a familiar scent of roses came through the air. There was sense of light and space all around him. They must have put him in a private room. Poor bastard, they probably said, it's the best we can do for him.

I don't want to be pitied, he thought. I want to be treated like a human being.

He knew he wasn't being fair to the nurse, who had only wanted to help. But all he wanted was to be alone. What does the future hold now? He thought. I expect Mother's money could make me comfortable, as they say. But who wants to be comfortable? If Oliver could see me now . . . He winced at the thought. It was too painful. He raised his hands and ran them over the bandages that still covered much of his face. How wounded am I? he wondered. Don't mince words, Sebastian. Am I a monster? Is that what you want to know? Would Oliver turn away in horror from my face? But he never can. I will never see him again. I would not risk the chance that he would see me as a responsibility, as a burden. I may have lost my sight, but I will not be a burden to anyone. I will kill myself rather than be a burden.

A man cleared his throat behind him. Sebastian jumped. He was ashamed at being caught like this, furtively and vainly trying to find out how disfigured he was. No more privacy, ever again, when anyone could sneak up on you without warning. No more safety.

"Who are you and what do you want?" he said roughly.

The man walked toward him. "I am sorry to disturb you, Corporal."

Sebastian guessed from his clipped accents and his neat footsteps that he was an officer.

"I have come to see you directly from London." The man paused. "From His Majesty."

Sebastian was silent for a moment in surprise. The officer hurried on.

"It is my duty—no, my honor and my privilege—to tell you that you have been awarded the Victoria Cross, for your heroic actions in the line of duty. His Majesty will present you with the medal at the palace as soon as you are well enough to travel. I do congratulate you most heartily—"

"A medal?" Sebastian interrupted.

"The Victoria Cross," said the officer, his voice hushed with awe and admiration. "It is more than a medal, Corporal."

"Well, I'm glad for that." Sebastian was shocked at the ease with which he found himself speaking his mind. After all, what did he have to lose? "What else does it do? Does it come with powers of resurrection, perhaps? Restoring sight to the blind?"

"I—"

"Because I don't want a bloody medal. I want my eyes back. I want my mates back. If His Majesty can do that for me, I'll crawl to the palace on my hands and knees if I have to. If he can't, he can go to hell and take his medal with him."

The silence was complete. Even Sebastian could hardly believe what he had just said. Telling the king to go to hell was probably something in the region of high treason, he thought. He might be in the interesting position of being one minute nominated for the country's highest honor and the next being clapped in irons and shut in the Tower.

The officer broke the silence, very carefully, as one would break something of which one wished to preserve every splinter. "I understand your feelings." His voice was soft and quiet. Sebastian was surprised—he hadn't expected as much from him. His respect for the young officer rose somewhat. "I see it is too early, still. I shall take a lodging in the village, and hope to speak to you again in a few days, when you have had time to think."

Sebastian sat, silently, as the man walked away. He heard him pause, close to the door. Then the sound of his voice made it clear that he had turned back.

"We have all lost people. It's hell. There is no bringing them back. But don't throw your life away after theirs, Corporal. If your mates were here today, I'll bet you they would say you deserve that medal, and you should take it. Let's get as much good out of this war as we can."

Then he was gone, the door closing behind him.

Sebastian sat silently, wrapped in thought. The young officer was right. He recognized that. But he had lost so much. His future was so uncertain. He could not look forward until he came to terms with all he had lost.

The birds were singing, and distantly in the fields the lambs bleated. Wind rustled in the branches outside. Sebastian sat back in his chair. He could dream he was sitting here with his eyes closed, that outside, Oliver was waiting for him, that it was summer, and he was back at Somerton.

CHAPTER
FIFTY-SEVEN

Rebecca set the teacups down by the countess's chair, thinking as she did so that it was hardly worth her efforts to move silently and not make a sound by allowing the fine china to rattle on the saucer—not when the thump of heavy footsteps from the billiard room upstairs was so obtrusive. From the expression on the countess's face as she glanced upward, she could tell she was thinking the same thing.

"I know it is all for the war effort, Lord Westlake," she said to Captain Wyndham, who was sitting beside her—here yet *again*, Rebecca thought, in resentment—"but oh dear, it feels positively suffocating to be limited to two rooms downstairs. And wherever one goes, there is the tramp of boots, or some distressing medical smell, or a VAD lost and wandering palely about. You must admit that sharing one's residence with two hundred soldiers is exhausting."

"I would never seek to deny it," Francis replied gravely. "In my view Your Ladyship's sacrifice is nothing short of heroic."

The countess did a good impression of blushing.

"You are generous. I only seek to do my bit, as they say." She paused, then went on in a lower voice, "Lady Georgiana has grand ideas, but she is naïve . . . flighty."

"Oh?" Captain Wyndham said warily.

"Yes, I like the girl well enough, but she is barely out of the nursery . . . hasn't a serious thought in her head."

Rebecca almost spilled the tea in her indignation. The countess went on: "Indeed, both the Averley girls have always been terribly jealous of my Charlotte. I can tell you this because you are family; I am sure you will let it go no further."

"Miss Templeton is nursing at the front, I hear? Admirable." She could hear in Captain Wyndham's words that he was trying to steer a tactful middle course between the rocks of the countess's disapproval and the whirlpool of losing his standing with Lady Georgiana.

"She was, but I have asked her to come back to Somerton. I expect her any day now. Now that we *are* a hospital, what need to go all the way to France to find one? I am sure you will like her very much."

"Indeed," said Captain Wyndham hesitantly.

Rebecca suppressed a smile. She was not unhappy with the countess's plan, despite her annoyance at hearing Lady Georgiana slandered. The man was so clearly a fortune hunter, and Lady Georgiana was . . . well, not anything that the countess said, but she *was* inexperienced, and kindhearted. If Captain Wyndham could be distracted from his pursuit of her, so much the better.

The doorbell jangled, and the countess looked up, startled.

"Who can that be? We are not expecting anyone, are we?"

"No, my lady," said Rebecca. "Shall I go?"

"Thomas can answer it," replied the countess.

"I am afraid he is in Palesbury today, at the dentist."

"Oh really! Very well, do answer it."

Rebecca tidied her cap and apron and opened it, wondering as she did so how Thomas was getting on at his interview. It was a painful thought, and she pushed it away as quickly as she could.

A pretty, blond young lady—certainly a lady—in a dove-gray traveling suit and a black velvet hat adorned with pale pink roses, stood outside. She met Rebecca's eyes with an easy smile, and yet Rebecca thought she looked deeply tired, and not merely from traveling.

"Good day," she said, coming up the stairs confidently. "You must be new. Is my mother, the countess, at home?"

Rebecca took her case, but before she could reply, she heard footsteps behind her. "Charlotte!" the countess fairly gasped, and came rushing to the door. Captain Wyndham was just behind her. The countess held her arms out wide. "My dear girl, why on earth didn't you wire?"

"Oh, Mother, how lovely! I prefer to make my own way nowadays. I have grown used to a certain amount of independence."

Charlotte allowed her mother to embrace her. When she released her, Rebecca was astonished to see tears in the countess's eyes. Charlotte seemed equally surprised. "Poor Mother," she said, "you have had a hard time of it."

"Very hard." The countess's voice quivered, and she spoke in tones so low that Rebecca could hardly hear them. "You don't know what it means to see one of my children safe again."

Charlotte looked both astonished and pleased. Rebecca was touched. Her own family had been so loving and close, it was moving to see how much this little proof of the cold countess's affection meant to her daughter. But the countess had already recovered her poise and stepped aside, revealing Captain Wyndham, who was hovering by the door.

"Well, here is someone you certainly must meet." The countess turned with a flourish to Francis, who seemed wary but prepared to be charming. "The new Earl of Westlake. What a delightful chance that he should be visiting just as you arrive!"

Charlotte began a polite smile, but as Rebecca watched her face the smile vanished—replaced with a look of genuine and extraordinary joy. Rebecca turned instinctively, as did the countess and Francis, to see what had caught her eye. She was looking beyond them, down the corridor to where the door was open onto the ballroom ward, and some soldiers were sitting and standing around, chatting and joking. The sound of rich laughter pealed down the corridor; the scene caught Rebecca's eye like a photograph, white and light and sunny at the end of a dark tunnel.

"Flint," Charlotte said. "Flint!"

She raced down the hall, toward the men. The tall one—the American, with the red-gold curls and the twisted arm—turned in surprise. A moment later Charlotte was in his arms. Rebecca, caught between laughter and horror at the breach of convention, saw their embrace and heard the American exclaiming, "Charlotte! Hey there, beautiful!" Rebecca did not dare look at the countess. The silence was as huge and frosty as an iceberg. Desperately trying not to laugh, she murmured, "Will that be all, my lady?" and dipped a curtsy.

The countess took a moment to answer. "Yes, Rebecca, you may go. And Rebecca . . . I shall expect you to say not a word of Miss Templeton's disgraceful behavior below stairs."

"Of course not, my lady." Rebecca hurried off. The countess was safe. The only person she was likely to want to tell was Thomas—and, she remembered with a sudden pain that took all the laughter out of her, they were perhaps not on such intimate terms as she had imagined, after all.

CHAPTER
FIFTY-EIGHT

"Is there any more news of Alexander?" said Georgiana, as she sat down at the breakfast table.

The silver and china were set out, and the crystal bowls filled with roses. Rebecca made a point of creating a little oasis for the family every morning, away from the bustle of the hospital. Georgiana appreciated it.

Rose sighed. "The hope of leave is still there, but there are no fixed dates yet. And the army are very cagey about where their forces are concentrated—it is a security risk, of course, but it is so hard not to even know where he is. He writes very reassuringly, but I know that he would do that anyway, to spare me. I feel that all the real truth is hidden by the censor's pen."

"Oh, Rose." Georgiana placed a hand on her sister's. "How I wish I could do something to help."

"It is enough simply being here," Rose replied warmly. "I wondered if I was wrong to leave Alexander, even though he was adamant that I should take Edward to safety, but I think I made the right decision. I want Edward to know Somerton, so much. It was my home, and I want him to love it as I do, as we all do."

Georgiana was about to reply, but she looked up to see Captain Wyndham entering the breakfast room. She removed her hand from Rose's, feeling awkward, as if she had been caught talking about Captain Wyndham behind his back.

"Good morning," he greeted them. He seemed in good spirits, but his smile to Rose was forced. Georgiana, searching for a subject to change the conversation to, said, "Has anyone seen Charlotte? I hoped she would be down for breakfast."

Rose made an expressive face. "She is still in disgrace. I think the countess is keeping her upstairs for a stern talking-to."

"I think she is quite right to do so," Captain Wyndham said, as he buttered his toast. "Of course, her nursing is admirable, but perhaps it has encouraged her to become a little too, shall we say, informal in her relations with the other sex. Men don't like such behavior, you know. They may encourage it in a girl, but they will never marry where respect is lost."

Georgiana looked at him in surprise. She was sorry to notice that she felt distinctly less liking for him after his little speech. Rose caught her glance and hid a smile behind a raised teacup.

"I do not know what men in general may feel," Georgiana said, "but I thought he seemed delighted to see her. I don't see why he shouldn't marry her. Of course the countess will not approve of it, but if he has his own means—"

"A very big if," Captain Wyndham said, with a tone that was close to a sneer. "I understand the man is a penniless cowboy. I suppose since she has the manners of a cowgirl, they may suit."

Georgiana blushed with annoyance. "I'd be glad if you would not speak about my sister that way."

"I beg your pardon." Captain Wyndham looked startled. "I understood you were not on the best of terms."

"We have not been," Georgiana said as politely as she could, "but we hope to be on better terms—and besides, I don't want to hear her maligned for something as innocent as falling in love and having the heart to show it."

"No, of course. You misunderstood me. I—"

"Kearney is free!" Rose exclaimed. She was still holding the newspaper, and she looked up over it, eyes wide.

"Free!" Georgiana exclaimed. "Are you sure?"

"Yes, it says so here. He was cleared of all charges."

"How dreadful!" Captain Wyndham leapt into the conversation, trying to echo the tone of their voices. "I find it quite incredible that this government is prepared to allow a known firebrand like that to go free."

There was an awkward silence. Georgiana could not find words to express her indignation. Clearly, he had mistaken their excitement for shocked disapproval. Finally, she managed to say, as calmly as possible: "Captain Wyndham, as it happens, my sister, Lady Ada, has been instrumental in the legal defense of Mr. Kearney. I understand you do not approve?"

Captain Wyndham looked completely crushed. Georgiana was not happy. She hated losing her temper, and hated losing respect for anyone. Luckily, at that moment a voice said, "Good morning, everyone," and all looked up as Charlotte entered the room. She was dressed in her VAD uniform.

"Charlotte!" Rose exclaimed. "I thought the countess had ordered you to stay upstairs."

"Oh, she did," Charlotte said, smilingly taking an apple from the sideboard and sitting down to the table. She sliced it delicately into pieces. "But I feel that it is my duty to continue to help while I am here. After all, that is what she called me home for. So I shall begin this morning."

Georgiana and Rose exchanged a glance. Charlotte had certainly been changed by her time abroad—and for the better.

CHAPTER
FIFTY-NINE

Rebecca stifled a yawn as she reached up to lock and bolt the back door. Outside, the night was black as velvet. Upstairs, she could still hear the floorboards creak as restless patients stirred. There was no silence in the house anymore, she thought. Before, it had seemed full enough, with staff and when the family were all at home, but now there wasn't a still moment. There was no ignoring the war anymore, no hoping it would go away. The war was here, all around them, in these missing limbs, in these ruined faces and broken minds. She pushed the sad thoughts away. At least the kitchen was spotless; everything was running well. She went to the door, pausing only to tidy away an apron that one of the maids had left on the table.

"Rebecca, could I speak to you before you go up?"

It was Thomas's voice. Rebecca could see him, sitting by the light of a single gas lamp, in his pantry. Her heart skipped a beat. He had said nothing about the interview; there had been far too much for them to do, on his return, for her to find a moment to ask him how it had gone. Besides, she thought, crossing the corridor to him, she was not sure she wanted to know. She wanted him to get it, of course—but she didn't want what it would mean, him leaving Somerton.

"Please sit down." He got to his feet as she entered, and drew out a chair for her. Rebecca sat, aware that he seemed both nervous and excited.

"What is it?" she asked.

"I wanted to tell you." He drew his chair close to her, and said in a low voice, "I got the job."

"Oh!" Rebecca didn't know whether the exclamation was of joy or pain. "I—I congratulate you."

"I can't leave until they've found a replacement, of course. I've told them that. But it's a dream come true."

"I am so happy for you." Rebecca spoke fiercely, angry with herself for not being more certain that she was pleased for him. Thomas deserved everything good, of course he did, and if he didn't love her back—well, you couldn't force love. That, at least, was how she knew she had to think. "We will miss you very much here at Somerton, but I'm sure—"

"Wait," he interrupted her. He reached out and took her hand. Rebecca was startled. He pressed her hand, looked into her eyes. "I hadn't finished."

Rebecca was silent, wondering what he could be going to say.

"I don't want you to miss me. Indeed, I don't want to be apart from you. The job pays enough to support both of us. Will you marry me, Rebecca? Will you come with me?"

Rebecca was silent, in shock. He hurried on.

"I know this may come as a surprise. I'm not one to speak my feelings, and I know we—I know we've always had a very professional relationship, but I do feel that there's something there between us. Well, there is for me. I think you're the most beautiful girl I've ever seen, the most intelligent, and the kindest. I wouldn't be happy without you, and that's a fact. And I . . . I've sometimes thought that you might like me too." He hesitated. "Am I wrong?"

Rebecca still couldn't find the breath to reply. Tears were running down her cheeks.

"I'm wrong, aren't I?" Thomas's voice was loaded with disappointment. He sat back, relaxing his grip on her hand. Rebecca, startled into action, caught his hand again.

"No. Oh no! You're not wrong," she sobbed.

Thomas looked at her in astonishment, and then pulled her toward him and kissed her. Rebecca tasted tears as they kissed. She could not stop crying.

"So it's a yes, then," he said finally, releasing her.

She shook her head. She was still crying, but now it was not from joy. "Mr. Wright. Thomas. I do love you. I want to marry you. But I can't leave Somerton. Not now."

"Not leave Somerton? But—"

"It's not that I care for you less than I care for this house. I don't. But all my life, I've wanted to do work that I'm good at. I know I'm good at this, and I love it here, what's more. I'll never find a job I love so much if I look all over the world. I don't want to be just someone's wife, even if I get to live in more comfort. I want to do what I'm good at. I'm so happy here, you see. I am sorry. I don't suppose you understand, but I can't marry you if it means leaving Somerton."

"I do understand," he said after a long pause. "I do. It's only what I feel myself, after all."

"I am sorry." She dried her tears. "I can hardly believe I'm saying this, doing this—throwing such a good man away." She almost started crying again at the thought of it.

"Dry your eyes," he said gently. He reached up and touched her tears away. "It's not the right time, is it?"

She shook her head.

"Well, one day it will be. That's what I believe. I'll wait for you, Rebecca. I may be on the other side of the world, but I'll wait for you—if you'll wait for me."

"Of course I will," said Rebecca. This time there were no tears as they moved together to kiss.

CHAPTER
SIXTY

Sebastian lay in bed, propped up on pillows. The morphine always wore off early and left him to wake in pain. The thoughts that accompanied his waking were even more painful.

There was a gentle knock at the door. That would be the nurse, come to change his bandages. Sebastian hated this part of the day. In the silence of the nurses he always suspected disgust. He was too proud to ask if he was disfigured. He didn't want them to think he cared. He wished the woman would go away, but he knew that if he did not answer, she would think he was seriously ill and come in anyway.

"Come in," he said heavily.

The door opened, and he heard her coming across the room toward him.

"Good morning," she said. There was the sound of curtains opening, and white light flooded his vision. He turned away from it. "I have come to change your bandages."

Sebastian did not reply. Her voice reminded him distressingly of Charlotte's. So much here was like Somerton, as a church bell's echo might remind him of the bells near where he was born. But it was a more pleasant voice than Charlotte's, he thought. It did not sound as bitter and sarcastic as hers always did.

"Would you like to get up?"

"Into that bloody chair? No thanks."

"I thought you might like to walk around."

He laughed. "I expect they value their ornaments too much for that."

There was a confused silence in response. He was sure she was staring at him; he almost felt the weight of it.

"Have we . . ." The girl seemed to shrug off her confusion. "Never mind. I have a cane for you, and it would be good for you to begin learning your way around." When he did not answer, she went on. "You will not always be so immobile. In time, some sight may even return."

This was the first time that Sebastian had heard this. He did not reply. He did not want the hope she offered. But he did sit up, and swing his legs so he was sitting on the edge of the bed. He heard the nurse preparing the bandages and the swabs. A moment later, her gentle fingers began unwrapping the bandages.

"I understand you have been awarded the Victoria Cross," she said as she worked. "I congratulate you."

Sebastian did not reply.

"It's hell out there. I know. But you made it back." Her voice was soft and soothing. And he had a strange feeling of déjà vu, as the nurse gently continued unwrapping the bandages, peeling them away so the light grew stronger and stronger . . .

The last ribbon of bandage fell away. There was a split second of silence, and then she gasped.

"Is it that bad?" Sebastian said savagely. He hated her for showing her shock and horror. None of the other nurses had done that.

He heard her breathing, ragged, and a black pit of fear sank inside him. It was worse than he had thought. So there was no hope with Oliver; he could not ask him to come back to someone who was helpless and hideous to boot—

"Sebastian," she whispered.

His name ran through him like a sword.

"Sebastian. It's me. Charlotte. Your sister."

"Charlotte? But how—" Sebastian was thunderstruck. Charlotte nursing?

"You're at Somerton," she went on. "Did you not know?"

"Somerton!"

"They converted it into the hospital. The earl is dead. Oh, Sebastian! How could this happen? Mother, she thinks you're dead. She—"

Sebastian reached out, fast as lightning, and grasped her wrist, guessing where it would be and guessing right. He heard her gasp again, this time in pain. His mind whirled; of all the luck, to end up at Somerton! The one place where people would recognize him.

"Tell no one," he managed. "I don't want anyone to know."

"But—"

"I don't want to be anyone's burden! I don't want the pity. I just want to disappear. Charlotte, promise me."

"Sebastian—"

"Promise me!"

"Sebastian, Mother loves you. *I* love you. You can't ask me to keep this a secret. You can't. You are wrong about this. Please believe me."

"If you love me, you'll do what I tell you. Promise!"

"I—very well, I promise!"

He heard a sob in her voice and released her wrist. "Now put the bandages back on," he said quietly.

He sat in silence as she bandaged him once again, her hands trembling. He felt her tears falling on his skin. Inside him was a whirlwind. He did not want anyone from the old days to see him like this, did not want to be a burden, did not want to spend his life being wheeled here and there. And yet the thought of his mother's feelings . . . She did love him. He knew it was the truth.

Finally the bandaging was done. Charlotte straightened up. "Our mother thinks she has lost you, and it has broken her heart," she said. "Please, Sebastian, I beg you to change your mind."

He did not reply. After a long time she turned and went out. He heard the door close behind her and was alone again.

CHAPTER
SIXTY-ONE

The motorcar glided down the long drive Somerton. Ada looked out at the trees that lined the path, the sweeping green lawns, the distant hills dotted with sheep. Opposite her sat Connor Kearney and Mr. Bradford. In her hand she held a large envelope. It was strange to think that what was in the envelope would determine the fate of this great house they were approaching. She felt triumph, but it was not a pleasant feeling. She would rather not have had this journey to make. As dearly as she loved Somerton, she had begun to feel that for her, it meant the past. She would spend the summer at Somerton, but she would always feel that her life was elsewhere, and until she could have the independence that Hannah had, she knew she would not be satisfied.

"You have been to Somerton before, Mr. Kearney?" Mr.

Bradford spoke to him over the noise of the engine. He had been very deferential to Connor—almost awestruck, Ada thought with amusement. The man's reputation preceded him.

"Once only. It is a beautiful place," Connor replied. "I'm sorry that I am not returning for a more pleasant reason."

Ada smiled at him teasingly. "Liar," she murmured.

"I beg your pardon, Lady Ada," Mr. Bradford said, sounding shocked.

"Indeed he is. Mr. Kearney loves a confrontation, don't you? I expect you have been looking forward to this for days."

Connor's amused glance told her she was right. The chauffeur drew the motorcar up in front of the grand entrance, and Thomas, smiling, came down to open the door for them.

"Good morning, my lady. Welcome home," he greeted her as she stepped out.

"Thank you," Ada murmured. Sudden memories of being here with Ravi caught her heart. Gathering her composure, she walked up the wide stone steps and into the house.

"Ada!" Everything else was forgotten as she heard Rose's voice. She looked up to see her on the landing, framed by the shining window, as beautiful as ever, beaming with joy and holding a bundle wrapped in a white lace blanket.

"Rose!" Ada ran up the stairs and into her sister's arms. She came to a halt, speechless with delight and admiration as she saw the little face and fists poking up from the blanket at her. "Oh, Rose, he's perfect! He has Alexander's eyes, I can see them at once—and isn't that the perfect grip to hold a paintbrush with?"

She kissed Rose on the cheek. "I can see we have so much to talk about. Well, I shall be here for the summer, so there is plenty of time."

"I am so happy to see you!" The tears in Rose's eyes underlined her words. She walked downstairs with Ada by her side. "Come in here—it is the last drawing room left to us. The soldiers have occupied everything else."

"May I present Mr. Kearney," Ada said quickly, "and of course you know Mr. Bradford." She almost wished both men were not there; all she wanted was to hear Rose's story. Georgiana had given her the outline of it, but she longed to hear it from Rose's own lips.

Rose smiled at both the men. She took a seat on the sofa and Ada sat down beside her, cooing over baby Edward in delight. "My first nephew! I promise to spoil you beyond belief," she said to him. "But tell me Rose, when will we see Alexander?"

"Soon, I hope." Rose's face showed her emotion. "I have just heard that he has finally been granted home leave. He should be here in late July, though the transport makes so much unsure."

"What a blessed relief!" Ada took Rose's hand. "Oh, you must have gone through so much. And with a baby!"

"I could not have done it without Noor," said Rose. "She is my maid; I engaged her in Cairo. She discovered I was to have a baby before I even knew it myself. Once I knew that, I felt I could not leave Alexander, that I was not prepared to risk that he should die without seeing his child." Her voice trembled. "So when he was dispatched, I used all my influence to make the general bring us along too. Luckily he was a keen amateur musician and he had heard some of my compositions, so he was sympathetic. I am glad I did not know the hardship we should go through, or I might not have dared to undertake the journey. And I am so glad that I did, because now at least I know that Alexander has seen his little boy." She stopped talking, clearly close to tears. Ada pressed her hands; there were no words that could express her feelings. She knew what risks Alexander faced. It was impossible to ignore the facts: young men were dying in the hundreds every day.

"Your courage is formidable," said Connor, his serious gaze on Rose. "But how did you make your way home?"

"Once Edward was born, Alexander became very concerned for his safety. There was a passage on a boat that could take us to Italy. Alexander begged me to go. So to oblige him, I took it. But the ship was torpedoed and we were shipwrecked "

"Oh, Rose!" Ada exclaimed. Rose paused only briefly before going on, with just the merest tremble in her voice.

"We were lucky to be rescued by a British vessel. The captain was heading to the Eastern Mediterranean but took an interest in us and helped us get ashore at Spain, which is neutral, of course—and then we traveled overland. Luckily, Noor speaks some Spanish, and we were able to get to the British ambassador's residence, and he arranged travel for us to England." She fell silent, clearly exhausted by the memory.

"My poor Rose." Ada embraced her. "I am almost relieved we did not know at the time what was happening; I would have been petrified with fear."

Rose smiled wanly. "I am glad, in a way, that I have experienced it. I feel I know better what the people displaced by this war are suffering. And we were as close to Alexander as we possibly could be, for as long as possible, and I am . . . I am grateful for that."

"Oh, Rose." Ada pressed her hand again, wanting to say that she was sure he would be safe. But she knew that nothing was guaranteed.

She heard running footsteps coming closer, along the corridor. She looked up, and Georgiana burst into the room, followed by Michael.

"Ada!" Georgiana came to kneel by her. "What a pleasure to see you, and to know we have you for some time. Your room is all prepared. And Mr. Kearney—my sincere congratulations on your victory. Michael, be a dear and ring for some tea, will you?"

"Michael," said Ada, remembering what she was here for, "will you ask your mother to come also? And Captain Wyndham. I presume he is visiting?" She glanced at Connor, who agreed with a slight nod.

"Is this about the will?" Rose looked up, wide-eyed. "I was sorry to hear that it had caused tension. I have been so concerned with little Edward, and with writing to Alexander, that I have not really been following—" She broke off as Rebecca entered.

"Rebecca, please ask the countess and Captain Wyndham to come here," Michael told her. After she had gone, he turned back to Ada. "So you have found something out, Ada? What is it?"

"I would rather not say until Captain Wyndham has a chance to answer me face to face," Ada replied. She glanced at Georgiana, whose expression was hard to read. She looked pained and concerned, but softhearted Georgiana would feel the same for anyone, Ada thought, who was in trouble. It did not mean she had lost her heart.

She looked up as she heard the countess's authoritative tread coming down the corridor. Everyone was silent as Rebecca opened the door for her and, with a quick curtsy, backed out again.

"What is the urgency?" The countess looked around. "Goodness, I see everyone is assembled." She looked at Connor and raised an enquiring eyebrow. "Directly from the Old Bailey, Mr. Kearney?"

"And most refreshed by the experience, thank you for asking, Lady Westlake," Connor said with a grin. The countess pursed her lips.

Ada noticed a shadow at the door and looked up. Francis Wyndham stood there. There was a sullen expression on his face. At last we are seeing the truth, thought Ada.

"Captain Wyndham, please do come in, and close the door if you would be so good," she said pleasantly. "May I present Mr. Connor Kearney."

Captain Wyndham hesitated, and then did as she had said. He was clearly reluctant to be there. He gave Connor the briefest of unsmiling nods.

Ada cleared her throat and got to her feet. The folder was

still in her hands; she held it carefully. She did not have a court-room, but she would make the most of the drawing room at her disposal.

"Captain Wyndham," she said, with her most pleasant smile, "I fear you have not told us the whole truth."

CHAPTER
SIXTY-TWO

Charlotte gently removed the last bandage from Sebastian's eyes. The room was quite silent, only the drip of water into the basin as she wrung out the cloth. The light came through the windows, and the muslin curtains stirred in the summer breeze. It was so pure white that it seemed blinding.

Carefully she cleaned his eyes. The blue was clouded, the skin around the eyes reddened and puckered here and there with scarring. Sometimes cases of gas blindness regained their sight. Charlotte knew that was true. But she also knew it was nothing to count on.

Sebastian was still as a statue, gazing sightlessly ahead of him. He did not flinch when she wiped his eyes. At least, she thought, he could go without the bandages now. The cane that the officer had brought still leaned by the door, untouched.

"There," she said quietly. She got to her feet and went to the door and opened it.

Flint was outside, just as she had asked him to be.

"Is he here?" she whispered. She was shaking. Was she doing the right thing? Would this end well or not?

"I'm here," said a voice from the shadows. Oliver stepped forward. He looked different in uniform. Older, more serious.

Flint pulled him forward. "Go on in, pal," he whispered.

Oliver hung back. "Miss Templeton, I still don't know why I'm here—"

"Go in!" Charlotte pushed him through the door and shut it behind him. She looked at Flint wordlessly. Flint caught her hands and held them comfortingly.

"Come on, let's get out of here," he murmured.

"What if it goes horribly wrong? What if . . ." Charlotte murmured as he led her down the corridor, toward the garden room.

"Then you've done your best, and you can't do any more."

"But was I right to telegraph him? Do you think I was right?"

"Yes, I do." Flint put an arm around her and turned her to face him. "Charlotte—Nurse Templeton—you're always right. That's one of the things I like about you."

"Not always." Charlotte smiled, remembering some of the many times she had not been right.

"Well, you are when you're listening to your heart, and that's what counts." His smile lit his eyes.

Charlotte couldn't help smiling back.

"Listen, I think I owe you an explanation," Flint went on, seriously. "You must be wondering why I haven't come up to scratch. I mean, why I haven't asked for your hand."

"I . . ." Charlotte realized that she had been wondering no such thing. She had expected that he would propose, certainly. But she had not been wondering why he had not. She had not had time.

"It's unforgivable of me, I know. I'm not one of your English gentlemen, but I hope I am a gentleman where it counts, and I know I should have said something by now. The thing is," he sounded embarrassed, "I didn't expect to find you living here. I suppose I should have known you were from an upper-class family, but accents and so on don't mean much to an American, I'm afraid."

"That's not important," said Charlotte, and was surprised to find she meant it.

"It took me so long to write because I was ashamed—hell, *ashamed* is the wrong word—but I didn't like to think you'd see my writing and see what an uneducated man I am. I do some things well in this world, but composing a letter ain't one of them. That's not the kind of schooling I've had."

"I—"

"The truth is, I don't see how I can ask you to marry me. Not looking around at this place, not seeing how you live. I have nothing to offer you, just a life that's harder than any you've lived before."

"Harder than on the front?"

"In some ways, yes. Poverty is different than war."

"But you won't be poor. You're drawing a captain's pay."

"And what's that compared to what you're used to?"

"Flint, I have plenty of money!"

"That's exactly it. I don't want to be seen as some kind of fortune hunter. I can't ask you to marry me until I have something to offer you that's as good as what you're used to!"

"So I should wait until you have risen to brigadier general in command of the Royal Flying Corps?" Charlotte could hardly stop herself from smiling. "If the war lasts long enough, I quite believe you could do it."

"Don't make fun of me, Charlotte. I didn't think you would do that."

"I'm sorry—but, darling, you are so amusing. You have put your case quite clearly, so I had better do the same, hadn't I?" She paused and went on. "The simple fact is, I am not going to be denied the love of my life because of your scruples. I have waited a long time for happiness, and I am not going to give it up when I find it. I understand that you can't propose. I do respect your position. So, I shall make things easier for you." She stepped closer to him and put a hand on his shoulder and whispered in his ear. "I am quite determined to marry you, Captain MacAllister. I shall marry you, and live in a tent, or a hovel, or whatever you prefer, and clean and cook and all the rest of it, and be quite common and perfectly happy, on a single condition—that I see your smile every day."

"Charlotte—"

"Do you understand now? *I* am proposing to *you*. What about it, pal?" She couldn't stop her smile now. "And I warn you that if you refuse, I shall simply follow you about in the most disgracefully abandoned fashion, until you, as a gentleman, have no choice but to make an honest woman of me. Is that clear? What do you say?"

Flint had been staring at her in astonishment, a huge smile breaking across his face. Now he burst out laughing, and took her in his arms. "Ain't got much choice, do I?" he said, and the tenderness in his voice told Charlotte that if she'd needed any confirmation that she'd made the right decision, this was it.

CHAPTER
SIXTY-THREE

"Who's there?" said Sebastian.

He cocked his head, listening. Charlotte had gone out, and someone had come in. He didn't know who. The person, whoever it was, had not spoken or moved. A stab of unease hit him—or not unease, exactly, but something that shortened his breath. A kind of wild happiness, without reason, like a child waking early on the first day of the holidays, not yet remembering why he was so excited.

"Who's there?" he said again, and a sudden fear that he would be disappointed made his voice sharp.

The person at the door made a slight movement toward him. It was at that second that Sebastian knew. Of course he didn't need to see Oliver to know it was him. Just the rhythm of his breathing, a sound so beloved and familiar, a sound he had dreamed of, imagined, longed for, throughout his time in the trenches, told him who it was. He automatically put a hand to his face to hide himself, sick at the thought of Oliver seeing him like this. Then there were running footsteps, and Oliver reached him. His arms were around him; he was on his knees before him, sobbing. Sebastian reached out despite himself to touch Oliver's soft curly hair. How he had longed for that touch, that sweet smell.

"Sebastian—" Oliver gasped through his tears. "Thank God. I thought I had lost you." Still kneeling at his feet, he took Sebastian's hands and covered them in kisses.

Sebastian lingered for a delicious, beautiful moment, then forced himself to pull his hands away. He had to be strong. He could not allow himself to give in to this wonderful temptation. "I can't," he said. "You shouldn't be here."

In answer, Oliver reached up and drew him down into a kiss so long and passionate that Sebastian lost all his breath, all his resolutions not to be a burden. For a long time they only kissed, and Sebastian did not try to fight it. He knew that he was not strong enough to resist this.

Finally he gained the strength to draw back. He felt Oliver's fingers caressing his hair, stroking the puckered skin around his sightless eyes. He tried to fight down the happiness that was threatening to overwhelm him. "You shouldn't have come," he repeated. "This is impossible."

Oliver gently kissed his mouth again. "Don't keep saying that."

"She shouldn't have called you."

"Of course she should. You don't know how hard I've tried to find you. I never imagined you'd gone into the ranks." His gentle fingers traced Sebastian's eyes. "Your beautiful eyes. Do they hurt you?"

"No." Sebastian cringed inside himself. "But you must find me repulsive now."

"Do you really think so?"

Sebastian was silenced by the weight of warmth and love and reproach that was in his voice.

"I don't want to be a burden," he said. "Not to you, not to anyone."

"A burden? Sebastian, finding you again has lifted the only burden I was carrying."

"But I don't want you to give your life to looking after me."

"That is exactly what I want to do. And I want you to look after me, too. That is what we should do, just as you said—and I was too proud and silly to know what a treasure you were."

"What do you mean?"

"We'll live together. We'll live in retirement. No one will suspect I am anything other than your servant. One day this war will be over, Sebastian, and when it is, the world will be a better place. Nothing will be the same, and perhaps things will be easier. But even if they are not, we will make it work. Whatever the future holds, I know we can face it—together."

Sebastian touched the khaki of Oliver's shirt, his rough braid. He did not reply. He knew that Oliver was giving him the best thing he could ever have hoped for. It was only a tragedy that it had taken a war to realize it.

Oliver's kisses touched his hair. He turned his face up to them. This was how a dying flower must feel, he thought, when the rain, finally, falls.

CHAPTER
SIXTY-FOUR

"I do not understand your insinuations, Lady Ada, but I feel they are in the worst possible taste." Captain Wyndham's voice was raised. Ada saw Georgiana wince and glance at the door. It would not be good for the servants to overhear this scene.

"I think Lady Ada is quite clear. The document you produced to support your claim that the estate was entailed was a forgery." Connor's voice was cold and calm.

"Nonsense," Captain Wyndham blustered. "It is an old document—"

"It does look old, certainly. There are people who can do that, for a price."

"I don't see how you can know—"

"Captain Wyndham, I've dealt with matters like this before."

Connor's voice was full of cold contempt. "The clues are easy to see, especially when left by a bungler. You might have paid more money and got a more convincing forgery."

"I cannot believe it of you, sir," Mr. Bradford spoke up. "And for Lady Georgiana's sake in particular—I could not be more saddened."

"Why?" said Ada sharply, at the same instant that Georgiana said. "Oh? Why for me, Mr. Bradford? That is, I thank you, but—"

"Well, your engagement . . . I expect things can hardly be the same now?"

Georgiana looked back and forth between Captain Wyndham and Mr. Bradford. Captain Wyndham was by now looking extremely red in the face, Ada was intrigued to see.

"I am not engaged to Captain Wyndham," Georgiana said, her eyes wide.

"Oh!" Mr. Bradford exclaimed. "But the earl gave me to understand—"

"And you advanced him money from the estate on the basis of it," Connor interrupted with a sarcastic smile. "Of course. *Châpeau*, Captain Wyndham, you think of everything. Have you done this before?"

"Not very much money." Mr. Bradford blushed.

"Well, let us be thankful for small mercies," Ada said dryly.

"I don't understand." The countess put a hand to her forehead. "But I am sure that if this is true, Captain Wyndham can have had no idea that his lawyer was mistaken."

"Unfortunately, a letter written in his hand would seem to

suggest otherwise," Connor said. He took a sheet of paper from the folder and held it up so that everyone could see the bold signature: *F. Wyndham.*

"I am sure Captain Wyndham has an explanation," Georgiana said, looking at him. Ada wondered how anyone could have the heart to betray her trust. Captain Wyndham seemed to feel it too, because his eyes flickered, and for the first time in the conversation Ada thought he looked ashamed.

"I shall need to consult my lawyer," he mumbled.

"Let me tell you what you will do," said Ada, finally losing patience. "You will sit down here, now, at this writing desk, and write a letter that explains that you understand the document you based your claim to Somerton on was a forgery. You therefore withdraw all your claim to the property."

"And you will leave it at that?"

"I do not want my late father's title dragged through the mud." Ada glanced around at her sisters and the countess. All of them nodded agreement.

Captain Wyndham took a deep breath. Ada watched him carefully, sure that his mind was working very hard beneath the smooth exterior and seeking the best way out of this situation.

"Of course I have no desire to profit from my lawyer's roguery," said Captain Wyndham finally. He bared his teeth in a smile. "He has been a servant of our family a long time, and no doubt he thought I would approve of his action. But I am prepared to take your word as a gentleman, Mr. Kearney, that this document is not what I believed it to be."

"Mr. Kearney's word, and the proof of your letter!" Ada exclaimed, furious at the way he so coolly seemed to be shrugging off the guilt.

Captain Wyndham crossed the room to the escritoire, sat down, and glanced at her with a knowing smile. "Letters can be misinterpreted. I might have been writing to him on quite a different matter."

Ada was breathless with indignation, but she caught Connor's glance and swallowed it down. *You have won your case,* his eyes said. *Do not undo the good work by losing control of yourself.*

There was silence except for the pen scratching across the paper. Finally Captain Wyndham rose and handed the letter to Ada. "Will this do?" he inquired with a sarcastic smile.

Ada read the letter. It seemed plain, but she passed it to Connor. He read it too, and indicated approval with a brief nod.

"Very well. I shall take my leave. Lady Ada. Mr. Kearney."

Ada acknowledged his bow with the frostiest tilt of her head. Connor was a little more generous.

Captain Wyndham turned to the countess with the same sarcastic smile. "I shall not expect to be invited here again soon, Lady Westlake. I thank you for your hospitality. Lady Rose, I wish we had known each other better; I do hope your husband survives the war. And Lady Georgiana—"

"Don't push your luck," Michael said between his teeth.

Captain Wyndham hesitated, his smile died, and he darted for the door. Ada was not surprised; the look on Michael's face was enough to make any man turn tail and run.

"Well," said Rose, with a sigh of relief, as they watched Francis's car roll off down the drive. "At last that is over."

"To think I was encouraging Charlotte to marry him! I think he got off too easily," the countess said.

"But how could we do more against him? We could not involve the police."

"Oh goodness, no. The newspapers would be full of it."

"Let us simply be thankful that Lady Ada's intelligent research has paid off," Connor said. "He may be Earl of Westlake, but he will never be master of Somerton. And even an earl can be blackballed at his club." He raised an eyebrow.

"You can arrange that, I suppose?" Michael looked at him in amused admiration. "You seem to be able to arrange anything."

"But you are not going," Georgiana exclaimed. "You must stay, Mr. Kearney."

"Thank you, but I must get back to Oxford," Connor said. "I have some business still to tidy up, in preparation for the new term."

"So odd to think of teaching and learning still going on, as if there were no war," Georgiana said with a sigh, as they walked down the stairs to the waiting motor car.

"But life does go on. Isn't that what we are fighting for?" Ada smiled at her sister as Connor got into the car.

"It goes on, but not unchanged, I fear," Georgiana replied.

Ada touched her sister's hand lovingly. From the car, the familiar smell of warm wood and leather, and the aromatic scent of Connor's cigar, wreathed her.

"Good-bye, Connor," she said. Georgiana echoed her farewell.

Connor, inside the car, raised his hand in farewell. "Good-bye, Lady Ada. Good-bye, Lady Georgiana. Until the next time we meet."

He knocked on the partition, signaling his chauffeur to drive on. The car moved slowly away, crunching across the gravel.

Ada watched it go.

"All things change," she said to Georgiana. "But perhaps some of the changes will be for the better."

CHAPTER
SIXTY-FIVE

Charlotte held Flint's hand tight and peeped around the edge of the door. Ada and her visitors had left the room, and so, it seemed, had Captain Wyndham. She guessed that something big had occurred, but she could not settle her mind on anything until she had done what she knew she had to do. The countess was sitting by the window, silent and clearly lost in thought. The evening light was unforgiving; for the first time, Charlotte thought of her mother as a woman on the brink of old age—for the first time, she felt sorry for her.

Flint pulled her back as she was about to speak. "Are you sure about this?" he whispered. "Because, from what I've seen of Her Majesty, I don't think she'll be rolling out the red carpet for me."

Charlotte smiled. "I'm sure," she replied in the same whisper. "We have to let her know, and the sooner the better."

She stepped through the door and cleared her throat. "Mother, may I speak to you for a moment?"

Her mother looked up and saw Flint, and Charlotte saw her expression sink into long-suffering exhaustion. "I expect I am not going to like what I hear," she said, rising to her feet.

"That's exactly what I told her, ma'am, but she wouldn't listen," Flint said wryly.

"I don't believe we have been introduced, Mr. . . ."

"No, but I'm guessing you have some idea of who I am, given that you saw your daughter jump into my arms like a cat off of hot coals, just a few days ago."

"That is not the same thing as a formal introduction," the countess said frostily.

"Mother, that's exactly it. That's exactly why I'm here, now," Charlotte broke in, before things could get out of hand. "You see, I know that wasn't the best introduction, and I'm sorry. But I want to introduce him properly now. This is Captain MacAllister. He is an American, but he has been heroic in his defense of England, flying with the RFC. In fact, he is to receive the Military Cross."

"That is admirable, but does it make him a gentleman?" the countess replied.

"I don't give a damn if it does or not," Flint said. "I don't aspire to be a gentleman. As far as I can see, it means not being able to dress yourself or speak to any fellow unless you've been introduced to him first. Ma'am, if the world went on like that, nothing would get done at all. I figure the world needs some commoners like me to keep it turning."

Charlotte stifled a smile at her mother's expression.

"Mother, I know you're not going to like it. I know you have invested a good deal in my successful marriage, and I understand how disappointed you must be. But I love Flint, and I am going to marry him."

"I see! Well, your fortune is yours in your own right, from your father, once you are thirty. But that is a long time to live in poverty."

"I don't think of it as poverty. I can work and so can Flint. His arm only keeps him from flying, not from doing an honest day's work."

"I never thought I would hear you say this, Charlotte."

"Neither did I," said Charlotte softly. "But I am saying it. And it's what I want. Flint makes me happy, and that is all I really need." She took his hand. "Mother, I wish I could make you happy too. I am sorry that I've been such a . . . such a disappointment." Her eyes filled with tears she hadn't been expecting. "I know you wanted a great marriage for me, and I'm sorry." She managed a smile, through her tears. "I think Flint and I *will* have a great marriage—perhaps not in the world's eyes, but in our own. Can you forgive me?"

Her mother sighed. "Oh, Charlotte. I love all my children, though perhaps I haven't shown it well." Her voice trembled. "Yet Michael does not trust me, and Sebastian is gone—" She stopped abruptly, and Charlotte heard tears in her voice. "I can't bear to be estranged from you also. I will not prevent you from this marriage, though I think you will regret it."

"Ma'am," said Flint abruptly, "Charlotte has something else to tell you. Something that will put a smile on your face, I promise."

Charlotte looked at him swiftly. She was not sure that this was the right thing to do. Sebastian had been so clear. But another look at her mother's face told her that Flint was right.

"Oh?" The countess recovered some of her poise. "May I ask what?"

"Mother," Charlotte said, taking her hand and leading her to the sofa, "I want you to sit down next to me. This may come as a shock . . ."

CHAPTER
SIXTY-SIX

PALESBURY

The train whistled and steam filled the platform, drowning the bright red geraniums planted in tubs, the stationmaster's raised flag, and the polished sign that read *Palesbury*. Georgiana waved her handkerchief as the engine picked up speed and chuffed away into the distance, leaving behind a few soldiers, kit bags in hand, and ordinary travelers with cases to make their way to the station exit.

"So," Georgiana said with a small sigh, turning to Rebecca and Rose. "Thomas is gone."

"He'll be back, my lady." Rebecca smiled through her tears.

Rose took Rebecca's hand and gave it a kind squeeze. "I know how hard it is to be parted from someone you love," she said.

"It is hard," Rebecca said, "but I know I made the right decision. I don't want to leave Somerton, not now."

"We are glad to hear it," Georgiana said. "We wouldn't lose you for the world—not till Thomas comes back to claim his prize, that is."

"Thank you, my lady. It means a lot to hear you say that. Now, if you'll excuse me, I really should be getting back up to the house." Rebecca smiled and turned away to get her bicycle, which was leaning by the railing. Georgiana watched her go. Rebecca paused only to flutter her fingers to baby Edward, who was on Noor's lap in the motorcar, looking out of the window with wide eyes. Noor waved his hand back to her as she bicycled away along the shady lane, toward Somerton.

"How sweet he is," Georgiana said with a smile. "To think what those eyes have seen already, and yet I expect he looks at Palesbury Station with the same wonder with which he looked at the Pyramids."

Rose laughed. "Yes, he is a joy. I wonder if he will recognize Alexander? I suppose not, but I can't help hoping he will." She added in sudden anxiety. "Oh, I do hope nothing is wrong. His train is late, I'm sure."

"I believe it's just the station clock," Georgiana said. "Don't fret, Rose; I am sure the train will be here soon. We should cross to the other platform."

They walked over the bridge together, to the platform where the train from London would arrive. Soon after they reached it, the bell on the platform rang. Rose gasped, and caught hold of Georgiana's arm.

"I'm so silly—forgive me. I don't know why I'm nervous," she said with a slight laugh. "It is just to think how he may have changed . . ."

"You are thinking of Sebastian, I know."

"I am. I am so grateful that he is alive, of course. It is a piece of luck that we never dreamed of, to find him here at Somerton under our very noses. . . . But . . ."

"It breaks all our hearts, that he is blinded," Georgiana said soberly.

"Not only that. He is different. Sadder and older, somehow." Her voice trembled. "I could not bear it if Alexander had been changed in some way, had become different, so that we no longer understood each other. . . . There will always be things he cannot speak to me about."

Georgiana looked at her in sympathy. "However he may have been changed by the things he has seen and suffered, I know that his love for you will not have wavered. Besides," she said thoughtfully, picturing Sebastian, guided by Oliver and Ada, walking in the garden just that morning, "despite everything, I think Sebastian is happy, because of Oliver. That is all one needs really, isn't it? To have the people one loves close, and safe. . . ." She broke off as she heard the distant whistle of the train.

"Oh, the train is nearly here!" Rose caught at Georgiana's arm. "If only he is on it as he said he would be. I've heard of men who were killed the day before they took their leave. . . . Oh, I am silly, forgive me. Please let him be on this train!"

The train was in sight now, a plume of white clouds over its head, glinting in the sun as it sped toward them. A wild hoot, and then it was pumping into the station, steam embracing them like friendly ghosts, and the smell of soot everywhere.

"I can't see him." Rose peered through the steam. "Oh, what if . . ."

Then the wreaths of steam dissolved, and Georgiana saw someone coming toward them along the platform someone with an unruly mop of dark hair under his cap, dressed in khaki and loaded with kit bags. He was thinner than she remembered him, and wore a tired, serious expression on his face, but there was no doubt. It was Alexander.

Rose released her arm and ran toward him. He dropped his bags and swept her into his arms, their lips meeting. Georgiana's eyes filled with tears of happiness as the steam veiled them once again. Then, after a long moment, she heard their voices, their happy laughter mingled with Rose's sobs of joy, as they came along the platform toward her. They appeared through the steam like spirits coming from another world in the clouds, their arms locked together tight as if they would never let each other go.

Georgiana smiled at the sight of the happiness on both their faces. "Don't spend a moment with me," she told Alexander at once. "Only let me say how glad I am to see you—and now you must go to the motorcar."

"Oh yes, you must see how much Edward has grown!" Rose said, still wiping the tears from her face. "I don't know why I am crying! It must be the relief."

Alexander gave Georgiana a warm smile and then went to the motorcar. Georgiana was struck by the exhaustion on his face. It hadn't been more than a year, but she could already see he was deeply marked by his experiences. At least, though, he was safe. Full of sympathy, she followed them to the motorcar and spoke to the chauffeur. "Please drive the duke and duchess back to Somerton. I will walk—it's a pleasant day for it."

Rose and Alexander were already in the car, Alexander with Edward in his arms. Alexander looked up. "Are you sure you will walk? It is a long way—"

"Nonsense!" Georgiana interrupted, laughing. "It isn't at all, and besides, can you imagine that I would intrude on your reunion?"

Alexander smiled gratefully, and then turned back to his son. The motorcar drove off, and Georgiana lifted a hand in farewell.

Left alone, with the birdsong and the distant bleating of lambs the only sounds to stir the peace, she sighed, all at once feeling a little lonely.

She turned to the gate that led from the lane to the fields, meaning to walk back across the sunny hill, which was covered in buttercups and daisies, rich with the humming of bees. But as she unlatched it, she saw that someone was coming down the hill toward her. She needed to wonder only for a moment before she recognized the figure. It was Michael.

"Hello," he greeted her, out of breath as he hurried to meet her. "I expect Alexander's train has arrived? I saw the motorcar in the lane, from the top of the hill."

"Yes, it has, and they are going back to Somerton. I'm sorry you missed them."

"Oh, I didn't come for Alexander. I shall see him at dinner, I'm sure. No, I thought you would probably walk back—and I thought you might like some company."

Georgiana was startled, but pleased. "Of course, I'd be delighted."

They set off up the hill, Michael walking with his hands in his pockets. Georgiana glanced at him sideways. "It's not like you to be so chivalrous," she teased him.

"No, I know—but perhaps I should be more so," he replied. "At any rate, you deserve some chivalry, so I should make an effort."

Georgiana found a blush on her face, and looked away. He probably meant nothing by it, she scolded herself. They walked on without speaking, Georgiana's skirt swishing through the grass. It was pleasant to walk in this comfortable silence, with the sun warming them. She smiled to herself, thinking of the way that Thomas had said good-bye to Rebecca. There was true love there too, she was sure of it. Once she had been romantic, now she was not sure what she was, but she still believed in true love.

"A penny for your thoughts," Michael said.

"Oh . . . I was just thinking how much we have to be grateful for."

"A good deal indeed," Michael said gravely. They walked on in silence for a while. Georgiana had the feeling that Michael was trying to find the words to say something; he frowned, and his hands were dug deep in his pockets. At last he glanced at her, and said awkwardly, almost angrily, "I hope you are not too disappointed in Captain Wyndham."

Georgiana was surprised. Surely, she thought, Michael knew by now how she felt about the man. "I certainly am disappointed. How could he be so lost to all sense of honor, all decency, all—"

"But I meant," said Michael, breaking into her speech, "that I hope you are not too greatly disappointed yourself—your heart, I mean."

"Oh!" They had reached the top of the hill, which was crossed by a hedge. Georgiana followed Michael up onto the stile. Michael jumped down onto the grass, but she stood where she was for a moment, poised at the highest point for miles around, looking down at Somerton Court's great beautiful sprawl of stone, embraced by the fields and the stream. The wind ruffled her hair and the leaves of the hedge. She spoke without thinking. "Oh, dear Michael, if only you knew how little my heart cares for anything, so long as I'm with you."

She almost bit her tongue. She had not meant to be so frank. But Michael turned to her with a smile. Georgiana, still perched on the stile, found herself looking down into his handsome face, his warm eyes. She was conscious of how close he was, the wind freshening his cheeks and tousling his hair, and the way his eyes were shining as he looked at her made her blush.

"I wonder what the future will hold," she said quickly. "For us, and for Somerton. I've often thought how sad it would be if the war meant I were never to dance here again—at Somerton, I mean."

Instead of answering, Michael reached up and took her hand. She stepped down from the stile onto the grass as if onto the polished floor of a ballroom.

"No war will ever stop me dancing with you," he said. Then he took her in his arms, and they were waltzing, on the top of the hill where the wildflowers bloomed. The wind and the lark's song all danced together through Georgiana's heart as he kissed her, like the most beautiful music any orchestra could ever have played.

CHAPTER
Sixty-seven

Somerton

The long hot day was beginning to tell on Ada's spirits. After their joyful welcome of Alexander, he and Rose had disappeared with little Edward for a long walk on the grounds before dinner. Michael and Georgiana, who had come back quite flushed and tired after their walk, had vanished too. That left her to while away the afternoon in the conservatory with the countess. She had some letters to write, but the countess was in the mood for talking—more specifically, in the mood for complaining about Charlotte.

"It is very hard to feel that she has made this foolish choice, after all my efforts," she went on now, continuing a conversation that Ada had tried not to encourage.

"But do you really think it foolish? Captain MacAllister seems a very solid man, and they are certainly in love."

"Love is all very well, but Charlotte is brought up to be a lady. She will not be happy for long, with just one maid and living in that poky little cottage near the aerodrome that they expect to move into after they are married."

"I think it is a delightful place, so convenient and easy to manage." Ada was aware she wasn't pleasing the countess, but she was not willing to criticize Charlotte. She had never liked her stepsister before, but it was easy to see that her experiences had changed her profoundly—or perhaps just drawn out the good qualities that had always been there. She had always suspected that much of Charlotte's unpleasantness had been created in her by her mother's fixation on marrying her off.

"Oh! I daresay you do. I daresay you think that anything is good enough for Charlotte, since she is not an Averley."

"I didn't say that. I—"

"Of course *you* have nothing to worry about," the countess went on poisonously. "Your father was very generous to you in his will."

Ada swallowed. The countess did not know that all her inheritance had gone to the bottom of the sea with William, and the memory of it stirred Ada's insecurity. She had more to worry about than the countess realized. Certainly the question of how she was to support herself was not at all answered. Without a degree, which Oxford would not award her or any woman, she could not practice as a lawyer.

The countess saw that her blow had somehow hit home, and pressed on. "Yes, you are quite a catch now that you have your inheritance, so I don't expect you will be at Somerton Court much longer, expecting me to feed you and house you. I should advise you to use your fortune to settle yourself swiftly in a comfortable future—I mean marriage, of course. Ten thousand pounds does not go as far as you think it does."

"Not half as far," said Ada wryly. It hadn't even made it to America.

"Exactly my point." The countess gave her a piercing glance. "What *do* you plan to do, Ada? When will you give up Oxford and find someone to marry? To be sure, having refused Lord Fintan it is hard to see who could please you—just imagine, if you had married him, you would be a very rich widow by now."

Ada swallowed her anger at the countess's insensitive words. Yet she knew that the countess had a point; that was what made her words so painful to hear. She did need to find some way of keeping herself financially maintained. It was not as if she needed much—just a modest amount for lodging, books, clothes, and food—but at the moment she had no idea how she would even find that small amount. Her father had set up a fund to pay for her remaining years of education, but after that, she did not know what she would do. It was out of the question to accept Connor's generosity, though she knew he would always give it. It was equally impossible to impose on Georgiana or Rose. No, she had said she wanted to be independent and earn her own money, and she would stick to that. The question was, how? She did not like to admit that she did not have perfect faith in the future—but she was anxious.

"I don't want to marry at all," she said to the countess. She tried to keep the resentment out of her voice. "At least, not now. I would prefer not to speak about it any longer."

The countess looked annoyed, but before she could reply, Mollie the maid appeared at the door. "A letter for you, Lady Ada," she said with a curtsy that was much more polished than it had been when she arrived. Rebecca had clearly been training her.

"Thank you, Mollie." Ada took the letter, glad of the distraction. Neither the postmark nor the handwriting was familiar. She took the silver paper knife from the table and opened the enve lope. A quick glance told her that it was from someone called the Marquess of Castlehardie. The name was vaguely familiar, and after a few moments she remembered: she had once heard Hannah mention him, though she could not remember in what context. She wondered why he was writing to her. They had never been introduced, and she knew nothing about him.

The first few paragraphs of the letter gave her little clue; they were the usual: condolences on her father's death, greetings and pleasantries. But when she began reading the second sheet, she froze. She had to read the words over again before she could dare to believe them.

I do not involve myself in public life, and so you may not know that I am a keen supporter of women's emancipation. I therefore like to employ women where I can. I am funding a defense of two prominent suffragettes who have been accused of conspiring against the Crown—quite unjustly, I believe—and

I was very impressed with your work on the Kearney case. I wondered if you would allow me to retain your services for the duration of the case? I would, of course, remunerate you appropriately for your time and expertise. If this offends you, I apologize. However, if you have the time and inclination, I would be very grateful for your help. . . .

Ada needed to read no more. Instantly she had realized what it meant. It was her first paid work, and it meant that the long, hard struggle for an education equal to a man's would be worth it. It meant success. It meant hope. It meant that when she completed her course of studies, there would be people who would employ her and enable her to earn a living independently.

She folded the letter, aware that the color was high in her cheeks. She looked up at the countess, who was watching her closely. "I understand your concern for your daughter and appreciate your concern for me," she said, hearing the ring of quiet confidence in her own voice for the first time. "But you must understand, I shall never marry for money. I shall earn my own. I shall be independent."

The countess gave a disbelieving sniff. But Ada did not care. She had seen the future. She had seen it between the lines of the old marquess's letter. And against the darkness of the present, it shone like a jewel with promise.